OLIVIA RENNER

THE
SACRIFICIAL
ROSE

BOOK ONE

Cover by Miblart

Copy/line edit and Proofreading by Tabitha @tabs.edit

Formatting by Vanessa Mena, Inkspark Digital

Content Notice

Please flip to the back after the acknowledgments for themes that may be upsetting for some readers.

For those who ever felt they lost themselves to trauma. You'll find yourself again. Beneath the rage, you can find the softness.

And to my husband who held me up through the constant self-doubt. You're a real one for that.

Seasons in the Realm of Nesrin:

Sprouting season - Spring
Flowering season - Summer
Harvest season - Autumn
Wither season - Winter

The deities:

Akuma - god of death
Aeterna - goddess of the earth
Cordelia - goddess of the sea
Esen - god of the sky

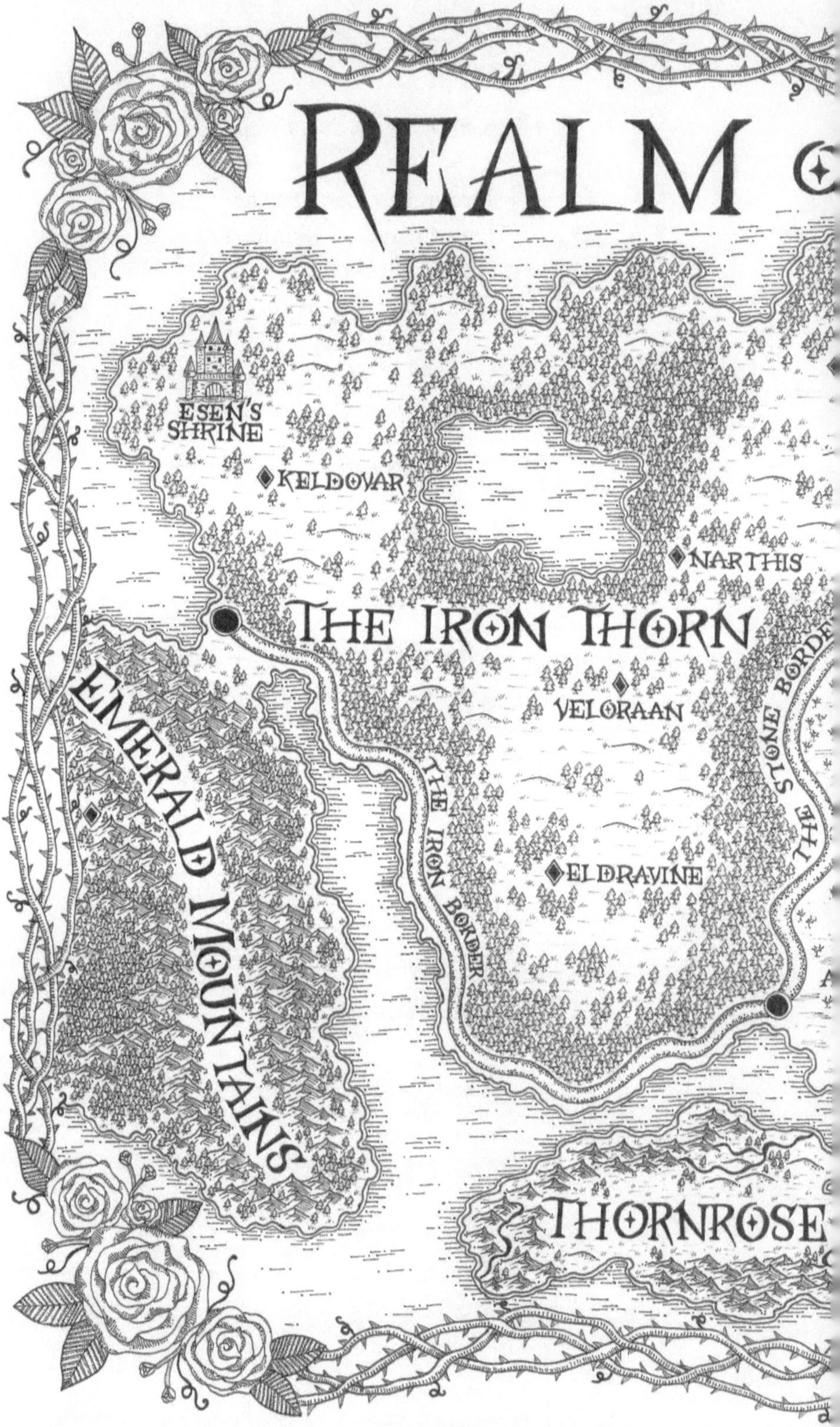

REALM (

ESEN'S
SHRINE

KELDOVAR

NARTHIS

THE IRON THORN

VELORAAN

EMERALD MOUNTAINS

THE IRON BORDER

ELDRAVINE

THE STONE BORDE

THORNROSE

NESRIN

THE FORGE BORDER

CORDELIA'S RUIN

EVERBLOOM

ORONDAL

RIVEN

...OLIA

CURSED SEA

MISTVALLE

N
W   E
S

Prologue

When death came for me, no one in the realm would notice my absence. No one except my mother and father. The ghost told me as much. Though I didn't trust him, did I? *Do ghosts die with you? If they tethered themselves to you?*

My musings seemed to conjure him, and the hair on my neck raised as his presence followed me outside the confines of my dream.

I stood at the top of the stairs and glanced behind me. The ghostly boy was nowhere to be seen. The only proof he'd been real was the item I held in my fist.

Black curls drooped over my forehead, obscuring my vision. I pushed them back before I wrapped a small hand around the wood railing. I shut my tired eyes for a moment and rubbed them with the heel of my palm. The movement brought the boy and his scarlet gaze flashing through my mind.

Panicked, my eyes snapped open. I gulped and took a cautious step down the stairs. My small feet pitter-pattered on the wood boards, which creaked with every shift of my weight. The farther I descended, the brighter the soft glow of the candle in the kitchen became.

The remnants of the ghost's presence followed me like a shadow. No matter how much I wanted to avoid alarming my parents, I scurried down the stairs. I had to tell before it became too late.

Urgency quickened my pace, and I pressed my hand on the wall and felt my way to the bottom of the steps, my nightgown swishing against my ankles with every footfall.

I froze when I heard Mother talking in a hushed voice. Halfway in the light, Father stood with his back to the stairs.

The desire to run to him couldn't outweigh the fear of upsetting Mother. If I told them both about the item from the boy, I worried it would be more than they could handle. Mother would send me away.

"It does her more harm to continue putting it off, Aedric." Mother's voice echoed from the landing. Her tone was the stone-cold one I had become accustomed to since the nightmares started. My ears tuned in to their conversation.

"What do you suggest we do, then? It'd be wrong to send her away for something she can't control. How can you be okay with the awful things they'd put her through?" Father's voice teetered on the edge of disdain.

"You know that's not what I'm saying. Why do you twist my words?"

Though she hadn't outright said it, I understood her clearly. A nine-year-old child shouldn't know what it feels like to have their mother resent their existence. The rejection stole pieces of my innocence. Lullabies and joy exchanged for slammed doors and cold shoulders.

"I'm not trying to twist your words. But she's just a child, Riona. I know it's difficult for you, but how would sending her away help? Do you expect to forget her existence when she enters the Temple?"

Mother bristled. "What difference does it make? I can't bring myself to look at her. Knowing what awaits her is unbearable. We should have alerted the council when she was born. Now we risk punishment if we continue to do nothing."

The room fell silent. Of course, Father knew she was right. I didn't blame her for her fear. It was something we shared, and it echoed in every moment of my life. I didn't want to be cursed. I didn't want to die. Warm tears welled up, blurring my vision.

After a pause, Mother braced her hands on the kitchen table. Her blonde hair brushed her cheek, and the candle illuminated her features, revealing a look of dismay.

"The council may know what her nightmares mean. A child shouldn't dream such horrific things. It isn't normal, even for a Rose." Her voice held a tremor—proof of her unrest.

"You know she can't do anything about them, but we've been working on it. It's been almost two weeks since she has come to us with a nightmare. I think the herbs are helping, but we have to give it time. If we alert the king, there's no going back," Father pleaded with her, and I saw the love in his stance, the one which looked ready to fight for his daughter.

Guilt overwhelmed me.

I almost turned to go back to my room. It made me sick to prove my mother right and disappoint my father. But the object I held tightly in my fist made me afraid. I didn't understand. I'd never had a dream so real. The boy had never broken through in such a way.

Father would want to send me away, too.

"You honestly think they've stopped? Are you so blind to her suffering? I'm hardly around her, and even I can see she's struggling to hide it. They haven't stopped." She paused, and a heavy exhale caused her shoulders to hunch. "She isn't normal. Her life isn't meant to be. The council knows how to deal with this far better than us both. We can't help her."

The floor scuffed beneath Father's foot when he took a step closer to her—a finger jabbed in her direction. "How could you speak as if she asked for this life? She's afraid, and all you can do is feel pity for yourself. *You* brought this upon her."

Mother pushed away from the table, her face twisted with unbridled rage. "Don't you dare pin this on me!"

"You take no accountability when you're the reason she's cursed!"

Tears clouded my vision, and I couldn't take another moment of them fighting.

I stumbled the rest of the way down the stairs, nearly falling when I ran toward the light. Father turned at the sound, his eyes wide. It happened within a matter of seconds—his arms reached out, and his hand dwarfed mine when he pulled me close.

"Elita, what's wrong?" Father squeezed my hand and crouched to my height. His appearance was unkempt, and his mousy brown hair was a wild tangle atop his head.

"The dreams—" The words wouldn't come.

Mother came closer with her arms crossed over her chest and a scowl on her face. Similar to my father, she looked nothing like me. Short blonde hair framed her scowl, and while she typically appeared kind and pretty, her face distorted into something frightening in the low lighting; her normally bright blue eyes now dulled and stormy.

I struggled with the words, not wanting to disappoint my father. But I had to say something.

"I had the dream again, Father," I whispered. My head hung low, and my voice broke under the looming glare of my mother.

Father sighed and released my hand, putting his palms on my shoulders. He smelled of cedarwood, and the scent soothed me.

I glanced at him then, bleary-eyed. I had proven my mother right, but he was not angry with me. Worry etched his brow.

"I woke up, and he wasn't there," I said in a hushed voice, concerned if I spoke any higher, it would conjure the boy who haunted my dreams.

"Who wasn't there?" Father's brow creased in confusion, changing from the worried expression he had given me.

It was the first time I had identified the boy to them. Though he had haunted me for many nights, he had only ever been a wisp of smoke in my dreams. That night was different, and the silky item in my hand grew damp with sweat.

"Casimir," I croaked out.

"Casimir?" He peered over his shoulder at my mother.

She shook her head in response.

My chin quivered when I spoke. "He told me it isn't safe here—that if I stay, something bad will happen."

Father appeared shocked, but his expression softened again in an instant. "It's simply a dream, little flower. It'll be fine." His tone was gentle, and he kissed my forehead before standing. He turned to my mother. "We'll go on a walk. It'll all be forgotten in the morning."

I trembled, breath as shaky as a leaf in the breeze.

For a pause, I shut my eyes as hard as I could before I found the courage to speak again. "He scares me, Father. He gave me something. See?" I put my hand out to reveal the small, thin rose petal. It gleamed crimson in the moonlight, delicate and foreboding.

They both whipped toward me. Mother grabbed my arm and sucked in a harsh breath as she ran a finger over the wrinkled petal. She dropped my arm as if it had been a hot coal, her eyes wide.

"Elita." Father spoke firmly to draw my attention.

"Yes?" I murmured.

Mother slumped in the corner by the hearth. The hem of her linen gown brushed close to the fiery edge, threatening to dip into the flames.

"What did he look like?"

I peered over my shoulder and up the stairs, where a cool breeze emerged, dusting tangled tendrils in front of my face. The candle on the kitchen table trembled as if sensing the ghostly boy who walked among my sleep. I faced Father, who gazed at me in worry.

Swallowing the fear, I leaned in close to his ear, my voice the lightest whisper.

"He looked like me."

Chapter One

12 YEARS LATER

Emerald pine whipped past me. The thunderous fall of Mora's hooves drowned out the tranquility of the forest, matching the rush of my heart. It hammered inside my ribcage, erratic and wild.

Wisps of black curls blurred at the edge of my vision, catching in the low branches. It didn't deter me.

Not when the ache of petals preparing to bloom followed me through the woods. No matter how fast I rode, I couldn't outrun the weight of it. The lack of control made me tighten my fists on the reins. *If I ride faster, perhaps I can forget.*

I whipped the leather in my fists, and Mora responded in kind. My breath caught in my chest and I held back the emotion that bit at the edge of my eyes.

My bloom had haunted me since birth—a destiny carved in stone. With each year that passed, I clung to the hope that there had been an error. The goddess simply made a mistake when she gifted me the features of a Rose.

The tiny black buds among my hair mocked me now.

Mora came to an abrupt halt at a stream, and the damning curls flew forward, blocking my vision. I huffed a frustrated breath, pushed the strands back, and tried to compose myself.

There was nowhere far enough in all of Nesrin that I could ride to hide from the petals that prepared to bloom.

Mora snorted, unimpressed by my temper that led us so far from the village. In the distance, the Stone Border stood at the edge of the Iron Thorn. I had set out before the sun rose without a word and aimlessly wandered. I needed to clear my head.

Father would be furious that I didn't say anything.

Ignoring the worry, I dismounted. My boots sank into the damp earth, and I straightened my lopsided cloak. I clicked my tongue, and Mora followed me to the water. She dipped her head and drank, disrupting the peaceful stream.

I sat in the grass at the edge, my gaze fixed on the surface as it shimmered. In the soft, lapping waves, I met my reflection. Too strange to overlook and no way to hide what I was.

Scarlet eyes stared back at me, resembling drops of blood in the water. A few freckles dotted the space at my temples and the upper half of my cheeks. They scattered like stray flecks of paint.

I stared a moment too long before the resemblance to the goddess made my blood run hot.

My hand searched the grass, and a rock brushed my fingertips. I plucked it up, threw it, and disrupted the surface once more. It distorted my face. A mirror to the chaos in my head.

Beside me, Mora scuffed the dirt. Her black coat pulled in the streaks of sunlight that poured through the trees. The unusual chill at the end of the flowering season couldn't prevent the sweat that peeked beneath the saddle. Guilt tugged at me. We'd gone too far. She wasn't used to such a long ride.

But to stay at the cottage meant to stay in my mother's company. If she noticed the buds throughout my hair, she'd be the first to alert the king. I wondered how she'd lie her way out of treason.

I sighed and stood, brushing the dirt from my trousers. If we didn't return to Eldravine in time, the markets would close, and I wouldn't have a chance to waste the day browsing. Though, I never did get to purchase things on my own. No, I had to inform my father of what I found in order for him to return later and deal with the merchants.

It wasn't safe for me to speak, let alone lift my head and meet someone's gaze.

My palm stroked the curve of Mora's neck, and I adjusted her bridle. "Sorry, girl. We'll take our time heading back," I said. In a single fluid movement, I mounted the gray and silver saddle. My boots ducked into the stirrups, and I clicked my heels.

Though I'd already been absent from the morning meal, the thought of returning to my mother's cold presence made it easy to put off the hunger that twisted my stomach.

Had it not been for the Rose curse, I would've left home when I turned eighteen to be free of her. But fear crippled me, and nearly four years passed since the prospect dangled before me. To leave meant to spend my last years alive away from the only home I'd ever known. A life away from my father.

The fear of loneliness solidified my choice to stay.

If only Mother didn't loathe my existence. Then, in my last days before the petals bloomed, we could've had time to mend the shattered fragments of our relationship.

My knuckles turned white around the reins.

No. There wouldn't ever be enough time to recover the years she spent pretending I had already died. A bitter truth that nearly made me turn back to sit by the stream until the sun died down.

Though my mother was the reason I was cursed, she chose to see herself as a victim. There was a line of Roses before her, but she had hoped that since her parents weren't cursed, and neither was she, I would have had the same luck as her—that I would be skipped straight out of the wretched Rose gene pool like a sharp, flat rock.

I was not so fortunate.

The moment I entered the realm, I looked nothing like my parents. Outside of small features, such as the shape of my mouth or the curve of my nose, I didn't fit. My irises echoed the bloodshed of centuries in them. Crimson to mirror the deity responsible for the curse that diseased the realm.

It was said that the earth goddess, Aeterna, created the Rose people to spite the other deities. When the first petal bloomed among a Rose's hair, they could harness abilities in the likeness of Aeterna. It was one of the few things to be considered powerful from a curse destined to kill you. Normal Roses bloomed and wilted at age twenty. Their life sustained the Iron Thorn, a sacrifice the Rose would pay, willing or not.

Despite my promise to Mora, I clicked my heels until she picked up a gallop. The silence, the stillness; they offered too much room for thoughts of my impending sacrifice to creep in once more. The buds were a taunting change that made it harder not to dwell. When they didn't appear after I turned twenty, it had given me too much hope.

Favor did not find me, and after a night of terrifying visions and another haunting by the man with crimson eyes, I woke to a new ache. Thirty pin-sized buds to count down my bloom and inevitable wilt.

I grunted and ducked under a low branch, my face close to Mora's neck. She kicked up mud, leaving a trail through the forest.

We broke through the edge of the woods, and the cottage I'd spent my entire life in came into view. A pit grew in my stomach, and I slowed our pace.

Gray moss covered the top of the black cottage. Clouds passed over the sun while we approached the gate to the backyard, casting it in shadow. Vines twisted their way up the fence posts. Tiny red flowers crawled across the greenery, and despite how much despair filled the walls of our cottage, it appeared enchanting from the outside.

We neared the gate, and I hopped off the saddle and walked Mora the rest of the way. I flipped the latch on the gate, which swung wide to welcome us in. It didn't take me long to get Mora back into the small open stable.

Father's horse was absent, and I sighed. I'd only just returned, but I wouldn't spend my day in the stiff quiet with my mother.

My plan to go to the village became a necessity.

After I poured feed for Mora, I shut the stable and made my way toward the backdoor. Exhaustion ran bone-deep, and I yawned, wishing the ghost would leave my dreams alone. I hadn't slept a full night in over three weeks, and it made it much harder to bear Mother's company.

Black stones paved the way, and bat orchids dotted the edge. I brushed a hand along them and made my way to the stairs. The door opened silently, and I crept inside.

"Take off your boots."

I jumped at my mother's voice. It trailed from the kitchen, and I fought the urge to keep on the mucky boots. A small act of defiance. I'd outgrown such behaviors, though, and I left the riding boots beside the backdoor and removed my cloak.

The mouthwatering aroma of midday meal wafted through the cottage. The scent of freshly baked bread grew stronger as I trudged further inside and my stomach grumbled in response.

Mother stood in the kitchen near the wood stove, kneading dough at the counter, her tan apron covered in flour. She left out a tray of food filled with rye bread and an abundance of strawberries. Beside the tray, steam swirled from a cup of tea, filling the air with the scent of lavender and mint.

"Where's Father?" I asked, not bothering with pleasantries.

She glanced over her shoulder, then returned her attention to the dough in her hands, flipping it to knead the other side. "He's with his students at the Temple. The prince requested their help. He'll be back soon."

"Oh..." I cut off a large piece of the bread and took a bite. "When he returns, can you tell him I'll be back later today?" I asked her around a mouthful of food, trying to hurry our interaction. I eyed the tea she hadn't touched yet, half tempted to take a sip since I didn't want to stay long enough to make my own.

Mother sighed and barely looked my way. "You're leaving already? You've just returned and barely eaten."

Any time Father was absent, the day always unfolded the same. Either I left the cottage or Mother would hide in her room to avoid me until he returned.

Since she was occupied with baking, I took a step out of the kitchen and said, "Yes, I planned to browse the shops for new fabric in Eldravine. Have you planned something else for today?"

She gave me a look of disapproval. "Is that really necessary? King Lendorr has increased guards in all the villages. Your father threw a fit this morning after you left without a word. He's worried you're not being careful enough."

I ducked my head, feeling guilty. I stared at the edge of my black tunic and ran the pad of my thumb over the red embroidery.

The kingdom was on the brink of collapse as they awaited a Rose with a mature bloom. Their desperation turned into scouring for hidden Roses from Keldovarr to all three borders. We'd been fortunate enough to not be searched yet, as the guards began to go door to door.

Soon, our kingdom would resemble the Drought Lands if they didn't have a bloom.

I clenched my fists until they ached.

Our kingdom would not fall. No, not when my bloom had begun. I bit my tongue to prevent myself from telling Mother. I wasn't ready, and I needed time to process death arriving at my door.

Releasing my fists, I whispered, "He shouldn't worry himself so much. I'll have to go one day, regardless of who takes me to the Temple."

She paused midway through kneading the dough. Flour clung to her hands. "He's still your father, Elita. He's spent your entire life trying to keep you safe from their awful practices."

I bit back a retort about how flippant she was being. As though 'awful practices' were enough to describe the act of being bred after the age of eighteen in hopes of securing the next Rose. Then having their bloom sheared for all to see in a torturous ceremony.

She never did speak of it with the full weight in her words.

When the brief interaction ended, I strode over to the door. The threat of guards noticing me wasn't enough to keep me there.

"Don't forget your shawl," Mother chided.

In a rush, I wrapped the black shawl around my hair and clasped a clean cloak over my shoulders. The gray fabric fell to my calves. The hood did nothing to hide my eyes, but I was accustomed to avoiding eye contact with anyone. Learning to do so was crucial during my childhood and remained a condition for me to leave the cottage.

With my boots on, I stepped back outside and was met with the fragrant aroma of blossoming flowers, and the burgundy, black, and white hues made me grin. I passed the crimson ninebark and ran a hand over it, the cluster of petals soft against my skin.

Pine trees split open at the end of the pathway, leading to the crumbling black cobblestone sidewalk.

The scorching sun cast its rays upon the well-trodden stone path as I made a turn. A familiar twisted black archway captivated my attention, beckoning me into the village center.

Eldravine was only one of the many villages sprawled throughout the walls of the Iron Thorn. It was crowded with taverns, markets, and shops. Cottages dotted the streets in an array of bland hues: black, gray, and some made of dusty limestone. Their roofs pulled to sharp points, onyx and burning in the afternoon light.

The only thing to break up the monotony of the structures were flowers that dressed the windows and paths.

Ashen wisteria trees lined the streets, their white flowers drooping over lantern posts. Black-lace bushes and bloodroot wildflowers took up space among the many flower beds. They worked hard to keep it that way. The council oversaw a group of skilled gardeners who were assigned to tend to the plants. They held them with such reverence as if the deities had placed them there.

I approached the market, which buzzed with people as they scurried along the cobblestone paths. Horses and carts zipped past me while laughter and chatter thrummed through the masses.

Merchants crowded the edge of the streets and set up their stalls wherever they would fit. Despite its modest size, the market became a chaotic hub of activity as bodies filled the available space.

Across the street, a large group of guards moved in organized lines, searching the crowd. It would've been smart to remain at the cottage, but something about the buds made me reckless.

I kept my distance from them, grateful for the chaotic market.

People scrambled about in a rush to prepare for the upcoming festival that loomed a few days away, one the Iron Thorn took great pride in. I was never allowed to attend, and Mother used to scold my father any time he mentioned going to see the exquisite art and dancing meant to honor the deities.

Someone's shoulder brushed mine when they jogged past me, but I didn't look up. Instead, I walked closer to the shops to avoid the busy flow of bodies.

From the corner of my hood, I noted the children who ran around at the feet of their guardians, laughing with unbridled joy.

A young couple paused at a stall adorned with flower arrangements, and I watched as the woman's face erupted with delight when her partner handed her a bundle of them. She pecked his cheek, and he turned a subtle shade of pink.

The fleeting exchange left my chest hollow and aching for a life I knew I would never have. Loneliness was my oldest friend, and it followed me in the streets of Eldravine.

I continued down the path, leaving behind the heart of the village. My hands pulled at my hood, obscuring more of my face. I tuned out the people around me and focused my attention elsewhere.

The scent of wildflowers threatened to overwhelm my senses when I came across a stunning array of white blooms. They popped up wherever they could, and some flowers extruded through cracks in the stonework, and others lined the edge of the street.

Close by, the Temple's grandeur paved the rest of the way, its architecture towering above the surrounding trees. The council remained there as the caretakers of the Rose children who used to roam the area.

Though the kingdom used to have many young Roses, our race had mostly died out. The fate forced upon the Rose people was more than any parent could bear, and having children with someone who carried the curse became something many sought to avoid.

It was what drove them to the choice to arrange suiters for the groomed Roses. That way, they could secure and control Roses in their Temple. However, that didn't always work out, and they suffered now for relying on such horrid methods.

The Temple stood before me in a foreboding manner; the spires jutted out in sharp inclines toward the sky. It devoured the sunlight in the black, twisting structure. Silver iron vines contrasted the onyx and twisted up the spires. It was both magnificent and ominous.

Black agate walls enveloped the Temple. A silver gate stood as the sole barrier to keep people out, and to keep Roses in. Four Temple watchmen guarded the only entrance and exit.

I quickened my pace to avoid getting too close to the Temple and their watchful eye. Overhead, a raven called, nothing more than a blur of black above the trees. My feet carried me along opulent white wisteria trees that lined the stone walkway to the gardens.

The village garden was the most magnificent in the Iron Thorn, tended by my father and his students. Among the gardens was where I felt most at home.

I held my head high on the secluded path, and sunbeams danced on my cheeks as the wind swept some clouds away. Everyone was much too busy with the preparations for the festival at the market. I had no fear and no need to hide my face on the vacant path.

The twisting archway to the garden appeared luminescent in the glittering sunlight. When I walked through it, my heart sank, and a soft gasp escaped my lips.

Everything was dead.

All of the flowers wilted as if Akuma's hand of death had swept over it, draining away all life. The irises were gone, fallen to the ground in a heap of brown, which crinkled under my boots when I stepped through the arch. Once crimson rose bushes laid wilting, becoming one with the dirt. The sight was haunting.

Dry and desolate, it could've easily been mistaken as part of the Drought Lands.

I scanned the garden, and the contrast of a marigold cloak grabbed my attention. To my dismay, it wasn't my father—who typically wore the same type of horticulture cloak.

A man crouched among the bed of lifeless flowers, his golden brown hair held back by a tie. The man's shoulders slumped, and dead leaves fell from his clenched fist, meeting the withered grass beneath it.

I held my breath and turned to leave, when my gaze was drawn to another vibrant speck of color in the garden of death.

In a wilted bush, there was a single bright rose basking in the sun, still soft, with no sign of the same decay awaiting it.

Despite the urgency to leave before being noticed, I couldn't resist making my way over to the bush in the barren garden.

Carefully treading to avoid the crinkled leaves, I halted in front of the peculiar, solitary flower. I lowered myself until my gaze met the bush's empty branches, once teeming with life. My hand trembled when I reached out to touch the delicate petals of the rose.

I grasped the stem and pulled it out, eyeing it with curiosity. In an instant, the moisture stripped from the petals, leaving a crumbled mess in my palm.

A startled gasp left my lips and I released the wilted rose. My skin burned where the stem had touched and I glanced at my palm to see a pinprick of blood. The same raven called again, swooping close to my arm. Its wings flapped, a slick, black shadow as it flew away.

I stood and looked around. My attention fell to the man on the other side of the garden. He watched me, his eyes a captivating azure that swam with keenness, causing my stomach to twist.

He rose and let more dead leaves fall from his fist. A knowing look flashed in his gaze, and ice twisted every knot in my spine.

I turned in a rush, picking up a sprint when he took a step toward me. Blood rushed in my ears, dead flowers crunched under my boots, and I stumbled through the archway.

"Wait!" The man called from the garden, but I didn't stop.

Terror clutched my chest, and as I ran past the Temple, the pathway lost its magnificence, replaced with dismay. If he recognized what I was, it wouldn't be long before I found myself back there.

The white flowers on the trees rushed past me in a blur. I tried to listen for someone in pursuit, but I heard nothing past the hammering of my heart and the rasp of my breath.

Dark gray clouds swept in with sudden howling winds. It was going to storm; I could feel the stickiness in the humid air. The rain swept in with the wind, whipping the shawl from my head. I scrambled to pull it back on, throwing the hood from my cloak over it for good measure.

When I returned to the market, it was nearly deserted as the villagers sought shelter from the storm. Rain pelted hard on the stone paths, painting them dark and slippery. My clothes clung to my skin, transforming my shawl and hair into a sodden mess.

A small shop jutted out at the corner of the street, and I darted around it, pausing to catch my breath.

I placed a trembling hand on my chest and gasped for air. My head remained low. I listened for sprinting or guards shouting nearby. To my relief, it never came.

Daring a look around the shop, all I saw were frantic villagers trying to stash their wares out of the abrupt rain.

It would be foolish to stay close to the gardens, and with a long inhale, I picked up a sprint once more. My boots struggled to find solid footing on the stones that swam in puddles of rain.

Before long, I reached the familiar dirt path, which split four ways. Straight ahead of me and then to the left was the black moss-covered cottage I called home.

My body flooded with exhaustion, which left me panting and my tunic clinging uncomfortably to my damp skin. I jogged the rest of the way up the path despite the fatigue.

I glanced back over my shoulder, half expecting to see the man from the garden following me with guards in tow.

The only thing that followed me was the image of blue eyes.

When I lifted my gaze to the cottage, the warm glow of lanterns flickering in the windows caught my attention. A sense of relief washed over me, and I entered the cottage without looking back.

Chapter Two

I stood in a puddle inside the cottage, trembling as my body tried to shake off the chill. The door shut, and warmth enveloped me as a fire crackled in the hearth—an oddity during the flowering season.

When I glanced around the entryway, I noticed Father's tattered boots were still missing. I groaned and removed my sopping wet cloak, which was once gray, now appearing black.

Footsteps followed the sound of my soaked boots hitting the wall. Mother came around the corner and gasped when she found me dripping onto the floor.

"By Esen's light, you're soaked through," she scolded. She approached me to take my wet shawl off and hang it on a hook. Shaking her head, she said, "Wait here while I grab a rag. You'll soak the floors."

She disappeared, and I heard the linen closet next to the washroom open. The iron hinges closed with an unmistakable squeak. She returned with a worn gray cloth; the fabric appeared soft and frayed from years of use. She handed it to me in haste, and I wrapped it around my shoulders, shivering in my heavy clothes.

"I'll have to boil some water for a bath. You need to change in the meantime before you freeze to death," Mother muttered.

I nodded and waved her off before sauntering through the house, leaving a trail of wet footprints behind me.

The stairs moaned, yearning to be left alone after years of use. The hallway's scuffed and splintered wood was covered by a red woven rug, leading to the sole room on the second floor—the place in the cottage where I was most at ease.

Inside my room, the heat from the hearth no longer reached me, and I wrestled with my wet clothes, trembling as they fell to the floor. I slipped into black linen trousers and a loose tunic to match.

After I grabbed a hairbrush and dry undergarments, I went back downstairs. The cottage remained silent. When my father was absent, it gave the impression of an abandoned home. Only furniture to fill the space, without the warmth of personal artifacts.

In a way, my mother and I mirrored each other. Lives consumed by a curse. Isolated with days spent in near-constant silence. Ghosts among the empty walls.

Father acted in stark contrast. He was the sun beaming in through the windows. The laughter that echoed in the emptiness. He brought warmth and love, regardless of a curse or my mother's indifference.

I passed the kitchen and noted a trail of droplets from where Mother brought in a pail of water from the well. I stared at the mess for a moment before turning at the sound of the washroom door opening.

She emerged from the room, an empty pail in one hand while the other wiped sweat off her brow. She glanced at me, never truly meeting my gaze, while she dried her palm on her emerald linen dress.

Barely addressing me, she said, "Your father wanted me to tell you he won't be back till late. I had to take him something to eat while you were out. He was distraught over the Temple gardens."

At the mention of the garden, I glanced at my hand, seeing the small red prick on my skin where the thorn had poked me. I ran the opposite thumb over it.

"I've just returned from there."

"Elita Fullan," she scolded under her breath.

I sighed in response to her theatrics, bothered by her use of my middle name. I walked further into the sitting room, fiddling with the frays of an old quilt.

"Everything was dead. I've never seen anything like it. And on top of that, the sudden cold during the flowering. I don't know if the kingdom will make it through another wither season without a bloom."

I waited to see the realization. To watch her glance over my hair for the buds in a panic. Anything to show that the start of my bloom made her feel something. Sadness. Grief. Desperation to retrieve the time lost, which she spent as if I were already gone.

Years of anger boiled over, and I balled my fists. "Though, I wouldn't worry. The buds appeared this morning, and you'll be free of me soon enough." It came out shaky. My chin quivered as the rage tried to release all at once. Visceral and white hot.

There was no change in her face. No sense of loss. She knew what the budding meant, and the reality of my imminent death couldn't alter who she was.

She wouldn't even look me in the eye as she said, "Your father will want to know."

The anger melted until it became another layer of grief.

"It won't change anything," I said quietly.

"He'll want to spend more time with you."

"And you?"

Mother's jaw clenched, and her gaze fiercely avoided mine. "Don't make it worse for yourself. We knew this day would come."

Wincing, I clutched my arms around my body. The weight of bitter disappointment made me long to disappear.

It was a foolish notion, but as a young girl, I always imagined that when the day finally came, she would be beside herself with grief, that perhaps she'd regret the years of callousness. It was nothing more than childish hope. I had grown too old for such things. And yet the ache didn't dissipate.

Mother pursed her lips and turned to go back outside with the empty pail. Without another glance my way, she paused in the doorframe.

Horrible, misplaced hope sparked in my chest and snuffed out just as quickly when she spoke. "I added the hot water. The bath should be warm enough." She disappeared out the back door.

Her indifference stung, but it didn't bring me as much pain as knowing how Father would fare when my wilt came. Unlike Mother, he made an effort to be present as much as possible before my sacrifice. Until recent years, with the state of the Iron Thorn.

With the decay in the kingdom, Father was being called in to help at the Temple more often. He was skilled in horticulture, and they wanted his input, his studies, and his entire mind. They were going to pick him apart, separating him from us daily. The king wanted a solution to prevent the decline of the kingdom while they searched for a Rose.

When the last Rose was impotent and failed at securing a replacement Rose, he was sheared at the end of his bloom, and their careful planning to ensure a future sacrifice died with him.

While it was ideal for them to raise Roses in their Temple and have them bred after the age of eighteen, practically guaranteeing a Rose child, there were still normal families whose children were born with the Rose curse. Families like my own.

Fate chose for them, cursing them with a sacrifice instead of a normal child.

Father never did treat me as if I were cursed. It was thanks to him that King Lendorr didn't know of my existence. He wanted me to experience a life beyond the Temple walls, even if the gods would require my sacrifice. A life in solitude since birth, marked by the king, and bred with a stranger to carry on the sacrifices wasn't something he wanted for his daughter.

If nothing else, I would allow myself to be grateful for the time I had with my father. I was more fortunate than most Roses; twenty-one years without a bloom was unheard of. But selfishly, it felt like it wouldn't ever be enough.

I wanted so much more.

The bath grew frigid not long after I got in. Our cottage did little to keep the cold out, and I hurried to be done with the icy water.

My linen sleep clothes were a kind respite once more when I slipped them on and left the washroom. I hung out my towel to dry near the hearth and walked through the orange hue of sunset that poured through the windows and stopped at Father's study to look for a book to sit down with.

When I tested the door handle, it was unlocked, allowing me to slip inside. With a soft click, I shut the door and ventured deeper into the study, observing the abundance of books strewn in disarray. Many were left open on his desk, with paper and quills scattered across the top, obscuring the scratched wood.

Dusting my fingers over a page, I noticed glasses and a quill in a book's cracked spine, indicating his most recent read. Reading the faded words presented a challenge, but it appeared to recount the history of the realm.

I glanced over the story, noting the mention of the sea goddess, Cordelia, and the sky god, Esen. Scratched from the paper until nearly illegible, Akuma, the god of death.

One name on the page jumped out to me more than the rest: Aeterna, the earth goddess. Next to her name was a faded painting that showcased a sketch of her.

Once black hair had turned charcoal on the page. Only the red of her irises remained vivid like pools of blood dried onto the paper. The white of her eyes was painted black, a chilling depiction and something the Rose people did not share with her—a feature belonging solely to the goddess.

A diadem rested at her brow, made of thorns and roses, and a wicked smile adorned her face. It was meant to appear kind and inviting. Instead, it resembled something out of a child's nightmare.

Uncomfortable rage boiled beneath my skin. Soon, I would be forced to atone for her arrogance, as many Roses before me had.

I released a heavy breath, took the quill and glasses off the page, and closed the book.

No longer in the mood to read, I left the study and shut out the image of Aeterna's wicked grin. I trudged upstairs, taking my time. There were no paintings or decorations on the walls. They were empty and gray, with no family portraits or art to fill them. My death would leave no trace of my presence on the earth.

Leaving the emptiness behind, I stepped through the door to my frigid room and stalked over to my bed with sluggish limbs. The mattress held little padding, but I fell onto it anyway.

I stared at the onyx ceiling and burrowed deeper into the bed, tugging the patchwork quilt to my chin.

Exhaustion pulled my heavy eyelids shut, and in an instant, panic quickened my pulse. If I fell asleep, he'd return. Worse yet, I knew the visions would as well.

But it'd been far too long since I'd gotten decent rest, and the bed cradled my aching body after a day spent riding and running.

A shaky breath parted my lips, and the black and crimson swirls filled the edge of my vision until it devoured everything.

An endless stream of torment disrupted the once-peaceful forest.

Hair and petals fell in flashes of red and black as icy tears coated my cheeks. My body jolted while I tried to fight my way free. I pushed and kicked, crying and screaming for something, anything.

The anguish was unbearable, coursing like relentless waves. No break. No reprieve. And as I writhed on the ground, I understood my mother's inability to love me. How could you allow yourself to care for someone, knowing the horror they would one day endure?

I yearned for the pain to swallow me so I would be free of it.

He sneered at me, eyes like flames.

"Elita." The voice cut through the nightmare, pulling me into the dreamspace.

I straightened against the headboard, causing the wooden bedframe to creak beneath me. Like always, the moment he materialized in the strange state between sleep and waking, the air thickened.

Casimir leaned against the windowpane. The curtains fluttered in an ethereal, shimmering breeze. Though I knew it wasn't real, merely a side effect of his disturbance.

His black hair lay in a wavy mess, and some of the dark strands came close to his eyes, their irises like crimson embers. A smirk tugged at the corner of his lips when he pushed away from the window.

He moved across the room, appearing more shadow than man—a stark contrast to the boy who once haunted my dreams. We were no longer children or uncouth adolescents, and his presence no longer brought me fear. Only vexation.

I peeled the worn-out quilt from my body. My skin was scorching, and the cool air made me shiver with relief.

"I'm too exhausted to do this tonight. My answer hasn't changed," I said. The dreamspace radiated with my annoyance.

Casimir sighed. "How you manage not to bore of such a redundant life never ceases to amaze me."

"This has nothing to do with how redundant my life is. For how persistent you are, you've never given me a good enough reason to leave."

"Outside of the fact that if you stay, you'll be used in unimaginable ways?" He quirked a brow. "That's not reason enough? Shall I beg?"

I rolled my eyes. "The alternative is running and allowing the kingdom to suffer. I wilt either way. Might as well do my part," I said, resting my head on the headboard. Though the idea of it all made my insides coil, it hurt more to pretend I had a choice.

Casimir shook his head and glanced at the ceiling. "I thought you had more fight in you than that." His gaze met mine. "You seem so certain it has to be you. As if there aren't other families who harbor Roses." His tall figure moved like a wisp of fog, and he stopped beside me, gesturing to the empty spot at the end of the bed.

I made room, and he lowered himself onto the mattress a few spaces from me.

Having him so close again felt odd. It had been five years since he last visited me in a dream—until a month prior when he wedged his way back in. I didn't resist. Loneliness left me weak and in need of company, even if he wasn't my first pick.

Casimir shifted on the bed next to me, and I knew what he was going to say before the words left his lips. We'd had the same conversation nearly every night since his return.

"You need to cross the Forge. The buds change things, and you're out of time to second guess. Eventually, the guards will find their way to you. Their search grows closer every day."

"There's no point in prolonging the inevitable. My wilt will happen, regardless of what I do," I argued back, sounding more akin to a child than a grown woman. I shied away from his piercing stare. The back of my neck grew warmer.

Casimir gave me a knowing look. "Never thought you'd so quickly choose to be a martyr," he mused.

I averted my gaze and wrapped my arms around my torso. "Don't be daft. If there's a better path that doesn't involve dying in the Drought, I'm willing to listen."

Casimir studied me, mulling over what to say. He knew there wasn't an answer that would convince me, but he tried anyway. "You know what they will require of you. Are you prepared to pay that price so willingly?"

The weight of it wasn't lost to me, and I despised that he stooped to such tactics to get me to leave.

To carry a child, not one brought from love, but one required by duty. Fathered by a stranger then torn from my arms, and groomed from birth to be the next sacrifice. It was horrific to imagine, and I hoped the existence of my buds meant there wouldn't be time for them to consider me capable of carrying the next Rose.

My hands knotted into the sides of my tunic. If I lingered on the cruel realities that had befallen many Roses before me, it'd conjure more nightmares.

I steadied my emotions before I spoke. "You know that's the last thing I want, and you have no idea how much the prospect haunts me. But I don't know if I can trust you. How do I know something terrible isn't waiting for me when I make it to the Forge?"

Casimir leaned back as if I offended him. "I have no intention of putting you in harm's way, El. I only mean to help." His posture relaxed, bringing his shoulder closer to mine.

The proximity became too much.

I stood, no longer desiring to be near him. It was strange to see such a different version of him.

Until his recent visits, he was merely a boy or a lanky adolescent who wasn't so sure of himself. He appeared hardened by the passing of time. All sharp edges, scarred hands, and confidence I envied.

In the years he was absent, Casimir changed. Whereas I struggled with feeling perpetually stuck.

He took in my appearance and his expression went grim. "It won't be long before the petals bloom. How will you ever make it to the Forge if you're locked away?"

"Why must I be the one to leave? What happened to the promise all those years ago when you said you'd come for me?"

Part of me knew the answer. An apparition couldn't truly take me away from the confines of the cottage.

"You know it's complicated," Casimir dismissed. "We're running out of time, and I can't help you from here."

"And where is 'here'? Why won't you tell me?"

He sighed at my question and ran a hand over his face. "I have to go." He stood and glanced over my hair once more. "You'll find me where the water is black, but the moon does not reflect on its surface. I'll be expecting you by the fourth bloom near the Forge. Don't linger there too long, or you'll run out of time."

"Casimir—"

True to form, he vanished.

Sweat drenched my body, causing my linens to cling to my skin. Black curls lay flat to the back of my head, matted from the moisture. A heavy breath shook my shoulders as I sat. Tangled hair overwhelmed my vision as rogue tendrils fell over the bridge of my nose. For a moment, I pushed them back and allowed myself to catch my breath. My palms were damp, and every thud of my heart threatened to make me dizzy.

Casimir hadn't stayed long enough to ease the thick cloud of unrest that followed my visions of death. The nightmare held on to me like a fearful child to its mother, and I tried to shake off the overwhelming sensation.

I inhaled slowly through my nose, attempting to steady the thrum of my pulse. When the shaking in my limbs ceased, I let my hair fall onto my shoulders and down my spine. I stood from the bed and straightened out my wrinkled gown.

It was routine, walking out of my room and into the empty hallway. I had done it plenty of times before. The darkness didn't phase me anymore, even as the moon hid behind heavy storm clouds. I had grown accustomed to tiptoeing through the hall in the pitch black.

A single candle flickered downstairs as darkness settled over the realm. The hour was late, and I hadn't intended to sleep the day away.

Sneaking into the kitchen, I approached the stove to start a pot of tea, in hopes a cup of chamomile could lull me back to sleep. Someone cleared their throat, and I yelped, whirling around to find Father on the settee. His glasses perched on his nose, and I noted multiple thick books sprawled out on the table in front of him.

I placed a hand on my chest and took a steadying breath. "You scared me."

He chuckled and set his notebook on the stained table. "More trouble sleeping?" he asked, though he already knew.

"Unfortunately," I muttered, avoiding the conversation of Casimir.

He had vanished when I turned sixteen, giving me a few years of silence until recently. They were unaware of Casimir's return. I hoped to keep it that way.

"Do you want to talk about it?" Father took off his glasses and set them next to his worn-out notebook. I saw it in the way his shoulders drooped with exhaustion—he wanted the distraction and no longer desired to be knee-deep in his work.

I decided against a pot of tea and instead poured myself a mug of water from the pitcher and made my way over to the chaise. I sat on the side closest to the hearth and sipped at the mug.

"After all these years, it's nearly time," Father said, leaning deeper into the settee.

I choked on my water, sputtering and coughing.

"By the gods, not that." He shook his head and ran a hand over his graying hair. "Once I finish training my replacement, I'll finally be taking a long leave." He chuckled apologetically. "That prince has about drove me mad. He's run us all ragged."

I watched him pause, swallowing thickly before he stared at the flickering hearth. "Plus, this extra year without you blooming has been a gift. I'd hate to squander more time away from home." His voice grew thick with emotion, and he cleared his throat.

Not wanting to talk about such morbid things, I tried to change the subject. "You know, a great way to spend some of that time could involve the festival," I suggested halfheartedly.

Father chuckled, and wrinkles fanned around his eyes. He met my gaze, his smile clinging to sadness at the edges. "If it weren't so dangerous, I would. But the guards are getting too desperate. They've begun to target people with black hair. It's madness."

The hope of lightening the conversation evaporated.

If I could stay hidden until the petals bloomed, there was no way for them to complete their wicked ceremonies. And if I continued to tempt fate, the consequences would be unbearable.

I sipped at my water, then set it down on a small table. It felt like defeat to admit how afraid I'd become, but it became impossible to pretend.

Quietly, I spoke the humiliating truths to the one person I could. "As a child, I was never scared of going out in the village. I couldn't grasp what it meant to be discovered. But now..." My fingers picked at the hem of my tunic. "Even in places I used to feel safe, the need for my bloom becomes more evident each passing day."

Father nodded in understanding. "Your mother told me you went to the garden. Did you see?"

"Yes, I did." I tried to ignore the increasing weight of dread despite how it warped my words. "I didn't think it could get worse than last year's early wilt." Absentmindedly, I glanced at the prick on my palm. "There was only one flower left in the entire garden, but it wilted when I touched it. And there was a man there who saw it happen. One of your students, I think—"

"Someone saw you?"

"I mean, I go to the garden often—"

"No, did he see *you*? Did he see your eyes?" Father's posture went rigid.

"I don't know. I noticed his so I'm sure..." The entire kingdom was on the hunt for Roses. I knew how dangerous it was, but there was no way to undo it.

Father ran a hand over his face, and panic overwhelmed his features as one of his worst fears came to fruition. He refrained from scolding me, but his expression betrayed his upset. I had agreed to keep my head low and avoid any interaction with people. That I would watch my feet, and that's all I did. But he wouldn't lecture me. He knew how much I needed time outside of the cottage, and I wasn't a child anymore.

We both allowed the conversation to fade, and sensing he no longer wanted a distraction, I stood to leave.

"Elita," he called as I began my walk up the stairs. I glanced back at him. "I don't want you to spend the rest of your life in fear. You have a choice. You always will."

"I know," I said with a soft smile, then went to leave.

"And Elita?"

"Yeah?"

"I see the buds." He struggled to say it, his voice broken. "You don't have to carry that burden alone."

Sudden tears sprang to my eyes. The weight of it hunched my shoulders, and I kept my face obscured in a curtain of black curls that fell from behind my ear.

Something about his acknowledgment made it feel real.

My time had run out. Soon, I would die.

Stray tears escaped, and I was grateful my father couldn't see them.

Steadying my voice, I whispered down to him. "I know, Father." Before he could say anything else or notice my tears, I climbed the rest of the stairs.

Part of me wanted to assure him his fear was unnecessary and that I would be fine, irrespective of the outcome. When my bloom wilted, I would at least have the gift of drifting into nothingness. My body used and sheared, but I would be free from it. Carried away by Akuma to a place where even the memory of a child born to shoulder the burden of a sacrifice could not follow me.

I told myself that I could endure it with the promise of an inevitable death within a year.

If only lying to myself worked.

Chapter Three

Morning light poured over the garden and illuminated the remaining flowers of the season: bat orchids and black velvet petunias. Dew clung to the grass as I made my way through the backyard, a basket held tight in my hand, ready to collect eggs and vegetables.

Chickens clucked impatiently while they waited for their feed. Only to be outdone by the horse's whinnying. I chuckled at their incessant noise and took my time to go through the garden, watching for vibrant vegetation apt for picking.

Leaves and stems plucked at my hands while I searched through the garden. I found and retrieved the few figs, which looked ready, along with a handful of strawberries. When I reached for a tomato, the light pressure of my grasp made it crumble. Heat rippled through my palm.

I gasped and dropped the rotten fruit. The tomato didn't have its usual spoiled squish; it felt as if someone stripped the moisture from it. The center was hollow, and the outer skin flaked away in the garden bed.

My hands shook when I dusted them off on the edge of my dress. I stared at it, bewildered. Memories of the barren garden were fresh in my mind, and when a breeze dusted away the remnants of the dried tomato, it replaced it with another wave of foreboding.

A raven whistled when it landed among the vegetation, trying to pluck at the leftover pieces. I shooed it away with a wave of my hand.

One of the hens' relentless clucking brought me out of my daze, and I stood with the basket in my hand, unwilling to grab another tomato.

The plush grass flattened beneath my shoes as I made my way over to their coop. When I glanced inside, I huffed a breath of frustration, noting the absence of eggs.

"Lazy girls, Mother won't be happy with you," I said as I dipped my hand into the feed bag attached to a loop on my vest.

The breezy cream linen dress I wore swayed with each step I took. I topped it off with a floral vest, which was one of my favorites. After many mornings spent with hands too full in the gardens, I sewed a leather loop to the side of it for convenience' sake.

I tossed a handful of grains into the coop and watched the chickens scramble and cluck.

Grinning, I stood, and my gaze fixed on the horses waiting at the stable door. "You two are next," I assured them.

The backdoor shutting caught my attention, and I turned to see Father walk out of the cottage, his riding clothes on.

"Up already?" he asked.

I lifted my shoulders nonchalantly before I made my way to the cottage, clutching the basket. "I didn't sleep well. But now that you're here, you can take care of the horses," I teased.

Father chuckled and shook his head. "Shoulda known you'd make me finish the chores. And on my day off, no less."

I feigned hurt. "How rude of me. Despite doing the morning chores daily, with no days off."

He rolled his eyes in response and walked over to the horses. Feeling accomplished, I turned to the cottage, which caused the dress to twirl at my calves. Upon reaching the steps to the back door, I opened it and placed the basket inside.

I didn't bother to carry them to the kitchen, and instead, I turned back to my father with my arms crossed over my chest. "The chickens still aren't laying," I said, ignoring the topic of the tomatoes. Another conversation about my inevitable bloom and death wasn't on my list of things I wanted to happen.

Father shrugged. "Ah, they'll lay when they're ready. I think they do it to spite your mother."

"If that's truly the case, I have no complaints."

He laughed in reply and grabbed a bucket of feed. It poured out into the horse's trough, making a melodic tune as it bounced off the empty bottom.

When it ceased, Father set the bucket down. "You up for a hunt today?" he asked.

My interest piqued. "Really?" I couldn't hold back the giddiness in my tone. It had been a month since we were able to hunt or forage, and the days spent in the stuffy cottage or wandering the village were beginning to seem endless. Getting out into the woods brought me a sense of freedom I never felt in our little pocket of the kingdom. As my bloom closed in, the distraction was what I needed.

Father approached the faded black fence where the horses were kept and retrieved a saddle from a nearby post. "You may want to change before we head out," he said, noting the dress I wore.

I glanced at the cream fabric, more upset to part with the red and green floral vest than anything. "I put so much effort into making these and never have anywhere to go but the backyard or the markets." It was mostly in jest, but I saw the way Father's expression fell.

It wasn't his fault I didn't have many places to go. I reserved my bitter resentment for Aeterna.

"We don't have to hunt today if you aren't up for it. I've felt bad for how absent work has made me," Father said.

I shook my head. "No, I want to hunt, really. I've missed it. Just give me a minute." With a grin, I darted back into the cottage to change.

At the kitchen table, I caught sight of Mother going through the basket I had set inside the door. She grumbled something to herself and appeared upset. I assumed it was regarding the lack of eggs, and I made my way to the stairs as quietly as possible to avoid the blame.

I made it to my room without making a sound and went straight for my chest of clothes. A black pair of leather riding pants sat at the top of the mess of clothing, and I grabbed them out.

Working in a rush, I found a linen top and threw my vest over it, not willing to part with the floral pattern yet.

It only took me a few minutes to get ready and tiptoe back out of the cottage. Once I was outside, Father had already saddled his chestnut horse and was adjusting its bridle. I grinned and grabbed the items for my horse, Mora, walking over with a skip in my step. Mora's slick black coat glistened in the sun.

Father glanced over his shoulder and smiled. "I hope you're actually ready to look for animal signs," he said.

"I couldn't help it last time. I was exhausted," I replied with a rise and fall of my shoulders.

Father laughed. "You fell asleep against a tree and left me to hunt on my own."

"Lucky for you, I'm mostly well-rested. Kind of." Even though I tried to make my tone light, I saw the knowing look in his expression. When his hands froze on the leather strap of the bridle, frustration replaced the excitement.

His hands released the bridle, and he faced me. "Did your ghost finally come back?" he asked, though he didn't need to. The exhaustion that followed Casimir's recurring presence was impossible to hide.

I tried to play it off with a shrug and threw a saddle blanket over the back of my horse. "It isn't anything to fuss over," I said.

"Elita, you know that isn't true. It's been years. What has it said this time?"

I groaned. "Can we focus on the hunt? There isn't anything new to tell. It's always the same ramblings conjured by my mind. I'm not sure why it would mean anything." Even as the words left my mouth, I knew they were a lie. It was easier to ignore the strange presence in my dreams, but Casimir had given me a clue to where to find him—if he were indeed real. A reflectionless pool of water. It was too vague to make anything of it, and I wouldn't worry my father with such a silly riddle.

It wasn't hard to get him to let it go. Much like my mother, any mention of Casimir made him uncomfortable. Despite all my father knew about the Rose people or what his books told him, there wasn't anything about spirits haunting Roses or strange dream delusions. No, that was a product of my loneliness. Not a trait Roses shared.

The fact did little for my unease.

We both finished preparing our horses without a word. When Mora was ready, I swung my leg over her saddle and sat. I waited while Father fumbled into his own. The bow on his back made the task more difficult.

I stifled a giggle when he got flustered with the gear he had on, and I guided Mora toward the open gate.

Once Father finished settling into his saddle, he mimicked my movement and followed me out of the wooden fence.

Silence carried on between the two of us. I was grateful for hunting and its ability to free me from having to discuss the matter of Casimir any more than I wanted to.

We needed to stay quiet if we were to catch anything. The sole noise we could afford was the hoofbeats of our horses. Something louder would scare off any deer or other decent game in the area.

The back of our land led straight into the Iron Forests. While we were but one village in the kingdom, there were many more spaced throughout those same woods. Some villages would take a week-long journey or more to get to. I didn't concern myself with them since it wasn't wise for me to travel throughout the kingdom.

The woods that surrounded our cottage were familiar to me, and Father trusted me enough to take the lead. Scouting for tracks became a habit after many times being responsible for the task, and my eyes scanned the forest grounds while we made our way in.

I watched for branches snapped, berry bushes that appeared bothered, or paw prints among the dirt. The relentless search paid off when I came across the unmistakable mark of a deer hoof. I swiftly reined in my horse, bringing us to a stop.

Father copied me, and we both dismounted silently. The sole of my boots sunk into the damp earth, and I glanced around the area before spotting more deer signs.

While I surveyed our surroundings, Father tied the horses to trees and joined me where I crouched behind a bush. I gestured for him to follow me through the trees. We remained low until we were further from the horses. I rose with caution and glanced around once more.

I noticed more disruption through the foliage, followed by more hoof prints. I pointed out what I saw to my father, and he nodded in response.

The quiet of the hunt never bothered me. It gave me a sense of pride to track for my father, especially when it all paid off and the hunt was a success. Hunting had become a pleasant escape from the mundane.

We made our way through the trees, and I noticed my father scanning the forest along with me. He paused and directed my attention toward a cluster of mushrooms. I glanced between him and the fungi, and my brow quirked.

He gestured at them. "Would you eat those if it was all you could find?" His question confused me.

"This has to be a joke?" I scoffed. I glanced over the seemingly harmless mushroom and its off-white cap. "If I yearned for a painful death, I suppose I would eat it."

Father gave me a stern expression.

I sighed. "No, I wouldn't eat it, Father. It's death cap."

He nodded. "These things are important to know, Elita. What's fit for consumption, and what's not. It may save your life one day."

I groaned, not wanting another survival lecture.

"Now, don't sulk. I only want to teach you important things that can keep you safe," Father pestered.

A branch snapped somewhere nearby, and I crouched lower. I searched through the trees but couldn't see the cause. Judging by the volume, I suspected it was the deer.

"Tracking isn't just meant to be for entertainment," Father said, his tone not low enough. I gave him an exasperated look, but he waved it off. "These skills could save you. Knowing these things could be the difference between life and death."

I flinched and stood. "The chances of me running into something dangerous in these woods are minuscule—"

"That isn't true, and you know it. A single villager could see you in these woods, and all it would take is one look before they notify the guards to take you away."

An icy sensation ran down my spine. "We're hunting for food, Father. No one said anything about knowing how to hunt *people*."

"You know that's not what I meant," he said.

"I'm aware. But I don't see how you expect me to protect myself in such a way. If I'm to die by a bloom soon, I will do so with innocent hands, regardless of what a villager does to me."

A haunted look crossed his face, and he shook his head, averting his gaze. "This realm is filled with cruel and sick people. Try to remember that."

"I know, Father."

In spite of himself and the grim topic, Father smiled. "I'm not a very good father if I don't teach my daughter to protect herself," he said, his tone lighter. "I know you're grown now, but you're still my little flower. It's my job to keep you safe. It goes without saying, but the realm doesn't just need a bloom; it needs you."

The intensity my father spoke with brought me more unease. I didn't know if I could protect myself if I faced a choice of someone else's life or my own. Mine was already on borrowed time. There was a chance for the kingdom to find another Rose, and I didn't want to die with blood on my hands.

I huffed in frustration, and without having to look, the sensations in the earth made me tune in to the stillness.

Branches snapped to our right, and I pointed in the direction. I didn't have to tell my father. We had hunted many times before.

He pulled his bow out, adorned it with an arrow, and let it fly.

Chapter Four

The earth shuddered beneath my feet. Dust and spatters of blood painted a horrific tapestry on every inch of my exposed skin. Wisps of the torn black dress whipped at my calves in the sour breeze, brushing against the broken ground. I ripped my gaze from the jarring sight, and when I tipped my head skyward, my heart sank, going heavy in my chest.

A towering figure draped in onyx stretched its arms out over me, its fingers contorted sickly as it clawed through the sky. From the figure's palms rained crimson rose petals, spinning to the earth in a delicate dance that felt misplaced in the desolation around us.

One of them landed on my cheek, warm and wet. I flinched and wiped my face. When I pulled my hand back, I stiffened.

Blood coated my palm.

I stumbled back, feet bare and bloodied as they caught on debris. The earth cracked and trembled, turning black with rot.

The figure followed me, its scarlet eyes illuminated beneath the drape.

When I tried to breathe in, the air evaporated. My mouth gaped, and I clutched my throat, staring at the draped figure.

The arms reached for me.

Black vines wrapped around my feet, and I fell backward onto the *rotted ground. The impact of the fall rang in my head. Too real, too tangible.*

My attempt to flee was futile as the vines tightened, and the figure closed the space, shrinking to the size of a human as it hovered inches from my face.

"They search for you." The voice echoed as though a thousand spoke at once.

It raised a hand, its nails like claws. The same black rot that devoured the earth twisted up the figure's skin like corrupted vines.

Heat rippled through the air, and quick as a whip, its palm pressed against my chest. The weight crushed me, and I opened my mouth to scream.

The corruption wrapped around my throat and choked me.

"Elita?" A breath of relief filled my lungs when Casimir's voice brought me out of the nightmare and into the dreamspace.

I lay there, pulse racing. I didn't respond at first. Instead, I rolled my ankles, flexed my hands, and gulped another greedy breath.

When I shook off most of the leftover panic, my head lolled to the side, and I met Casimir's gaze. He sat by the window, a fist under his jaw.

Casimir tipped his head, giving me a strange look before he chuckled. "You're pleased to see me?"

I groaned at his tone and sat up despite how I continued to tremble.

"Hm, nice nightgown," he said, voice dripping in sarcasm when he glanced at the sleep clothes I had put on before bed. It extended to my ankles, with long sleeves to match. Lace adorned the top, and the color was a soft periwinkle. It appeared more suited for a grandmother's nightgown, but I found it comfortable, so I scoffed at him.

"It's rather comfortable," I said, voice still shaky. "Plus, I don't recall caring what an imaginary man thinks of me."

"Sounds a *little* like you do." He raised an eyebrow. "And you're still stuck on the imaginary thing, huh? Yet you continue to indulge me."

I bit the inside of my cheek and faced away from him. His awareness of my thoughts bothered me. And as if I wasn't flustered enough, he read my mind once more.

"I don't read minds. I do, however, have more access to your stream of thoughts—while I'm in the dreamspace, at least."

"Very comforting."

"I can tell you mean that," Casimir said, unfolding himself to stand. He walked over to me, and his grin fell into something more grave. The intensity of his crimson gaze made me fidget. He ran his hand through his hair and left it on the back of his neck. "Nightmare?" he asked, taking on a gentle tone.

A lump formed in my throat, and I bunched the quilt over my lap, then proceeded to pull my knees to my chest. I rested my chin on the warm fabric, not bothering to watch him. He never did stay too far, and I made room for him to sit.

"Well, is there a reason you seem relieved by my presence? Or do you intend to keep that from the imaginary man?" he asked while leaning back in my bed. His arms stretched out behind him to hold his torso up.

When his movement settled, I looked at my hands and realized they were trembling.

"Not sure what you mean. Your interruptions do a number on my sleep, and I'm fairly certain you're proof I've either lost my mind or I'm being haunted. I find no relief in that."

By his expression, Casimir found my answer entertaining. "So you say. Although, typically, your frustration is palpable, and your face does that thing when you're pissy." He shrugged.

My teeth ground together, and any comfort I initially experienced dissipated.

Casimir raised a brow and proceeded to sit back up. "Or is it that you've finally decided to be reasonable and you're relieved to be free of Eldravine?"

"You aren't helping." I paused and ran my fingers over the fabric of the quilt. "It was a nightmare." The very mention of it made the hair on my arms raise. "Only it didn't *feel* like a nightmare. It felt more real than being in the dreamspace."

His weight shifted the bed when he turned more of his body toward me. "Was it the same one you've always had?"

"No." When I answered, the memory of the figure's voice made me ill. "I wasn't alone in the nightmare. There was a figure with me. It said someone was searching for me."

Casimir's eyes narrowed. "It was likely just a dream. I wouldn't try to make something out of it."

Beneath the erratic flutter of my heart, the pressure from the figure's palm remained. I rubbed at the spot and tried to forget how the black vines crept under my skin.

"El?"

I hummed in response.

Casimir's expression mirrored my confusion while he watched me rub the sore spot in my chest. He hesitated before he spoke. "This figure, what did it look like?"

A field of goosebumps erupted across my skin. "You said not to make something out of it."

"Humor me."

The tension made the dreamspace flicker around us.

I choked back the fear. "It was draped in black, but its eyes...they were vibrant red. Whatever it was, its skin appeared diseased. Like black vines—"

Casimir recoiled as if I'd spat at him. His expression flashed with alarm, making my heart hammer in my chest.

"What did I say? What is it?" I asked.

He tore his gaze from me and stared at the wall, his jaw tense. He stayed that way for a moment when, without warning, he began to fade.

I sprung up, panic replacing comfort. "Please, stay," I said, my voice trembling. I reached out to grab him, but his hand, like smoke, passed through mine.

"I can't stay. When you're afraid, it makes it difficult to hold the connection." He tried to explain, but it didn't register with me. I stared at him, pleading.

A muscle in his jaw twitched, and I sensed his remorse. It warped the dreamspace until it resembled a blurred painting. He evaporated in front of me, fast and cruel.

I didn't sleep again after Casimir left. The fear of the figure returning kept me awake and made it difficult to function when the sun finally rose.

The light that poured in the windows at least offered me a break from the shadows my lantern cast. The darkness felt too suffocating after the nightmare. For once, I wished my ghost had stayed.

When I heard my parents stir downstairs, I got out of bed. My muscles were stiff after lying rigid for hours.

I threw on a black tunic and an emerald leather bodice over it and left my room, determined to escape the cottage for the day. The visions increased with the presence of the buds, and I needed time to sort through them without the weight of my father's grief.

I bounded down the steps, and Father glanced up from his breakfast, grinning from ear to ear as he stood from his stool. The chipper attitude wasn't what I had expected from him.

"Not so fast," he said, pulling me into a tight hug before I had a second to reply or dart out the door. "The buds may have shown up, but that doesn't mean you get to hide and wallow."

The rough fabric of his marigold work cloak brushed at the edge of my cheek, familiar to me since he had spent most of his time in it lately.

He smelled less like himself, and I wondered if the Temple would also steal his comforting scent.

I smiled and embraced him. "I'm not trying to hide." A poorly executed lie. "I just thought you two would have left for the festival by now, you know, to avoid hurting my feelings since I can't go," I joked as he pulled back.

He shook his head and gestured over his shoulder. "Wouldn't count on it. You know this one doesn't like fun," he said in jest, pointing at my mother. She rolled her eyes, but a small smile betrayed her when it disrupted her serious demeanor.

She returned to the whistling kettle that blew steam on the stove. Father moved back to his stool and pushed his plate my way, nudging me with his elbow.

"Eat before you go out. No sense in going hungry because of...well, you know." Father wouldn't say it outright, and we didn't need him to.

When she finished pouring the kettle, Mother turned from the counter and glanced at me, observing my clothes. "Are you certain it's wise to head out?" she asked, a steaming teacup in her hand. Orange and honey filled the space when she stirred it.

"I was going to go for a walk through the woods and avoid the village for a while. You're both welcome to come along," I said.

Father's mood shifted, and his head dipped down. "I'm needed at the gardens. I've been trying to train a replacement so I can have more time here. The young man I'm training doesn't seem to take it seriously enough." He sounded upset.

My attention went to my mother, and she shook her head. "I have things to do here."

The answer wasn't shocking, though with the presence of my buds, I had hoped it would change.

I snatched a piece of buttered rye off of Father's plate and turned to leave.

"Don't forget your shawl," they said in unison.

"I know." I grinned and grabbed it off the hook. I wrapped it around my hair, tucking pieces in as the curls tried to poke out. "You know, I envy you both and your straight hair," I grumbled, peering over at them after I slid my boots on.

Father grunted in response while he rummaged through papers near his plate.

"Before you go, you haven't seen my notebook, have you?" he asked, his gaze fixed downward in the mess of pages.

"I haven't." I swung my cloak over my shoulders.

Father muttered to himself and glanced at my mother, hoping she knew. She simply shrugged.

"It's fine, I'll check my study. Don't stay out too long. Oh, and avoid the garden," he added while he shuffled through the disarray of papers and books. I nodded and waved before darting out the door.

The leaves whirled in the trees, turning over in anticipation of the incoming rain. Clouds made a wave of gray through the skies, moving with the strong breeze. I secured the shawl over my hair to prevent it from flying off and started down the path.

My heart tugged at me. I wanted nothing more than to sneak off to the festival. I ignored the temptation and went towards the forest, a familiar path my father and I took many times after the nightmares.

Pine trees and heavy foliage swallowed me when I ducked through the archway, which led further from the street and to the woods. It smelled glorious—the rich and earthy scent before the rain.

The small path weaved its way through tall emerald trees. Brush grew up at the edges of the trail, making it easier to follow. I scarcely needed it after trudging through those same woods many times before. Somewhere in the dense foliage, the Iron Border stood not far from our cottage. The only border wall I had ever seen when my father and I hunted a little too far.

My mind wandered to Casimir and I forced back the memories of his alarm when I described the figure. Instead, I lingered on Casimir's previous instruction for me to go to the Forge Border. The further I walked, the stronger my desire to be brave enough to make the journey grew. It would be easy to slip away. Leave while Father taught his students and Mother avoided me.

Twenty-one years spent in seclusion, with no other company than my parents or my ghost. It pained me, despite knowing my father did his best to protect me. It was unwise to trust people in the Iron Thorn. I was aware, but it didn't erase the longing.

Every moment brought me closer to my bloom. The buds had their own pulse, unable to be ignored. If I left, my last moments would be spent alone. And the realm would perish because I was too afraid to die in the same garden where countless other Roses were sheared.

A heavy lump formed in my throat. My gaze fixed on the tranquil stream I stumbled upon, its gentle ripples mirroring the echo of yearning in my chest.

The water rushed over the rocks, submerging them entirely after the previous day's rain. Tall grass at the edges of the stream bent sideways with the power of the water and wind. No matter how hard I tried, the thoughts of solitude persisted.

I sighed and glanced upward to be greeted by the sight of brooding dark clouds dominating the sky. Thunder cracked in the distance and rumbled through the trees. I pulled the hood of my cloak over my shawl and waited for the rain.

After some time passed, drops gradually disrupted the stream, rippling the water in its wake as it fell. Until a few turned into many, and the rain surged. Mother would be furious at me for returning soaked through once more, but I didn't move. Not yet.

I watched it fall for a long time, the feeling of it on my cheeks soothing despite the frigid bite in the air. I tucked my arms into my cloak, wrapping them around my torso while my gaze was transfixed on the rain bouncing off of the water.

A bird squawked close by, followed by pattering. Slick black wings flapped as a raven perched on a rock close to the stream. I watched it twitch and try to shake the water off, to no avail—the rain continued to rush in, soaking the raven. It remained and cocked its head to the side, staring at me with beady eyes.

Bells tolled in the distance, disrupting the tranquility and mixing with the sound of the thunder. I spun around and looked back at the trail, the Iron Thorn far from the small pocket of peace I found. My pulse thrummed with the peculiar sound.

Once more, the bells reverberated, something I had heard only twice in my entire life. Eeriness disrupted the woods. Despite how serene the forest appeared, I couldn't shake the feeling.

I looked back at the raven. It jumped from one stone to another, pausing to glance at me. It stared at me like it expected me to do something. My brow pulled together. Then, as quick as it came, the raven cried and lifted itself with soaked wings, disappearing into the forest.

The tolling ceased, and just as I let my shoulders release the tension, Casimir's presence hit me like a wave—overpowering and unfamiliar in its intensity.

"*Run.*" Casimir's voice made my pulse quicken. I didn't hesitate. I started sprinting back down the path, slipping in the mud and picking myself back up in an instant while I stumbled through the trees. The sound of the bells resounded louder and more frantic than before.

"*Elita, no. Don't go back.*" Casimir pleaded in my head. Desperate, pained.

A sour scent overwhelmed me. The air was thick, causing my lungs to work harder as I persisted along the trail, with the archway leading back to the street visible. My limbs burned with exertion, but I pushed myself to move faster, my heart pounding while the rain pelted my skin. The emergency bells blared, echoing dreadfully throughout Eldravine.

Mud coated my boots and trousers. Branches ripped at the fabric of my cloak. The hood fell back as I sprinted until I broke through the trees.

Heat overwhelmed me.

Smoke twisted sinuously in the sky as flames licked up the mossy cottage I had left no more than an hour before. I stared at it in a mix of disbelief and horror. The pounding of my heart drowned out the sound of the bell tolling.

Frantically, my eyes searched for my parents, trying to find them somewhere outside of the destruction.

There was no sign of them.

"*There's nothing left. It's not safe.*" Casimir's voice echoed in my head, louder than normal.

My chest rose and fell so quickly, I thought I might be sick. I shook my head vigorously, screaming inside my mind, telling him to leave. His warning meant nothing to me.

The upstairs windows of the cottage bled flames, creating a terrifying display. It resembled a horrified face, fire spitting out of the windows like burning tears.

My feet carried me forward. The sound of the emergency bell continued to ring close by. The thrum of hoofbeats grew closer, but they wouldn't get there in time. I had to make sure they were safe.

The heat nearly knocked me to my knees when I got closer to the cottage. I pulled my shawl down over my mouth and nose, throwing the front door open no matter how my mind begged me not to.

Smoke billowed out of the door, blinding me. I raised my forearm over my face and pushed through into the sweltering heat.

"Father, Mother!" Fabric over my mouth muffled my words. The cottage shuddered as it fell apart, creaking and groaning while the fire ate at its bones. Flames crept down the stairs, a waterfall made of ember and ash.

"Father—"

"Damn it, Fullan."

I whipped around and scanned through the smoke in desperation. Near the table, a body lay sprawled on the floor. My stomach twisted at the sight, and I swooped down.

"Mother." My voice broke. Her pale face glistened with sweat. I tugged on her arm, trying to get her out.

She groaned in protest. "Please, no." Her arm moved out of my hand, and it brought my attention to where she tightly clutched the fabric of her tunic. Blood painted her skin in a horrid display of scarlet. My vision distorted in a blur of smoke and ash.

"What—I don't understand." I moved her hand and lifted the edge of the tunic, exposing a jagged wound torn through her abdomen.

I gasped, inaudible over the sound of the cottage slowly collapsing. The shawl on my face grew damp, and it took me a moment to realize I was crying.

"You shouldn't be here. Go," she rasped, blood sputtering when she spoke. "You can't be here when he comes back."

"You're not making any sense, Mother." My voice trembled, muffled by the shawl.

She grabbed my hand, smearing it with warm blood. "Leave, Elita. You need to cross the Forge." She grimaced and squeezed my hand. I never noticed how nimble and delicate her fingers were. "They'll find you if you get over the wall. Tell them you knew Valor."

Every inch of the cottage shook as memories turned to ash, rendering me unable to think clearly.

"Let me get you and Father out, please."

She let out an agonizing cry, shaking her head. Her head lolled to the left, and I followed her gaze, releasing a strangled sob.

Crimson stained in harsh contrast to the familiar marigold cloak. It splattered the fabric and strewn papers. Father's body lay in a pool of blood. No twitch left in his ink-stained fingers.

Frantically, I tore the shawl from my mouth. "Father! Can you hear me?" I cried.

"Your father is gone." She glanced behind me at the door. "He came for your father. He came for you." I stared at her, my tears wetting her tunic. "You can't let him get to you."

I shook my head and stood. Throwing the closest cupboard open, I grabbed a tea towel and dropped back down to her side, applying gentle pressure to the wound on her stomach. She winced and grabbed my hand.

Stormy blue eyes found mine. She looked younger than I ever noticed. Freckles dotted her face, reminding me of my own. It was the first time she gazed back at me, *really* looked at me.

A bloodied hand lifted to my cheek, brushing a stray hair from my face. Another bout of tears fell at the touch. She left her palm on my cheek, a sad smile tugging at her lips.

"You look so much like your father," she said, tears trailing down her temples. Her chin quivered when she took a shaky breath. "You'll be okay, Elita."

My tears coated her hand. "Please, I need you."

"I know." Her hand left my face, shaking as it rested on my arm. Her breathing shuddered, but she didn't look away from me.

The heat in the cottage grew until it became unbearable. I coughed, the smoke thick enough to suffocate me. I had to get her out.

Debris fell from the ceiling, crashing into the sunroom in a bout of smoke and flames. I screamed, throwing myself over my mother to shield her from some of it. Embers singed the fabric of my cloak.

When it settled, I straightened and looked back at Mother.

The heat of a blazing fire couldn't stop the ice that filled my veins. She stared back, but she wasn't there.

"No, no, no, please," I whispered through the sobs, pulling her limp body closer to me.

The stillness swallowed me in a cloud of torment as I wrapped my arms around my mother for the first and last time in years.

I let my head fall back, and a guttural sob ripped through me, threatening to tear my chest open. Despite the roar of the fire, my limbs went numb. Leaving my parents to the flames was unfathomable. I couldn't bring myself to move.

The fire continued to creep down the stairs, eating away at the moisture in the air. I held onto her, heavy and limp in my arms. Her body shook with my weeping, and the tea towel rolled off of her abdomen.

"I'm so sorry. I shouldn't have left." Apologies fell from my lips in fervent prayers. I begged the god of death to let my parents hear them. The smoke made my voice hoarse, but I echoed my apology.

Another burst of flames bled through the ceiling. While it rained down, rough hands tugged at me. My mother rolled off my legs and back into a pool of blood on the floor. The hands pulled again before they gave up and hoisted me off the ground. *Please, let me stay with them.*

Words evaded me, but my body fought the arms wrapped around my waist while they attempted to pull me from the cottage. In the grip of anger and grief, I kicked and thrashed without stopping. I screamed and wailed the further they took me.

The hazy sky burned my eyes when they got me out. Guards and healers surrounded the burning cottage, and horse-pulled water tankers crowded the yard. They all watched in bewilderment at the destruction.

I pounded my fists on the person who held me. "Don't leave them!" My voice cracked, fists covered in blood and soot.

When our eyes met, an icy shiver ran down my spine.

A Temple guard dressed in all red held onto me, carrying me from the cottage as the front door collapsed with a puff of black smoke.

I shrieked, fighting harder until he had no choice but to drop me on the ground. The pain of the fall didn't register, and I bolted up from the muddy path, running for the cottage.

Another body collided with mine, catching me at the waist. "We need a sedative!" A voice yelled over the ringing bell. I fought the new set of arms, trying to get free. Flames bled from every opening of the cottage. It looked as if it were screaming.

My bloodied hands stopped clawing at the arms. The adrenaline dissipated when the realization hit me. *They're gone.*

Fetid aromas mixed and filled my nose when a healer brought an amber glass to my face. Her hand shook and she stared at me with unease. I tried to push back from her to rid myself of the scent of hops.

A tingling sensation crept through my body until every limb went slack. The cottage swam in a vision of tears and fuzz. I blinked hard to combat it, but each closing of my eyelids made it harder to open them.

The emergency bells tolled, a raven called in the distance, and flames sizzled in protest at the rain. Yet nothing outweighed the sound of my heart shattering.

Chapter Five

W hen I was a child, I used to wonder what the inside of the Temple looked like. I imagined intricate designs of silver and red. Lavish curtains of velvet embroidered with roses and swirls. Floors that shimmered with colorful arrays of sunlight from the stained glass windows.

I never envisioned it being dark, damp, or smelling of copper and rotten fruit. Cages of iron and stone never crossed my mind. It was too cruel of a place for a child to be raised in.

The Temple was meant to be a place to honor the deities. Somewhere for Roses to live from infancy into adolescence. In my ignorance, I imagined beds stacked with lush mattresses and silk blankets. A scenery to rival a bedchamber that belonged to a queen.

Reality was always much more cruel.

My cheek rested on the wet stones when I stirred awake in a cell. Iron bars caged me in with a single wooden bed frame that lacked any padding or blankets. Every guard had a clear view of me in a heap on the floor, missing my boots and cloak.

None of it mattered. Not anymore.

Smoke swirled in the sky outside of my barred window. It met with heavy storm clouds, and even the rain couldn't rid the air of the acrid aroma. It wafted into the cold room, a cruel reminder. A punishment and a lesson for defying the gods and the king—for thinking I could escape penance for my arrogance.

Keys rattled nearby, pulling me out of my listless state. The aftereffects of the hops clung to me, and it made it hard to do more than turn my head in the direction of the guard. He sneered at me; his face pinched in a way that made him appear more akin to a pig than a man. Alarm flashed on his face when I glared back at him.

I had grown so accustomed to the scarlet in my reflection that I forgot perhaps others might have been afraid of my gaze. Much like my mother had been. She avoided looking into my eyes my entire life, and she would never have the chance to again.

The air pulled from my lungs, and my nails dug into my palms.

I stood on quivering legs, and before I took a step, the guard linked a chain to the shackles around my wrists. The metal was cold, and I made the mistake of glancing at my hands, which were covered in dried blood and the remnants of ashes.

When the guard tugged at the chain, I stumbled forward. The soles of my feet grew sticky from dragging them over the stone floor. We left the confines of the cell, and even then, no relief came.

Another Temple guard stood close by, and she opened the wooden doors that separated the cells from a massive hall on the other side. I followed the pig-like man out into the hallway made of stone. In front of us stretched an immense staircase winding upwards into the unknown. Torches perched on the walls, offering little visibility.

We approached the steps, and I followed him without a word while we ascended the stairs. The further we climbed, the air shifted. It went from sour and earthy to crisp, and lavender overwhelmed my senses.

We reached the landing where people shuffled in organized lines. They resembled ants trailing each other in their silky black robes. The edge of their robes dusted on white marble flooring, a jarring contrast.

A few of them froze, appearing bewildered as if they'd never seen a Rose before. Surely, they had seen the last Rose who walked those daunting halls. Even though it had been thirteen years since the last sacrifice, they all appeared old enough to have been present.

The guard led me to another set of doors which extended to the height of the ceiling. The dark cherry wood was opulent, with elaborate floral designs swirling through the dense lumber. It was immaculate and well taken care of, and it didn't fit in the realm we lived in anymore.

The doors opened, and anger threatened to spill from my tongue, but the sight snatched my words away. If it weren't for the relentless grip of grief, I would have let out a gasp.

Two enormous stained-glass windows adorned the stone walls on both sides of the vast room. The stones were their own magnificent display, a strange mixture of white and pale red stone.

Eleven seats stood at the far end of the council hall. They all appeared made of cherry wood, except for the glimmering marble throne in the center of them all.

Temple and Iron Guards lined the walls of the room, swords attached at their hips. Every eye trained on me as I gazed forward to the man who sat on the largest throne.

He stood, his robe as red as the windows. His hair showed significant signs of graying, with scattered streaks of brown amidst the silver strands. He had a beard down to the collar of his robes and beady dark eyes. A black crown with red jewels sparkling throughout it adorned his head, resting on his wrinkled brow. King Lendorr stared down at me with malice in his eyes, his skin almost translucent.

"Elita Blackthorne, daughter to Riona and Aedric Blackthorne. A Rose birthed at home and hidden from the king's orders." The king looked at the council members, pausing on the man closest to him, who had a smaller crown in his blonde hair—the prince—before he glowered at me. "Do you know how many crimes your parents committed?" Gold and silver rings adorned every finger on his hands. Their shine glared as he gripped the arms of his throne.

"Have you cried your voice away?" he mocked. "By hiding the fact your mother was with child and birthing without a healer present, she broke one of our most sacred laws. To hide a Rose child and leave the kingdom to suffer is punishable by death. Does this make sense to you?" he taunted.

The room spun in a horrible display of white and red. Disbelief and anger welled in my chest. I struggled to make a sound, gaping at the king. "But the guards, the healers, they were trying to help," I said, my voice hoarse.

"Do you truly think we can publicly execute a family? That the people of this kingdom would feel safe if we did so, to their knowledge? Don't be naive." King Lendorr's eyes danced with pleasure. The prince mirrored his father, taking delight in my sorrow.

"I don't understand—"

"It had to be done," he snapped. "We can't have traitors living within our kingdom. Least of all, one like your father, who had such a high position. How arrogant of him to think we wouldn't discover a rat in our midst." He tossed a notebook onto the floor at my feet. The familiarity of it made my stomach twist in knots.

"By decree, a healer must deliver every child born in the Iron Thorn to avoid parents harboring Rose children. It is an act of treason to falsify or hide the status of a Rose. The death they received was a mercy compared to being forced to witness your shearing and live their days haunted in a cell. You should be grateful."

I choked on my words. Grief tightened its grip on my throat until my chest burned and tears blurred my vision. I took a step forward as if there were something I could do. The guard yanked me back, and I lost my balance, stumbling.

"Away with her. I want her prepared for a suiter, and I don't want to see her until she's produced the next Rose and it becomes time for her shearing." The king turned with a swift twirl of his robes and strode out of the room without another glance.

The prince followed his father out, a smug grin on his face.

Each of the council members rose from their seats, their posture perfect. They left the room in uniformed lines.

I didn't look up on my way back to my cell. I kept my eyes down, no longer enchanted by a building where such evil could exist.

When they released the chains from my wrists, I slumped to the damp, hard floor of the cell. The metal door squealed shut, the guard locking me back in.

I let the salty tears trail over the bridge of my nose and stared at a single stone on the wall.

My parents' lives were spent for nothing. Twenty-one years all for me to wallow on the floor of the Temple cells regardless—my bloom and sacrifice an inescapable destiny written by the gods.

For every moment I thanked my father for keeping me safe from a life in the Temple, my mother lived in misery, knowing what awaited me. Rather than having to witness my wilt, she was killed for my very existence.

Born into my mother's hands, and in turn, she died in mine.

The rays from the sun turned into scattered moonlight pouring through the bars welded into the stone of my cell. Sinister shadows danced within the cramped space, trying to pull me into the nothingness.

Exhaustion turned into delirium. I couldn't sleep. Not with the way the moon illuminated everything around me. And not with the promise of more nightmares. I couldn't endure to witness my mother dying again, her hands and mine stained with her blood. Even the fleeting thought made me flinch. I shook my head to rid my mind of the images. If only it helped.

Sorrow wedged its way through every bone in my ribcage. Twisting and tightening until every breath seared my lungs. If there was any reprieve, it was that I didn't have to see my father's face void of life.

I tried not to think about Mother's plea for me to leave and go over the Forge. She was the second person to instruct me to cross the border. I longed to know what it meant—what awaited me there.

Thunderous footsteps jolted me from my thoughts. They reverberated through the main hall outside of the cells. With every pounding footfall, I recoiled deeper into the cell.

The guards stood straighter and appeared surprised when the door burst open.

Pale green eyes flashed as they scanned the three different cells. The prince who had been present in the throne room stood in the doorway, his white and silver garb a blunt contrast to the surroundings. Ivory fur lined the top of his embroidered cape.

"Prince Talos," both guards bowed at the waist, stunned. "We weren't expecting you. We apologize for not being prepared for your arrival," one of them said, his hair short and black, nearly shaved down to the skin.

Prince Talos waved them off with a single gloved hand. "No need for apologies. I merely wanted to speak with the Rose before returning to Keldovar."

I grimaced and wished I could vanish the way Casimir did. A puff of smoke, leaving the prince bewildered. But only a ghost could be so lucky, and I was left to tremble in the corner of my cell.

Talos found me cowering in the only occupied cell, a sinister smile on his lips while he made his way toward me.

"My, what trouble you have caused." He spoke smoothly, like honey to mask the poison on his tongue. Blonde hair shimmered in the lantern light, pristine. The years of being spoiled were visible on every inch of him.

Talos approached the bars, glowering at me. He slid a finger over one of the bars and pulled it back to glance at the grime that painted his ivory gloves brown.

"My father insisted speaking to you would be fruitless." He scoffed, gazing with hunger. "I'd have to disagree. A Rose who spent her life in hiding? She is a Rose of high value. The information you may possess, the secrets your family clung to. It has piqued my interest."

Despite the way he stared at me in expectation, I didn't make a sound. I had no information to share. I lacked any secrets outside of a spirit that haunted my sleep. Even so, something told me not to tell him about Casimir's presence in my dreams.

Prince Talos snarled, his patience worn thin within seconds. He slammed a hand against the bars. The sound rattled through the stone room. I grimaced, which brought him joy.

"You wretched girl, you will acknowledge your prince," he snapped, some of his blonde hair falling into his eye and out of the slick way it was pushed back.

I swallowed the lump in my throat. "What you're asking makes no sense." My voice quivered.

Talos's nostrils flared, and he turned from me, stalking over to the guard, his footsteps resounding in the small space. "Open her cell," he demanded, nose to nose with the guard.

Alarm coiled in my body until it felt as though I would burst from the tension. There was nowhere to hide and no way to escape.

The guard gave a single nod and approached my cell, his hands scrambling through the keys until he found the right one. With a click and squeal of iron, it swung on its hinges, allowing the prince to swoop into the cramped space. He stormed over to me.

I sprung from the floor, afraid of being so low.

Regret flared the moment I realized the mistake I made.

Talos's gloved hand grabbed my chin, his grip tight on my jaw. I whimpered and tried to settle my body.

"You think you're clever?" he hissed, hot breath fanning across my face.

"I have no secrets. My only company was my parents." I tried to explain, nearly unable to speak around the way his hand held my jaw.

"Do you think it wise to lie? Your father's notebooks told enough of what knowledge he possessed. You expect me to believe you were not aware? That you have no idea where the other Roses are hiding?"

My brow furrowed, and doubt gripped my throat. "There are no other Roses." The ache in my face was unbearable.

Talos glowered at me, digging his fingers deeper. He looked me over as if appraising me. His glower turned into festering anger. "Useless. You've already begun the budding. Your selfish family has robbed the kingdom of security by hiding you." He pushed me away, causing me to stumble and collide with the bedframe in the corner.

The unforgiving texture of the wood scraped my skin. I caught myself before I landed flat on my back, rapid breaths nearly making me sick.

Prince Talos glared down at me. "Though you may be of no use in procuring the next Rose, I'll find use for you yet," he said, then slicked his loose hair back into the neat strands. "You will remain here until you die in the sacrificial gardens. The guards will have plenty of time to force any information out of you." He grinned, pleased with the idea. "Of course, the choice to give locations, names, it still stands. It would be the smart choice, girl." The word stung like an insult, though he merely appeared ten years my senior.

"I have nothing to give you. There are no other Roses."

"Do you take me for a fool? Do you think yourself special?" he snarled.

"My family and all I've ever known are gone. Why would I lie?"

His rage steadily rose, and in turn, my nerves intensified. Despite how honest I tried to be and how calm I kept my tone, he took offense once more, his lip curling.

"You assume we know nothing of revenge? What better retribution than to go to your grave with your secrets, thinking it was payback for what was done to your wretched family?" He licked his lips, his demeanor frightening. "I seek the Rose people in hiding. And I believe you will lead me to them." He grinned, sure of himself and his accusations.

Except there was nothing to tell. The king did not capture a Rose who held realm-shattering secrets. His prisoner was nothing more than a lonely girl who had long ago lost her mind. One who talked to herself and took the company of plants the same as one would a friend. Every assumption the prince made was wrong, yet his madness continued.

They had me. How was it not enough?

"Whoever it is you seek, I can't help you. I wasn't allowed companions."

A frustrated breath hissed through his nose. "Do not expect peace here, Rose. I would first cut off my own arm before I allowed you to wait quietly for your bloom. By my order, you will be questioned daily. Tortured if need be."

My mouth went dry, panic itching beneath my skin. The threat hung over my head, but I had nothing to give him. There were no other Roses. And had I known for certain if Casimir were real, I wouldn't have given him up, anyway. Not for my gain or freedom. The very thought made me ill.

The urge to lie, to lead him on a pointless manhunt, made me bite my tongue. It would only bring me more pain. There was no place far enough in the kingdom for him to search that would give me time to bloom. No answer to satiate him.

I hoped that regardless of him being the king's heir, a demand for my torture wouldn't be approved. They needed me; they needed my bloom. In the event of my demise, the king would have to recommence his search for a Rose, causing a significant setback. I tried to hold on to the hope it would be enough.

The guards shuffled behind the prince, watching the interaction unfold. Part of me questioned if they would step in should Prince Talos go overboard. Their first duty was to the crowned king, not an heir. And my life meant something to them. The king wouldn't be happy with his son if he were to kill me for being a nuisance.

It gave me some courage when the thought crossed my mind, and I sat straighter. "I don't possess any secrets or names. Do what you wish." The words shook as they left my lips.

I experienced the full force of his fury when his gloved hand struck my cheek. My head jerked to the side, and bone on bone grated in my ears when my teeth ground together.

"Rest assured, I will do as I wish. You will regret giving me that permission." He spat at the floor near my feet and turned on his heel, his cape a flash of white and blinding silver embroidery.

The guards scrambled to close and lock the cell, leaving me to my own company once more. I sat in shock, the burn still crawling through my skin and the fear like a rock in the pit of my stomach.

A prickling sensation ran across my skin, and I raised my hand, pressing it against my cheek. There was no need for him to suppress his anger. There was no fear of being reprimanded. And he would unleash his wrath on me tenfold.

Talos left, but relief never came. Even with his confirmation that my buds rendered me useless in regards to their line of Roses. There was no room for relief in such a place with the threat of torture hanging over my head.

I laid on the uncomfortable, creaky bed—I stared at the ceiling, imagining a life where I was free to live without fear and had a hand in my fate. Parents who didn't worry every time I darted out the door. A haven for my family until my bloom came.

That was never meant to be, and I laid there, the sorrow spilling over in tears that wouldn't stop flowing even if I tried to prevent them.

Chapter Six

Prince Talos kept his word.

A shallow breath left me lightheaded as I slumped onto the stone floor. Sweat dripped from my forehead to my lips. Salt filled my mouth.

Flinching only made it worse, but on instinct, my body tried to jerk out of his rough grip.

Talos had visited my cell four times since my capture eight days before. The healers insisted if I didn't have some reprieve, it would be detrimental to my bloom, so every other day, I dreaded his arrival. Heavy footfalls storming toward my cell became committed to my memory and echoed in my nightmares.

Talos's nails dug into my forearm again, and I gasped.

"You know, Rose, I've begun to believe you," he said. The scent of cloves overwhelmed me when he moved closer. "But I think I've started to enjoy these visits. A suitable punishment for your profitless womb." His laughter brought a chill up my spine.

When Talos first threatened me with torture, I had imagined something more straightforward. Beatings, depriving me of food, perhaps holding my head under water.

Instead, Talos brought another tincture with him, and—despite how I tried to yank free of his grasp—he held me tighter. Delight flickered in his eyes as he dripped the tincture into my mouth.

Sparks erupted in my throat, and I wanted to scream. I desperately tried to. Only an anguished groan escaped my lips as I fell onto the stone floor. I struggled to catch myself when his hand released me.

My body heaved with the sensation of sobbing, but no tears came. Agony echoed through my body until it seared the very marrow of my bones.

Whatever herbs Talos used to make the tincture torched my nerves and vaporized the moisture in my body until I resembled the dry and dead flowers in the Temple Gardens.

"While I know the answer likely won't change, do you have anything to tell me?" Talos asked with a face-splitting grin.

I trembled and sweat left darker drops on the stone beneath me. It poured down the sides of my face and down my back. I waited for the initial shock to dissipate. After the first two times, I knew not to speak until the scorching in my throat settled some.

The horrid liquid moved through me, a tangible sensation. It fell from my throat and lit my limbs on fire.

I grimaced. "There's nothing," I rasped. The words barely escaped my lips before the sensation of my blood boiling made me scramble away in a panic.

There was nowhere to go, yet my body tried to flee every time the force of the tincture reached its peak. No tears fell. I couldn't scream.

I thrashed helplessly, begging for an outlet for the sensation. Prince Talos wouldn't allow me the courtesy of writhing on the damp floor. Like the previous times, he grabbed my forearms and forced me to stand. My legs tried to give out beneath me.

"Please." The word tumbled out of my lips. It did nothing to make Talos back away or change how the liquid rippled through me.

He smirked and pulled me to the wall. I winced when his nails dug into my arms, knowing the aftermath would reveal a patchwork of purple marks. Just as the other bruises started to fade from purple to green, new ones would take their place.

The chains rattled in the room over the sound of my gasps and whimpers. Tears refused to fall, and I wished for the sensation of them dripping down my cheeks.

Talos brought my arms above my head, locking my wrists into the chains. Until it wore off, I would stand and writhe. He always stayed and watched. My eyes shut as hard as they could while I tried to fight off the inferno that coursed through my skin.

The tincture turned into pins and needles in my blood and the chains rattled. They shook and smacked the wall, but I refused to look at Talos. I heaved for air, and when it finally reached my lungs, screams reverberated off the stone and iron. It split my skull and tore through me until my throat was raw.

Minutes felt like hours before it began to fade. Perspiration coated every inch of me, causing the fabric of my clothes to cling to my skin. I went slack in the chains. I opened my eyes, and sweat dripped from my brow, burning in place of tears.

Talos stood before me, pleased. He released my chains, and I fell in a heap on the floor, unable to catch myself. The scent of cloves inched too close when he leaned down beside me, next to my ear.

I couldn't even recoil.

"I think I liked that one better, didn't you?" His voice grated like nails on stone. "I may adjust the herbs next time. It didn't seem to last long enough."

I listened to him stand and leave. The iron squealed when it closed behind him. Even in his absence, relief never came.

When the tincture wore off, a torturous sob ripped up and out of my chest. The solace of tears pouring down my cheeks again made me shiver despite causing the ache in my bones to worsen.

Before I choked on my sobs, I laid on my stomach and let the weeping lull me into a state of listlessness.

Sleep remained elusive as the persistent throbbing continued to torment me.

I begged Casimir to visit me and take some of the pain away.

In another layer of torture, my father appeared in my delusion. He smiled softly, his gaze lifeless. *"It's okay, little flower."*

For the first time in my life, I begged the goddess to let me bloom and end the anguish.

Chapter Seven

Maids flooded the cells in the early morning. They skittered around, white linen gowns swishing at their ankles. Their arms were full of black fabric, washcloths, a basin, brushes, and other items that filled me with dismay. Talos stood in the corner of the room, watching.

Sleep weighed on my eyelids and I struggled to keep them open despite the company. It had been nine days since the fire, and each night, more visions of flames and bloodied hands filled my sleep. Casimir never appeared to offer reprieve. Every time I attempted to rest, I prayed to the gods for him to materialize. I even tried to conjure him on my own, sure that if he were someone I created in defiance of seclusion, it would've been easy to do. I held onto the hope he would block out the night-mares. Or fend off the inferno in my veins that remained after Talos's torture.

But he never came. It stung worse to feel his absence among the other losses. I had no one, nothing.

I pushed the thoughts of Casimir from my mind and tried to prepare for whatever Talos had planned.

The keys clicked in the door of my cell. There hadn't been enough time for the last tincture to dissipate before he returned. A day of rest wouldn't come. Not while Talos watched from across the room, arms folded over his polished attire. He looked prepared for a ceremony, and the realization didn't take long to settle over me like a blanket of dread.

For centuries, the sacrificial Roses were presented to the kingdom donned in all black. The marking ceremony took place when the Roses were children. At age five, they announced the next Rose in waiting. Now my time had come to do the same.

A maid approached me and held up a black gown. She nodded to herself after gauging the length and stepped back. It wasn't in Talos's nature to let me evade any of their traditions I had time for, and the dress was another piece of the part I had to play.

Silence filled the room. Each article of clothing that left my body and hit the floor made me wish I could vanish. The maids created a small barrier around me, shielding me from most of the guards. It didn't ease the humiliation while I stood among the stone and iron, stripped of everything I once was. Cold air filtered in through the barred window, and every inch of my raised flesh was on display.

Two of the maids took a moment to wipe my arms from the grime that clung to them. A third handled my unkempt hair, brushing through the long tresses—every stroke caused the buds to ache. The two maids moved from my arms to my nails, ridding them of their blackened appearance. The only relief came from my mother's blood being washed from my skin.

When they finished, the fourth maid stepped forward with the lump of black fabric. The gown slid on me like buttery silk. It was misplaced, too extravagant. Long billowing sleeves stopped at my wrists with tight silk cuffs that rubbed on my raw wrists, and the bodice hugged my chest, stretching halfway up my neck until it felt like it would choke me. The flowing skirt of the dress fell to my feet, now clean after the work of the maids.

After the remnants of fire and blood were washed away, all four women stepped back and bowed their heads at Talos. I fought the urge to avert my gaze from him. Shame coiled in my chest and I stamped it out as quickly as it appeared.

Talos appraised their work. Unsatisfied, his lip curled. "It'll have to do."

The maids straightened and folded their hands in front of their bodies, shuffling out of the cell. It left me alone in the middle; bare feet the only thing to ground me. My mind clung weakly to reality. Every second, it slipped and blurred in tincture until I felt detached from my body. It worsened when Talos strode into the cell.

His gaze flickered over my hair. He sighed, displeased. "Isla." The name brought one maid to a screeching halt.

She faced Talos and bowed. A few blonde ringlets fell from her slicked-back bun. "Yes, my lord?"

Talos flicked a curl off my cheek and I winced. "I need the hair away from her neck. Fix it."

Isla entered the cell with us and dug around in the apron tied at her waist. She pulled out a handful of pins and eyed my hair. When she circled me and paused to style my curls, I barely felt it. Numbness pooled in my limbs, my gaze never leaving Talos's. My sense of self became more distorted, splitting into fragments of the tincture. A hallucination bleeding into reality.

Lifeless eyes watched from over Talos's shoulder. They mirrored my mother's stormy blue before they turned crimson and black.

When Isla finished, Talos snapped in front of my face. It did little to break me out of the trance, but I took a step forward. They never offered me shoes. I couldn't bring myself to care.

We left the cell, chains nowhere in sight. Temple guards and council members lined every inch of the hall. Their gaze followed Talos as he led the way out of the cells and to the upper floor. Marble with swirls of silver blinded me, and focusing on Talos in front of me didn't help—his alabaster cape amplified the light pouring through the windows, tainted crimson by the stained glass.

The walk through the halls passed in a haze. White and black gowns fell in line behind us with each person we passed. It was meticulous and haunting. Their footsteps disrupted the silence. I focused on the click of their shoes and tried to calm my erratic pulse.

Wherever Talos led me, it wasn't the council room they brought me to before. We turned down another hall, leading to a pair of massive onyx doors etched with silver vines. Four guards in all white stood watch and bowed their heads when we neared.

Two of the guards lifted their heads, and each opened a door, allowing sunlight to filter in and reflect on the marble floors. I squinted, stumbling behind Talos.

The prospect of being outside didn't excite me. My eyes gradually adjusted to the harsh change to see that we had left the Temple and entered a walled off garden. In the center, there was a large circular platform made of polished black agate. Rose bushes encircled it, and on either side stood two statues of the goddess Aeterna weeping over the platform.

Despite years spent trying to buy more time, fate brought me to the sacrificial garden.

I froze in place, horrified when I noticed the people on the other side of the platform seated on stone benches, prepared to watch whatever Talos planned.

Someone prodded me forward. I fell behind and Talos ascended the steps onto the agate. He turned, eyes lit with fury when they locked onto me. The closest maid rushed me to the platform. My bare feet caught in the grass and tiny gray pebbles.

The crowd of people watched me scramble up the stairs. Talos reached out a gloved hand, and I wanted nothing more than to slap it away. Instead, I took it, shaking the entire time.

He pulled me to the center of the agate, beneath the weeping goddess statues. I scanned the vacant faces, praying to the gods that someone would see the fear, the reluctance.

They watched, emotionless.

In the sea of bodies dressed in black and scarlet, I noted a flash of color that caused my chest to contract with grief. The marigold cloak matched my father's—the cloaks worn by the horticulturists.

The man stood at the back of the crowd, appearing stunned with a notebook in one hand and a flower still attached to a bush in the other. His azure eyes locked with mine and a terrible familiarity came over me.

It was the man from the garden.

Talos cleared his throat and pulled my attention. He stood in place of the council members who handled such matters. The small crowd of people from Eldravine seemed enthralled by the change.

Talos wouldn't relinquish the opportunity to humiliate me himself.

"The crown takes notice of your answer to our call for attendance." Any hushed conversations died when Talos spoke. "While such an abrupt call is unprecedented, we are delighted to share with you a spark of hope." Talos smiled in my direction, the sight unnatural, a cat pretending to befriend a mouse. "Our search for a Rose has come to an end. We rejoice and thank Esen for His guidance in our endeavors."

The watchers erupted in joyous chatter; some even applauded. It shouldn't have shocked me to witness them celebrate my imminent death. My role was clear from the day I was born. They didn't look at me as one would a young woman being groomed for her death. To them, I was nothing more than a means to an end. Their brief salvation bought with my blood and all the Roses before me.

I trembled, barely noticing when another person joined us. They stood at Talos's side, offering him items cradled on a small red cushion. Steel glinted in the light.

Desperate, I searched the crowd, pleading for someone to help. None of them acted uneasy. No, they looked *eager*. Excitement made them clutch their hands together in anticipation. Many of them grinned, and part of me wondered if they reacted the same when a child stood on the platform.

Talos dismissed the council member and addressed the crowd once more. "We discovered a Rose raised in secrecy. Hidden by the Temple Garden caretaker, Aedric Blackthorne," Talos said, false pain in his voice. "To be betrayed by one of our own has been hard to accept. But he finally brought his daughter before us, ready to pay the ultimate price."

A flash of marigold caught my attention again, and I watched the man step closer to the crowd. Strands of wavy chestnut hair escaped the attempted half-up hairstyle he wore, and they settled along the edges of his sun-kissed face. A breeze tousled the disheveled hair. He didn't pay it any mind, gaze trained on me while his brow knit together in confusion. It wasn't hard to guess why he stared in such a way.

I thought then of my father and how he'd been in the process of training someone to replace him in the gardens. I wondered how it felt to watch his secrets come to light, but it did little to dwell. Not when I'd experienced something similar when Talos dangled my father's note-book in front of me, claiming he knew things he shouldn't have.

The man stopped at the back of the crowd and folded his arms over his chest, watching. It was foolish, but part of me hoped perhaps he'd say something—try to stop Talos. There wasn't a person in horticulture who hadn't trained under my father. I wanted that to be enough for him to step in or question the ceremony.

It was nothing more than a fool's hope.

Talos grabbed my arm, and my head whipped in his direction. Loose curls brushed my temples. Ice crept down my spine when I noted the small blade in his other hand.

A look of delight flashed across his face.

He won't kill you. You haven't bloomed yet, he can't kill you...

The pressure on my arm increased until I fidgeted, wishing I could get away. Talos grinned. "Kneel, Rose." He hung onto his facade, his voice eerily gentle.

His soft-spoken command settled like a fist around my throat. The crowd silenced, and I waited for someone to put a halt to his actions. To show any sign it brought them unease to witness another person subjected to such harsh treatment. The notion was naive, and I paid for my hope with a hand to the back of my neck.

Talos shoved me until my knees smacked the agate. I gasped and my palms flattened on the slick surface. When his hand released me, I stared into the complicit faces. The only one to show an ounce of humanity was the man in marigold. He wore a look of disgust without shame, focused on Talos. I didn't let myself hope again. He chose not to vocalize his disapproval.

"Due to the nature of finding this Rose, the sacrificial ink will not be ready for some time. Today, by Esen's word, we mark her regardless. The debt paid for Aeterna's destruction."

My stomach dropped. The delicate blade reflected the sun in the corner of my vision. Before I had the chance to move, shackles fastened on my wrists. Panicked, my attention flickered to the length of chains tied from me to the feet of the goddess. Forever burdened by her fury.

The muscles in my chest burned when heavy breaths constricted it. My shoulders shook, and the numbness of loss wasn't enough to prevent the endless pit of fear I tumbled down. I stiffened when Talos tucked the loose curls behind my ear.

"Try not to move," he taunted.

The blade came dangerously close to my neck and I thrashed against the chains. "No, please."

"Keep moving, and I'll be sure to take my time," he hissed, yanking the black fabric further down my neck. I panted and sweat beaded above my lip. My pleading gaze wasn't enough to make the people step in. They watched, enthralled by Talos. Eager to witness my torture.

Without warning, Talos dragged the edge of the blade over the side of my neck, just breaking the skin, and my mouth gaped open. Screams tried to claw their way out. Only a pitiful groan escaped the confines of the fiery shell I remained trapped in.

Tears streaked my cheeks, and when I found the garden keeper, his arms fell to his sides, fists clenched. He stared back at me, sadness sweeping across his face. If only it were enough to make him step in.

Each flick of the blade hurt a little less until my body became entirely numb, and I slumped against the chains, sitting on my heels.

Talos finished carving into the skin beneath my left ear. "Perhaps one day you'll receive a proper marking. That should do fine for now," he said, sneering.

Blood trickled down my neck and caught in the fabric of the dress, making it cling to my skin. When they released my chains, the sound echoed through the silent garden. Blurry-eyed, I wiped at the blood with my hands, aimlessly trying to rid my skin of it.

I couldn't see the mark left by his knife, but I knew enough about the sacrificial marking to understand what he'd done. The Iron Thorn insignia the guards wore in the form of a silver broach—a blade going through a rose.

Roses raised in the Temple were all given a much more uniform black marking on their neck. The king's property and the kingdom's sacrifice. The people of the Iron Thorn saw nothing amiss with Talos's cruelty, and the reality of what I was to them sank in.

When Talos straightened, crimson dripping from his blade onto the agate in inky blots, the people stood and celebrated the spilling of Rose blood.

Chapter Eight

Clouds blew in front of the sun and drenched the halls in shadow. The guards held me up by my arms behind Talos. They moved in a rush, and the marble beneath my feet grayed in the dim light until it appeared sickly. It didn't resemble the slow march to the garden. It was different, rough. The cheering outside turned into white noise the further we went.

Rain pattered on the windows when we passed them, and they resembled tears of blood. I wondered if the goddess wept for her people or if she'd grown numb to our pain.

The guards brought me down the staircase, and the air changed with the scenery. It became cool and damp, and I shivered when familiar stones touched my feet.

They hurried through the door to the cells, trailing Talos the whole time. He stood by once more while the room broke into chaos. The maids crowded behind the guards as they pulled me back into the cell. Hands tugged at me, taking pins out of my hair, undoing buttons on my dress, and ripping it off over my head.

It happened in a blur, and it left me dizzy when they threw a linen shift over my head. The scratchy fabric only went halfway down my thighs, and when I went to adjust it, a maid slapped my hand away.

Strands of wavy black hair fell into my eyes, some catching in the raw skin on my neck. I tried to brush it away, but Talos was in the cell the moment the maids gave him enough room.

I recoiled when he closed the space, cloves burning my nose.

His gloved hand untwisted a bottle of tincture, and he grabbed my chin. It took me off guard and I tried to jerk away. He gripped tighter, and the pressure on my jaw wouldn't allow me to speak.

It hasn't been a full day. Please, it's supposed to be a full day.

The tincture poured and he slammed my jaw shut.

The pitter-patter of rain ceased when the sun died down. After Talos left, I didn't get up. I stared at the wall until my vision turned hazy, and watched spiders and other small bugs skitter over the stones and in the corners.

A tray of food lay at my feet, the scent acidic. It made my stomach roll with nausea and I continued to ignore it. If I ate too soon before the tincture wore off, the meal would be back on the floor in no less than five minutes. Not like I was eager to eat it.

When my hip ached from lying on it for so long, I turned over, resting on my back. The lone light came from a lantern near the guards, and it left the room dark enough that I shut my eyes, hoping for rest.

Goosebumps rippled to life when I shivered, and I longed for a quilt or the comforting warmth of a hearth. The shift offered little help, and despite the pain, I rolled back on my side and curled close to my legs. My hands tucked to my chest and I waited for sleep to come.

A soft knock sounded at the door to the cells. It was faint but enough to make my heart race. *He wouldn't come back already. The healers wouldn't let him.*

Talos wasn't the kind of man to wait for permission. Rules didn't apply to him. I stayed curled on my side and waited. Pity he came back just as the exhaustion overwhelmed me enough to promise some sleep.

The guard grumbled under his breath, and the chair scraped the stones when he stood. Iron hinges squealed when he opened the heavy door, and I waited for the familiar aroma of herbs to fill the cells.

"I didn't think the prince wanted personal deliveries here—"

Iron sang when something slammed into the side of my cell. I turned, blood rushing in my ears. I watched the guard struggle against the bars of my cell, his head forced back by a hand holding a cloth.

Shouts ensued, and I rolled as quickly as I could until I was on my hands and knees.

Another guard appeared behind the intruder and tried to grab him. She earned an elbow to the nose and stumbled back, holding her face.

The guard that was pressed to the bars fell limp with a resounding *thud*. Lantern light trembled, revealing the intruder's face. His azure gaze met mine for a moment before he turned to the other guard.

She got her bearings and went to swing at him, shouting for someone to help. Before she could finish begging for aid, the man from the garden covered her face with the same cloth. She flailed and tried to fight him off, but whatever he had on the cloth made her limbs slow, and eventually, she fell limp. I watched in horror while he laid her next to the other guard.

My ears rang and I raised up, sitting on my feet. I pressed my palms flat to my thighs, sure I was hallucinating again. The man from the garden stood, shaking stray hair out of his face. He stared at the guards, their chests rising and falling as if they were in a deep sleep.

Herbs still crept in my bloodstream, and I tried to fight the abrupt wave of dizziness. *Perhaps I should've eaten the food.*

The man dusted off his tunic and faced me, keys in his hand. I stared, confused, as he approached my cell. He struggled to find the right key to open the door to my cell, but when he got it, the click made me shudder.

I scrambled away from him, and he paused, eyeing me. "My apologies. I didn't mean to frighten you." The man brushed a hand through his hair, and I noticed the drugged cloth tucked in his trouser pocket.

A shaky breath parted my lips, and I pressed a palm to my chest. My heart stuttered. "You—what did you do to them?" The question sounded foolish. But regardless of how much I despised the guards, they were at least charged with keeping me alive. Now, I was alone with a stranger whose intentions were unclear while herbs still thrummed in my veins.

The man ignored my question and crouched in front of me. He

cocked his head to the side, surveying me as if I were a spooked animal. He appeared not much older than me, though his hands showed scars and calluses from years of working. My father's skin had been similar. Days spent handling the gardens, the stone planters; his palms stayed dry and cracked.

When the stranger reached out to me, my brow furrowed. "I'm Ronin." His grin was soft and warm, friendly to a fault. "Oh. I suppose that doesn't help." He ran his other hand over the back of his neck. "I'm a friend of your father's. Or, perhaps student would be a better word."

I remained motionless and baffled. After a shallow breath, I sat straighter and said, "You didn't answer my question."

Ronin chuckled nervously. "Yes, of course. I used hops to have them sleep for a bit. I couldn't help get you out if they were awake."

Another wave of lightheadedness made me sway, and my fists clenched on my thighs, barely covered by the shift. No matter how much I tugged at it, the length remained the same. Ronin pursed his lips, watching me fiddle with the bothersome excuse for a dress.

"You do want to get out...don't you? After the ceremony—" My head snapped up and I met his curious blue gaze. He swallowed hard. "Sorry. It was difficult to witness. I'm just glad they didn't make Aedric watch."

"Excuse me?" The room fell silent.

Ronin shifted his feet, still crouched just inside the cell. "Your father is Aedric Blackthorne, is he not?"

I glared at him. "*Was.* My father is dead." The words were like poison on my tongue.

Ronin clumsily stood, staring at me in disbelief. Shaking his head, he said, "No. He can't be. The prince said—"

"Every word out of Talos's mouth is a lie." My voice trembled, and I tightened my fists on my legs to steady the panic.

Ronin sank back down, both of his hands running over his face. I took a moment to watch the guards, hoping one of them might twitch or show a sign of waking. *What am I doing*? If the guards woke, I'd go right back to lying on the floor—there and not—drifting in the strange in between. And if they got their wits about them quick enough, the man before me would likely die.

After a long pause, Ronin uncovered his face. "When did he die?"

The question made my shoulders hunch. I tried to recall how many days it had been. Talos's visits stole so much time from me. "Over a week ago, I think. I don't remember." My voice was distant like it belonged to someone else.

"Why wouldn't they have told us? All of his students have been awaiting his return until I heard what Talos said today. I thought he would be held here with you."

The fury sparked in an instant. "Because they murdered him. How are you so blind to their evil?" I spoke through clenched teeth.

"I didn't know, Elita. I'm so sorry."

When he said my name, I jumped. "How—"

"I've been your father's apprentice for two years now. He mentioned he had a daughter before. Never that you were...you know." He gestured at my hair and face.

The fact my father mentioned me to Ronin made my apprehension worse. Not for the stranger in front of me, but of my father and his secrets. While Talos lied as easily as he breathed, he had my father's notebook and claimed it held information no one should've known. Things he never told me.

I watched Ronin peer over his shoulder at the door. The two guards lay unconscious, unmoving except for their soft breaths.

The fear began to sizzle out, and the exhaustion almost knocked me over. I ran a hand through my hair. "So, you intended to help me get out?" I asked, letting my head lean on the wall behind me.

Ronin met my slitted gaze. "Well, yes." He surveyed the other cells. "Did they take your mother?"

I sighed and closed my eyes, regretting it in an instant when it felt like the floor disappeared beneath me. "You think they would let her live?" My voice sounded muffled, and I fought the pull of fatigue.

Tense silence amplified the abrupt sound of clambering on the floor above. When I met Ronin's anxious expression, my heart dropped. He had to get out before they saw what he'd done.

"Go," I said.

Ronin shook his head. "You'd let them continue to torture you?" His voice caught. "The prince has been demanding more from the herbal gardens. The plants he's inquired about...you shouldn't stay here."

I chuckled weakly. "What difference does it make?" No matter how much I didn't want it to bother me, it made my skin crawl to think of Talos making a tincture that was worse than what I'd consumed. Sighing, I said, "If they see us leaving, we're both dead. Why would you help me?"

Ronin flinched. "He carved into your skin with a smile on his face." He sounded haunted. "Please. I didn't have the chance to help Aedric. Let me help you."

"I don't think—" Thunderous footsteps interrupted me and my head snapped up. I eyed the door, my heart in my throat.

Ronin pursed his lips and extended his hand to me. "It's now or never, Elita."

Shouts from the Iron Guard ensued, and I didn't have time to contemplate anymore. I grabbed his hand, standing on legs still leaden from the tincture. Ronin watched me steady myself before he let go.

Feet bare, I shuffled out of the cell. No guards, Talos, or chains. The freedom wouldn't last long. The buds in my hair continued to ache and soon, they would bloom. I remained chained to my destiny. Running didn't offer me an out from my bloom, but when I thought of Talos returning to torture me, I quickened my pace.

Ronin fell in step behind me. I tiptoed over the sleeping guards and didn't glance back. My pulse thundered in my ears, and beneath the thrum, I heard the guards shouting at the top of the stairs.

I froze and the marble chilled my feet. When I turned to Ronin, he was across the room, opening a side door. "There's a way out through here," he muttered.

Intuition told me to hesitate before trusting a stranger, but there wasn't any time to think it through. The guards broke through the door at the top of the stairs. Whatever Ronin had done to delay them no longer held them back.

I darted for the open door, too clumsy on my shaking legs. The edges of my vision blurred and the effects of the herbs caused a cold sweat to bead on my forehead. I stumbled through behind Ronin, smacking my head on the doorframe.

Stars burst behind my eyes, and I groaned, pressing a hand to my forehead. The hall I stumbled into swallowed me in darkness when the heavy door closed behind me. Damp stones rubbed against my knees.

"Elita?" Ronin's voice came in a raspy whisper. When his hand found my shoulder, I held back a squeal and shook it off.

"I tripped through the door. It's fine. We need to go."

Ronin didn't reply, and his boots scuffed when he started to move. I stood and pressed a palm to the wall of the hallway. My pace wasn't fast enough, and any second, my escape would be over before the wind even hit my face.

I made it a few feet down the hall before the door burst open behind us, filling the hall with light.

The guard's gaze met mine and my heart stopped.

Adrenaline took over, and I ran through the dimly lit hall, a hand still holding my forehead as sticky blood dampened my skin. Ronin wasn't too far ahead and continued to sprint down the hall. He peered over his shoulder to make sure I was following and skidded to a stop, horrified.

"Elita, duck!" he shouted.

The second it took me to duck, a guard's hand brushed through my hair, not quick enough. I scrambled to regain my footing when the guard pinned me to the wall, a forearm to my throat.

If they weren't supposed to keep me alive, I would've been dead.

The anger seethed from the guard while he snarled at me, forcing me flush to the slick stones. I remembered some of the self-defense my father had taught me and brought a knee up between his legs.

He yelped and stumbled back.

It wouldn't take the other guards long to get to me. We needed more time. I regretted talking for so long in the cell. Bells echoed nearby, sounding muffled. *The emergency bells.*

Before I sprinted after Ronin, I brought my knee to the guard's chin as he went to stand. The sound made me tremble. His body slumped to the ground, knocked out with blood trailing from his nose.

I stared, wide-eyed. "Oh, gods..." I couldn't take it back, and thinking of all the times he smirked while Talos poured tincture down my throat, I let the guilt die out.

The guard's body laid across the hall. I hoped the other guards wouldn't trample him, and my desire for escape cost his life. It did me nothing to linger on things I couldn't control, and I sprinted toward Ronin, who waited close by, watching with exasperation.

When I reached him, he huffed an impatient breath. "We need to get out of here."

"I didn't see you helping," I bit back, keeping pace with him.

Over a week in the cell wasn't enough to erase muscle memory. Years of running and tracking in the woods echoed through my body. Gods, it felt good to run again. The lean muscles in my legs stretched and burned with the exertion, and I basked in the sensation.

I caught sight of another door at the end of the hall just as the inky black consumed us again. The door slammed shut, but the guards continued their pursuit.

At the other end of the hall, soft moonlight poured in. Ronin gestured for me to hurry, though I was only a few paces behind. When I made it through the threshold, he shut it and went to pull a large stone bench in front of it. Despite how my hands shook, I bent beside him and pulled. It scraped through the grass and dirt until it blocked the door.

Ronin straightened, panting. He ran a hand through loose hairs. "We have to go. Those bells will signal everyone in the kingdom. Word will be out within the hour."

I nodded, not needing to be told twice.

We got out. The guards wouldn't be far behind, but for a moment, I was free again.

The door we left led straight to the woods at the back of the Temple, and I hoped it would be enough to keep the guards off our trail. Ronin jogged in front of me, leading the way. I followed without a second thought, only glancing back once when we reached the forest's edge to see if the guards had gotten out yet.

There were enough exits in the Temple, they wouldn't be far behind. But with the darkness and the thick foliage, it would be impossible for them to find us if we ran far enough. My body just needed to fend off the exhaustion the tincture left behind.

Twigs and rocks scraped at my feet, but I kept a steady pace. Adrenaline would carry me far enough. Unless the king burned the entire forest down, there was no way for them to track us.

I panted and sweat dripped down my spine. The chilly breeze didn't offer enough relief when the fever still crawled across my skin. It grew more difficult to keep track of Ronin the darker it got, and after we ran for half an hour, he slowed his pace.

He glanced back at me for the first time since we left the Temple. My breathing was loud enough he likely never thought for a second I got lost or left behind. It gave me the chance to catch up, walking beside him.

"Do you intend to keep aimlessly running, or do we part ways now?" I inquired, wiping droplets from my forehead.

Ronin quirked a brow. "Oh...I thought you may have needed help finding somewhere safe to hideout. I suppose that was a poor assumption."

I pursed my lips. "You intended to harbor my entire family?"

"Aedric was my mentor. He may have had his secrets, but he was a good man. Yes, I wanted to help him and his family."

Another twig snapped beneath my bare feet and I grimaced. The foliage was growing too thick to navigate in the darkness. I came to a halt, lethargy overwhelming me.

Ronin watched me for a moment. "Listen, we can part ways if you want. But for now, I gathered some supplies and left it in a barn not far from here. Clothes, food, healing supplies..." He stared at the spot on my head, which continued to throb. "Whatever you decide to do, at least let me give you some things that'll help."

It would be another day before the effects of the tincture finally wore off, and there was no benefit in carrying on alone. Not until my body returned to a normal state. The dark of the forest already made me afraid of hallucinations that might follow me.

We weren't far enough from the Temple for me to think it over as long as I wanted to. My muddled brain made it too difficult to sort through it all. After a brief pause, I sighed. "Okay. We'll go to the barn, and then I'll figure it out from there."

Chapter Nine

I t didn't take long to find the barn after I agreed to follow Ronin. The forgotten structure hid well among the forest. Old paint peeled off in chunks. It appeared liable to blow over, but when Ronin swung the doors open, it held firm, and we ducked inside as rain began to fall.

Abandoned and rotting, it still smelled foul, like livestock and blood. Hay covered the ground, gray and damp from the holes in the roof where water leaked through.

Ronin went further inside, but I stayed back by the doors. Within a few moments, a lantern flickered to life after he fumbled around in the dark. It shuddered on the walls of the barn.

Droplets clung to some of my hair and skin. Further away from the Temple, it didn't take me long to grow uncomfortable with the shift I wore. Running through the forest left my legs covered in dirt and scrapes.

The journey to the barn was hushed, and the tense silence followed as I stepped inside. Ronin rummaged through a crate and pulled out three leather packs stuffed with items. It piqued my curiosity, and I walked closer, peering into the first pack he opened.

Inside appeared to be lumps of fabric rolled up tight. He shuffled through it and grabbed a few of them out, offering them without sparing me a glance. I took them from his outstretched hand, one article of clothing at a time.

I found a secluded part of the barn without a word to him. It was far from the lantern, but after the previous day at the Temple, even changing in the rain tempted me—if it meant having the privacy back that had been stolen from me in the cells. Ronin continued to search through the packs, and I inched further out of sight.

Ronin's presence continued to bring me unease, and trusting the word of a stranger had to be a horribly foolish decision. It made no difference that he helped me escape the Temple, and I worried it was the wrong choice. But he had assured me he meant well, and I didn't turn down the offer.

Part of me was selfish and didn't want to live the rest of my days in the Temple, with the promise of more visits from Talos. I didn't deserve a peaceful death, not with the fate I brought upon my parents. But I didn't know how I could endure more torture. I told myself leaving was the payback that Lendorr and Talos got for the callous way in which they killed my family. Maybe then the guilt wouldn't eat me alive.

I shifted my thoughts from the grief and tried to ground myself. Taking in the sights around me, I noted lofty walls—old and made of blackened wood with the same peeling green paint, rotted down to the bone in some places. Holes and missing planks of wood littered the roof.

A moment later, I removed the shift. It slid off effortlessly and I shivered when the cold caressed my skin. I unraveled the first roll of fabric to reveal a pair of women's trousers. Apprehension bubbled in my chest, but I slid them on, added the ivory tunic, and tied on the brown vest after. Then came the cloak, dark green and thick. It dwarfed me, the only item which appeared to belong to a man. With the cloak secured over my shoulders, I walked back over to Ronin, feet still bare.

He heard my approach and looked at me. "Huh, they fit better than I anticipated. Boots are there," he pointed by the crate, "but they likely won't fit as well. Options were slim."

I bent to retrieve the brown leather boots and sat on a crate to put them on. "The clothing. Where did you get it?" I asked, confused as to why he had an assortment of women's clothes. I regretted asking when he frowned.

"They belonged to my late wife."

"Oh." Curiosity had me on the verge of prodding. The urge to ask him prying questions took me off guard, and I stifled the nosiness. With the appropriate clothing and boots on, it would've been smart to make my way further from the Temple.

Wind and rain howled outside of the barn. It wouldn't be an easy endeavor, but staying in Eldravine wasn't an option.

For twenty-one years, I never left our quiet village. I wasn't ever truly alone, despite how lonely I felt. My parents had always been a constant. For the first time in my life, true isolation settled on my shoulders with a heavier weight than I anticipated.

It didn't matter how ill-prepared I was. Fate decided my path, and stalling wouldn't change it.

Ronin continued to organize pieces from the bags, and while he was distracted, I took a step further from him toward the open barn doors. "While I'm very grateful for your help, I need to get as far as I can from the Temple before morning. If we somehow cross paths again before my wilting, I'll be sure to return your wife's things."

His head snapped up, appearing confused. "You're leaving?"

My boots shuffled in the damp straw. "I intended to, yes."

"Where will you go?"

His concern surprised me.

The destination remained unclear, but when I thought of my mother's last words, it gave me a starting point. "The Forge." It came out more like a question than a statement. I didn't know the way to the Forge Border, and all of my father's maps burned in the fire. I ran a hand through my hair. "If I can find it, that is."

Ronin stayed silent, observing me. Outside, the rain slowed. If I didn't make a choice, it was possible I'd get caught in another downpour. Soaked clothes would make the journey much worse.

A few minutes passed before Ronin spoke. "I know it's not the most ideal situation, but I had hoped I could help you find somewhere safe." His gaze fell to my neck, and I bristled.

"Why would you continue to help me? You've given yourself a death sentence. It's hard to believe you did that solely out of kindness."

Ronin flinched. "You think so little of other people?"

"The same ones who watched Talos carve into my neck while they applauded and smiled? Or the people who have let innocent people be used and sacrificed for centuries without a shred of guilt?"

His fists curled, and he looked at the ceiling of the barn. "It doesn't help if you continue to make assumptions about people you don't know. I wanted to step in when he left the marking. But you know where I'd be right now? A cell beside you. That garden was flooded with guards."

Years of skepticism made me question Ronin's intentions. But everything my father taught me about trusting people in the Iron Thorn became a stark contrast to my encounters with Ronin. He saw me in the garden weeks before and never told the king. Rather than stay complacent, he helped me escape.

Finally, I said, "You didn't tell me what your intentions were. I just want an answer. I don't think that's too much to ask for."

Ronin sighed and took a seat on a crate. He ran both hands down his face. "I know it's hard to trust what I say. Believe me, I get it." He plucked up a piece of straw and ran it between his fingers. "It's been two years since I lost my wife, Melody."

I pursed my lips, still shocked that he already carried the title of widower. He didn't seem much older than me.

Moments ticked by before Ronin continued. "Aedric was the first person I met when I came to the Iron Thorn. I left my old life behind after Melody died. I knew her since we were children, and staying there caused me more pain." He swallowed, the topic difficult for him. "King Lendorr's cruelty is partly to blame for my wife's death."

"How—"

He lifted a hand, eyes glossy. "Now that part I won't be sharing with someone I just met." He chuckled softly. It couldn't hide the pain in his voice, and I bit my tongue.

"I worked alongside Aedric almost every day for two years. He shared some about your family. I think he did it to get me to open up. Sly old man." He grinned, and I couldn't help but smile softly in return.

"I helped you because the king and his son are cruel. I may not know anything about you, but what they were doing to you in that cell...Elita, I know about the tinctures he was giving you." Ronin sat straighter, looking me in the eye. "The horticulturists were the ones delivering the herbs to the Temple."

I took a step back, my fists loosening. The awful question popped in my head: had my father been responsible for the herbs grown and used by Talos? Had he been complacent in the torture Talos was well versed in?

Ronin pulled a pack onto his lap and patted a crate next to him. I stared, unsure. "Now, before you decide, can you let me patch you up? You hit your head pretty hard in the Temple."

Proclivity told me not to stay. Exhaustion made me sit down.

Grinning, Ronin pulled out healing supplies, laying out a jar of comfrey salve and some bandages. He contemplated over a suture kit, but to my relief, he put it back.

Wind whistled through the rotted barn. I tried to tune into the sound and ignore how close Ronin leaned in. He stood from his crate, leaving the bandages and salve next to my thigh.

He narrowed his gaze and moved closer. My entire body tensed in response. The last person to get that close was Talos. I tried to remind myself that while I didn't trust Ronin, he wasn't Talos. And when his fingertips brushed my forehead softly, it was the contrast my body needed to release some of the tension.

I swallowed hard and inhaled through my nose. Ronin froze, watching me. "Sorry. Does that hurt?"

Uncomfortable heat crept across my face. "No. It's fine."

He nodded and grabbed the comfrey salve. When the lid came off, the scent overwhelmed me. I watched him stare at his dirty hands and then the scrape on my forehead. There weren't many options, and he made a quick decision, dipping his fingers in the salve.

The slather of comfrey stung the raw skin. It didn't compare to what my body endured over the past ten days in the Temple, and I allowed him to finish applying it.

Only when he reached out to apply some to my neck did I recoil. "What are you doing?"

Ronin paused. "It doesn't look like anyone tended to the marking yet. The edges are red. It'd be smart to clean it."

"I—" The words caught in my throat. I couldn't find the right explanation, at least not one that didn't unearth things I wished to bury. No one in the Temple asked before they touched me. Every hand brought me more pain or humiliation.

I let out a shaky breath. "Just ask before you do something next time, please," I said, pushing the hair away from my neck.

It made my stomach twist in knots when he touched the marking and I focused on the ceiling of the barn, trying to distract myself. I counted the holes in the roof while he bandaged my forehead and neck. When he opened the bandages, the sweet aroma of honey filled the space, and the sticky substance adhered it to my skin.

After he finished, he gathered the supplies and put it back into the open leather pack. He tied it shut and went to another pack, shuffling through it. I watched, more tired than I'd ever been.

He returned with a cloth bag and offered it to me. I took it, untied the top, and the scent of rye bread filled the air, accompanied by the vibrant colors of a few scattered pieces of fresh fruit.

I glanced at Ronin, my brow furrowed in confusion.

He shrugged, a mischievous look in his eye. "Grabbed a few things from the Temple. Hoping Akuma doesn't smite me for it."

I scoffed and took the bread out first. My mouth watered, and I tore into the rye. After days of eating the acidic slop the healers gave me, it tasted divine. The fresh fruit called to me, and when my teeth broke the juicy surface, I sighed.

Ronin watched, amused. While my mouth was full, he said, "The village I plan to hide out in is near the Forge. If you want, we could go that way together, since I know how to get there. And when we reach the village, we can go our separate ways. If that's what you want, of course."

There was no one else to decide for me. No one to point me in the right direction. Perhaps the fear of being alone again clouded my judgment, but it didn't take me long to choose my path. Ronin offered me an out, and at the very least, I had someone to lead me to the Forge Border.

Unwilling to be forgotten, the herbs also needed time to leave my system. It would be difficult to defend myself, and Ronin proved to be somewhat useful in that aspect.

I had contemplated long enough, and we needed to get far enough from the Temple that I could find a moment to rest. "Okay," I said, breaking the silence. "We'll go together toward the Forge. At the first sign of something off, I won't hesitate to protect myself from you."

Ronin fought back a grin. "I don't doubt that for a second." He offered me a pack to carry. "You have my word. No funny business. As long as you promise not to turn me over to the council."

I chuckled dryly and stood from the crate. "There's nothing in all of Nesrin that could make me return there." I put the pack on my shoulder and pulled the hood of the cloak over my hair. "I do have one request, though."

"And that is?" Ronin raised a brow.

"We find somewhere safe enough to sleep before I keel over."

His expression softened. "Deal."

Chapter Ten

Hours spent trudging through the woods took its toll on my feet. The night wore on at a snail's pace in a blur of towering black trees. Branches, brush, and rocks, all new and unknown to me, tripped me up, a small curse escaping my lips often. Ronin was quick to catch my arm several times before my face hit the dirt.

Icy air bit at my cheeks, the cloak not enough to protect me from its harsh sting. I kept my hands tucked into the cover of the fabric to seek some respite. The strange cold settled deep in my bones.

We had barely made it out of the village before a raven followed along. It whistled in the trees and swooped close a few times. Its sleek, onyx wings caught my attention when it dove again, close over Ronin's head. He shooed it away and grumbled under his breath. It wasn't the first time the bird had gotten so close to us.

The foliage broke off into less overwhelming brush as the tree roots ate them up, giving us more room to walk. Mossy rocks dotted our path, small white mushrooms popping up on them—poisonous from the look of their gills.

Warm puffs of breath formed clouds in front of me. The cold in my lungs had become painful not long after our trek began. No matter how

I fought to keep my mouth closed, I reached a point of constant panting as the journey stretched on.

I stumbled once more, too exhausted to pay attention, tumbling forward over a stump. I grunted and caught myself, my hands skidding through the dirt and brush.

Frustrated, I huffed out a breath and kept my head down. I heard Ronin turn, his footsteps quickening as he hurried over to me.

"Are you okay?" he asked, his hand resting on my shoulder. I groaned in frustration and leaned back on my heels. The hood fell from my head, releasing a mess of curls.

"Fine," I ground out, ignoring his attempt to help while I brushed the dirt off my hands. I stared at them for a moment and noted a few scrapes on my palms. Anger welled in my chest, the exhaustion and hunger catching up to me all at once.

Ronin stood next to me, making no sound. For someone who didn't know me well, he at least had the sense to notice the frustration radiating from my body, and he gave me a moment to breathe and fend off some of the embarrassment.

I sat back more, letting my legs come out in front of me. "I need a minute. My feet are killing me," I said, annoyed. I reached down to take the boots off, hoping for some relief. My feet didn't have time to break the shoes in before such a long trek, and the way they looked showed as much. Blisters formed on my toes and heels, my skin scraped, and it left a bright pink tint. I grimaced; they were worse than I had expected.

Ronin sucked in a breath and knelt beside me. "Sorry, I wasn't thinking. I was trying to get us as far from the Temple as possible."

I threw up a hand in a dismissive gesture. "I'll be fine. The further from the Temple, the better. I just need to rest for a moment."

He nodded in agreement and began shoving sticks away with his foot, creating a spot to sit down across from me. He relieved his back of the bags he had, undoing the clasp on one of them to pull out a water-skin, which he handed to me.

Despite not wanting to look pitiful, I ripped it from his hands, opened the top, and chugged it with abandon. The water wasn't too warm; the cold temperature outside was enough to make it bearable.

Though had it been lukewarm river water, I would've gulped it down all the same.

I gasped for a breath, replacing the cap on the waterskin. Ronin suppressed a small smile and took it from my outstretched hand. "I gave little thought to how this trip would be for you. I haven't meant to disregard your needs."

"It's okay," I said sheepishly. "Honestly, I don't know how I'll ever repay you. I owe you so much more than a mere thanks." I rubbed at my arms, still purple and sore where Talos dug his nails in.

Ronin's smile fell. "What you said, back at the barn, you were right. People in the kingdom have been complacent for too long. What kind of person would I be if I knowingly left you to be tortured? Sacrifice or not, it was wrong."

I bristled, and for the first time in the past few hours, I noticed the herbs had worn off. "I've not meant to seem unkind," I said. "But what I endured in the Temple—"

He shook his head and offered me a somber smile. "Don't apologize. You've been through something awful. No one would blame you for having your guard up." Ronin pulled a pack over his lap. "Now, any chance you might be hungry?"

On cue, my stomach twisted, growling with hunger. I nodded and took the pack off my back, setting it to the side. Ronin searched through his and after a moment, he offered me half a loaf of rye bread, keeping the other for himself.

I ripped off hefty chunks, shoveling the bread into my mouth as if it were a rare delicacy. I had lived my life in blissful ignorance, shielded from the harsh realities of hunger and thirst, and it showed.

Ronin watched me while I ate, and the attention made heat prickle in my cheeks. His focus went to the spot on my temple and I absent-mindedly touched the dried honey bandage.

"How does it feel?" Ronin's gaze flicked from my temple to the matching bandage on my neck.

"Not too bad. The headaches have stopped."

His brow raised. "You've been having head pain and didn't say anything? Are you sure you feel fine?"

"We had to get out quickly. I didn't want us to slow down on my behalf. I'm fine, truly."

He nibbled at the skin on his lip before scooting closer. "Could I take a look at them while you finish?"

My fingers paused when I went to break off another piece of bread. "I suppose that would be fine." I dreaded the invasion of space but allowed him to come closer.

His boots dug through the dirt as he brought himself to my side, a bag dragging beside him. The contents clattered while he went through it until he brought out the kit that held the bandages.

I tried to ignore his proximity and continued to eat. His calloused hands brushed at the skin of my temple before he removed the first bandage. It pulled away black with dried blood.

The bandage on my neck was worse. It adhered too much to the torn flesh and tugged at scarcely healed edges. The top of my cheek twitched when he removed it.

Ronin released a heavy breath. "This one may need more help." He unraveled two new bandages and took out a container of comfrey salve. He applied a thin layer of salve to the wound on my neck, apologizing under his breath when a gasp hissed through my teeth. Honey wafted through the air, and he fiddled with the bandages until he secured one to my temple and another to my neck.

"Hopefully, those will help. I'll need to check them more often."

He moved back to his previous spot and wiped his hands off on his trousers before he grabbed the slice of bread left atop a pack, tearing back into it.

We finished with the food, and I closed the pack, sliding it back over my shoulders. My muscles complained, but I ignored it and stood.

Ronin watched me with a brow quirked. "Do you intend to finish the journey without shoes?" he asked, eyeing the boots on the ground.

If not for the cold, I would've thrown them into a bag and forgotten about them, but the way the air bit at my skin, I needed them. "Right." I sighed, stooping to pull the boots back up, flinching when they pulled over the sore skin.

Ronin stood and tugged his supplies back over his shoulder. "Are you sure you're ready?" he asked, adjusting the straps across his chest.

"Yes, I'll be fine." Because I had no other choice, I wanted to say. But I left it, allowing him to lead the way, and with a quick glance toward the compass he had in hand, Ronin started to move.

The sun rose high, offering little relief from the frigid chill in the air. It seemed like it fell as soon as it appeared, plunging us back into darkness the further we walked. The lack of sleep made me delirious, and I stumbled through the woods with a hand gripped on Ronin's cloak in front of me to avoid getting lost in the dark forest.

His footsteps never faltered while he led the way, and I was starting to believe he must not be human with how he trudged through, never the one to suggest rest, always quick to end a lapse in our journey. It left me drained.

The unforgiving terrain grew more hostile, with jagged rocks that protruded from the ground, altering our surroundings the more we distanced ourselves from the king's reach.

After a few hours into the night, Ronin slowed his pace, casting a glance back at me. He looked apologetic but didn't speak a word. With a quick survey around us, he veered right and pulled us toward a small cluster of rocks and trees, which made a makeshift wall between parts of the woods.

Relief swelled in my body when he brought us to a stop. He rolled his shoulders, trying to relieve how tight they were—the lone outward sign he struggled with the effects of the journey.

"We'll rest here for now. We have a few more days before we reach the Forge Border, though. But we've made a lot of progress."

I nodded, my head lolling to the side.

"You can let go now," he said with a chuckle.

My face flushed, and I released my grip on his cloak.

He took his bags off and set them near the trunk of a tree before scanning the ground. I watched him gather sticks and twigs, feeling their bark to determine if they were dry enough for a fire.

I slumped to the dirt with a grunt and tore the pack off my shoulders, the movement quick and full of pent up frustration. When I discarded the boots, the scrapes went from pink to red, where small patches of blood covered my feet. I struggled to give them attention as my eyelids grew heavy to the point of being painful.

I brought my cloak around my shoulders, draping it on top of my body. A yawn made my jaw ache, and I leaned my head back against the tree. Worry wrapped around my mind, but I couldn't avoid sleep forever.

Through slitted lids, I watched Ronin drop a bundle of wood that he'd gathered before he kneeled, brushing the leaves and grass away to create a clear spot. He placed the misshapen wood in the center and stacked some of them while leaving the rest off to the side.

Exhaustion pulled at me until my vision turned blurry, and Ronin's features swam.

My eyes opened to my room.

The curtains shuddered back from the windowpane when a harsh wind howled. Movement near them caught my eye, and I jolted at the sight of Casimir striding toward me, urgency in his step, no longer a slow-moving ghost.

My heart rate quickened when he stopped in front of me, grabbing onto my shoulders. The sensation of his hands prickled through my skin.

"Fuck, Elita..." Relief filled his voice, his usual calm demeanor gone. "I thought you'd died."

I shook my head, knotted curls brushing my cheeks and forehead.

Some of the tension released from his shoulders, and his grip loosened on me. "Where are you?" He scanned over me until his gaze froze on my neck. I tried not to recoil when I thought of the sacrificial marking—not yet healed and slathered in comfrey.

He hesitated before he reached out and brushed my hair back for a better look.

The ghostly touch made me shiver.

"I'm somewhere in the Iron Forests," I replied, my breath hitching. I glanced down, noting my dirty attire and the leaves knotted into some of my coiled black hair. The blisters on my feet were worse than I had realized, and I pressed my lips into a thin line at the sight.

Casimir's gaze found my battered skin on the soles of my feet, and he grimaced. His hands dropped away, and the dreamspace shifted around us. The heavy emotions rippled in visible waves.

His familiar presence became a soothing balm, and tears distorted my vision while I stared at him. He was more frazzled than I'd ever seen him—his stubbled jaw had become a short beard, his hair a mess.

Casimir took a steadying breath, and I watched the dreamspace sharpen again. Cautiously, he asked, "What happened? How—" he stole another glance at my neck, his fists curled. "After the fire, where did you go?"

The question threatened to pull me out of the dreamspace. My tongue pressed to the roof of my mouth, trying to fend off tears.

When I shoved down the memories of Talos, I finally said, "Guards got me out of the cottage. They kept me in a cell for nine days before I got out of the Temple. I've not slept in over three days." My voice trembled.

Casimir's fists clenched. He hesitated before he spoke. "Did they—the buds, they didn't allow enough time for them to attempt to secure another Rose, correct?"

The question made my skin crawl. If there was one thing I was grateful for since the fire, it was that I had missed the window to be bred.

"No, there wasn't time. I think that upset the prince more than anything," I said quietly, not meeting his gaze.

Casimir swallowed thickly. "I should have come for you after the fire."

His guilt rippled around us. The scene swirled with the stronger emotions, and I tried to ignore the way my head spun.

I reached out to him, my arm shaking. I brushed a hand over his sleeve and he felt there and gone. No warmth to him. It stung to not be able to feel him, and I pulled my hand back, looking at my fingertips as they tingled.

He stared at my hands, his features more distraught. "It's difficult to become fully tangible. The night I gave you the petal, I didn't wake up for days."

I looked at him, wiping at the sudden tears on my face. "It's not very fair you're able to do...whatever this is, yet I've never been able to summon you of my own accord. The days in my cell were—" I fought the urge to say terrifying when I thought of the way the tincture seared my blood. "They were difficult."

Casimir's gaze went anywhere but me. He tipped his chin up to glance at the ceiling, and I followed his gaze, noticing the holes in the roof, the rot, and the black. No, I wasn't home. My mind so desperately craved for me to be.

"Where are you planning to go?" he asked, taking in the broken room. The dreamspace tried to hold the illusion, but nothing in it felt quite right or real.

"I've not thought it through yet, but I think I'm going to the Forge. There hasn't been much time for me to consider other options. Escaping from the Temple wasn't something I had planned." I sighed and leaned back into the bed, the frame deteriorating beneath me in slow motion as the illusion started to evaporate.

"Care to elaborate?" he prodded.

"Someone saved me," I explained hesitantly, not quite ready to recount the past two days. "He came for me after the marking ceremony." The wound on my neck sparked with pain. "A man broke into the cells to get me out. He knew my father." There was too much to explain and the exhaustion I felt was bone deep, still palpable in the dreamspace.

Casimir's face contorted in confusion. "He knew your father? That's why he got you out?"

I sensed his disapproval, his skepticism like a cloud of negativity. I recoiled and stood from the bed, watching it crumble into dust beneath Casimir, sending him to the floor with a grunt.

"At least someone helped me. Would you have preferred I stayed?" Anger replaced the comfort he brought, sudden and white hot. I clenched my fists. "All those years ago…you said you'd come for me, so I didn't have to go alone. You never did. If you had, then maybe—" The words caught in my throat, my voice dying out with the anger. *Maybe my family wouldn't have died.*

Casimir peered at me beneath messy black waves, the moonlight catching in his fiery ember gaze.

"Are you even real?" I whispered, wrapping my arms around my torso.

He huffed and stood. "Don't start this again. I'm *real*, Elita."

I pulled back when he stretched out his hand. My heart sank, and I whirled, unable to look at him. Uncomfortable panic tightened my chest.

"My gods, all this time, and sure enough, you're a figment of my imagination. All those years I spent with no company except for my parents—it was too much for my mind to handle."

Casimir flickered, his presence waning. "Why do you always insist on making this more difficult? You'd rather believe you've lost your mind than listen."

"If you're real, then why didn't you help me? How did you even know enough to tell me my family was gone before their bodies were cold? *What are you?*" I asked, hot tears welling up. My pulse thrummed harder until the sound echoed in the dreamspace.

The look on his face was one of remorse, and I bit the inside of my cheek, stepping back from him. He ran a hand over his scruffy jaw, his features wild with panic.

"Elita, please."

With the panic came the disappearance, my sorrow too much for him to bear. He faded, his eyes like flickering flames as he turned to smoke in front of me.

I choked out a sob and covered my mouth, relief and familiarity replaced with more despair.

Stars greeted me when I opened my eyes. Tears trailed down my temples, falling into my hair. The chill in the air had me worried the show of grief would freeze on my skin, despite the fire a few feet away, or the cloak resting over my body.

I wiped at the tears with icy fingers, then ducked them back into the cloak. Movement caught my attention, and I noticed Ronin standing on the opposite side of the fire, his back to me as he surveyed the woods, vigilant despite how tired he must have been.

When I sat upright, it didn't take him long to notice, and I was grateful he still had it in him to be leery. He faced me, the flames illuminating his confused features.

"Up already?" His voice was low, only carrying the words so far.

I shook off the remnants of disappointment after Casimir's visit. It hadn't been the relief I longed for and expected. Instead, it left me with more despair that I didn't have the energy for.

The warmth of the fire pulled me in, and I shrugged off the cloak and stood, reaching my hands out in hopes it would ease the cold that stung my skin. I felt Ronin's gaze but didn't meet it, knowing it'd be swimming with questions.

My avoidance proved insufficient as he shuffled my way, coming to stand beside me.

"With how exhausted you were, I half expected you to sleep for days. Are you too cold?" he asked.

"Just can't sleep," I whispered, refusing to meet his burning stare.

Ronin hummed in response, but he didn't prod. We stood quietly for a good span of time, the fire comforting. My vision turned blurry as I watched the flames, never finding a focal point. Until, eventually, I saw my mother's face in the flames, a hallucination, but it made my blood run cold, and I turned away.

I wrapped my arms around myself and went back to where I'd been sleeping, plucking up the cloak. While I fastened the clasp, I finally met Ronin's quizzical stare. The single glance appeared to be enough, as I watched understanding sweep across his face.

He began to put out the fire. "If you're rested enough, we can continue toward the Forge."

I muttered a quiet "okay", and he finished covering the fire until only a thin wisp of smoke rose to the blackened sky.

We prepared to leave in silence, and for a moment, I wished I hadn't gotten so angry with Casimir. Blaming him for any part of my parents' death was nothing more than a poor attempt at rejecting blame.

Had I gone to the Temple years ago, knowing the stress I caused my mother, they both would have lived.

As we resumed our trek to the Forge, I tried to make room for the guilt. I worried if I continued to bury it, it would eat me alive.

Chapter Eleven

Ronin sat across from me while he rummaged through the pack that once held all of our food. Crumbs dropped from the bag, landing in the grass below.

"Our food supply is sadly gone," he said.

I pressed my lips into a tight line. If either of us were to blame for the lack of food left, it was me. I had to fight off a blush when I realized how irresponsible I'd been with what we had.

Two days in the woods and I cleared out what little supplies we had. He had warned me about how long the journey would be, but I'd never gone so long without a meal.

Boots scuffed through the dirt when I shifted. "I hadn't meant to eat it so quickly," I said sheepishly.

Ronin shook his head and glanced up from the bag. The corners of his lips lifted in a soft grin. "It's fine. But we need to figure something out. We won't be at the Forge for a few days still." He appeared thoughtful when he broke my gaze to scan the forest.

After a pause, he put down the food pack and picked up another one, his hands shuffling through it. While he searched, his brow pulled together, and he swiftly replaced it with a satisfied smirk. Something glinted in the light when he pulled it out of the pack. The sight of the gleaming dagger made me recoil.

Ronin's gaze flicked to mine, and he dropped the small smirk. "Sorry, Elita," he chuckled apologetically. "Our options are slim, and we may need to hunt or fish if possible. Something sharp will come in handy."

My fists relaxed at my sides, but the tension lingered in my shoulders. I took a deep breath and allowed my pulse to slow. "It's okay," I said. "Do you know what there is to hunt in this area?"

Ronin shrugged. "Rabbits, deer, or other game similar to those."

"My father always insisted that the animals far from Eldravine were cursed. I never did hunt this far out."

Ronin didn't hide his shock. "You hunt?"

A sudden heat crept up my face. I turned my gaze back to the woods. "Just something I did with my father. He said survival skills were important for anyone to know. I suppose he was right," I said. The thought of my father held on to its sting. Uncertainty and questions flooded me, with nowhere to go and no hope for answers. To experience so much grief and unanswered questions, I didn't feel like my body had the capacity for anything more, lest I burst at the seams.

Even so, fond memories began to turn sour as they blurred with more wondering and apprehension. When my father told me that knowing how to hunt and survive was important, and how *I* needed to survive, I hadn't thought much of it. But after the harrowing events I endured, the memory sparked uncomfortable emotions.

When Ronin stood, it broke my train of thought.

I wanted to hunt and forget the memories which plagued me. Something familiar, even though I yearned to be accompanied by the one I always hunted with. It became an opportunity to put the skills my father taught me to use.

I copied Ronin and dusted off my trousers when I stood.

"I'm not sure where to start," Ronin said, scanning the woods.

The Iron Forests were vast, and I began a mental checklist of things to keep in mind. We had put little effort into being quiet when we trudged through the area. It was daylight. And to add to our misfortune, we lacked weapons suitable for long-range hunting.

My lips pursed together, and I surveyed our surroundings. The trees swayed in a soft breeze, and the bushes rustled. I searched the greenery and came up empty-handed. There were no animal signs in our immediate area.

At my side, I noticed Ronin observing me. I turned to him and felt a sudden swell of nervousness. "I don't see any fresh signs of animals coming through this way. And our presence here likely scared off anything close by. We'll have to go further and be as quiet as possible," I said.

"Consider me impressed." He grinned. "Your father taught you well."

In response, I gave a quick, dismissive shrug and faced the mass of pine trees, hoping to conceal my face. Compliments were foreign to me, and I worried it would show in my expression.

Ronin stepped closer, with the pack returned to his shoulders. "Do you want to lead the way?" he asked.

Despite my nerves, my footsteps were sure. The boots rubbed against my skin and created more discomfort, but I ignored it and allowed Ronin to follow the path I chose.

From the way the branches sat to the berries which coated a few bushes, it appeared to be our best bet. Ronin didn't question me or offer any input. Something about his faith in me gave me the confidence I needed.

My father always led our hunts, but my skills were in tracking, and it was familiar as I searched for signs of disruption in the area.

We trudged through the wood further from our makeshift camp. If it weren't for Ronin's compass and map, I worried I would get us lost. I tried to tune my fears out and focus on the ground.

The first sign of animal life was a simple rabbit print, but it was enough to give me hope. I glanced over my shoulder and pointed it out to Ronin. He gave me a nod of acknowledgment and waited beside me.

Bushes rustled to the right of us, and Ronin froze, his gaze flickering in the direction of the sound. Before another second passed, he lunged. Then came my least favorite part.

· · ·

Ronin chuckled at me again as I grimaced.

I held the prepared rabbit in my hands, unable to take a bite. I never had an issue with meat, but something about seeing him skin the rabbit put me off to it. He had taken the time to do the dirty work and cook it over a fire, and I continued to just stare at it.

"I thought you said you hunted," he mused.

"Yes, I have. I never helped my father with preparing it. Plus, the rabbit was adorable. It's unfortunate." I shrugged and took a reluctant bite of the meat. It was bland and gamey, but it beat going hungry.

Ronin watched me, and the scrutiny made me uneasy.

"What?" I muttered around a bite of meat.

He shook his head. "Nothing. When you're finished, we should probably head out. I don't like how visible the smoke is during daylight."

I nodded in understanding and went back to eating.

Silence swept through the forest while we ate. I noted the blood on Ronin's hands and made a mental note to locate water as soon as possible.

Once we were done, Ronin took care of the fire and tried to cover our tracks by scattering dirt over it. I went to stand when a noise resounded somewhere much too close for comfort. My head snapped toward the rustling.

Ronin didn't remove his attention from the woods when he whispered, "We need to leave."

I rose, threw my pack on my shoulder, and pulled the hood of my cloak over my hair. My hands shook while I tucked the loose strands further into the green fabric.

Ronin grabbed my wrist, and it took me by surprise. I didn't protest when he led me from the area. The sound was too loud to be another rabbit or something else small. I held onto the hope perhaps it was a bear or a deer crossing through. Because even a bear would have been better than what stalked out of the trees.

Four men donning bows approached us from our left. One of them had a dead deer slung over his shoulders, and blood coated his hands. They spotted us immediately, their gazes falling to me first.

I ducked my head and moved closer to Ronin's side in an attempt to shield my face from them.

"These are private hunting grounds."

My body ran cold when Ronin tensed beside me, and his hand tightened its grip on my wrist. Not enough to hurt, but enough to keep me secure to his side.

"We weren't aware, our apologies," Ronin replied. I heard the panic in his tone, and I hoped they didn't pick up on it.

One man scoffed, and I heard leaves crinkle beneath his boots when he came closer. My heart hammered beneath my ribcage with such intensity, I worried he'd be able to hear it.

A pair of boots became visible from the corner of my eye, and I recoiled further into Ronin's side, causing his balance to shift.

"We'll be out of your hair," Ronin asserted while he steadied us both.

"Well, hold on now. You can't expect to get off so easy after ruining our hunt. Your fire will scare off any animal for miles."

The rush of adrenaline ignited in my veins, causing my breaths to come out in rapid, shallow puffs through my nose.

"Ah, give it a break, Lorn, you've gone and frightened the girl," the one closest to me mocked.

Ronin's grip on me tightened even more. The tip of my nose brushed the fabric of his cloak the closer I ducked into his shoulder. Sweat moved over the edge of my hairline.

"We were just passing through, and we will be leaving now." Ronin's tone clipped.

The man huffed, and I flinched, bumping into Ronin when I tried to move further from them. I kept my head down and hoped they would decide to move on.

He stepped closer to Ronin, his hands covered in blood. Despite having his kill slung over his back, the sight made me wince.

Ronin moved to the side, further shielding me from their gaze. I wrapped a fist into his cloak, trying to stay as close as possible. Panic continued to build the longer the men refused to depart.

"Odd area to pass through," a raspy voice said from behind me. I yelped when a hand grazed my arm, and my head jerked up, catching sight of the burly man's face. Recognition stormed his features, and I pressed into Ronin when the man tried to grab me.

"Keep your hands off of her," Ronin snapped, bringing me closer.

"She's a Rose!" the man thundered, stumbling even closer, a dagger in one of his hands.

Ronin didn't hesitate. He grabbed my arm and tugged me forward, sprinting between two of the men. They shouted and reached out, missing my body and gripping onto the edge of my cloak.

My hand slipped out of Ronin's and I fell to the ground as the clasp from my cloak dug into my skin. He froze, turning on his heel with his own blade in hand. Ronin lunged at the man who had pulled my cloak, slamming into his gut with a fist. The dagger trembled in Ronin's other hand, but he didn't use it.

I rolled on the ground and stood, throwing my hair back from my face. The scrape on my neck stung, but I ignored it, eyeing the men who circled us. By tossing away my hood, the man proved he had been right. The curse of the Rose was unmistakable.

They stared at me hungrily, poised to attack.

Ronin used one arm to put me behind his back, and with his free hand, he took back out his dagger.

"Let us leave." Ronin's voice dripped with malice.

The man who held onto the deer dropped it. An amused grin flashed across his face. "I don't think so. The king would pay a hefty reward for that girl."

I nearly retched.

Ronin shook in front of me, surging with adrenaline. I stared at his back while the seconds ticked by. Everyone paused, waiting to see who would lunge first.

To my dismay, the man closest to me did, yanking me in his direction. I screamed when he forced me into his chest. He smelled foul, like sweat and copper. Crimson stains dried to his hands, which roved over my cloak. He tore it off of me and let it fall.

Ronin turned in an instant, livid.

The man who held me chortled when another hunter rammed into Ronin, preventing him from getting to me.

I used what little movement I had and stomped down on his foot, hoping he would release me. Instead, he held me tighter and his fingers dug into my arms, breaking the skin. Panic set in and my surroundings became a jumbled mess, blurring my vision.

Despite being outnumbered, Ronin held his ground against the other men, while the one who held onto me seized the opportunity to escape without hesitation.

The fear ripped through me. My limbs thrashed, hoping to find a target, but I missed as he cackled and tugged me further from Ronin.

Ronin's gaze found mine, brimming with anger. The man who held me continued to disappear further into the woods while the other hunters pulled Ronin's attention.

"Ronin!" My voice caught when the man yanked my head back, his hand wrapped in my hair. I lost sight of Ronin and felt my chances of getting away slip through my fingers the more distance the man put between us.

My hands clawed at the man's arms in desperation. I tried to dig as deep as I could, and my dirty nails scraped at his skin. He was relentless, and instead of letting me go, he jerked me around to throw my hands off of his arm.

The forest swallowed us in its sinister embrace.

I need to try harder. They'll take me back to Talos.

A new wave of desperation bubbled to the surface. I kicked and thrashed in his arms until finally, an elbow found his ribs and I slammed into them, bone against bone.

He hollered and released some of his grip on me.

I broke free of his arms and went to sprint when he pulled me back by my hair, sending me to the ground with an awful thud. Sparks speckled my vision while my head throbbed.

My lungs begged for air, but it evaded me. I sputtered and rolled until I was on my hands and knees. The man didn't take long to recover and came over to me. His hand wrapped around my upper arm, and he jerked me to a stand, snarling in my face.

The expression went slack as quick as it appeared.

Wide eyed, he gasped and fumbled forward. I jumped out of the way and he fell on his face. A lone dagger stood in the center of his back.

My chest heaved with harsh and quick breaths while I scrambled back from his limp body. I looked up to see Ronin leaned over, one hand on a knee, his breath ragged.

The other men were nowhere in sight.

Despite how labored his breathing was, he ran over to me. I stared at him, bewildered. Ronin brought a bloodied hand up to me and froze when I flinched.

"Are you hurt?" he asked. He scanned over me for any visible injuries. The skin on my neck burned from where the clasp had scraped me, and the flesh on my arms ached. But I was alive.

"I think I'm okay," I replied.

Ronin didn't appear convinced. The concern only deepened when his stare flicked to the scrape across my collarbones.

"I'll be fine. We need to go." I couldn't bring myself to glance down at the man dead on the ground. Nausea swept over me at the thought of it.

Ronin let go of a heavy breath and, without a word, he stooped and pulled the dagger from the man's back. I tried to block out the way it squelched when he retrieved it.

Once he had it back, he wiped the blade off on the man's tunic.

Sweat dripped down the side of my face and my pulse hammered in my ears until everything else muffled. It was hard to steady myself while the forest spun around me, making me sway.

A hand grabbed my elbow to steady me and I glanced at Ronin—worry etched his brow. "Elita, we're okay."

Somehow, the words made it worse.

I sucked in a shuddering breath and tears coated my cheeks. "He's dead," I croaked. Despite my efforts not to, my gaze found the man's lifeless body on the ground. Crimson leached through his tunic as he continued to bleed.

Ronin sighed and bent to retrieve my cloak.

Fear and disbelief gripped around my throat, and I couldn't speak another word if I tried to. The tears fell silently while Ronin replaced the cloak around my shoulders. Bloodied hands fastened the clasp and pulled the hood over my mess of curls. It barely registered with me.

"Are you fine to walk?" Ronin asked. He pushed his hair back from his face and I winced when it left a trail of crimson through it.

When I used to wonder what it would be like to adventure out in the realm, among the vast forests the Iron Thorn had to offer, I often imagined it as enchanting. A whimsical journey among the trees.

The reality of the realm outside of the safety of the cottage left a sour taste in my mouth and more haunting visions of blood and death.

My voice trembled when I spoke. "We need to find water."

Ronin didn't have to ask me why. He stared at his own hands for a brief pause before he nodded. We turned to leave, and I forced myself not to look back. I couldn't stomach the sight of the man's lifeless gaze.

Ronin led the way through the woods. Peace whistled in the trees with birdsong and the rustling of leaves—it was misplaced.

We lingered close to where our fire had been, and went back toward the water Ronin had cleansed his hands from the remnants of the rabbit he skinned.

Every twig that snapped or leaf that crinkled beneath our boots sent my skin prickling with anticipation. I waited for another group of stragglers to jump out of the trees and attack, but they never came.

It didn't take us long to find ourselves back at the same body of water we had stumbled upon before. It remained unoccupied, and I sighed.

Ronin dropped his things in the dirt with a huff and strode to the pond's edge. The water ran crimson when he dunked his hands in. The blood rushed from his skin, carried away in the lapping water.

I stood close by with my arms wrapped around my torso. The green cloak clung to my shoulders with remnants of red streaked on some of the fabric from where Ronin had touched. Despite how much I longed to scrub it away, I didn't want the cold clinging to me.

The breeze grew cooler by the day, and I dreaded it as the harvest season swept in. Soon, the leaves would change, and I wondered if it meant my bloom would wait until the next sprouting. It was a foolish hope. I was well aware a bloom didn't obey the rules of nature.

The thought made me shiver, and I ducked further into my cloak while Ronin rubbed furiously at his skin. My movement caught his eye, and he turned to me, which caused hair to fall into his line of sight. He blew a breath at it to get it out of his face.

"Cold?" he asked as he straightened. He dried his hands on his trousers and left the edge of the water to stand beside me.

I brushed my hands over my arms and sighed. "I've forgotten what day it is. But I think maybe harvest season has begun."

"It's hard to keep track of time out here," he replied. "It's not the most ideal weather for such a journey."

My gaze shifted to him, and I gave him a small smile. "Hopefully, we can find somewhere warm to stop on the way."

He grinned in reply. "Are you having second thoughts about leaving the Temple?"

I faltered, my eyes going wide. Talos's torture was never too far from my thoughts. "Not in the slightest."

Ronin chuckled, missing my reaction as he bent to retrieve his cloak, which had been thrown over the bags. Instead of putting the cloak back on, he tucked it over my shoulders on top of the green one I wore.

I looked at the cloak, then met Ronin's kind expression. "I can't use both, Ronin. You'll be cold." My fingers tugged at the edge of his thick gray cloak to remove it.

He shook his head and threw on both of his bags. "I'll be fine. Let's go find somewhere to make a camp. A fire will do more to fend off the cold than an old cloak."

Ronin led the way, and I stumbled close behind him, never too far. Despite how guilty I felt, I tugged his cloak tighter around my body as the trees began to swallow us.

The woods appeared more dangerous after the men crossed our path, and the worry of what else could be lurking in the vast Iron Forests had me on high alert, watching for threats at every turn.

With any luck, we would find the Forge soon, and the threat of being caught and returned to the Temple wouldn't feel as though it were breathing down my neck.

I trusted Ronin to keep me safe until we got there, and as the trees began to distort in blurs of black and emerald, I hoped that the Forge would be the answer. He would get me there, and I could bloom and wait to return until the last petal was ready to wilt.

Silently, I prayed to the gods that my mother and Casimir had told me to cross the Forge for a reason, and I could find solace on the other side.

Chapter Twelve

The days began to blend into one another, with the swirl of changing emerald leaves, black bark, and gray rocks creating a blurred tapestry. It was all too similar; it felt like walking in circles. Nightmares of horrors that were all too real made it difficult to sleep, and made it even harder to keep track of the time.

Ten days came and went since Ronin and I embarked on our journey to the Forge. Ronin's initial path was taking days longer than expected due to how fatigue overwhelmed me. We spent many hours in the dirt, taking a break from the constant walking.

The stops weren't always my doing, though, and after finding another spot to rest for the day, I sat behind a tree while Ronin bathed a few feet away in a pond we stumbled across. The proximity always made me uncomfortable, but it made both Ronin and I feel safer if I wasn't too far from him, in case more hunters came along.

Sunlight dappled through the trees and reflected off the dagger in my hand as I turned it over, observing the intricate details on the hilt. The steel was cold and unforgiving, well crafted with great care. Though it made me uneasy, it was better than sitting unguarded. Ronin had taken the time to show me how to properly use it for self-defense after our run-in with the men, but it still wasn't something I took pleasure in holding. Not after I'd seen it coated in blood.

Water lapped behind me, the distinct sound of Ronin clambering out of the pond. Then a muttered curse at the icy breeze followed before the flick of a cloak caught the air. He was drying off.

Tension I hadn't noticed released from my shoulders, leaving the knot between them sore from being rigid for so long. But he was out, and it meant our protection was no longer left in my hands. He simply had to dress himself, and the responsibility was no longer mine.

"Elita?" Ronin called from near the water.

I scrambled up, the dagger in one hand, and a pack in the other. My head peered around the tree, and I yelped as heat traveled across my face, painting me red.

"By the gods!" I sputtered, dropping the pack. I pressed a palm flat to my chest as my heart threatened to burst. "I thought you were done. I wasn't thinking."

Ronin laughed, the sound much too loud as it cut through the previously tranquil forest. "I was mostly covered. No harm done." He assured me, though the sight of his nearly bare frame was burned into my mind.

I tried to shake it out.

"When you said my name I figured—gods, I'm sorry." I slumped back to the ground, relieved my hand of the dagger, and pressed my cold palms to my cheeks as they blazed.

A softer chuckle came from beside me, and I tentatively turned to see Ronin there, his chest bare, but he at least had his trousers on. The cloak he'd been using to dry off with had thankfully kept him decent enough, but it was still more than I had expected to see. Too much skin from his chest to ankle as his makeshift towel only covered half of his frame.

Ronin retrieved the dagger from the grass and tucked it into a sheath at the waist of his trousers. "It's fine, Elita. Truly. I apologize for startling you, I just hadn't seen you move, and you're an awfully quiet person. I thought perhaps you went back to where we left the other packs."

I lowered my hands, resting them on the sides of my flushed neck. "No, please. Don't apologize. It took me off guard, is all."

Ronin gave me a sideways grin, then tilted his head. "I think sometimes I forget how isolated you were. Your reaction reminded me, though," he teased.

A nervous chuckle made its way out of my throat. "And your level of comfort while indecent reminds me that we lived very different lives."

Ronin ran a hand through his wet hair while I fixed the pack over my shoulders. He reached the wet ends and squeezed the excess water onto the ground.

Shrugging, Ronin said, "I suppose that's fair. Although, my wife was the only woman I'd ever been that comfortable with." His face changed a subtle shade of pink. "I wouldn't say it's too different. Unless you're implying you thought that was a normal occurrence for me."

His tone was light hearted, despite the mention of his late wife.

I smiled softly, embarrassed by where I steered the conversation. "I hadn't meant to imply anything. I never had to worry about such situations before. A life in hiding doesn't really offer many chances to get close with anyone." The conversation felt too vulnerable, and I pursed my lips, lest I say something more uncomfortable.

Ronin's face lost the jovial expression, pulled down into a sadness that took me off guard.

I stood, worried I had somehow offended him. "Did I say something wrong?" I asked.

He shook his head. "No, it's just...that kind of connection, it's always implied it was never meant for Roses. Finding a spouse isn't something they're permitted to do. And yet the king uses them, has them birth children they don't even get to know." He paused, his fist clenching. "I'm glad your father protected you from that. The solitude may have been difficult, but the alternative sounds barbaric."

My stomach churned and I ducked my head, staring at the ground.

The leaves had begun to change, and red and brown hues scattered over the stumps and rocks. A vibrant blanket in the bleak woods. Weeks ago, when I first arrived at the Temple, I worried they wouldn't permit me to see one last harvest season before my death.

For a flicker in time, I sat with the odd gratitude. As if one terrible act never coming to fruition could undo the rest. The constant state of in-between, living in two truths, it was hard to shoulder.

I fixed my gaze on Ronin, releasing a quiet sigh. "Sometimes it's hard to see the small graces among all of the bad things that have happened. Thanks for reminding me." It was genuine, though it felt impossible to articulate how much I had once longed for that connection with someone.

It was a harsh reality that I accepted the moment the desire manifested. Pretending it was feasible for me to find someone to love caused me unbearable pain, and I had learned to shut it out in my adolescence.

Yet the way in which Ronin lived and shared his life with Melody, even if only briefly, made me envious. A bothersome feeling that did me no good.

I stuffed those emotions down and chose to be grateful that I at least had enough time left to have a friend. It was more than I ever thought I'd get.

We made our way through the woods in a comfortable silence until we found the spot we left our bags.

Within a few minutes, Ronin had a fire started and rummaged in a bag for whatever food we had left from foraging. We swapped the waterskin, built piles of sticks to replenish the fire, and cleared spaces to sleep for the night. At some point during our silent routine, I thought of Casimir and realized I hadn't been entirely alone all those years. At least, not for some of them.

Casimir didn't disappear until after I'd turned sixteen. For seven years he haunted my sleep, and beneath the wall of frustration I put up, when he did return, I was relieved.

The past few months with him back hadn't been enough, and I hoped they wouldn't be the last.

While I sat across from Ronin, whispering among the crackling embers of a fire, I felt pulled out of the moment, away from the company I had always wished for—and instead, I found myself missing a ghost.

Gentle hands ran over my arms. Warm. Scarred. Tangible.

Lips brushed mine until it changed from a caress to fervent and insatiable. It melted my limbs until it was as if I had become one with the floor. A puddle with a roaring heartbeat.

Fingers danced through my curls, pulling a soft sigh from my chest. The room spun with delight, and my eyes fluttered open.

Black hair filled my vision, framing an ember gaze.

My pulse faltered at the sight.

The face flickered until Ronin appeared before me. He grinned. Kind and comfortable. The scene distorted until it burst like a bubble to days sitting in the grass among a river, trekking through the woods. Real, tangible. Not a ghost. Only Ronin and his laughter and warmth.

I sat from my spot on the ground, shivering until my teeth chattered. I scanned the woods while tugging my cloak tighter over my shoulders to block out the frigid air that swept through the trees.

The remnants of the dream flickered through my head, and I used grief and the uncomfortable conversation with Ronin to explain it away.

Casimir hadn't visited me since that first time after the Temple, and I longed for his familiar company. There were no tinctures or fragments of grief freshly shattered in my chest. Nothing to explain his cruel absence. It left me hollow in a way I never prepared for after years spent convincing myself he was a curse.

A ghost or illusion; it didn't matter anymore. I begged for another interruption and the distraction his presence offered, sat at the end of my bed with his sole purpose seemingly to vex me. No matter how perturbed I became or how he found it entertaining, he always made an effort to pull my mind out of the chasm it lived in—with a sarcastic remark made in jest to brush off the cobwebs spun by loneliness.

Casimir was once a thorn in my side. Over time, he became embedded and less of a nuisance compared to the hole in my chest and the repetitive nightmares.

I rubbed the heel of my palms into my eyes, hoping it would ease the ache he left behind. For the first time in my life, I had to learn how to shake the discomfort alone.

Standing on shaky legs, I racked my fingers through knotted curls with a sigh. I needed to find a way to ease the thrum of my pulse and ease the sorrow spent on a ghost. For a moment, I watched Ronin to see if he'd stir awake. He had his back rested on a stump, a pack in his lap, and the dagger at his side, asleep though he was meant to be on watch.

The guilt I experienced over his lack of sleep never waned.

I left the makeshift camp and Ronin behind, cautious of where I placed my feet to avoid the leaves and brush on the ground. I didn't want to wake Ronin, not when he avoided rest most nights. The years of hunting aided my footwork, and I snuck away.

Soreness down my back and hips caused my body to yearn for the thin mattress I used to sleep on. Despite its lack of comfort, it was heavenly compared to the hard ground.

The cloak over my shoulders wasn't enough to block out the chill in the air, and I shivered, my arms dipping further into the confines of the green fabric. Water trickling acted as a guide through the trees. I wandered toward the sound, hoping to alleviate the tension in my body.

Moonlight shimmered on the pond. A stream flowed from elsewhere in the woods, refreshing the water. The calming sound echoed around me and caused my shoulders to droop. It was much colder near the water, but I didn't mind. Goosebumps pebbled across my skin, from my neck down to my legs. I shivered when the cloak fell from my shoulders, thin as a feather, making no sound.

If I had known how to swim, I would've gotten right into the water to wash away the weeks of filth on my skin. Another thing that was easy for Ronin, but an obstacle for me.

Beneath the sound of the water lapping, wings fluttered close. A familiar raven landed nearby. It stood at the edge of the pond and stared at me, its head turned to the side.

I sighed. "I have nothing for you. Quit following me."

The raven squawked and flapped its wings. I stared at it, wishing I knew what it wanted from me. It had followed me from Eldravine. A bad omen, a spirit—it was never too far.

Its persistent presence reminded me of Casimir, and the desire to have him visit me again threatened to overwhelm me. I longed to speak with someone who knew me and who I didn't have to be so wary of.

But he didn't return. Never had I experienced such a sense of distance between us. His presence felt like it belonged to another realm. I closed my eyes and fought back the wave of grief for a ghost.

"Elita?"

For a moment, I imagined the voice was Casimir's. A call to bring me back from the brink. But Ronin's voice was distinct, and not only in my head.

The raven cried and lifted from the ground, disappearing into the night. I watched it go until the blackness swallowed it.

Ronin shuffled toward me. His presence was different from Casimir's. The sound of him at my side was real and not an echo inside my dreams. Ronin was closer to me than typical, his heat palpable. When his hand softly touched my arm, I almost jumped. The touch was foreign.

"It's a bit cold," he said, kneeling next to me to retrieve my fallen cloak. I offered a small shrug while he laid it back across my shoulders. "Probably not ideal for a bloom." His tone was gentle. We stood at the water's edge, close enough that my back almost touched his chest.

The only sounds to break the silence were the gentle gurgle of running water and the melodic chirping of bugs. I was accustomed to most of it and found it beautiful in its own way. The specks of yellow glowing bugs lit up the night for them to communicate with each other in the darkness.

"I didn't mean to wake you," I said softly.

Ronin chuckled. "Perhaps we should swap who sleeps during the day and who sleeps at night. I don't think you've slept a full night this entire journey."

"Sorry," I whispered, afraid to say too much.

"No, it's okay." He inched closer. "More nightmares?"

My cheeks blazed red at the reminder of the dream.

It wasn't much of a nightmare.

"I've had recurring night terrors since I was a child," I said, avoiding a direct answer to his question. "My father used to take me out on walks to help clear my head. I've never had to deal with the nightmares on my own until the fire. There was always someone there to comfort me. I miss him."

I didn't mention Casimir, though he was the one who often

brought me out of my visions of death. Whatever Casimir was, he wasn't someone I wanted to mention to Ronin.

"The ache of missing those we've lost doesn't ever truly leave, but it gets easier. Some days, at least," Ronin said, breaking the quiet while doing the one thing he could to comfort me.

I offered him a halfhearted smile. "Sorry for waking you...but I appreciate you coming to find me. It's difficult being alone."

He offered a small smile and nodded. "Of course. Now, is there any chance you may be able to get some rest? We have a long way to go tomorrow." Ronin's walls went back up, and he tucked the emotions away. He seemed to handle his grief with ease, or perhaps it was the opposite, and like me, he had to conceal it so it wouldn't engulf him.

I released a heavy breath and pulled the cloak tighter around my shoulders. Part of me was exhausted and needed rest. But deep down, I knew sleep did not offer any relief.

Ronin turned to head back, and I followed, silent while I trailed his footsteps. The heavy weight of darkness appeared more sinister than it used to. Where a walk through the night used to bring me relief, it made me uneasy.

The campsite appeared before us, tucked in a peculiar circle of trees and brush. The thought of sleep filled me with dread.

I stared down at the spot on the ground where I had been lying, and my pulse rushed in my ears. It was easier to never hope for sleep or relief from the constant exhaustion.

Ronin glanced over his shoulder, studying me. He sighed, then sat down on the ground. "Sit with me," he said, gesturing to the spot next to him. I stared at him, shocked, but I obliged.

I lowered myself next to him, the ground cold beneath me. He patted his shoulder, looking over at me. It took me a moment to realize he wanted me to lean on him. Tentatively, I rested my head on his shoulder.

"Try to get some sleep, okay?" Ronin shifted until my head leaned halfway on his chest.

Despite how hard I tried to keep my guard up, his body heat brought me comfort in the harsh cold. Maintaining my walls became an unattainable task, and I rested further into his side, shutting my heavy lids and yearning for some rest.

After Ronin spent the night awake to give me a chance to sleep at his side—he sat across from me now, his back pressed to a rock while he took a few hours to get some rest. He frequently opted to forgo sleep, and he was adamant I required it much more with my bloom. But it caught up with him then, as his chest rose and fell in a slow and rhythmic way, his lips parted.

I had my cloak draped over my body and legs, my knees pulled up to my chest to hold in more heat. The dagger Ronin kept close for protection lay beside me in the dirt—as if I had any inclination of how to use it.

The sun was rising, casting streams of light through the few trees that surrounded our makeshift camp. I fought the urge to doze off. His company offered some relief, but not enough to fend off the worst of the nightmares and I spent the night plagued by visions of Talos.

I watched the small fire dwindle from bright orange flames to vibrant smoldering embers. The feeling of warmth began to wane, leaving a slight chill in the air.

The peaceful silence was shattered by a loud crack from the dense woods. I jumped at the sound, whipping around to glance behind me.

Ronin startled awake and I glanced at him. "What was that?" My voice trembled, and I watched him jump up and throw dirt on the fire, trying to smother it. The smoke continued to rise anyway, a thin trail twisting in the sky.

He watched it with frustration before throwing his cloak back on, and then his two bags. "We need to move. The sun is too high. They can likely see the smoke miles from here."

I shuddered and copied him, throwing my cloak and pack on before I shoved my hair back into the hood. Ronin rubbed at his face, still appearing half asleep.

"You need more time to rest," I said, though I knew our need to leave was much more important at the moment; the fatigue was obvious in all his features. Ronin shook his head and used his foot to break up the makeshift fire ring.

Utilizing the scattered rocks, he masked our presence, leaving no evidence behind. "If they get too close, we won't make it to the Forge. We can't have them following our tracks." The panic was clear in his voice.

The contagious unease emanating from him made me scan our surroundings. My senses heightened, and I looked for any indication of the Iron Guard or hunters. The cause of the sound remained out of sight, but the worry continued to intensify.

"Let's go," I said, pulling at Ronin's sleeve.

He glanced at me, and noticing the fear on my face, I watched his features relax. The concern in his own expression vanished. "We'll be fine. We're close enough to the Forge, and if we can get a start now, I can get you there by nightfall."

"But what about you?"

"The place I planned to hide out at is close. I'll be fine. Let's focus on getting you to the Forge first." His hand wrapped around mine and pulled me along, stepping up onto a large stone. He hoisted me up onto a rock, moving further from the safety of our camp.

Despite our lack of cover, there was no opportunity to pause and take in our surroundings and he pulled me along behind him. The minutes ticked on, and Ronin eventually slid his hand out of mine. I followed at his side, never out of his sight. He continued to glance behind us and up at the sky. The only thing out of place was the smoke that continued to swirl in the sky from the spot we left behind. I tried to disregard the guilt for letting it smolder so long, signaling with smoke to anyone who was out searching for me.

Not wanting to think about it anymore, I hopped on the rock in front of us. I looked down at Ronin while he climbed it, too.

"I've been wondering, what got you interested in horticulture?" I asked.

Ronin glanced up at me. A flash of pain crossed his face. "After Melody passed, I wanted to do something that made me feel close to her. She was a garden caretaker in the village we grew up in." Ronin dusted off his hands after climbing up the rock. "It ended up bringing me a lot more peace than I expected. A slower, less harsh, life. No sweltering forges or iron burning my hands. I think the pull to it was Melody's parting gift to me. The only solace I've been able to find."

"I didn't mean to dig up old wounds. I'm sorry," I said, tucking a loose curl behind my ear. "But I think it's a powerful thing—you finding purpose after such loss. It couldn't have been easy."

Ronin frowned, and for a moment, I thought I said something to offend him. It took me off guard when he reached out, running a piece of my hair between his fingers. The buds tingled.

"I wish you could have the chance to do the same," he said softly, letting the curl fall. He cleared his throat. "I imagine it must be hard carrying the weight of being a Rose."

Awful, morbid words threatened to spill from my lips. Truths I never spoke to anyone. That maybe wilting would be my gift—the release from such pain. A mercy. Rather than live with the grief or the memories of torture, when my wilt came, none of it would be mine to bear anymore. Death would be a silent escape, and sometimes, rather than scare me, it sounded like relief.

The secrets never had the chance to be spoken. I heard the soft *whoosh* through the trees before the sting registered with me. It whistled through the air, grazing my thigh through my cloak. I yelped at the sensation and dropped to the ground, my hand finding the cut on my leg.

Ronin whipped around, crouching to grab my arm. "Run, Elita!"

I grunted when he pulled me up, tugging me forward.

The sting disappeared from my mind as adrenaline pumped through my limbs, pressing me on faster than I should've been able to move. My leg stung, but whatever hit me had merely grazed my skin. Not enough to be lethal. I knew none of their efforts would be, at least towards me. But Ronin...

I heard the firing of arrows as they whistled through the air. I stumbled and ran, my vision distorted by panic. Ronin pulled me along while he tried to dodge, avoiding the open areas and ducking for the small trees or large rocks, trying to buy us any protection or time possible. Black wings darted in front of us. The raven cried out, never too far from me.

My pulse pounded in my ears while we ran, and my breathing turned ragged. We continued to sprint, struggling when the rocks rose too high to run over. Ronin propelled me up onto them and he followed behind.

He never let go of me, holding on while the shouts echoed behind us. Their voices grew closer, warning the archers to avoid me and aim for the male. It caused my stomach to twist with nausea.

I dared a glance behind us and saw the flash of red as the Iron Guard charged after us, a line of archers resting on a knee to fire before they rose and advanced. The sound of their bows releasing the tension from the pull rang in my head.

Ronin paid them no mind. He was quick and light on his feet, bringing me along with him no matter how much I slowed him down. I half expected him to throw me over his shoulder and sprint off, but he didn't. He just urged me on, never faltering or slowing.

I panted, and my limbs burned with the exertion. We scrambled over rocks until they finally died out; the terrain grew flatter the further we ran. It fueled my fear to know the guard was so close. All it would take was clear terrain to get a clear shot. My concern for Ronin grew. I knew they wouldn't hesitate to end his life if they had the chance.

Another round of arrows fired, catching the edge of my cloak, and one flew close to Ronin's cheek, almost grazing him. He didn't let his composure crack and did his best to keep us out of range. I tried to time the archers from their kneel to their sprint, but it felt hopeless as I counted the lapse. *One... Two... Three...*

I yelped when Ronin plummeted, his body vanishing with his hand still in mine, pulling me along as he fell.

His free hand clamped over my mouth as we rolled to muffle my shriek of surprise. Our bodies came to an abrupt stop when we hit something hard, and darkness engulfed us. Ronin pressed himself against me, his arm encircling my waist while his hand covered my mouth.

"Shh," he murmured against my ear.

I stilled and tried to get my bearings. We were buried in a strange pocket of earth, and an overwhelming musty scent smothered me. The only light came from above us. It came in through the place we had fallen from, partially hidden underground. Twigs and leaves shadowed the edge of where we'd just fallen, our bodies having cleared most of it.

I hoped it would be sufficient to keep us hidden.

Neither of us dare move or make a sound. Overhead, the sound of the guards shouting reverberated with groans of frustration and confusion at our disappearance.

Someone barked orders, a voice rough and full of rage. "Find them!" The voice sounded distant as the dense air carried it to the burrow, faint but audible enough.

I pleaded with the gods in desperation, hoping the guards wouldn't find us nor that we would be buried alive. I didn't know which one would be worse.

Chapter Thirteen

We remained in the burrow for hours, long after the voices faded into nothing. Ronin's body heat became a relief from the cold that crept into the burrow. The closeness provided a steadying heartbeat at my back while we stayed hidden. My limbs tingled and cramped, aching with the aftermath of adrenaline.

Ronin's breathing stayed ragged despite hours of silence after the Iron Guard moved on. Ronin fidgeted once more, unable to remain still. His hand no longer covered my mouth but rested on my shoulder, his elbow bent between our bodies. If it wasn't for the discomfort in my limbs, I might've nodded off when the sun faded overhead.

Time flew by in a blur before Ronin finally shifted his arm away from me, groaning as if injured. "We need to move," he ground out, pain in his voice. Alarm flared in my chest, but I nodded, doing my best to move my numb arms to crawl and pull myself out.

In an instant, the space became too small.

With my elbows in the dirt, I crawled up the slope, using my feet to push, while Ronin propelled me by placing his hands under my boots.

The frigid weather brought a nip to my skin when I reached the surface and gasped for air, falling on my back to lie out flat. I didn't pause to check if it was clear. Everything hurt more than I thought possible. But the cold grass was a welcome relief from being trapped in the burrow.

I remained there for a few minutes before it dawned on me I didn't hear Ronin follow me out. I sat straight and looked into the burrow at him. He had his eyes shut and paused halfway out. Pain etched his brow, and he huffed another breath.

"Ronin?" Apprehension filled my voice, and I reached a hand toward him. "Let me help."

He looked up at me, his eyes bloodshot. I stretched my hand further into the burrow, and he reached for it, his hand warm and wet, slipping into mine. My face paled when I saw the crimson on his palm.

I mustered all my strength and extended my other hand, gripping his forearm tightly to pull on him. He groaned and gritted his teeth while pushing up and out of the burrow, panting. I scanned over him in a panic and found a tear through his cloak and tunic. Blood stained the fabric.

"My gods," I muttered, scrambling closer. "Ronin...what do I do?" My voice broke as I searched his face.

"We need to go. You can't stay here."

I stared at him with uncertainty, glancing from his wound to his face. His resolve was sure. Regardless of my hesitation, I wrapped an arm around his torso, careful not to touch his wound.

"Focus on holding pressure on it. Tell me how to get to your hideout," I said.

Ronin tensed. "But the Forge—"

"It'll still be there in a few days. You're hurt. I'm not going to abandon you in the woods."

He stared down at me, searching my face. Our gaze locked, and a second later, he nodded and pointed us deeper into another stretch of woods. I let him rest some of his weight on me and did as he instructed. One of his hands continued to clutch his side, and the other held the shattered compass against my shoulder.

We stumbled along, and the trees began to swallow our surroundings and offer us some cover from anyone who may have still been searching.

Ronin and I traded places—him stumbling while I helped him

along, my footsteps more sure than they had been for most of our journey out of the Iron Thorn.

The sun disappeared and drenched us in darkness. The weight on my shoulder grew heavy, but we pressed on. Until the course changed, a shape taking place in the woods as if the path were purposeful.

Ronin sighed, and his body shifted from mine. I stayed close, but my shoulder slumped, relieved of the weight. He walked on, keeping me close to his side despite no longer needing my support.

If I weren't trying to look for it, I would've missed it. A dark wood structure stood misplaced in the bark of the trees.

The tiny cottage appeared before us. Vines grew over it, the roof painted in a fluff of green moss. Trees stood close to it and helped to camouflage it in the forest. Abandoned and neglected, it appeared as if time had forgotten about it, on the brink of disintegrating. Yet the sight of it brought me a sense of comfort like I hadn't experienced in a long time.

"This is it. My father's old cottage," Ronin said. I looked over at him to see a smile of relief on his clammy face.

"Good. Now, we need to handle your wound."

The inside of the cottage was small. There was a single old cot, a wood-burning stove, a small table near the back door, a lone sink, and, according to Ronin, a pot outside meant to be used as a latrine. The cabin had belonged to his family, but his father almost solely used it for hunting.

Ronin went with his father a few times, and though he hated being cramped in such a tiny space back then, he knew it was safe and well-hidden.

We had a small lantern lit on the floor, too afraid to use the wood stove, knowing it would put off smoke. Rust covered the lantern, left beside the cot and forgotten for many years. But it was enough.

Making myself comfortable on the floor by the cot, I unclasped one of the packs Ronin had carried. He sat on the edge of the frame in front of me, the blood now crusted on his hands. The lantern flickered, casting shadows over him as it shifted.

After searching, I pulled out the small cloth bag filled with the only healing supplies we had on hand. I hoped it would be enough to tend his wounds. The graze on my thigh was long forgotten; it was just a minor scratch in comparison.

"Let me see," I said timidly, looking at him after I laid out the bandages, a glass bottle of cypress oil, and a few other items I hoped I wouldn't need, like the suturing supplies. At the bottom of the bag, I retrieved a container of comfrey salve. It would have to do.

Ronin clenched his jaw and grabbed his tunic, pulling it over his head. As it fell to the floor in a feather-like twirl, my attention shifted to his right side. It looked jagged where the arrow had run through the edge of his skin, leaving a gash.

Wide eyed, I looked at him. "And you laid in the burrow for hours?"

He shrugged, then relaxed his arms behind his torso. I shook my head and glanced down at the supplies. In an attempt to ward off infection, I moistened a cloth with the fragrant cypress oil, hoping it would suffice. I raised on my knees and brought the cloth to his wound, pressing it to the torn flesh with a delicate touch.

He hissed in pain, his knuckles turning white where he gripped the cot with both hands. I muttered an apology but continued to wipe the wound clean with caution, feeling awful with every breath he sucked in.

When I finished cleaning it, I looked at our remaining items. Though I didn't want to, the wound needed to be sutured.

"Ronin—"

"It's fine. I know."

He gritted his teeth and moved to lie down on his side to give me a better angle of his wound. My hands trembled when I grabbed the kit, my heart pounding.

"I hope you aren't intending to suture me while shaking like that," he joked, glancing over his shoulder. I shook my head, then my hands, trying to fight off the nerves.

Ronin averted his gaze from me and laid his head on his outstretched arm. I put the sutures back down and poured water from the waterskin over my hands before rubbing them in cypress oil. The smell was overwhelming, but the fear of causing him an infection outweighed the scent. It wasn't the best, but I had to stop stalling.

I sat straighter and threaded the needle with the sutures. I tried to imagine I was back at my family's cottage, preparing to stitch together another leather vest, not someone's skin.

Ronin gripped the other side of the cot with one hand, bracing himself. My pulse flitted with nerves.

"I've never sutured skin before." My voice shook, and I noticed Ronin tense—the muscles on his back coiled.

"Just be careful not to go too deep. You'll feel it when it breaks the skin. Don't keep going deeper."

"I don't think I can do this."

He sighed and glanced at me again. "I'll tell you if you go too far. It'll be okay."

My gaze flicked back to his wound, and I wished his words gave me some comfort. "I'm sorry," I said, sick to my stomach, when I pointed the needle at his skin.

With the first pull, Ronin let out a sharp hiss of pain. My hands threatened to tremble, but I steeled myself with a grounding breath. If I shook too much, it would only hurt him more.

He ducked his face into his arm and clenched his jaw. I took a shallow breath and tried to distract him.

"When I was a little girl, I cut my shin badly enough to need a healer," I said, my voice timid, trying to fill the silence as I worked the sutures. "My parents didn't take me in for obvious reasons. So, my mother sutured it herself." I grimaced at the memory. "It was awful. And I can't tell you how sorry I am to not have a way to numb the pain."

Another pull, a breath through his teeth, and I finished suturing the wound. I reached down for the small dagger and pressed it against the hanging suture, cutting it off from the needle. I saw Ronin release a sigh, and as soon as I put the needle and suture thread down, I grabbed the bandage wrap with bloodied hands.

"Can you sit up?" I asked. He nodded and shifted until his legs dangled off the side of the bed. I tapped his elbows so he would raise his arms and began to wrap the bandage around his torso.

I went around from his side to his back, my arms going behind him. His breath moved across my cheek as I grabbed for the other side. I pursed my lips and focused on my work, going around him twice before the wrap was almost gone.

Using the blade, I severed the bandage and adjusted it snugly around his body. After I finished, I sat on my heels.

Ronin slid his tunic back on and released a shaky breath. "You say your mother sutured you herself? How old were you?" he asked, pushing his messy hair out of his face.

I bit my lip and looked down at my hands, which were painted crimson. "Just a child. Not my favorite memory."

He patted the cot next to him, and I stood, putting my weight on the old frame with caution, afraid it would turn to dust beneath me. It appeared on the verge of falling apart, but it accepted my added weight, and I leaned back as well, resting against the wall.

"I can understand their apprehension of taking you somewhere, but I also can't imagine putting a child through that kind of pain." Ronin's voice caught, and he cleared his throat, fidgeting beside me.

I glanced at him, watching him fidget, his mind elsewhere. And despite how nervous it made me, I reached over and rested my hand on top of his, drawing his attention back toward me. His expression distorted with grief, a painful memory bubbling to the surface.

"Ronin?" I whispered. In an instant, his walls came back up and he looked away from me.

Silence lingered between us. The lone sounds came from outside of the cottage as the breeze whistled through the holes in the old wood.

Moments passed by before Ronin moved his hand from mine and got up from the cot, his movement sluggish. I wanted to reach out to him and ask if he was okay, but refrained. Instead, I pulled my legs up onto the cot with me.

"You can have the bed. You could use some sleep. Tomorrow, we'll need to gather supplies from the village nearby. Once we've refilled everything, I can take you to the Forge."

I stared at him in shock. "You can't truly expect me to let you sleep on the floor with your side mangled," I said, exasperated.

He just chuckled, tossing his cloak into a wad on the floor. "Out of anyone I've ever known, you sleep the worst. You'll take the cot."

"But you slept so much less on our journey here. I can't in good conscience let you suffer even more. *Especially* with your wounds."

Ronin gave me a knowing look. "I'll be fine. What kind of man would I be if I had you sleep on the floor instead?" His lips turned up in a playful grin, and despite the guilt, I couldn't think of another solution. Other than me sleeping on the floor to be stubborn.

I watched Ronin adjust his makeshift spot on the floor for a moment before the unease at the prospect of going into a village crept in.

"Won't going somewhere with other people be dangerous?" The question was silly, but everything inside me fought the idea of willingly being around others, especially with guards on our tail.

"We're out of food, and our healing supplies are abysmal. I don't want to risk it, but we have no other choice. At this point, it's more of a risk to catch fish or hunt and cook over a fire. They'll be watching the tree line for any sign of smoke. And if you plan to make it in the Drought Lands, you'll need a lot of food and clean water."

I nodded in understanding and lay on my side, tucking my hands beneath my head. Ronin tended to the lantern, checking it was okay. I watched him stash all the supplies away, my body fighting sleep.

The adrenaline died down and the promise of more nightmares made my entire body tense. Every night, it got worse. Memories of my parents, dead in the cottage. Or Talos and the delight he took in torturing me. It was too much, and I longed for something to help me sleep. A cup of chamomile tea or a walk in the woods with my father. Even the ramblings of a ghost to distract me from the horrible memories.

Part of me feared I wouldn't ever see Casimir again. That my angry words were true, and he was merely something I conjured up in my dreams to ease the loneliness. I didn't know which was worse. Him being real and allowing me to suffer alone, or Casimir not being real at all.

The snarl of a prince haunted me when I finally drifted off. Cloves burned my nose in my nightmares. It threatened to cut off my oxygen when visions of Talos grabbing me flashed through the blur of distorted dreams.

The morning light brought no relief with it. Sleep eluded me once more, leaving me restless and drained.

Ronin stood on the other side of the tiny cabin, getting his things ready to head to the village. He had his hair pushed back into his hood in a low twist.

Another yawn caused my jaw to ache while I pushed my feet into my boots. I was thankful they were mostly healed. After days of walking and running, the leather was more familiar and worn to the soles of my feet.

The cloak draped back over me, the fabric swallowing my frame. After my boots were on, I started to braid my hair back in loose overlapping layers, the buds more noticeable than normal, some of them causing a strange twinge in my scalp when my hands brushed over them.

I didn't tell Ronin. I wouldn't speak a word of it to anyone. The fear of my imminent death continued to plague me, and I had to put it aside. There was no time to wallow. We needed to get in and out of the village, with the hope of enough supplies to last us until my bloom finished.

Ronin looked over at me when I finished my braid, tying it off with a piece of torn fabric. He straightened back up after he put on his boots, gaze fixed on my face. Insecurity got the best of me, and I ran my hand over the braid, feeling for stray pieces.

"It looks nice," he said with a sideways grin. He walked over to me to pull up my hood and tucked the flyaway hairs into the fabric. My stomach knotted, and I cleared my throat.

We got all of our bags layered on and left the safety of the cottage behind. Ronin took charge and led us through the woods. Though it was quiet, he stayed vigilant and continued to scan the forest while we put more distance between us and the little shack.

Ronin's attention flicked down to his compass while we followed the path that became a permanent part of the forest from years of use.

Smells from the village wafted through the forest and pulled me out of my thoughts. The closer we got, the more it continued to build. The scents of burning wood in the hearths, baking bread, and the recognizable aroma of boiling broth. After an hour of walking through the woods, the shift made me eager.

My stomach growled, the noise impossible to ignore. If not for Ronin, I may have sprinted right into the village. He grabbed my arm, stopping me for a moment.

"Let me talk to the merchants. Try to keep your eyes down and stay behind me if you can."

"So, like a normal day back in Eldravine. Got it," I joked lightly, a pep in my step at the aroma of food. Ronin didn't seem to be in a humorous mood, and he searched my face.

"If anyone notices you're a Rose, it's over, Elita. I can't protect you from an entire village of people who would turn you in for a few copper coins."

My mood deflated, and I nodded, recoiling into my cloak as Ronin led the way to the village.

The sounds and scents were overwhelming when we arrived at the stone wall, which appeared to be built from the same dusty blue rocks we had made our way across in the woods.

Between the walls were two large wooden doors held open by guards who didn't resemble the Iron Guard at all, their armor a harsher red with swirls of purple lining the edge of the cuffs and collar. They each had weapons strapped to them: a dagger, a sword, and a bow across their chest and back.

Villagers scrambled in and out of the gate, their heads low, bustling about. The guards paid them no heed, all of them virtually a sea of gray, tan, or black cloaks, coats, and leathers.

Ronin glanced over at me, watching me take it in. "Welcome to Woolfolk, the village I grew up in."

Chapter Fourteen

The wooden gates yawned open as we walked among the crowd, Ronin's shoulder bumped mine while I stayed close to his side. Dark green fabric blocked most of my vision, as my face remained hidden in the hood of my cloak.

The sound of lively chatter, children playing on the packed dirt road, and men laughing and shouting from a nearby tavern rang through the tiny village. People crowded around us, their carts and livestock jostling for space, while others leisurely strolled through the bustling street. Vendors scattered on either side of the dirt-packed road, offering a variety of baked goods, clothes, and blacksmith items. An enticing aroma emanated from a kettle as a fire burned below it close by.

With all the excitement, it was impossible to keep my head down. It was nothing like the Eldravine. It wasn't uniform and carefully polished and tended to. The atmosphere was cozy and inviting, filled with smiles and energetic activity. Parents pulled their carts along while their children sat on the back, swinging their legs and giggling with every bump of the cart.

I had to duck my head, aware of my carelessness.

The environment was intoxicating.

There were humble buildings throughout the village, made with stone foundations and wooden boards rising halfway up and topped with pointed roofs. While they lacked extravagance, the captivating charm surpassed anything I had encountered before. Inviting in a way the Iron Thorn buildings were not.

The dirt path wove through them, creating intricate turns to more cottages, shops, and the like. It bustled with life, people much too busy to notice us in the fray.

Ronin led me through the busy village center, eyeing the stalls and shops. We walked through until we came up to a small apothecary nestled between two taller buildings. The awning was a faded purple, damp still from a recent rain.

A large stone propped the wood door open, and we ducked inside, the busy noise dying down in the muted little shop. The walls were adorned with shelves full of glass bottles, wraps, a pair of wood crutches, and many other things to replenish our healing supplies.

In a whisper, the shopkeeper welcomed us in, sparing a quick glance from her work. Ronin nodded in reply, his gaze fixed on the shelves, scanning for things we needed.

I spotted a vial of frankincense and pointed it out to him, knowing he desperately needed it if he was going to avoid a nasty infection. He seized the vial with his free hand, then reached for additional gauze and a calendula healing salve.

I kept count of each thing he grabbed, eyeing the price scratched into the wood beneath them. Some were only two copper pieces. A few of the more rare items were over eight copper for a single vial. My eyes widened, and I glanced at him, unsure how he intended to pay for any of it.

After adding them to the small pack we had emptied before leaving, Ronin carried it to the woman sitting behind the counter.

Small round wire glasses perched on her nose, and her lips moved as she muttered something to herself.

When Ronin cleared his throat, she looked up; her face was young yet worn from years of work in the sun, appearing like warm honey in the flickering of the lanterns in her shop. "Is this all?" she asked, her voice hoarse. Ronin nodded, and she glanced in the pack, counting under her breath as she looked over the items. "Twenty copper pieces," she said, her tone suspicious.

I glanced at Ronin from the side of my hood, watching as he pulled out a leather pouch I hadn't seen before. It jingled with the sound of coins, full and plump in his hand. He opened it, counting out the payment. Sliding the coins across the counter, he watched as she counted by pushing the copper pieces around, catching the glow of the lantern on them as she did.

She nodded her head while she slid the coins into a hand and placed them under the counter, adding them to a tin that echoed the drop of each coin. "Thanks for coming through. The roads will turn muddy soon. Seems Esen is blessing us with more rain," she chimed, not sparing another glance as she turned back to her work, her gaze darting over the pages of a book.

"Thank you."

Ronin stashed his coin pouch out of view and hoisted the pack onto his shoulder, carrying provisions I hoped would remain untouched.

Upon leaving the shop, we noticed the skies were indeed gloomy. A dark, thick cloud moved near the mountains in the distance, like a bad omen manifested in blackened clouds.

We walked past many of the vendors and deeper into the friendly little village. The thought crossed my mind of what it would've been like to grow up in such a unique environment, far from the powers of the king. Maybe my life would have been normal. A young girl running through the streets with friends, laughing without a dark cloud over her head.

How I ached for my young self to have been able to have that. An ordinary life with friends and unbridled joy. Without the ache of loneliness or the persistent sense of impending doom. My life being my own, to learn and explore.

I spent every moment of my life hiding. Too afraid to look another person in the eye. Never speak to anyone, keep my head low, keep my distance. A lonely room with no one to keep me company but a ghost in my dreams.

My parents were their own kind of ghost even when they lived, the fear and the isolation affecting them in their own way. Their parents and families were gone, no friends of their own. They had no one else but each other, though they spent most of their time ignoring the other's existence.

But that wasn't my life. Not anymore.

The stark contrast between my comfort level with him now and when I first met him a few weeks ago was jarring. I thanked the gods Ronin helped me escape from the Temple.

My insides recoiled at the thought of being trapped there, arms bruised as I lay alone and afraid, awaiting another visit from the cruel prince with his bag of tinctures. I took solace knowing I wouldn't have to return there.

Ronin looked over at me and gave a kind smile. *Yes, much better than the sneer of a prince.* He had become a good friend, and I questioned my choice to go over the Forge. If I stayed, the fear of dying alone couldn't haunt me any longer. Crossing the border was a risk I didn't want to take anymore.

To my delight, Ronin led us toward the baked goods, the boiling pot now being dished out into large stone bowls. Villagers were all eager to get their hands on a frigid day.

The crowd was moving in a steady flow as people grabbed their goods and went about their day, quick to sip at the bowls, and from the look on their faces, it was still too hot to eat.

We approached the stall, walking amongst the different wooden stands, which were full of bread, rolls, and delicate pastries. I stared at them, mouth watering as I ogled the food. Ronin nudged me, and I turned to see a grin on his face as he offered me the pack to carry the food.

"Pick some things out. I'm sure you're starving," he said, letting me take it from his hand.

I felt like a giddy child, filling it with rye and sourdough and throwing in a few cinnamon-dusted pastries. Ronin chuckled beside me, watching with amusement as I shopped with abandon, hunger overwhelming my concern for coin. I was certain he had enough on hand.

After rummaging through the baked goods, I grabbed a few fruits, apples, berries, and some pears. I avoided other perishable foods like butter or milk, knowing they wouldn't last more than the day.

We approached the pot everyone had been eager to get a scoop from. The scent of spices and meat made my mouth water. "Two bowls, please," Ronin said while setting the bag of other foods down to be counted.

"It's fixin' to rain. May want to finish it quickly," the man muttered, making conversation as he filled the two bowls, steam swirling from them. A woman stood beside him at the other side of the table, counting the things we had in the pack.

"Thirty copper pieces, please," she said, tying up the bag and sliding it our way. I found the cost shocking, but Ronin had told me to pick out what I wanted. Thirty pieces were more than I had anticipated, though he didn't seem concerned.

Ronin dug out the coin to pay for it, and I grabbed the bowl from the man, my gaze low, breathing in the delicious steam. It appeared to be beef stew, with potatoes and carrots poking up in the broth, along with cuts of meat and a few floating herbs like thyme and rosemary.

I thanked him without glancing his way and stepped aside, using the wooden spoon to lift a bite, blowing on it. The sight of the village teeming with life filled me with joy. It was as if I had entered a different realm.

The stone wall hid the little gem well along with the thick emerald trees that towered past the gray-blue rocks. In the distance, the rolling hills created a mesmerizing pattern of dips and rises.

While the Iron Thorn had its own kind of beauty, with sprouting flowers at every corner and well-shaped roads of intricately laid stepping stones, the village of Woolfolk held a different, simpler beauty.

Just as Ronin walked over to me, his bowl in hand and stuffed to the brim, my heart sank when I saw someone catch his arm.

"Ronin? Ronin Woolfolk?"

The sound of my racing pulse drowned out everything else as Ronin turned to face the person who stopped him.

Ronin's eyebrows furrowed, his nostrils flaring. "You must have me mistaken for someone else."

The man, stout and a few years our senior, gave a look of surprise and pulled his hand back. "You don't remember me? I know it's been a while, with everything that happened with your family—"

Ronin gave a glare to silence the man, but he continued.

"I only meant to see how you were after losing them in such a way." His face flushed as he took a step back.

Visible rage seethed from Ronin the more the man spoke. "You have the wrong man."

"I worked with your wife, Melody Woolfolk, before your—"

Ronin got in the other man's face, and I gasped, my hand grabbing his upper arm.

"Ronin," I said in a soft voice as I pulled him back. The man flushed with anger and threw his hands up in disbelief.

Ronin turned to face me, his face red with animosity. I recoiled from him as his gaze sparked with rage. It took him a fraction of a second to notice, his demeanor melting in an instant and a heavy breath released from his chest. He turned back toward the man, waving him off.

"My apologies. Please, excuse us," Ronin muttered before stalking off, his strides long and quick.

I struggled to follow him, holding my bowl in one hand as the other grabbed onto my hood to keep it in place. Ronin's bowl spilled over the edges with every step, sloshing out, wasted in the dirt.

I heard the confused mutters follow us as I trailed him through the crowd. I huffed in frustration and slowed my pace.

"Ronin!" My voice carried further than I intended it to, but all the same, his head whipped my way, appearing shocked.

He met me where I stood, eyes wide as he searched my face.

"What was that?" I asked, my tone full of irritation. He glanced around for a moment, looking anywhere but me.

Finally, he sighed, running a hand through his hair, his hood discarded. "Nothing. He knew my father, my wife."

"Woolfolk?" I huffed. "Like the village of Woolfolk?"

He gave an exasperated noise and shrugged. "My father's family were descendants. It isn't anything to talk about."

"That entire altercation was something to talk about," I countered.

Ronin's focus flickered away from me, embarrassed. My patience wore thin, and I took a few steps toward him until we were nearly chest to chest, glancing up at him.

I watched as a rush of heat crept up his cheeks.

The village continued to bustle around us as we stared at each other. I waited for him to say something or explain himself further.

Yielding, he let go of a sigh, his hands fiddling with the edge of his cloak. "There are a lot of bad memories for me here. My father owned a homestead near this village. He was well-loved. My wife was as well. People knew them; they knew me...but that was before. I'm not the same man anymore."

I reached out a hand and put it on his arm, squeezing it. "And there's nothing wrong with that. But you can't let it get the best of you."

He glanced at my hand, his expression swimming with emotions I couldn't place. I released my grip, taking the time to adjust the pack on my shoulder.

"We should head back," he muttered, staring at the food he had spilled in the street, his anger on display for all to see.

I dropped my gaze back down to avoid any lingering stares as people passed us by. It wouldn't do us any good if someone saw my Rose features if they observed me a little too close. Despite how wonderful it felt to visit Woolfolk, I knew it wasn't safe for me to stay there long.

With a curt nod, I departed rather than waiting for Ronin to lead the way. The gates were still open wide, people coming and going in the crowd, bodies pushing against each other in the open gates.

Ronin was never too far, and his shoulder brushed mine when he caught up to me. His presence became a comfort, and I told myself that staying with him was safer than crossing the border. Despite Mother's wishes, or Casimir's insistence.

The fear of the unknown, no, the fear of *being alone*, held me captive. And for the time being, I would allow myself to stay inside the walls of the kingdom. Even as the voice of my mother, and the look of disappointment on Casimir's face, both haunted me.

When we returned to the hidden cottage, we shuffled through the packs without a word. I waited for Ronin to bring up a plan to go to the Forge, but he never did. And I wondered if he also didn't want to be alone. If what the man in the village said had any weight to it, Ronin's family was gone.

Our shared grief became an invisible string, knotting us together. I found comfort in his friendship, even though I had tried to fight it. Trusting him had felt unnatural, but something changed, and I watched him sort through our supplies, grateful neither of us had to be alone anymore.

Chapter Fifteen

shen trees bent. They twisted and clawed the dead earth below. A vicious chill permeated the air, like icicles scraping across my skin.

"Why do you run?" A shrill voice split my skull, and I clasped my hands over my ears, desperate to block it out.

Ice crawled through my veins, and I stared at the twisting trees. Their unnatural shape caused panic to build in my chest, suffocating me until my head swam.

Their bark peeled; the white turning to black rot. Every piece that fell brought disease to the earth until the black corruption flaked away, lifting from the ground and suspending in the air.

Vines tore through the earth, white as they slithered like snakes until they wrapped around my ankles. Crimson corrupted the ivory strands, coating them in blood.

"In your defiance, you will become death."

The dreamspace flickered.

It spun until it formed strange shadows and shuttering leaves. No longer my room, nor the cottage. Trees warped around the edge of my vision, like a smeared painting.

The sight of Casimir sitting on a fuzzy stump made my pulse quicken. Weeks faded into each other, but it felt as though an eternity had gone by since I had seen him last.

When he spotted me, he stood. A black tunic met with a pair of gray trousers. Tension pulled his shoulders tight. "Elita."

His voice swirled in my head, and for a pause, I closed my eyes. I had somehow missed it. It used to bring me nothing but irritation. Another haunting, another interruption. I welcomed it.

Grass tingled against my palms. A strange sensation. Not quite real or right. I glanced back at him, and a swell of relief loosened a knot in my chest I hadn't noticed before. Not until it dissipated.

"Hi." Embarrassment tinted my cheeks.

Casimir chuckled. "*Hi?*" He scratched his stubble-adorned jaw. "Interesting."

My fists clenched. "I don't know what to say to you. I thought you were gone."

He shook his head and walked closer. "You're the one with the stubborn blocks. I can't ever decide if you've finally gotten yourself killed or if you've shut me out."

I pursed my lips and took a quick scan of the dreamspace. The trees moved in unnatural ways. Floating, then grounded. Blurred, then sharp. Before the cottage burned down, it had always been my room. A space I longed for.

When the thought crossed my mind, Casimir sighed, and without warning, the scene shifted. It changed until it consisted of fragmented pieces from my old room. A bed here. A fuzzy tree there. Grass poked out of the floorboards.

I met his gaze, and he rubbed at his neck. "Yeah, not my best work." More pieces changed when he spoke. My bed turned into a mound of moss.

Even as it shifted, the few items from my old room brought me a comfort I had gone so long without. The longing twisted in my chest until I worried the entire space would evaporate from want.

Tears threatened to spill, but I didn't want it to disappear yet.

"Why are you here?" I asked. The question came out harsher than I intended, and Casimir froze. He tucked his hands into the pockets of his linen trousers. The sleeves of his tunic pushed up past his elbows.

"Oh, my apologies. I'll go."

"No." Nails bit into my palms. "Don't. Please." The desperation mortified me. But I didn't want to grieve for him anymore. My ghost wasn't gone. Not yet. I needed the familiarity.

Casimir appeared amused. "No need to beg. Though, I'm not opposed to it." He took a step closer, observing me. "Are there no baths where you're at? Or is the hair a choice?"

I blushed and reached for my tangled mess of hair. The matted curls were greasy at my scalp, and the discomfort followed me in the dream-space. It made it worse to think Ronin likely noticed the same but didn't have the heart to tell me.

Slowly, I stood. Casimir observed my every move, his gaze flickering from my hair to my clothes. Part of the surrounding scene shifted. A forest inside of a bedroom. Trees sprouted from the bed. Flowers grew through the windowpane.

"Mock my appearance all you want, but you seem to be losing your touch. This is sloppy."

Casimir's attention went from my clothing to my face. The scenery sharpened. My old room took on a solid shape. None of it broken or faded. Grief twisted like a knife in my gut.

A shaky breath fell from my lips. "That's better."

As quickly as it appeared, it evaporated. We were left in the blurred woods. Casimir pushed his hair from his forehead, and messy waves tried to fall back down.

"It's hard to hold a space for too long unless one of us is physically there."

"So...where are you, then? The afterlife? Or did you purposefully make the dreamspace appear like somewhere people go to die?"

Casimir bristled at my question. I watched the muscle in his jaw jump, and he turned from me. "Just in the woods. Not sure what difference it makes where I am. You, on the other hand, need to be on your way to the Forge. Clock is ticking."

"Not funny." My hands curled into fists. "I have no intention of going to the Forge anymore."

He clicked his tongue in vexation, and in a few long strides, he stood in front of me. "Don't be stubborn." A whisper of his breath brushed at the coiled curls framing my face. There and not.

"I'm not being stubborn. I simply don't fancy dying in the Drought Lands."

He ran his tongue over his teeth and looked at the sky. His frustration tainted the shaky scene. "No, you'd rather die in the woods with a stranger."

I wrapped my arms around my torso. "Why does it matter to you? If I die regardless, there's no point. And Ronin isn't a stranger. Not anymore. He's my friend."

Casimir scoffed. "Then why not have your *friend* help you over the Forge?" His anger caught me off guard.

Overwhelmed by the desire to curl in on myself, my shoulders hunched, and heaviness settled in my chest. Ronin didn't know about Casimir, and I intended to keep it that way. I didn't need him to think I was crazy or cursed. It had been a wedge between my mother and I. And I couldn't bear it if Ronin looked at me as if I were a curse.

I didn't say any of those things to Casimir, but the scene around us flickered as if to mirror my growing dismay. My emotions would break off the connection like they always did.

Casimir watched it start to fade before searching my face, curious. "You haven't told him, have you?"

In response, I shook my head and surveyed the blurry woods for a spot to sit. I settled on a patch of grass where no trees stuttered in and out of sight. When I took a deep breath, the dreamspace sharpened again. The air was thick and uncomfortable in my lungs, but I didn't want him to go.

Casimir followed me to the smooth patch. He watched me pull my legs to my chest. My emotions swirled in the space, and he remained quiet, letting me work through them.

The thought of telling Ronin about Casimir and his visits filled me with fear. Too many years of my life were spent with others afraid of me and my ghost. I didn't want Ronin to see me differently.

Absentmindedly, I ran my hands over my hair. The curls that framed my face tucked behind my ears. Every bud ached, and I let my fingers linger on one of them. It was hot to the touch.

The slowing of my pulse made the flickers settle. My shoulders fell from my ears, and I dared a glance at Casimir. The exasperation was gone, replaced by curiosity.

He let go of a heavy breath and sat next to me. Nothing solid to his shoulder when it accidentally brushed mine. Casimir scratched at his arm, pulling my attention. Scars echoed across his skin. Stories I never bothered to wonder about, written on his hands.

When he shifted again, fiddling with his boot, I focused my attention on his face. "What's over the Forge?"

His head snapped in my direction—an eyebrow quirked. "From where you're at, Orondal."

"The one that's decimated? Not helpful."

He smirked. "Why don't you climb over and find out?"

"And why don't you answer my questions for once?"

Casimir's amusement warped the dreamspace, swirling so quickly, it made my head spin. "Think back to your father's maps. His books. What do you remember about Orondal?"

My lips pressed in a line, and I laid back in the grass, my hands folded over my abdomen. Casimir's gaze followed me.

Flashes of book covers went through my mind. Maps, which made little sense to me. The kingdom of the Iron Thorn was the only one with any color to the paper. Everything in the Drought Lands was outlined with black ink and left appearing as an afterthought.

Beginning with Orondal, just over the Forge. Then came Tyvolia, over the Stone Border. There were mountains much too rugged and sharp for anything to survive scrawled on the thick parchment. Cursed water outlined the land of Orondal until it broke off at the rocky cliffs near Tyvolia. Trying to remember the books and maps did nothing to help me.

Thoughts of them only brought me back to the sight of my father with his face in a book, the comforting feel of the cottage's roaring hearth, and the sweet smell of my mother's baking.

Overwhelmed by grief, the scenery blurred again. Broken and faded. A testament to my every emotion.

Casimir lay in the grass beside me, his gaze on the night sky. A shimmering moon lit the black canvas. It burned bright before it spun, turning into dust. It glistened as it fell.

A smile curved my lips.

"Orondal was one of the ten kingdoms." Casimir disrupted the quiet. "It was also one of the strongest in its time. They had a formidable army. Castles made of gold." The dreamspace twisted until the blanket of onyx above us turned into a painting of golden castles, willow trees, and rivers running through the kingdom of Orondal.

"They were at constant war with Tyvolia and the Iron Thorn. The three fought for power in the region..." Casimir continued to retell the story. He spoke into the space, and the scene changed.

At the cottage, I had devoted much of my time to learning the histories and could recite them from memory. And Casimir knew that.

It was one of my favorite stories.

I laid there and watched him morph the sky into different scenes. His voice carried through the dreamspace, and he lifted an arm, pointing to the different pieces as the story unfolded.

"The selfish nature of the kingdoms displeased the earth goddess. The rulers waged war and brought death upon the realm. And in turn, Aeterna scorched the earth and cursed the seas. From the ashes, a new power. A sacrifice to heal the earth."

The Roses.

Scarlet eyes flickered across the blank canvas. Stars exploded into fiery, falling embers. They twirled to the ground, changing into crimson petals before they landed.

Casimir's voice echoed in the space, and I shut my eyes. The aches vanished—whisked away by the dreamspace, and the story which filled me with comfort.

When he finished recounting the story, my head lolled in Casimir's direction.

He searched my face. "Bored you to sleep in the dreamspace? That's a first. Didn't think that was possible."

I smiled and shook my head. "No, not at all. Thank you, Cas."

"For what?"

"I love that story. As absurd as that is. It brings me back to the cottage. I miss it." The dreamspace flickered.

Casimir watched as some of the pieces fell away. "I didn't intend to bring you more distress."

When I chuckled, it echoed and rang until it hurt my head. Casimir was undeterred by the sound.

"It's okay. I needed this." I turned my gaze forward again. The painting changed from the leftover ruins of the two kingdoms. Bat orchids dotted a misshapen stone path leading through a garden. A little gray shed sat in the far left corner of the backyard, and on the opposite side, my horse Mora stood by the stables.

Tears welled up and trailed my temples. They fell into my mess of hair, and I grinned. The garden smeared, and I turned to see Casimir already vanished, taking with him the visions.

I sighed and wiped at the tears.

When I woke in the cabin, grief echoed in every inch of my body. For my family. For the cottage. For a ghost.

I stared at the ceiling and noted the holes in the wood until my pulse settled. Soft, sleepy breaths filled the cabin, and I turned to look at Ronin, asleep on the floor.

His hair fell over his cheek, and his hands tucked underneath his jaw with the cloak he used for a pillow.

Part of me longed for my old life back. Quiet mornings in the garden. A ride through the woods with my horse and my father. Visits from a ghost every few nights. The scowl of my mother.

For a night, I allowed myself to miss it all.

Chapter Sixteen

Eight days came and passed, secluded in the hidden cottage. I never spoke to Ronin about my change of heart regarding the Forge. He didn't ask, and our fear of loneliness matched painfully well. It was easy to ignore the conversation that would leave us both alone once more.

I spent another morning in the sunlight outside of the cramped cabin. Despite the harvest season in full swing, some days, the warm rays continued to offer a kind respite.

Light poured over my skin as Ronin's hands moved through my hair in a dance that had become a part of our routine. Searching for a sign the buds would bloom or the petals I wouldn't have been able to see.

While it was tedious to sit through another examination over the pin-sized buds, the sun felt glorious on my skin. Every pore in my body soaked it in as if I were indeed a plant and needed the warmth to bloom.

After going through my messy head of hair, Ronin sighed and sat next to me in the dirt, his hands going behind his back to hold his torso up. The wound on his side was improving, albeit slower than I was comfortable with. He didn't appear to be in pain anymore as he stretched out with his face toward the sun, his cloak discarded, leaving him in a stained tunic and frayed trousers.

It was the warmest day in weeks, a welcome change to the endless chill. I closed my eyes and inhaled through my nose. Sunlight cast shadows from the branches onto my eyelids, illuminating them and making them appear red against the light. A strange sensation I loved. The silence was a comfort, just a moment swimming in the nothingness until Ronin cleared his throat.

I sat and glanced over to find him watching me. "My apologies for how cooped up we've been. If you're up to it, we've just about cleared out the food we gathered in Woolfolk. Would you want to make another trip with me?"

I perked up, nodding with enthusiasm. "A change of scenery would be nice." I grinned. The thought of spending the day somewhere different made me giddy.

Ronin smiled and leaned forward, dusting his hands off as he did. "I'll get the packs so we can carry enough supplies to last us another week or so." He stood, taking his time, stretching his arms over his head.

"If we have time, I may look for a clean tunic and trousers. I've never gone this long without bathing or fresh clothing before." My nose wrinkled when I ran a hand over the dirty tunic sleeves.

Ronin chuckled. "I would hope not. I may not look at you the same if I found out it was a regular occurrence."

I rolled my eyes, grinning when he bumped my shoulder with his. While it had been the least of my worries, the count of days escaped me. My own grime and smell did not. Among all the unpleasant clothing, the only exception was my cloak. It settled around my shoulders with ease, and putting it on had become habitual. The green fell over my back, and the clasp was effortless to fasten.

I pulled my hood up while waiting for Ronin to grab the things we needed, tucking each strand of hair out of sight. I tugged it forward so it would shadow my scarlet eyes, with the hope of keeping others from noticing me. The sun burned brighter than it had been, which meant increased exposure. I had to be cautious.

Ronin returned with the packs and gave me one to carry while he fastened the others over his shoulder and chest. He led the way, and I followed close at his side.

I wanted to enjoy the change of scenery, but every step closer to the village made me more hesitant. We hadn't been inside the village long before someone recognized him, and in our mutual avoidance of grief, I hadn't asked him about the man who had approached him.

In all the weeks we spent journeying together, he didn't prod when it came to my family. Even though he knew my father, he didn't ask me to divulge the details of his death. It was rude to not give him the same courtesy. The questions popped into my head each day, but I kept them to myself. And maybe the avoidance made the grief worse. But I couldn't bear to talk about my family, so I didn't ask about his.

Ronin kept his hood down, his hair catching the sun in a delightful way. The golden color in his hair shimmered—whereas my hair resembled a nest, despite Ronin's efforts to help manage it when he searched for the petals in my hair. The knots were firmly wound at the base of my neck, nearing the point of being matted. His wavy hair differed in texture, and it didn't suffer the same way mine did.

Moss dotted the trees, creating a lush, green canopy overhead, while droopy flowers guided our path through the woods. The narrow path we followed was mostly hidden, blending into the foliage. Despite being neglected for years, the narrow path was ample for us to navigate back to Woolfolk. The hour-long walk didn't bother me with the prospect of getting out of the cottage for a while.

The sense of wonder persisted as we approached the gate. In the places where the stones had been broken apart many years ago to stack, the wall shimmered. With the beaming light, it appeared enchanting.

The entrance wasn't as busy, with a few carts or villagers making their way in. It was midday, and most people were occupied with work and their stalls, which were full of patrons rummaging through their stock.

The large kettle boiled over coals once again, the steam rising as the same woman stirred the pot with vigor. I ogled it greedily, hoping we would make time to stop by. The stew reminded me of home, despite not being able to enjoy a significant portion of it after the altercation Ronin found himself in. I prayed to the gods no one would recognize him.

Like a well-oiled machine, we moved in unison, arms brushing as our hands swayed inches from each other. We walked a similar route through the village, stopping at a few stalls Ronin looked through. After a while, a garden caught my attention, a bit deeper into Woolfolk, an old wooden fence outlining it.

"Could we visit the garden?" I asked, my gaze never lifting outside the safety of my hood, not even to glance at his face.

"It's nothing special, not like Eldravine's garden. But if you would like to, I'm sure it wouldn't hurt anything," he said.

He led the way and avoided walking close to others as he kept near to my side. When we reached the garden, the sight made me grin.

It was simple in the most endearing way. Without flashy or intricate architecture, just simple small groups of flowers planted with intent along the small stream which bled through it. Cattails lined the edge of the water.

Stone benches sat in between some of the flower beds, and a few people occupied them. Some with their focus trained on little children who stood in the stream, playing in the cattails despite the chill that lingered in the air.

I envied their unbridled joy as they splashed about, their noses and cheeks red as they giggled.

The garden in Woolfolk was nothing like the one in Eldravine. It was simple but full of life. Nothing wilted or gray. As if the happiness in the village on its own sustained it.

"It's just as I remembered it," Ronin said in a soft voice. I glanced over at him, my hood shading some of his face from my view. But from what I saw, his heart appeared torn.

"It's bursting with life here compared to Eldravine," I said, taking in the array of flowers that all thrived amongst the village.

"Yes, it appears that way. I think the gods may have cursed the Iron Thorn long ago with the rest of the realm, despite how hard the king tries to hide it. There is nothing holy in what they do." There was disdain in Ronin's voice, a sentiment we both shared.

The mere thought of the king and his callousness made me shiver. I hadn't loathed anyone until he brazenly made light of killing my parents. Mocking my pain and every other Rose who had been a sacrifice for his kingdom.

"I hate to cut our trip short, but we need to gather a few additional healing supplies and head back. The village gets quite busy around this time."

I deflated but nodded in agreement.

We turned and left the garden behind, weaving our way through the crowd as it grew, heading toward the apothecary.

It was more hectic than our previous visit. The tiny apothecary held a higher amount of bodies than it meant to accommodate. Ronin grew rigid beside me, and I tried not to let the tension engulf me.

I ducked my head lower and watched Ronin's feet as I kept my hand tucked into the crook of his arm. He grabbed additional tinctures and herbs as he had before and added extra bandages to wrap his side.

We shuffled through the shop, trying not to collide with others, albeit my attempts weren't successful when I couldn't see, and I found myself running into someone.

They grunted as their armful of supplies fell to the ground, clattering against the old wood floors. "Oh, my apologies," I said, voice dripping with nervousness as I bent out of habit, trying to gather some things they dropped. The person also crouched and started to collect their fallen items.

Once it was all retrieved, I stood and set the rest of their things into their arms, offering an apologetic smile.

"Thank you—" They glanced at me, their brown eyes taking in my appearance. Confusion distorted the young man's face.

Before either of us said a word, Ronin grabbed my arm and pulled me back to him. "Our apologies," Ronin muttered, pushing me along. It took me a second to realize why he rushed me forward and away from the confused young man. His brown irises were a feature I shouldn't have known if I had kept my gaze averted.

Swallowing the lump in my throat, I prayed the darkness concealed my Rose features from him.

Ronin moved with urgency, pushing our way through to the woman at the counter, the same one we had seen on our previous trip. She made light small talk with Ronin, but I didn't hear any of it, tuning it out. The desire to turn around and check behind us to see if the man was following was impossible to ignore.

But I averted my gaze, scarcely seeing as Ronin paid the shopkeeper, who thanked him for revisiting. Her voice was chipper.

He led me out of the shop in a hurry, tugging me behind him. "Did they see you?" he asked in a hushed voice, not slowing his pace.

"I'm not sure," I said in a whisper, the knot in my stomach twisting. It was a fraction of a second. But it was enough for me to remember the color of the young man's eyes or to have realized he was perhaps sixteen years of age.

Ronin released a heavy breath and slowed our pace, glancing over his shoulder at the apothecary. "We need to get food and leave the village. If he saw that you're a Rose, it isn't safe for us anymore."

I nodded in reply and allowed him to lead me toward the stalls, which had an assortment of food. There was a twinge of disappointment knowing we wouldn't be able to grab clean clothing, but I couldn't linger on those emotions. Not with the worry the boy may turn us in.

We walked through the crowd as it grew, bumping into the shoulders of people I couldn't see. I was too scared to do anything except direct my gaze at my own feet as I depended on Ronin to guide us.

My heart hammered in my chest when I remembered a similar experience I had with Ronin before we knew each other. Our eyes met for a split second in the Temple Garden, but the brief instant was all he needed to see the red and to see I was a Rose. It was a feature that belonged solely to the Rose people. It was hard to miss.

We moved through the stalls with ease, regardless of the busyness in the afternoon—we followed a similar path as we had the first time in Woolfolk. Going through the foods that would last us the longest, Ronin stuffed his pack full to the brim.

If the young boy had seen what I was, we wouldn't be able to return to Woolfolk. And we wouldn't even be safe in the cottage, no matter how well it appeared to be hidden. I wondered if Ronin would accompany me over the Forge or if he would go somewhere else.

Ronin avoided small talk from the merchants, replying in single-word responses. Some merchants were offended by his standoffish replies, but they didn't prod or try to stop him.

At the very end, he grabbed me a bowl of the stew without me having to say a word, quick with every transaction. It was the least important thing at the moment, yet I had worried we wouldn't have had time. My stomach grumbled with hunger as I greedily grabbed the bowl from his hands, letting him pay the merchant.

Ronin added a few items to the pack over my shoulders, filling it while I waited to consume the piping hot dish.

"We'll need to make these rations last longer than the last trip. I'm not sure if we'll return here," Ronin said.

I glanced back at him, guilt-ridden, as I watched his face pull into a look of fear. "I didn't mean to look at them." My voice came out too small. It brought me back to the years I had to force myself to be softer, more meek, in the presence of my mother and her disapproval. The reminder bit at my emotions until the wound became raw once more.

Ronin sighed and pushed his hair back from his face. "You were trying to help. I get it."

"It took one glance for you to know what I was, Ronin." The fear crept up my throat, and I tried to stuff it back down. The boy was young. Maybe he wouldn't know. Maybe he wouldn't say anything.

"What's done is done. But we need to leave. The crowd is growing, and if we don't go, we'll get caught in a mess." He started to go the opposite way of the crowd as they flooded through the market.

The noises increased with every new person, all of them carrying on their conversations, their laughter echoing in the street. The sounds of the wheels on the carts became amplified and grew worse with each bump they encountered, resulting in the contents inside to clatter.

Ronin tried to move us out as quickly as possible, dodging carriages and livestock. The air was thick with chaos, making it impossible to take a deep breath. Every sense in my body became overwhelmed with the strange thrum.

As we hurried along, someone bumped the pack I had on me, causing some of the contents to spill out onto the road behind us, with the flap on top of it left undone. I stared back at it and tugged on Ronin's sleeve to get him to pause.

I opened my mouth to speak when the sound of glass shattering drew my attention.

Ronin glanced at me just as I turned, seeing a sudden flood of people swarm toward the market center. Concern and uncertainty marked every face as they joined the crowd—their focus pulled back toward where we had grabbed food.

The swarm of people continued to increase, the only noticeable difference being the harsh red and purple uniformed men, their faces wrought with discomfort as their hands gripped the arms of a familiar shopkeeper. It was the same woman who had sold us healing supplies.

My stomach twisted. The confusion froze over into terror when I saw the dreadful uniforms I had hoped never to encounter again. They were dark crimson, akin to pooled blood. Silver cuffs at the edges, and silver embroidery at the right side of the chest, the insignia of the Iron Thorn. A dagger through a rose. The Iron Guard.

The bowl fell from my hand, the contents spilling on my clothes and boots. I watched in horror as a red uniformed man pulled out a silver dagger, menacing in his hand as it glinted against the last remnants of the sun.

"The Rose. Where is she?" The man barked. Ronin pulled on me, his words drowned out by the sound of blood as it rushed in my ears.

"She was spotted in this village not long ago, with another sighting last week." His smile twisted, which made him appear more frightening. "This woman was said to be selling to her, yet she says she has no recollection of a Rose in your midst."

The sound of murmurs filled the air and blended with the growing panic of the crowd. Ronin pulled on me, but my feet stayed planted. It was as if I turned to stone.

Everything inside me screamed to turn and flee. To not face what was about to happen, to leave and forget the woman's face. The tears streamed down her cheeks, her expression wrought with terror.

The village people gathered, sounds of distress and protest building. The woman pleaded, her voice broken and lost in the thrum.

No one moved, too frightened to intervene. The Iron Guard invoked fear as they held her for all to see, making an example of her.

"No one has anything to say? You know the punishment of harboring a Rose." The guard raised the dagger and pressed it to her neck. Her eyes slammed shut. Her lips moved as if she were muttering a prayer to the gods.

My body screamed at me to run, to stop the guard. Panic flooded my veins. In the crowd, the sound of gasping sobs filled the air as a man and two children were held back, desperately reaching out for the woman. I stood frozen, fear splitting my resolve. *I need to stop them.* They wouldn't kill me. They couldn't. But they were going to kill her.

I took a step towards the crowd.

A firm grip jerked me back and sent me scrambling. I fought against the arms, barely glancing up to see Ronin's gaze as it swam with apologies. He wouldn't let me go, holding on to me as he tried to retreat from the masses. His hand covered my mouth when I opened it to shout for the guards to stop.

Screams of horror erupted.

The wails of the crowd were piercing as his dagger ended her life. Blood pooled from her neck and her body fell limp.

Icy horror rippled through every inch of my body. My hands went numb as I fell to my knees, Ronin's arms releasing me at the sudden dead weight.

The screams and cries echoed through everyone; the man's cries were a shriek of sorrow I never wanted to hear again. It rattled my chest, my heart hammering so hard it felt as if it would burst.

Arms wrapped around me a second time, pulling me up and over their shoulder. Ronin whispered apologies over and over as he carried me away while the village continued to weep, grieving for a woman who had done nothing wrong.

Ronin ran, his breath coming in gasps as he tried to keep a quick pace with me over his shoulder. The sounds of horror started to fade until they were a faint groan amongst the trees, scarcely a scream to be heard. But they continued to echo around my skull, threatening to split it.

The woods consumed us and moved in a blur until I couldn't take it for another moment. I hit Ronin's back a few times, wiggling my legs until he stopped behind a large tree and set me down.

Immediately, the contents of my stomach were on the ground, my body curling over. Ronin pulled my hood and my hair back and gave me a chance to catch my breath.

My body quivered, and my legs appeared ready to give way at any second. Ronin grabbed me by the shoulders and turned me toward him. He scanned my face. "We have to go, Elita. We won't be safe this close." He spoke with urgency.

Tears cascaded down my cheeks as I stood, my body unstable.

"I have to go back, please. I can't—" I gasped. "I could have stopped them! They wanted me! Why did you stop me?" I cried, pushing at his chest. He appeared pained as he grabbed my wrists when I went to push him for the second time.

"I'm trying to protect *you*, Elita. They would have killed her regardless, for the simple fact she offered us her services. There was nothing to be done. We have to go." He searched my face, desperate for me to understand.

The shame and guilt hung heavy over my head. Each second of my hesitation brought her closer to her end. I didn't try hard enough. She was gone, and it was my fault. I wanted to turn around and run back, to end the hiding, to prevent anyone else from suffering the same fate— another dead body at my feet.

Ronin squeezed my shoulders, trying to snap me out of my thoughts. I swallowed the panic in my throat and tried to gather my composure.

Without another word, we took off. We ran through the woods, snapping against branches and brush, the forest sinister. I had to fight the urge to be sick yet again as the horrific sight played in my mind while we ran. The screams burned into my memory.

We sprinted until my legs yearned to give out. The adrenaline carried me on, just beside Ronin, never losing sight of him until we found ourselves back at the cottage. An hour vanished before I had any time to catch my breath.

The silence that followed us carried an eerie presence.

With the last bit of strength I had, I entered the cottage, my hands the ones truly covered in blood.

Chapter Seventeen

T he roof of the cottage stared back at me as I lay on the cot. The quiet lingered since we left the village behind. Screams echoed in my mind, the horror too much to shoulder.

There were pieces of broken wood on the roof, the sky scarcely visible through them. I didn't let my focus shift. If I closed my eyes, if I averted my gaze, I feared I would see the woman's face staring back at me, her terror tangible.

The silence was the only thing that appeared appropriate. The guilt continued to drown me. I had wanted to stop them, to run forward and prevent the execution from happening. I would have given myself to them in exchange for sparing her life. Maybe I would have been able to negotiate for Ronin's life to be spared.

My cowardice and hiding cost a woman her life. Those children lost their mother, and a man lost his partner. All so I'd die another day, my bloom killing me as swiftly as the guard chose to take her life. More blood spilled on my account.

I tried not to think about my mother or my father; it was torture. I wanted to yell, to throw something. Lives lost to prolong my death. It was sickening, and I fought the urge to retch once more.

Part of me wished Ronin had never rescued me. Or my father had let my mother bring me to the Temple many years ago. Perhaps my bloom wouldn't have taken so long, and my wilt wouldn't have been so bad.

The guilt threatened to engulf me.

I shuddered, trying to shake the thoughts and images from my head as I jolted upright. Ronin looked at me from where he was applying ointment to his sutures. He frowned and pulled his tunic down, standing.

The way his face softened threatened to make the flood of tears fall, but I had exhausted all I had left. Hours spent without a word, the cottage ridden with sniffles and sobs.

"They're all dead because of me." My voice cracked with the first words I had spoken since we left Woolfolk. A village that was once happy, alive with the sound of laughter and friendship. Now haunted by a crimson stain in the dirt and horrified cries echoing inside its stone gates.

Ronin knelt in front of me and put his hands on my shoulders. "This isn't your doing. Don't carry that burden." He spoke with conviction, the belief true in his heart. I wished I believed the same. But the shame washed over me like a wave.

Tremors ran through my hands as I lifted my gaze to the ceiling. "I should have screamed for them to stop. I should've done something more. If I had just stayed at the Temple, she wouldn't have died."

Ronin tensed and put a hand on my cheek, pulling my attention to him. "So they'd torture you? So they'd make your wilt as painful as possible?" His voice hitched with anger. The flame from the lantern flickered in the reflection of his eyes.

"What does it matter? When my bloom finishes, I die regardless. Instead, I allow innocent people to be killed on account of me. What kind of person does that make me?" My voice quivered.

Ronin shifted closer. "It makes you human, Elita. Being afraid of torture, being afraid to *die*, it doesn't make you a bad person. It's instinct."

I grimaced and averted my gaze, focusing on the flame.

"My parents are gone. They wasted their lives trying to stop a sacrifice I'll have to give, anyway. And the woman in the village—" My voice broke, and I shook my head, trying to empty it of the images. "She's gone. Dead because she sold us bandages. Her life ended for me to have maybe another month or two if I'm lucky." I chuckled darkly. The thought of a wilt didn't seem so bad anymore.

Ronin's hand cupped the curve of my neck. My attention flickered back to him, caught off guard by the touch. His eyes searched mine, and I gulped.

"The king will not have you. Your petals will come, and you'll bloom and wilt in peace. Not in their sinister garden. Don't choose to bear the sins of the king."

For a moment, I chose to believe what Ronin said of me, that I was acting on instinct—I wasn't a monster. It couldn't erase the horrors of the day, but it provided me with some reprieve.

The stillness settled over us. With Ronin close, the only sound was the gentle rhythm of our breathing. The flame reflected in his vivid blue stare as the shadows it cast danced on the walls.

Ronin's fingers moved from my neck, and he brushed the hair away from my face, tucking it behind my ear. His hand cupped my jaw. I froze when he leaned in, causing him to hesitate, unsure, before his lips brushed mine.

I never gave much attention to the idea of a first kiss. The reality of my fate always stifled any thoughts of affection. It was cruel to search for that kind of connection, knowing I was going to die.

But the little thought I had given to it didn't match the odd pit in my stomach. I tried to release the tension and melt into him. His other hand grabbed the side of my face, tender and sweet.

My lashes fluttered shut, and my hands pressed against his chest, resting below his collarbones. His heart thumped beneath my palms like a steady drum. He held me with a delicate touch as if, at any moment, I would shatter.

In an instant, it was over, and he pulled back from me.

I stared, wide-eyed and insecure. "Sorry," I blurted out. "No one's ever kissed me before."

Ronin chuckled without mocking. "You have nothing to apologize for. It may seem foolish, but I think perhaps it's ingrained in us. The instinct written on our lips long before we share a kiss."

I nodded sheepishly, afraid if I spoke, I'd embarrass myself. The kiss was sudden, and I struggled to make sense of it.

His hands left my face and trailed down my arm. "You should get some sleep. I'll keep watch so you can rest. Today has been long."

Words failed me, and I nodded once more. Ronin gave my hand a soft squeeze, then stood, pushing his hair back from his face.

I scurried away as my fingers trembled. The cot creaked when I curled on my side, facing the wall. My pulse raced, and I didn't know what to feel. Shame coiled in my chest when I thought about the woman who died senselessly in Woolfolk.

Her family continued to live their worst nightmare while I sat in a cottage, hiding from the inevitable. I closed my eyes, knowing the woman's face would haunt my sleep.

The images of the woman dying haunted me when I fell into a deep sleep. The screams were deafening as I stood in place, my mouth open, but no words came out. Complacent. Guilty.

I was well acquainted with nightmares, but the fear became tangible, and I walked among my nightmares wide awake.

I woke in a cold sweat, the cottage pitch-black.

My head throbbed, and a splitting headache spread along my entire scalp. Dizziness blurred my vision, and heat licked up the back of my neck. Stiff and sore. I sat up in the cot, my body drenched in sweat. I ran my hands over my tunic, shocked at the dampness.

I made my way to stand, but the piercing pain caused me to lose my balance, and I fell back onto the cot, short of breath.

"By the gods... What is happening?" I ran a hand over my face, wiping sweat droplets.

After a quick survey of the cottage, I noticed Ronin's absence. With the sun not up, it wasn't unusual. He took his watch outside most nights to keep an eye on the woods in case we needed to escape out the back. It gave us more time.

I cautiously gave standing another go. My limbs all trembled when I did. The wood creaked beneath me, my weight shifting the rotten bones of the cottage. A spark echoed from my neck to the crown of my head, and I swayed. The walls warped around me.

"Ronin?" I spoke hesitantly, my voice close to a whisper while I stumbled through the cottage.

When I reached the door, I opened it and peered outside, only to find Ronin's usual spot empty. I took a step back and shut myself inside. The uneasiness sat in my body like a stone.

My hair matted to the back of my head from the sweat, and I ran my hands through the curls to free it from my skin, gasping when they snagged on something soft. It throbbed from the lightest touch.

A million horrible feelings rushed me.

I held the delicate petal with a tender touch. The odd and soft texture was out of place amidst my hair, a couple of inches below my shoulder. My hands shook as I pulled my hair forward and searched through the black curls to find a white rose petal contrasting against the onyx, bright in the night.

I ran it between my fingers once more, noticing the way it caused my scalp to tingle, as equally a part of my body as any of my limbs.

My hair slipped from my fingers, and as it fell, a wave of realization washed over me, replacing the awe.

In a surge of panic, I opened the door and scanned the woods. "Ronin?" I called, voice shaking. I shouted his name a second time until my voice carried, despite how wrong it felt to call for him with such intensity. Branches snapped, and Ronin stumbled out of the woods in a rush.

"Elita?" He froze a few feet away, and worry etched his brow.

"I didn't mean to frighten you." My voice quivered, giving away my unease. His expression of concern grew, and he reached a hand out toward me. "My bloom," I blurted, stopping him in his tracks as the statement hung between us.

"Your bloom?" Confusion replaced his concern.

"My bloom, Ronin, it started. The first petal." My vision blurred, but no tears fell. He stayed rooted to the spot and took in my appearance until he found it—the white petal tucked into my hair, misplaced and, at the same time, destined to be there.

The first of thirty petals before I would die.

Timidly, he approached me, his features sharper in the moonlight. He reached for my hair, grabbing it with careful fingers before he ran a thumb over the petal. It didn't burn as much. Only a ghost of the sting remained.

"It's so white," he breathed, not meeting my gaze. Tension pulled his shoulders upright, and he cleared his throat. "You should go inside to rest. I'll be in after I grab my pack," he said abruptly, his voice catching.

"Ronin—"

"It'll be okay. I'll be there with you in a moment." His reassurance did little to fend off the fear.

"I'm not ready." My voice was thick with unshed tears. Years spent waiting and dreading that day. The pain still radiated through my scalp, unwilling to let me ignore the bitter truth.

Ronin's features softened as he noted my fear. He came closer and softly touched the lone petal. "I was beginning to hope the bloom wouldn't come." His hand trembled when it dropped and brushed my arm. "Get some rest. I'll come sit with you after I get the supplies back inside."

I stared at him with tears welling up but nodded all the same.

The cottage filled with eerie silence when I shut the door behind me. A heaviness settled in my chest and I stayed rooted to the spot. My vision went out of focus while I stared at the rotten planks, barely visible in the darkness. The walls closed in around me, and I stifled a pitiful sob with my palm.

A nerve in my scalp twinged, running the length of the strand of hair until it caused the petal to sting. I took a steadying breath and ran the pad of my thumb over it—soft in contrast to the coarseness of my filthy hair. It was radiant. The veins of the petal were no different from one plucked out of a rose bush. It stood out with an obnoxious bright-ness while somehow appearing intricately placed, as if hand-picked by the goddess Aeterna herself.

If only my father were alive to see it. I yearned to witness his amaze-ment and curiosity or his compulsion to examine it—taken aback by the abnormal color, strikingly different from the expected scarlet hue.

The loss stung. A wound that refused to close. I took comfort in the fact I wouldn't have to endure the pain much longer. The petals would continue to bloom, and in due time, the last would grace my head, the beginning of the end.

Voices outside broke my train of thought, and I glanced toward the cottage door. Footsteps sounded close by before Ronin raised his voice, the sudden volume giving me pause. "What are you doing here?" The disdain as he spoke carried into the cottage.

"I don't forget a face, Ronin. And I didn't forget your Rose friend, either. You let Lenora die to protect that damned woman. And you'll both pay for it."

My stomach twisted. The voice was familiar from the village, belonging to the man who had approached Ronin over a week ago. And with him, I heard more footsteps. Twigs and branches snapped as they surrounded the cottage.

"Whatever you think you saw, you're mistaken," Ronin spat back.

"Save it. The Iron Guard is already on its way."

I backed away from the door and scanned for the bags that were left in the cottage. I flung the lone pack over my shoulder with caution to not alert those outside to my presence. With shaking hands, I threw my cloak on and hood up, my pulse racing.

"There's no one else here. It's just me." Ronin's voice raised louder, and I realized he did it for my benefit, the only warning he could give me. The moment I realized he wanted me to leave without him, the weight of it crushed me. I wouldn't leave him to die.

Yet my feet continued to carry me in reverse. Walking to the door in the back of the cottage—to the exit I prayed to the gods wasn't surrounded by guards who waited for me.

Muffled words continued to be exchanged until I heard the impact of bodies, their shouts erupting in chaos.

"Bind him! The king will want a word with him."

My face paled, and I retreated more until I found the door, my back turned to it. Sounds of struggle disrupted the night.

"Run!" Ronin's guttural cry reached me like a slap across the face.

Icy blood ran through my veins as the sick sensation continued to grow. I didn't have time to think. The footsteps approached the door, and I had to make a choice.

Panic ruled my feet, and I flew out the back door, the overgrown vines snapping as I threw it open and sprinted with everything I had. Tears blurred my vision until they spilled over, guilt, rage, and fear all intertwining. Ronin's face followed me in the back of my mind while I fled from the cottage, leaving him behind.

My cowardice haunted me, but I let my legs carry me onward.

The chaos diminished as I sprinted, my muscles burning with exertion as I fought through the trees, unsure where I would go. I was lost without Ronin beside me. My resolve split in two, wanting to turn around for him.

He didn't want that.

I continued to tell myself the same thing over and over. I held onto hope my escape would buy him time. Perhaps they wouldn't kill him if they believed for a second he knew where I was going.

My escape could buy him time. I could save him for a change.

The lies ran through my mind, trying to push me forward, toward whatever survival it was I hoped to find. A life running until I died against the earth, my petals wilted in the dirt.

Ronin risked his life to help me. And as a thanks, I left him behind to die.

Four lives to spare one. My hands dripped crimson.

Chapter Eighteen

The moon followed me until the sun broke the horizon. Every few minutes, I glanced over my shoulder. In search of the Iron Guard, in search of Ronin. I begged the gods he would escape and catch up to me. But I was alone. My cowardice carried me further from the cottage.

I watched the tree line for the Forge Border while twigs scraped at my bare feet. It would be a death sentence as much as a sanctuary. If I made it over the Forge, I could hide. I could choose not to let the Iron Thorn have my sacrifice, to make them have to hunt for another Rose, for someone else.

Talos would never lay another hand on me. No tinctures to burn through me. The king would never have the satisfaction of witnessing my wilt. A quiet death far from those who sought to bring me pain.

The thought shocked me, shame filling me once more. I was selfish. King Lendorr and Talos weren't the only people who needed my bloom to survive. But the families, the people who gave so much every day to keep the Iron Thorn together, and those who protected it.

What am I doing?

The further I went, the more my mind wandered until my thoughts drifted to Casimir, and I wished more than anything for the ability to conjure him so he could tell me what to do. But he never appeared. His voice didn't carry in the breeze. The grief increased as it all tried to bury me under the weight. I fought it; there was no time to let myself drown. I had to find somewhere to rest. I had a choice to make: to go after Ronin and turn myself in or continue on the path so many fought to keep me on.

I stopped in my tracks, the wind rustling through the trees, loose leaves spinning to the ground. The tranquility was misplaced.

Fields of rocks continued to grow in size, their color ranging from dusty gray to a warm sandstone. A fetid scent carried in the breeze—sour as the Drought Lands grew closer with every step.

My skin prickled. Everything inside me longed to forsake the destiny I never asked for. I wanted to live. And with another step further from the cottage, from Ronin, my selfish choices continued to hurt the people around me.

Rain pelted against my cloak as I stood under a tree, the hood soaked to my head. My endeavor to traverse the forest on my own turned out to be more arduous than I had expected. Night came and went, but sleep never did.

Two more blooms opened, one near the crown of my head and another hanging on the bottom length of my hair. My skull ached and burned with the new petals, but little by little, the discomfort eased, and before long, I scarcely realized they were present, outside of the way the white would glare in my peripheral vision.

The rain roared in my ears, and thunder boomed overhead. The gods were displeased with me.

A death outside of the sacrificial gardens would wreak havoc on the kingdom. It wasn't what the gods required. They had spent countless centuries without failure, every Rose dead in the same horrifying ceremony. Painted beautiful by flowers, which adorned the circular onyx agate. The Rose lay in the center, where their bloom would be taken from them, falling to the earth.

It was anything but beautiful. My father had seen enough sacrifices to know it resembled torture as opposed to a peaceful death planned by the gods.

Out of the corner of my eye, I saw a shadow dart through the trees, quick and small, causing a rustle in the brush. It pulled me out of my thoughts, and I tensed, trying to find it in the midst of the rain as it surged through the blurred woods.

The animal jumped out from behind a tree, its ears perked up, golden eyes staring up at me. It was a small black cat, a cut through its left ear. Despite its soaked fur, it refused to shy away from the rain. It continued to stare back at me as my heart rate slowed.

Timidly, it made its way over to me, tail whipping around.

"Hello," I said in a whisper, feeling somewhat silly. The cat pitter-pattered over to me, its paws leaving tiny prints in the mud. I dropped into a crouch and put my hand out so the cat could sniff my skin.

It rubbed its wet fur over my hand and left some mud behind. In spite of myself, I chuckled, its presence soothing. "Want to find somewhere dry with me?" I asked as I rubbed under its chin, the cat purring. A small smile made its way to my face, and I stood to survey my surroundings for somewhere to go.

I clicked my tongue at the cat and walked in a different direction from the tree, toward some of the larger rocks ahead of me. It pranced beside me, seemingly unbothered by the intensity of the rain. I envied the cat and wished to be so unaffected.

We made it over to the rocks. Some of them came out in large, sweeping cliff-like edges. It was a better shelter from the rain than the tree had offered. The cat rubbed against my ankles as I paused to glance around.

A pit formed in my stomach at the sight through the trees.

The Forge Border was visible in the distance, stretching toward the sky, stones stacked on top of each other. Fires burned at small parapets near the top, housing guards.

Mother's dying plea became a pull to the wall so tangible, my body had a visceral need to go. After a short pause, I scrambled under the rocks overhang, sighing in relief as the weight of the rain disappeared. I slid off my cloak and tried to lay it out, hoping I wouldn't be as cold if I removed some of the soaked layers.

To my surprise, the cat sat outside the dry space, staring at me as it sat in the rain. "I thought cats hate water." I pulled my knees to my chest, trying to keep my body heat close.

The cat jumped above the rock to where I could no longer see it, and I sighed, unraveling my arms from my legs. It meowed out of sight, and I crawled back out, peeking over the rock.

It faced the wall, gazing at it as the rain pelted its fur.

An invisible string pulled at me as the cat watched. I must have been nearing insanity when the thought crossed my mind that perhaps the cat was there to show me the way.

"When the rain stops, and the sun is up. Maybe then," I said to myself. Dread pooled in my limbs. A dizzying sensation among my hunger and thirst.

I crawled back under the rock, the cat still not following me. I told myself if the cat were there when the sun rose again, I would go.

Chapter Nineteen

To my dismay, the rain stopped, and the sun came out the next day. Not a cloud in the sky to sway my decision. The cat remained perched on top of the rock, eyeing me oddly as I crawled out from under the ledge—patient despite how long I rested.

I shook out my cloak, trying to dust the mud off it. The fabric was still damp to the touch.

Everything clung to me with similar moisture, uncomfortable, and a hindrance. But I had made my choice, regardless of how insane.

The air was sickeningly dry, a stark contrast to the wetness and how humid everything was the night before. Something was out of balance within the realm as the weather shifted drastically. I held out hope that maybe the way the air stung with sudden heat and dryness, perhaps my clothes would dry, and it wouldn't be as miserable.

I folded my cloak and looped it over the strap of my pack, no longer needing it as the sun burned against the earth.

I had never seen the Drought Lands.

My father had told me stories, none of them good. He told me of how hard it was for the people of the Drought to survive such a harsh environment. Above all else, he warned me if I found myself over the Forge, my bloom may never happen, or I may end up dead. Either among the elements or by the hands of the people who resided in the barren lands. Their disdain toward the Rose people and the Iron Thorn exceeded my understanding.

I had undoubtedly lost my mind. Loneliness and lack of guidance led me to put my faith in a cat.

Gods help me.

The cat pranced in front of me as I walked through the woods, jumping with ease up onto the rocks I struggled over. I had no idea how I would make it over the Forge. The stones laid misshapen on top of each other, reaching toward the sky.

Climbing would be my best bet if I didn't find a ladder.

It could also be my demise.

If my father could see me, he would have fainted on the spot. With my pack slung over my back and a cat by my side, I eyed the Forge Border, eyes ready to pop out of my head. By the time I had made it to the Forge, darkness fell over the realm, which was something I would take. It made it easier to stay out of sight of the guards.

The pull never left, and I was drawn to the other side.

Many times, I considered turning from the wall and seeking refuge in the safety of the trees before the sun rose again.

I could hide out in a hole until I gathered the courage to give myself to be the kingdom's sacrifice. Too far into my bloom for Talos to torture me. Climbing the wall would potentially not just doom me but also spell disaster for the entire kingdom.

In the back of my mind, I thought of Ronin. Taken as a bargaining token, at least, that was what I chose to believe. I wouldn't let my mind go any darker. I wouldn't accept that I might never see him again.

I had to move. I couldn't let everyone's sacrifices be for nothing. And something told me the answers and help I needed were over the Forge, somewhere in the barren land of Orondal. Waiting for me in the deadly drought. It was utter madness.

The cat hopped up a few of the stones that stood out more, looking down at me as it did so.

"You make it look easy," I whispered.

A few feet away, I spotted a rope ladder that fell down the expanse of the stone wall. I made my way over to it and glanced up at the daunting border.

Every inch of my body ached from running and the constant panic, which continued to constrict my muscles. The climb wouldn't be easy. It looked impossible. The odds against me grew the longer I stared at the jagged border.

A soft breeze blew my hair in front of my face, flashes of white appearing in the corner of my vision. I took my cloak back out and tugged it on, tucking my hair into the hood to hide the petals to the best of my ability.

I tightened the pack and took a breath to steady myself.

The rope was rough and damp under my hands after they soaked in the rain the previous day. My palms would be blistered by the time I reached the top, but I started to climb regardless.

Unfamiliar aches erupted in my muscles with the new movement as I made my way up. I tried not to think too hard about how high I had to go. The Forge was meant to keep raiders out and keep our people safe. It was nothing to scoff at, and I wished for an easier way.

The cat followed along, hopping beside me on rocks which jutted out. Its glowing eyes watched each move I made. Despite being grateful for any company, I wished it was Ronin who accompanied me.

I pushed thoughts of Ronin out of my mind. If I let my thoughts linger on him, I wouldn't be able to focus.

The acidic air became difficult to breathe the higher I climbed and the more the muscles in my chest strained. It tasted odd, dirty and bitter, like something spoiled wafted in the wind. So close to the Drought Lands, I correlated the two.

As I ascended higher, a growing sense of fear wrapped around me. The fall was more likely to kill me than the Drought Lands from that height. Every time I looked down, I regretted it.

The cat was gone from my sight, which made me second-guess my choice. Perhaps it had been mad to follow it in the first place. But the absence of the cat was replaced by a familiar raven. It flew close by and, every so often, landed on a stone a few inches higher up—squawking whenever I paused.

Its company made it easier to continue on. Every time I wanted to turn around, its inky black feathers would shudder close by, and it would stare at me until I moved again.

The sparse light from a handful of torches on the top of the Forge made it significantly harder for me to go unnoticed. It wasn't ideal, but turning back felt impossible. It was hard enough getting up the ladder. It would be unfeasible for me to climb back down with how exhausted I was. I only hoped the guards were perhaps asleep or oblivious. None of them moved nor paced the length of the Forge. I would have to go on a whim.

Every inch of my arms smarted with strain when I reached out, continuing the climb. The rope swung, throwing me off balance, but I held on the best I could. It shuddered with every move of my body and became worse the closer I got to the top.

When white petals peered out of my hood, it startled me, quickening my breath. If only I had heeded Casimir's words sooner. I had reached the third one, the same amount he warned me against.

Maybe it was too late.

And perhaps I would die from my lack of coordination.

The climb continued to stretch on, higher and higher, as I struggled. My muscles were failing as I neared the top of the ladder, and I had to press my sweaty forehead to the rocks in front of me. A whimper escaped my lips, but I didn't let myself cry.

My raven called out close by. Its wings brushed my arm, and it landed a few feet higher.

The wetter my hands became with sweat, the harder it got for me to hold on. My mouth was dry and begged for water. How easy my life was before everything changed when I lost my family. Back then, my nightmares and Casimir were the only things I found challenging. That was nothing compared to what I had experienced out in the realm.

By the time I was on the verge of reaching the top, my body was close to giving up. I'd been climbing for what seemed like hours. It paid off as I scaled the last stretch of the rope, nearly there. One glance down and death was the only fate that would meet me on the ground.

As soon as I saw how far the fall would be, a wave of dizziness washed over me. I forced a breath back into my lungs and reached up once more, grabbing onto the next rope as my hands shook, and right away, I knew it was a mistake.

My hand cramped around the rope, and the rough fibers tore into my palm as it slipped. The raven screeched and flapped frantically. I cried out in pain as the fall jerked at my other arm, just shy of popping it out of its socket. My fingers barely held onto the rope when my feet lost their place. I scrambled with the ropes, trying to get it to steady back under me as it viciously swayed.

"Casimir, please, please..." I didn't know what I was asking for; I only hoped he would hear me and that he would somehow save me from such a gruesome death—the figment of my imagination appearing to rescue me. I imagined myself on the ground, like a fly who had been hit with a boot. My stomach turned at the thought, and the raven swooped, plucking at my sleeve with its beak.

Death was not my fate.

A jolt of disbelief came at the sight of someone reaching for me. My imagination quickly turned into reality as they grasped my tunic, followed by a succession of more people reaching out. Before long, four arms stretched out to pull me the rest of the way, saving me from the horrible fate below.

When I got to the top with the help of the guards, I sprawled out on the cold stone, gasping for air. I sensed their gaze on me but tried to tune them out. I took a moment to breathe, thankful that it was not my time to die yet.

They all spoke over each other, their voices merging in chaos. My hands were sore and blistered, and every fiber of my being screamed from the way my limbs burned.

A loud voice barked over the others to make way for them to examine the deserter, and it took me a moment to realize he was referring to me.

The sense of relief from evading death didn't last long.

A sinking sensation settled in my chest when I realized that once I opened my eyes, the guards would know what I was. All of my effort would be for nothing, shipped off to the Temple the second they had a moment to observe me.

A chill came over me with a strange thickness.

No, it wasn't a chill. Casimir's presence was unmistakable, and my breath hitched. The familiar sensation sent a shock through me.

"*Jump off the other side of the border.*" Casimir's instruction caught me off guard.

Surely, the other side was the same as what I had overcome. I envisioned the jagged rocks on the other side protruding out to scrape against me and bring me more pain as I fell to my death.

Casimir must've been out of his mind. But regardless, I was going to listen to a delusion, so perhaps I was the one who should have pleaded insanity.

I thought death was not my fate any longer.

It turned out that was my lone option.

I groaned.

Before the guards said anything else, I darted up and sprinted across the length of the wall. It stretched far, and I half wished it didn't. There was too much space to second-guess my choice.

I heard the shouting, but it was all white noise in the back of my head. Blood rushed in my ears, and I held onto the sound, knowing it was the last time I would hear it. Eventually, I would be nothing more than a lifeless body, limp and crushed on the ground.

All my faith was in a fictional man, and when I leaped over the edge, a yelp escaped my lungs. The raven followed me, flying close in the corner of my eye. It cried out into the night.

I wasn't ready to die.

Instead of a dusty, rocky death below, I was met with a cliff. I landed hard, and my ankles ached with the shock.

My chest heaved with agonizing breaths, and I threw my head back, feeling disdain for Casimir and his lack of warning about the cliff.

The guards stared down at me from above. I didn't have time to gather myself, and I crawled my way to the edge, seeing a pool of black water beneath me. I stared at the reflectionless surface—surely pestilent —with apprehension.

But it was the only way to get down and maybe have a chance. It was foolish to think I'd make it out of the water. And it was foolish to think I could escape the guards any other way.

As if the gods thought I needed more motivation, the raven jumped along the edge of the cliff, looking down at the water.

I had to jump before they captured me.

The scream left me prematurely, but I was sprinting and then falling once again. It became a burdensome habit. My limbs flailed, protesting against the sudden lack of solid ground beneath them.

The impact tore across my skin. Heat and ice in equal measure when I broke through the surface. Every inch of my skin burned from the cursed water, and the icy blackness swallowed me whole.

After the heat, my body was in shock at the change. My mouth gaped open as an empty scream tried to leave it. It acted as a way for more fetid water to make its way down my throat.

The endless cursed black pool scorched my lungs as I searched for its bottom. When my foot found it, I pushed with all my strength, but it was useless. I couldn't find the top of the water.

It was strangely thick, and it continued to leave a fiery trail over my exposed skin.

My arms tried desperately to catch the water and use it to get back to the surface, but they wouldn't move right. My body faltered—giving out after all I had put it through.

Dying at the hands of the king or a wild beast would've been more desirable than the suffocating terror of drowning. The pain was relentless as the water seared my lungs, trapping me in its grip.

"Swim, Elita! Get out of there!" Casimir became frantic, begging me to do the one thing my body couldn't figure out.

I hadn't ever learned to swim. A skill neither myself nor my parents ever saw a need for. My neglect of basic abilities the majority of people possessed caught up to me at the most inconvenient time.

I would die for it.

Chapter Twenty

The water pulled me deeper, drowning me in inky black as it rapidly changed from freezing to hot coals across my exposed skin. Putrid water filled my lungs as I flailed. The reality that I would drown only made the panic worse until it became all-consuming and my movement slowed.

Casimir seemed to sense it, evident by the way his once light presence transformed into a suffocating weight. But it was more than his intense presence.

The water trembled around me—breaking under the weight of Casimir's desperation. It wasn't right.

An arm wrapped around my waist, their grip firm.

I guess I will die by the king's hand.

The other body pushed off the bottom, as I had done, but they were much more successful in their effort. My body was limp, nothing but dead weight. Briefly, I hoped the guard would let me float to the bottom rather than return me to Talos. But they didn't let go.

The pressure of the water let up, and as if I hadn't escaped death enough, we broke through the surface, and air seared my lungs. I gasped and sputtered before we were out of the water, which lapped at my chin.

The guard wrapped both arms under mine and pulled me onto the shore, gasping nearly as much as I was. I wondered if they'd be offended when I didn't thank them for saving me.

When they released my arms, I rolled on the ground until I was on my hands and knees, coughing up cursed water from my lungs.

I could hear the guard panting behind me. It would've been easy to allow them to take me back to the Temple to use my bloom. Within a matter of weeks, it wouldn't matter either way.

But I would've first drowned before returning to Talos willingly.

Before the guard had a chance to recover or come closer, I whipped around—skin burned and muscles sore—with my fist raised and poised to strike.

I scarcely moved an inch before a hand grabbed my wrist, halting my momentum.

"Not exactly the reaction I anticipated. Is that how you intend to thank me for saving your life?"

The voice sparked recognition in my bones. An intimate knowing after years of it filling my head.

My vision adjusted to the night, and pieces of the face came into view. Familiar sharp features and gleaming scarlet eyes stared back at me —framed by wavy black hair weighed down by the moisture.

His fingers remained wrapped around my wrist, both of us inches away from the inky, reflectionless water. My breath was ragged, painful against the burning in my throat.

"Casimir." The name came out raspy, and I blinked in disbelief.

Casimir crouched in front of me, searching my face. He appeared akin to a soldier, donned in black leather armor and a cloak that draped over his broad shoulders, clinging to his soaked frame.

The night blurred behind him, and I couldn't peel my eyes away. My body trembled, realizing before my mind could that it was not a dream.

Any ounce of control left me, and I sprung from my kneel, breaking his grip on my wrist. My arms wrapped around his middle, and he almost lost his balance. Warm hands caught me, solid around my waist. My head spun as he steadied us.

Casimir's voice didn't echo around in my head. It thundered in my ear and made my skin prickle when he spoke. "You scared the fuck out of me." His chest vibrated, and the warmth of his breath coated my neck. "I started to think you'd never come find me. It was a little disheartening," he said.

I glanced up at him, noting the droplets that still hung off the ends of his hair, some dripping onto my shoulder.

"I can't believe you're—" For the first time in days, I chuckled. "You're here. You're real." My fingers twitched, nearly lifting to brush the hair from his forehead. I wanted to prove he was real, to feel the warmth of his skin. Not the wispy touch of a ghost.

I refrained, curling my fist.

Casimir moved his attention to my bloom, noting each rose petal.

"I should have told you to find me sooner. I shouldn't have let you wait so long," he said, taking on a withdrawn tone.

"To be fair, I convinced myself years ago you weren't real. I'm partly to blame." I sat back on my heels, drenched from head to toe.

Casimir appeared amused, until his features turned grim, and he moved closer. "The water did a number on your skin," he said, not taking his gaze off my neck.

I lifted a hand and brushed it over the exposed skin. Even the soft touch made it sting. The water had already left marks over me, and gods only knew what it did to my lungs.

Casimir reached out, almost touching the burns, but he froze. His lips pursed, and he pulled back. "We need to get somewhere we can tend to that. It can cause a nasty infection fairly quick."

I stared at him, wide-eyed. My heart hammered while I observed the way he moved when he shuffled away, adjusting his wet cloak. Nothing like the slow-moving ghost in my dreams. I wrapped my arms around my torso as a shiver rippled through me.

"It might've helped if you had mentioned the cursed water. Nasty infection does not sound pleasant." Strangely, I felt unsure as I made quips at him. But a lot like in my dreams—a hot-headed grin curved his lips.

"Your options were slim. I simply made a calculated decision. I hadn't accounted for the fact you couldn't swim." His shoulders lifted with a nonchalant shrug, yet I saw the tension they held onto. It occurred to me Casimir likely got burned by the cursed water as well. Guilt knotted in my chest.

I paused to assess my wounds and wrung some of the moisture out of my hair.

Casimir continued to observe me. "I couldn't see you for over a week. I waited here for days, hoping you'd stop being stubborn," he said.

My bottom lip pulled between my teeth, trying to hold back a grin. "You know, you're lucky I found my way here at all. Your cryptic instructions weren't very helpful."

His eyes blazed with amusement while he stood and offered me his hand. I tentatively grabbed it, worried he would disappear at the touch. He didn't; instead, his hand remained solid in mine, warm from the rush of blood beneath his skin.

"Now, we won't want those guards coming after us. I've got something to show you, and I wouldn't want them to discover it. We should be on our way." He paused and looked me over. "Of course, if you're alright. We can assess wounds at our destination if you think you'll be fine."

"Yes, I'll be fine." I offered a nod of assurance despite the pain crawling over my skin.

He pressed his lips together in what looked like an attempt to fight back a grin and led the way. He didn't hesitate, and I kept up with his pace, disregarding the inferno in my muscles and lungs.

I wanted to be far from the guards, and I needed to find somewhere safer to plead with Casimir for assistance in rescuing Ronin.

The thought crossed my mind as we distanced ourselves from the wall and the black water. I wouldn't allow Ronin to stay in the hands of the king. But I needed help, and I hoped Casimir could provide it.

Part of me dreaded asking, already hesitant to approach the topic. It would be fruitless to ask him for help to rescue Ronin, considering he hadn't crossed the Forge to come get me.

My pace quickened. The fear of the unknown was too much to bear. I had found Casimir, and that in itself was a miracle. I only needed one more to save Ronin.

When I found myself a short distance ahead, I observed our surroundings. Dead trees twisted and bent around us, crippled and lifeless, with no greenery to color them. Their bark took on a gray hue as dirt covered them in the sour breeze.

Rocks jutted out from the ground, stained from what I assumed to be blood. Some of them had odd markings on them, drawn into the dust. It appeared to mark the path we continued to follow.

Further off stood several old structures that were burned and barren. They barely held onto old wood, aged to the point of rot. The sinister-looking trees couldn't conceal anything in such a dreadful place.

Ruins rose and fell all around us. Gone were the castles made of gold and the willow trees that used to dance along the edge of the dry, barren rivers.

Some remnants of old life were still present. Shattered glass, old pots, and other items scattered the ground as we walked through the abandoned land of Orondal. My feet crunched on the debris, the only sound besides the wind that burned my skin.

The further we went, the more disturbing the desolate land became. Bones covered some of the way, and despite my disgust and groan of protest, Casimir and I walked through the piles of them. I had to stop myself from gagging.

When we came to a bridge over a cavern—the edges crumbled and fallen in places—I hesitated. Casimir walked onto it, which should've made me less anxious, but I continued to stare. Sweat dampened my palms. Over the edges, the fall was deadly.

Casimir seemed to sense my discomfort because he slowed and looked back at me. "El?" The shortening of my name startled me, having never heard it outside of the dreamspace.

My hands gripped the sides of my tunic to hide how they trembled. "I don't fancy falling through a bridge that appears ready to collapse."

He took a couple of steps back to me. "I didn't bring you all this way to have you die crossing a bridge." He beckoned me closer. A soft grin tugged at his lips, one of knowing. The same look once filled the dreamspace when I was too afraid to be alone—the nights he stayed with me the longest. "I won't let you fall."

"But—"

"Just trust me."

Sour wind dusted strands of petaled hair across my face. The white continued to be jarring, and I tucked it behind my ear. Deep in the cavern, the breeze whistled. Twisted trees framed the beginning of the bridge. Dead vines clawed up the columns below, gray and withered. It was a miracle it hadn't disintegrated in the wind centuries ago.

Even as I stared at it with apprehension, Casimir's presence offered enough comfort. The tug was visceral to follow him. It had been that way for many years. And so my feet shuffled through the dusty path he left, and I stepped onto the bridge with him.

The stone structure didn't collapse beneath us, and I followed close to Casimir, unwilling to go too far. He'd already rescued me from the water, and I chose to trust that he'd prevent me from falling.

We reached halfway across the bridge, and Casimir looked over his shoulder at me. "It may not be prudent, but on the days I didn't see or visit you, where were you?" he asked. It took my mind off the things around me and brought it back to everything that had transpired in the past few weeks.

Unpleasant feelings rushed me. I took a steadying breath and attempted to explain everything. I told him about the fire and holding my mother's body in my arms as she died, which he solemnly told me he knew. I omitted the details of days spent consuming sour food and enduring Talos's torture in the cells, and instead, I shared with him about Ronin and how he aided me.

I tried to explain Ronin's friendship with my father and how he rescued me from the Temple. I spoke about my nights spent under the stars, feeling one with the ground beneath me. Moreover, I told him about how painful it was when the first petal arrived. How it burned, and my entire body ached, and how I couldn't sleep for two nights after I left the cottage. The guilt and the fear were too burdensome to allow me any rest.

Casimir took most of it in stride, not asking questions. He interrupted me only once, and it happened when I made a passing comment about Ronin's familiarity with the Rose people.

"You had never met this man in your life, yet he knew more than any stranger should have," he said, exasperated. "And at what point did you see it fit to allow a stranger to take you captive and hide you in the woods? Even if he knew your father, do you have any survival instincts at all?"

I flinched and focused on my feet as they summoned clouds of dust on the forgotten bridge.

"When the fire happened, I didn't care an awful lot about what happened to me." My tone was more harsh than I meant. "And you have no idea how awful the prince was to me. Ronin was kind, and I don't know why, but I trusted him. I still do." I avoided meeting his judgemental stare. Saying it out loud, it sounded foolish—how careless I became after the fire.

Casimir didn't scold me again; instead, he brought us to a stop when we reached the other side of the bridge, facing me. "I should have come for you when the buds appeared." He looked over me, something unsaid in his eyes.

"I mean, it may have been a little helpful," I teased, trying to lighten the mood.

His tongue clicked in amusement. "You know, there are rules I'm meant to follow." He swiped a hand through his wavy hair, now dried. "But perhaps those should be questioned."

My eyebrows raised, confused but not willing to ask for further explanation. The exhaustion set in, and the fatigue was almost more than I could take. With the watchful eyes of the guards no longer a concern and the adrenaline faded, I longed for somewhere to rest my head. It had been far too long since I had slept.

Casimir remained silent until we came upon what appeared to be a dead end, the rest being a sea of black dead trees, old crumbling cottages, and a mountain of jagged rock.

"Casimir?"

"It's right up here." He picked up his pace, and I had to jog to keep up with his long stride as he hurried ahead. "The king doesn't know of our existence, and it remains that way for a reason." Excitement leaked into his voice. Knowing Casimir, cheating the king out of something likely brought him immense joy.

The unmistakable sound of trickling water filled my ears. The air became less stale, and I sensed the difference in it as I took a breath.

Curiosity engulfed me, and I walked a step behind Casimir, with the pulse of life echoing through my body.

We approached a massive opening in the mountain. There was a cave carved into it with jutting rocks that appeared like menacing teeth. Casimir approached the cave, and as we neared, I realized there was a path well traveled through the middle of it.

Water streamed out, and the rising sun glistened on it. It was nothing at all like the toxic waters I had read about in my father's books, nor what Casimir had pulled me out of.

When we came closer to the opening, our feet met with the water. The stream ran cold and clear, lapping at my ankles. I glanced up at Casimir, but his attention was fixed on navigating across a few larger rocks, venturing further into the cave.

I followed him wordlessly, suspecting that if I followed him, my questions would be answered.

Casimir looked back at me and smirked before he beckoned me forward. The resemblance to his visits in my dreams quickened my pulse.

I clambered over the rocks, grabbing onto some with my hands. The contrast between the thick black water I fell into earlier was striking.

The light vanished as we trudged deeper, making it difficult to see. One glance behind us revealed a glimpse of the sun shining outside of the cave.

I gasped when my hand fell on something I didn't expect. A soft clump of green moss pressed into my palm, and I drew it back, staring at the impossibility with wide eyes. *It can't be.*

When I faced Casimir, he gave me a knowing look, and then he vanished, going around a turn in the rocks.

I neared where he disappeared, and everything was muted compared to the sound of rushing water. A misty spray filled the air of the cave, and the rush of it overpowered the thrum of my heart.

When I turned the corner, there ran a magnificent waterfall illuminated by a large opening at the top of the cave where the sun shone through. The waterfall flowed down into a hole in the floor of the cave.

Throughout my life, I had been brought up with the belief that there was nothing in the Drought Lands. The water was meant to be cursed, and people couldn't live long in the barren lands without food or clean water, making the Iron Thorn the only safe place to reside. However, in that cave, I had seen life.

"You're somewhat of a legend here. Try not to let it get to your head, though, yeah?" Casimir grinned, causing a flutter of nerves in my chest.

With that, he walked through the rushing water until he reached the far side of the cave, close to the top of the waterfall.

A wooden ladder peeked out from the opposite side of the opening, away from the rush of water. Casimir started to vanish down the wall of wet rocks as he descended the ladder, with his back turned toward the waterfall that plummeted into the earth.

I watched him go, the sun leaving his skin as he descended. The stream rose to my waist as I followed until I stood at the edge of the hole in the ground.

Timidly, I reached down and grabbed hold of the wood with my heart in my throat.

Chapter Twenty-One

T he climb down the slippery ladder caused my stomach to twist in knots. The rickety wooden rails held to the rock wall with iron nails, and yet it shook as I clambered down.

I didn't know what awaited me below, but I had seen enough to make me question everything. The existence of running water—*clean water*—outside the Iron Thorn was proof enough that what I believed about our realm was a lie. Acknowledging it didn't prepare me for what was in the underground cavern.

Reaching the last rail, cold water lapped at my calves as the waterfall continued to rush behind me. I turned, meaning to face Casimir.

None of my questions ever made it past my lips.

A soft gasp escaped me at the sight of a lush forest of emerald pine trees. A stunning array of flowers dotted along a dirt path that led away from the water, and blooms sprung from the trees as well, bristling along with the leaves in the breeze, which no longer carried the sour scent of Orondal.

Casimir watched from the edge of the pond, his hand outstretched for me. I took it and clambered over slippery stones to get out of the cold water.

When I steadied on the solid ground, grass brushed my feet.

The landscape unfurled in a splendor of colorful hues. Grandiose tents scattered throughout the pine trees, somewhat hidden. A small stream connected to the pond snaked through the middle of the tents, adorned with quaint wooden bridges. The stream led to a large body of water in the distance, visible through the trees where they split open to make way for the rushing water.

Brown, tan, and a few green tents stood at different heights, which gave it the appearance of a muted sea made of fabric.

Sun-bleached fences lined the perimeter of a few large wooden structures off to the right of the path. Some linens hung on lines to dry in the sun, which poured through a massive opening in the earth above us. A dome beneath the ground, overflowing with life, hidden in the guise of a mountain in Orondal.

Casimir never took his attention away from me. A softer expression changed his demeanor, and for a moment, I saw in him the same disbelief I had felt since the water. After so many years, I had finally found him.

A soft chatter filled my ears, and with a startle, I noticed Casimir and I weren't alone. I turned to him, ducking my head when I realized we had drawn attention, my hood long ago discarded.

Casimir leaned closer at my side. "Welcome to Everbloom, Elita."

I gaped at him for a second before the people approaching us stole my attention. Eager whispers carried among them. The trees appeared as if they had begun to move, and it took me a moment to realize it was another group of people emerging from the foliage.

The unease sat like a rock in my gut, and my hands scrambled for my hood. When I glanced back at Casimir, I spotted a young woman jogging toward us, curly onyx hair brushing the dirt path. Twisty ringlet bangs nearly blocked her vision.

A wide grin spread across her face, and as she reached us, she swallowed Casimir in a hug, the impact audible as he swayed on his legs, arms squashed to his sides.

"You've found her!" the young woman chimed. She released him and enveloped me in a sudden tight embrace, which made my sore muscles ache and my breathing strained. After an uncomfortable pause, she pulled back and held me at arm's length. I was greeted by pale crimson eyes, bright and chipper, as though we were long-lost friends.

Bewildered, I looked to Casimir once more.

"Alba, give her room to breathe. I haven't had time to explain anything," Casimir dismissed her lazily as though her overbearing antics were a common occurrence.

"Nonsense. She's home here. We might as well act like it," she said, rolling her eyes at him before she released my arms. "I'm Alba, and we've been waiting so long for you to arrive. It seemed like Casimir was never going to pull through."

"Have I ever *not* pulled through?" Casimir snickered.

"Don't get a big head. It's not hard to recruit more Roses. But Elita's arrival is different," Alba said, unbothered by his ego.

Finding my voice, I tried to prod without sounding nervous. "What does she mean?"

Casimir gave me an apologetic look. I resented the fact that he told me nothing before our arrival. For how long we walked in Orondal, he had plenty of time to explain.

"You haven't told her?" Alba scolded.

I glanced between the two of them, apprehension taking the place of the previous awe.

"Casimir?" My voice held the slightest tremble. Beneath the worry, exhaustion flooded my body, mixing with the confusion until my head was a muddled mess.

"You idiot!" Alba smacked Casimir's arm. "Elita, you have so much to learn. This fool of a man clearly has not done his duty—"

"That will be enough for now." A voice from my right startled me. I turned and the flood of people parted to let a man through.

Pure white hair adorned his head despite his age being nowhere near that of an elderly man. He looked to be maybe ten years older than me, dressed in black leather armor similar to Casimir's but with a long gray cloak resting over one shoulder. He carried the air of a leader.

Alba moved back and pouted at him.

"There will be plenty of time to explain things this evening. She needs to see Taryn." A hush fell over the crowd when he spoke.

"Oh, Orin, I wish you'd lighten up." Alba walked over to him, patted a palm to his cheek, and sashayed away, taking a place in the crowd that continued to watch us.

"We'll give Elita a proper greeting later. For now, please resume the morning tasks," the white-haired man—Orin—said. No one besides Alba had a problem with the order.

The crowd split, some disappearing into tents and others went to tend gardens in the distance. I watched, waiting until most of them cleared out before Casimir took his place back at my side.

Orin offered a strained but polite smile. "The general and I welcome you to Everbloom, a sanctuary for the Rose people. Of course, more will be explained soon enough. For the time being, Casimir will escort you to our healer, and then he will show you to your sleeping quarters." Orin gestured to the tents toward my left.

"Until tonight, I'd advise you to remain close to Casimir. We will discuss things after the final meal of the day," he said dismissively.

I dipped my head at Orin when we turned to leave. He appeared to be a respected leader. Although, from Casimir's demeanor, he clearly wasn't liked.

Casimir led the way, and I kept close to his side. It embarrassed me how enthralled I was, but I watched him from the corner of my eye. No matter how anxious I grew or how tired I was, he didn't disappear.

"We keep our wounded far from the entrance," Casimir said, interrupting the quiet. "It'll be a long walk to the healer's tent." He ran a hand over his jaw before pointing to our left. "Through the trees here, we have the washing tents. There are two, one for clothing, and one for bathing. The two look nearly identical inside, so keep that in mind. You won't want to find yourself naked in the wrong one when someone comes in to wash their clothes." He chuckled to himself.

"Duly noted."

He smirked and focused on the path, leading me through a few different tents, some of them a dark, dusty green. Others were faded brown or dirty ivory. They ranged in different sizes, but the deeper we trudged through the woods, the larger they became.

Casimir pointed out the housing tents, which were buried deepest into the woods, and they were all the same color of brown, blending in with the bark of the trees. He explained how that was purposeful, and we were safest within those trees. Next to the housing tents stood a single black one, which had a red swatch of paint across the opening to it.

We walked up to the entrance, and Casimir paused, looking over at me. "We would like access to the healing headquarters. I bring with me tidings of joy," Casimir said with a wink. He seemed to think he was comical, and I had to suppress the urge to roll my eyes.

Loud footsteps stomped over the hard-packed dirt before hands appeared through the holes in the drapes, undoing the ties.

A face peered out, glaring at Casimir. "You always have something fun for me to work on, don't you, boy?" The woman huffed.

"This time, I've brought you something much more interesting. Taryn, meet Elita." Casimir dipped his head in my direction.

Taryn opened the drapes wider, revealing a long white healer coat over linen trousers and a tucked tunic. The woman had vibrant red hair that stretched down her back. The ringlets poked out as if they were trying to reach out and grab something. Her eyes were such a pale red that they appeared more orange.

After a moment of staring in shock, I realized her hair was filled with an abundance of red petals.

"By Cordelia's sea...you never disappoint." Taryn grinned, reaching a hand out for me to shake.

"You're the second person to say as much since we arrived," Casimir replied as I took the woman's hand.

"Well, come on in. Nice to have you here, Elita. We've been hoping Casimir wasn't lying about you coming."

I followed her in with Casimir in tow. Cots stretched on in intricately placed lines before the end of the vast tent. Healing supplies, tinctures, stacks of bandages, and linens all cluttered the tables.

I slowed my pace to walk closer to Casimir, observing the almost completed bloom in her hair. "Are there other healers here?" I whispered.

"No, just Taryn for the time being while others train. Why?"

"Her bloom..." I trailed off.

Before Casimir answered, Taryn chortled. I looked at her, shocked she was laughing, and embarrassed she overheard my question.

She turned around, appearing amused. "Did he forget to explain the purpose of this sanctuary? This is my fifth time in full bloom."

"It didn't seem appropriate to tell her," Casimir snapped.

I cast a glance at him, overcome by anger and bewilderment. Somehow, Taryn survived not only one or two but five blooms, and she stood there unaffected. Somehow, she hadn't died.

The disbelief bubbled over into white-hot rage. For centuries, all the Roses who died needlessly, sacrificed in a garden, told it was the sole choice. Taken from their families to be raised in a cruel Temple under the rule of an evil king. Their only other option was to be used, wilt, and die.

It was all a lie.

I seethed, unable to follow the two as they bickered at each other. They didn't notice at first, but when they did, they both froze.

Casimir searched my face. "Elita?"

"How could you not say anything?" My voice broke. "All the Roses murdered at the word of the king when they had another choice, and you just let them die? You knew how much stress it caused me, and you said nothing?"

Casimir crossed his arms over his chest. "It's not that simple. We've been bringing in as many Roses as we can. But the king can't know. It would do more harm than good. It wouldn't do any good at all, actually. He nor the council care about the Roses, and telling them we don't have to die won't change anything. They would require a sacrifice for the Iron Thorn, regardless."

"But Everbloom—"

"It's the beginning, but things take time. The Iron Thorn is different, and so is every living thing left out in the Drought Lands. You can't expect us to have not thought everything through. Not everyone can handle the knowledge we have."

I opened and closed my mouth, not sure what to say. Taryn gave me an apologetic look and gestured to an empty cot. I sat down, no longer willing to discuss the matter with Casimir.

Taryn pulled up a wooden stool and sat in front of me. "So, anything odd going on? Something specific you're worried about?"

I shifted on the cot, unsure where to begin. "I've had a headache since my bloom began, and there's a few rough scrapes on my legs."

"She also fell into cursed water and likely inhaled some," Casimir added.

After a bewildered pause, Taryn shook her head. "Cursed water? What kind of mess did you get the poor girl into?" Her hands reached toward me, stopping when I recoiled. "Oh, guess I should've elaborated. I'm a Rose healer. Which means I can scan you for injuries and offer a bit of help in the healing process. Make it a tad quicker."

I blinked, not understanding in the slightest. She chuckled and then put out a hand. Despite my hesitation, I placed my palm in hers. Her hand wrapped around mine, and she stared at me, her gaze unnerving before her eyes started to dart from side to side. I pursed my lips and waited for her to finish whatever she was doing.

Taryn exhaled and pulled back, her hand releasing mine.

"The ache from the bloom is normal, by the way," she said first, standing from her seat. "Those gashes will need a bit of help. Respiration is all good, but I'll have to focus more time on healing your lungs. The burns from the water will need to be watched for infection, but a salve spread over it before you sleep should do the trick. Now, let's see 'em." She gestured at my legs.

I stared at her with wide eyes before I rolled up my tattered and damp trousers to expose the cuts from rocks and brush. The tight fabric struggled to move higher than just below my knee.

Taryn reached over to a nearby table and grabbed a few different things. She opened an amber glass bottle and spilled some of the contents onto a cloth. The scent of calendula filled the tent. She pressed the cool cloth to one of the deeper cuts on my shin.

"Hmm, some of these are pretty deep. Sutures might be a good call," she mused, grabbing more supplies. "Now, we've run out of herbs to numb—"

"I can't," I interrupted.

Her brows raised, but she nodded all the same. I couldn't hold it against my mother. It felt wrong with her gone. But the memories of how badly it hurt when she sutured my leg had me willing to take my chances on ragged scars.

Taryn wrapped bandages around the two gashes and stood, happy with her work. "Those should *hopefully* heal fine, but I'll watch 'em and do what I can in aiding the process. Try to come back every day, or at least every other day, so I can change out the bandage to prevent infection. And don't fret, Casimir doesn't mean to be a pain in the ass." Casimir scoffed. "He means well, but we all got to abide by rules here. Keeping people in the loop is Orin and the General's duty." Taryn smiled and patted me on the shoulder. "It was good meeting you." She walked away, and I noticed someone else in the tent, holding their stomach as if in pain.

Casimir tipped his head toward the exit, his arms remaining crossed. I nodded and followed him out, feeling less enchanted with it all than when I'd first arrived.

When I was a young girl, I used to imagine what it would be like if Casimir were real and I found him. What would the experience be like to encounter him outside the realm of my dreams? It was difficult to experience the sour disappointment, the secrecy from him tainting it.

"Well, a bath or sleep?" Casimir asked, glancing over his shoulder at me. "Personally, I'd recommend a wash. You look as rough as you smell."

I came to a halt, not at all enthused by his jab. "Whatever gets me a moment of peace."

He pursed his lips, turning away. "Sleep it is, then."

Chapter Twenty-Two

We didn't speak while we made our way through the forest of tents. Their appearance continued to amaze me. They were tall and pointed, pulled at the top as the bottom of it ran in a loose circle.

My father would have been captivated by it all, the flora especially. His curiosity about architecture and plants was unmatched, and I shared a lot of that fascination—after many years of him teaching me and having me help him study the plants in the garden.

Thoughts of my father circled to Ronin, and the shame and guilt settled on my shoulders. I refused to accept that the guards would kill him. I held onto a foolish hope that they would keep him alive to get to me. Regret became an overwhelming consequence of my cowardice.

He was my friend, and I abandoned him.

If I could, I would make it right. Save him for a change. Hopefully with the help of Casimir. Naivety continued to plague me.

After walking a good distance in the stiff quiet, we approached a tent that stood out, the brown darker than the others. The fabric appeared freshly sewn. The markings above it showed it was a housing tent, and the tie was fixed in a bow to hold the two drapes together.

Casimir stepped forward and pulled the tie loose in one movement, the drapes cascading to the sides in a graceful shift. Inside the tent was a simple wooden bedframe with a cushion resting on it, a quilted blanket, and something that resembled a misshapen pillow.

Nothing had ever appeared so enticing.

The rest of the tent didn't interest me. Every part of my being begged for rest. The days and nights escaped me, leaving me nearly delirious.

I removed my cloak in a swift motion, the clothes mostly dry after leaving the waterfall behind. Casimir pulling me out of the cursed water felt like a lifetime ago as I scrambled over to the bed, forgetting anything else. Even Casimir, until I noticed he hadn't left and watched me with a questioning gaze inside the open drapes.

"This is your idea of giving me peace?" I asked. The sleeplessness caused the annoyance to be unbearable.

"Orin charged me with staying close until things have been discussed. Many people here get uneasy when newcomers arrive. Standard protocol," he said with a shrug.

I groaned and sat on the bed, too fatigued to protest it. I pulled the faded red and tan quilt over me, and the fabric was worn against my fingertips; used, but it made it more comfortable. I shifted my gaze from Casimir and settled onto the mattress. It cradled me, more comfort than I had in over a month since the fire. The pillow below my head resembled what I imagined laying on a cloud would be like after weeks in the dirt or an old cot.

I dozed off before I formed another thought.

The sun was almost gone from the sky by the time I woke. I jolted upright, alarmed by how long I slept.

"Nightmare?"

The voice startled me, and I glanced over to find Casimir sitting on the ground, his arms crossed over his chest.

I took a shaky breath and laid back down. My gaze flickered from him to the top of the tent.

"No. I slept well." An abrupt swell of emotions bubbled in my chest. I couldn't recall the last time I'd slept without nightmares laden with death.

When my head rolled back in his direction, he continued to watch me. The same question echoed in his stare. A strange phenomenon, and only he could understand the complexity. I had experienced night terrors for as long as I could remember.

My stomach rolled with hunger, too distracting to ignore, and my hair became an awful mess around me.

Casimir stood and stretched his arms behind his head. He froze mid-stretch, staring at me. "You have a new petal."

I ran a hand through my hair, and sure enough, there was one close to my scalp, at the very top of my forehead. I could only imagine how silly it looked.

"Any advice on brushing hair with petals in it?" I asked while I attempted to smooth down my messy curls.

"Carefully" is all he said, not offering much help. He pointed over his shoulder at a stack of fabric on a wooden chest. "Clean clothes are there; a brush and soap are all stored in the washing tent. I can't guarantee anyone will be there to get water boiling for a bath at this hour."

My cheeks flushed, the frustration slept off. I noted his clothing, the same ones he wore when he pulled me out of the cursed pool. More guilt piled on.

"As long as it isn't as cold as that water you pulled me out of, I'll take it," I said sheepishly.

He nodded and made his way to the drapes.

I grabbed the folded clothes and followed Casimir out. People bustled by, and children ran around the crowd's feet, the end of the day not enough to stifle their energy as they dodged parents' hands, laughter carrying among the dwellers. I smiled at the sight.

Everyone was on their way back to their tents, leaving behind the markets and mess hall, and I started to worry I missed the last meal of the day while my hunger pains grew.

I followed Casimir's long strides. When the crowd continued to grow, he slowed his pace until I walked close to his shoulder, watching out for the oncoming people while they made their way through the crowd of housing tents.

A few children paused as they walked past, and some pointed at us, tugging on their guardian's sleeve. A blush lit my cheeks, sure that they must be mocking my ragged appearance. Casimir observed the pointing, his gaze shifting from them to me.

"Nothing to be ashamed of. They've just never seen white petals."

My eyes widened, and I absentmindedly ran a petal through my fingers, glancing down at it as I muttered, "Oh." I tucked the knowledge away for later. Another question to ask Orin since no one else would give me answers.

We kept our pace until we arrived at the larger tents, finding Alba slumped in a chair in front of the wash tent. Her head snapped up when she saw us approach, and she stood, waving with enthusiasm. To my surprise, a familiar, thin black cat jumped off of her lap.

"I know that cat," I blurted. My attention went from Alba to the cat. Casimir gave me a knowing look.

Alba met us as we approached the tent. The cat followed at her feet, which I duly noted were bare by choice.

"Elita! We've been waiting for you; we've had water on a boil for a while in hopes you'd swing by—I mean, not trying to imply anything." She assured me, putting a hand on my shoulder.

I shook my head. "No, I understand. It's been a rough few weeks." I crouched, hardly paying attention to the conversation as the cat sauntered over, rubbing its cheek along my hand, its fur warm and soft. "Now, this cat, does it belong to you?" I glanced up at them.

Alba grinned, leaning down to pet the cat's slick fur. "This is Astoria, she's my familiar." She patted the cat on the head, to which Astoria replied in kind with a purr.

"She found me on the other side of the Forge. She led me to it. Persistent girl wouldn't even hide from the rain with me. But I owe her a great thanks. I wouldn't have had the guts to climb the wall had she not led me to it."

"That's my girl! She's so wise, always knows when there's a Rose in need. It's how she found me. Now, that's a story for another day. Are you wanting to use the bath?" Alba asked, standing.

I gave Astoria another gentle scratch of thanks and followed suit, trailing them into the tent. Steam swirled from a large stone pot close by, flames licking up the sides of it. Two other women stood in the tent, talking around it. When they noticed us, they stopped and offered a nod in our direction.

"This is Elrin and Lyleen. They helped keep the water ready to add. I'm sure you'll all become acquainted soon." Alba rushed it along.

The two women didn't speak. But one of them, Elrin, stared at me, a flicker of distaste in her expression. Light brown hair fell in loose waves down her back, framing a slow-growing scowl.

It was the first encounter I had where someone appeared displeased with my presence outside of possibly Orin. Though, it was hard to tell if he didn't want me there or if that's just how he was.

Lyleen, a woman with short cropped onyx hair, elbowed Elrin. The two whispered for a moment, and with one last glance of abhorrence, Elrin joined Lyleen in lifting the boiling pot, cloths wrapped around their hands.

Casimir jumped in to help, receiving a sharp glare from Elrin. "We don't need your help," she muttered.

Casimir rolled his eyes and helped them dump the pot of boiled water into what looked like a large trough for horses. Alba thanked them, and the two women scurried out, talking in hushed tones. The fabric of the tent billowed behind them when they left.

I watched Casimir after the two left and went to stand at his side. "What was that about?" I asked, tipping my head toward where the two women departed.

He shook his head. "Don't worry about them."

Alba never noticed anything amiss and bustled around the tent. She grabbed a bar of soap and set it near the bath on a small wooden table. Close by was a hairbrush and a cloth to dry myself off. There was a long, thin stone slab just outside of the trough-like tub.

I added my clothes to the top of a nearby chest and turned to Casimir and Alba. "I know I'm meant to be guarded, but could I do this part in private?" After my time in the Temple, I half expected one of them to say no. But they were nothing like Talos, and I had to remind myself most people couldn't be that cruel.

Casimir cleared his throat and nodded, turning on his heel. "I'll be close by," he said, leaving the tent. He held the drapes for Alba, who giggled at him. The cat, Astoria, followed them, prancing out of the tent. Casimir tied the drapes behind them, and their shadows on the outside of the tent disappeared.

My dirty clothes came off with a struggle. The fabric had dried in an unusual manner until it was stiff. When my body was bare, goosebumps covered me from head to toe, and I threw the dirty linens in a messy pile, hurrying to the water that my body craved. To have the grime and dried blood washed from my skin.

I lowered into the water, which was warmer than I had experienced in a long time, not since the day at the cottage when I got soaked in the rain. I let myself sink like a stone, my head bobbing under the water for a moment to soak my hair. The bar of handmade soap sat close by, and I dipped it into the water. The small square appeared unused and misshapen. I scrubbed it along my skin, trying to ignore how murky the water became as I did so.

The soap smelled faintly of geranium and sage. Small beads in the bar aided in ridding my skin of darker patches of dirt and dried blood.

My hair was harder to work with, but I lathered it all the same, carefully rubbing the bar through the soaked tresses around the petals. I rinsed it all out, let the water lap against my skin, and sighed when it was all said and done, the new cleanliness like a slate wiped clean.

The bandages on my legs held onto the water, so I removed them, cringing when the water and soap touched the tender skin. New bandages would have been necessary, regardless. I hoped Taryn wouldn't be too upset.

When I was thoroughly clean, I clambered out onto the stone slab at the side of the bath, patting dry with the cloth left out for me. I unfolded the clothes, revealing a loose cream linen top and faded green linen bottoms. It was the most comfortable I'd been in over a month.

The shock was overwhelming when I realized it had been over a month since my parent's death, and it nearly brought me to my knees. How fast the time flew by, stuck in places I had never imagined I would be. I missed them more than I had given myself the chance to in a while.

I took a steadying breath and grabbed the hairbrush. The bristles looked menacing, like metal claws. I took my time and started from the bottom of my hair and worked my way up, gentle around the petals and the buds that had yet to bloom.

My hair fell down my back, the curls taking shape while I shook them and used the cloth to squeeze the excess moisture out. The petals shimmered in the lantern light. By the time I finished, the sun had set, leaving only the flames to illuminate the tent.

There were no shoes, but my feet had grown accustomed enough. It didn't bother me.

I made my way over to the drapes, grabbed the tie, and gave it a tug, causing it to shudder open. Casimir stood a short distance away, his back to the tent while he spoke with Alba. To my relief, I noticed Casimir had the time to swap his armor for something clean. The black tunic and loose trousers were much more familiar to me.

Astoria spotted me first, and the cat pranced over to where I stood. I chuckled and leaned down to pet her, my hands much cleaner.

"Elita!" Alba exclaimed when she caught sight of me. "You look refreshed. I'm sure it feels much better."

I stood to my full height when they approached. "It does. Thank you, Alba, for staying so the water was warm."

Alba grinned and waved me off as if it were nothing.

I looked between Casimir and Alba as discomfort rolled through my stomach. "I hate to ask for anything more, but I'm quite hungry."

"Well, Orin is waiting at the mess hall," Casimir said. "We can find you food there. There's a lot to talk about, a lot of questions I'm sure you want answered." He turned toward the path and I followed, eager to eat something that wasn't plucked from the ground, a suspicious berry or a crunchy insect or two.

Alba stayed behind and waved us off. I looked at Casimir. "Is she not coming?"

"It's best if the crowd stays small."

We walked along the path through the tents and trees, the sun's warm rays no longer reaching the crater in the ground. There were a few lanterns lit, hanging from iron stakes in the ground. Enough to light our way on the path, which was no longer busy.

The nighttime in Everbloom had an enchanting atmosphere. With the absence of chatter—replaced with the echoes of chirping insects and the gentle glow of illuminated lanterns—it was somewhat whimsical; nothing cynical lurked in the trees.

Few people remained outside. The only ones out wore leather armor, black and ominous, along with bows and quivers slung over their backs. Their focus remained on the ladder which led out of the mountain.

It brought me comfort to know Talos and his father couldn't reach me. And I wasn't on my own. Each one of the Rose people inside the secret crater despised Lendorr and Talos. They would protect their own in a way the people of the kingdom would not. Not for the Roses. Not the way I desperately needed.

We walked for an hour's time before we came up to the mess hall. It remained lit by lanterns, the wooden doors propped open to reveal many circular tables covered in food scraps left in the wake of the dinner hour. Some people stayed behind to clean up, gathering what they could and disappearing out a side door.

Orin sat at a table with another man, his hair a deep brunette, shaggy, and chopped in a way that looked accidental. He wore a golden locket around his neck, which rested on his warm, umber skin.

The man and Orin were engrossed in conversation.

Casimir and I approached, and Orin glanced at us, his posture straightening. "Elita, nice of you to join us this evening." His tone had a bite to it. Patience didn't seem to be his strong suit.

The other man stood and pulled out a chair, gesturing to it. I met his gaze, the red of his eyes like a deep red wine. "My name is Galan Hayes. It is a pleasure to meet you, Ms. Blackthorne." Galan spoke as if in a hurry, his tone friendly.

I tipped my head at him in greeting and sat, feeling uneasy around so many people. Casimir sat in the chair next to me, bringing me more relief than I cared to admit.

Orin tapped his fingers on the tabletop, his gaze unnerving. "Shall we begin?" he asked.

Orin glared when Casimir put his hand up, interrupting already.

"Actually, Elita is pretty hungry, having not eaten in a few days. Someone should fetch her some food before we start," Casimir said casually. The tension was palpable when Orin glowered.

"I see. Why don't you get her something to eat, Casimir? We can begin in your absence."

Casimir fought back a smirk and shook his head. "Sorry, she's pretty spooked. Someone else should."

"I am not spooked," I blurted, adding another glare in Casimir's direction. He gave me a warning glance.

"Best to not leave you alone with this one." His voice in my head again was grating. But for the time being, his warning remained, and I turned my attention back to Orin.

Galan stood, his entire body rigid and his stance that of a soldier, although it didn't suit him. He was possibly a few years younger than me. "Sir, I will fetch food for Ms. Blackthorne. I would be happy to help," Galan said, his voice young but his tone full of respect for Orin. I bit back a smile.

Orin waved him off, not bothering to reply. Galan bowed his head and walked toward the exit of the main dining area. The quiet that followed his departure made me more nervous. I waited for someone to cut the silence.

Orin sighed and sat straighter, his hands knotting together on the table. "Elita, there are many things we need to cover if we could begin while we wait for Galan to return."

I nodded and clasped my hands in my lap to stop them from shaking. Casimir let out an annoyed breath and leaned back in his chair, preparing for a long conversation.

"I'm sure the history of the Roses is no mystery to you. Casimir has assured me you know a fair amount from the man who raised you."

My hands unfolded and fidgeted with the edge of my linen top. "My father?"

Orin's eyes bounced to Casimir and back to me. "Of course. The information he shared, the histories," Orin added.

"Yes, I'm aware of the history, the deities, how it all came to be. I've read plenty about it." Frustration dripped off my tongue. "What I don't understand, though, is how the Roses here seem to bloom without dying alongside their wilts. Not a single history book I've come across has mentioned anything like this."

Casimir snickered beside me, but Orin was unenthused.

"The people here are not asked to give their bloom as a sacrifice. Have you ever questioned why the council must raise Roses in their Temple? Why they breed them in a continuous cycle, never allowing them to leave, only to be sheared in the same spot every time? It's glaringly obvious."

I sat with it for a moment, my mind reeling. "King Lendorr has been knowingly killing Roses when their bloom isn't the end? That would make every sacrifice just a public execution." My heart sank.

Casimir's demeanor changed beside me, the atmosphere in the room going grim.

Orin observed as I processed it. "Every Rose that has entered the sacrificial garden has had their hair sheared. Their sacrifice is not a choice, not truly. When you're presented with a one-sided story, such as every Rose will die with their first bloom, what other choice is there? Die anyway but not give the Iron Thorn life, or kindly sacrifice yourself for the kingdom? It's a lie that is centuries old. A falsehood that the king has fought and killed to keep a secret."

Anger boiled in my blood, hot and sudden. "I've wasted my life waiting for a sacrifice I don't have to give? My mother and father lived in fear of a lie?" I faced Casimir, the fury unbearable. "You let me believe I was going to die. There was somewhere safe for my family and you never told me!"

Casimir's jaw clenched.

Orin took in my reaction, his emotionless stare maddening. "Casimir had nothing to explain to you, nothing to tell you. Nowhere for your family. Nowhere for *you*."

The anger died in my throat. Where Casimir refused to meet my gaze, Orin's eyes bore into mine, amused.

"There is a prophecy as old as the great drought itself—"

"Orin." Casimir's interruption caught me off guard.

Orin gave him a warning glance. "She must know."

Casimir scoffed. "It's nonsense written by people who died centuries ago."

Glowering, Orin leaned over the table and pointed a finger at him. "Your unbelief doesn't change her story."

My palms dampened and I ran them over the linen trousers.

They glared at each other for a long pause before Orin sat back and snickered. "Know your place. Now," Orin faced me, "it's imperative you know the histories taught to you are incomplete. Many are, including the knowledge we have here. Crooked kings have shaped the histories to their betterment for centuries." Orin reached forward, grabbing a mug from the table. He swirled it around, staring at the steam as it rose. "Surely that comes as no surprise to you." He peered over the mug while he sipped at it.

I thought back to the times my father reminded me that the stories I spent much of my time reading were one-sided—told by those who had something to gain.

Orin set his mug down and tucked a loose white hair behind his ear before he continued. "The reason for the norm king clinging to this prophecy remains a mystery, yet that doesn't change its existence. The goddess Aeterna gave our people this hope. Her parting words before her disappearance. The penance for her ruinous fury."

The air caught in my lungs and I waited, bothered by the way he took delight in taunting me. Shadows flickered on the walls of the mess hall, distorted by the flames that twitched in the lanterns.

Leaning closer to the table, Orin spoke without a shred of empathy. "The prophecy tells of a Rose who would be the ultimate offering. A bloom that would end the drought and restore the realm. Foretold to be a bloom as white as snow."

The room blurred and numbness crept through my body. I almost retched when the damning words fell from Orin's lips.

"You are the final sacrifice. As told by the goddess herself."

Blood rushed in my ears, and a horrible heat spread from my face down my neck. I stood so quickly that the chair fell backward.

Casimir jolted upright, a hand hovering near my elbow as I swayed. "Elita?" His voice sounded much like it used to in my dreams, distant and muffled as if he were talking to me underwater.

Orin rose from his seat, his hands folding behind his back. "Casimir was never meant to bring you here. This is no sanctuary for you. Your destiny is to set the Rose people free of their sacrifice by becoming the final offering yourself."

I turned my back to him before he said another word. Voices rang in my head while my feet carried me to the exit. My shoulder bumped into Galan's on my way out, but I couldn't muster an apology.

My vision swam, blurring everything around me until I barely saw where I stumbled. Nerves tingled from my temples down to my chin until it quivered.

The night air had a harsh, cool bite. Being far beneath the earth, it filled my body with ice. I shivered; my skin raised in goosebumps. My heart hammered in my ears as I wrapped my arms around myself, squeezing hard.

Thoughts raced from my mother and her dismay for me to my father and his determination to keep me safe. I wondered if they knew. Every waking moment, if they were aware, I had such a cruel blade hanging over my head.

Footsteps crunched behind me, Casimir's presence no longer as soothing but familiar all the same. "El?"

Some of the steel in my veins melted, and I whirled around, ducking into his chest. He faltered, shocked by the impact, but his arms tentatively wrapped around me all the same, a grounding pressure. One of his hands ran over my shoulder blade, gentle and hesitant. I tried to focus on his steady breath beneath my ear, hoping it would calm me.

I shook with the tears, surely leaving stains on Casimir's tunic. But the weight was too much, and I couldn't bear it alone anymore.

"I'm sorry," he whispered, the guilt thick in his voice.

I fought the urge to yell and take my anger out on him. It stung worse after the brief hope for a different life. A sanctuary meant for Roses to live without the fear of being used as a sacrifice. In the sinister part of my mind, I knew it had been too good to be true.

The realm continued to ask more of me than I wanted to give.

If I had only known sooner. My father, my mother, and Ronin, too; I could have spared them from protecting me from a destiny I had no hope of fighting.

Chapter Twenty-Three

I wore exhaustion like an old, worn cloak while I stalked toward the healer tent with Alba at my side the next day.

The night was full of dreamless sleep, something I wasn't accustomed to, and I felt somewhat guilty over how much sleep Casimir missed on account of me. But beneath the guilt, a cynical part of me viewed it as payback for the times he caused my sleep to be horribly unsatisfying. His interruptions of my nightmares only offered a small reprieve, considering his visits left me feeling as if I hadn't slept at all.

When the sun rose, Casimir ducked out with hardly a word, and Alba replaced him as fast as he'd left.

The events of the previous night suffocated me. I never had a chance to mention Ronin. It all fell apart when Orin spoke the damning words with a smirk of amusement on his face.

Alba walked beside me with a perpetual skip in her step. I was too aware of how my life had changed from constant isolation to constant company. It was a stark contrast, and I was grateful for the quiet month spent under the stars with Ronin. As if it could have prepared me for the amount of interaction Everbloom had.

When we entered the tent, Taryn sat among a pile of tattered washcloths. She didn't glance up from her task when we entered. Instead, she continued to fold the layers, her tongue poking over her bottom lip.

"Hello, gods to Taryn," Alba said, her voice a sing-song melody.

Taryn huffed a breath and whipped her head our way. She went from angry to sporting a wide grin.

"There she is! I was wondering when you'd return so I could swap those nasty buggers for you. Pick a cot; I'll come take a peek at your wounds in a minute." Taryn's accent reminded me a lot of the people from Woolfolk, and a pang of sadness rippled through my chest despite how chipper she greeted me.

I gave her a nod and sat down on a cot, still dressed in my sleep clothes. Alba placed her hands on her hips and stared at Taryn—her lack of patience dripped from every pore.

"Don't leave Elita waiting. Let me fold them," Alba chastised. "We're trying to get to the mess hall before all the goodies are eaten up. Poor Elita here has had nothing to eat yet."

When Taryn glanced over at me as if I were the impatient one, my face turned splotchy with warmth. "It's really no trouble. I'm not in a hurry," I stammered.

Alba giggled, my embarrassment entertaining to her.

Taryn stood and allowed Alba to replace her previous task.

I dreaded the next part as I shuffled my thighs further onto the cot. My hands worked at the bottom of my linen pants, and I pulled them up past my knees to give her a better view of the nasty cuts.

Taryn brought over a jar of salve and plopped down next to me. Her hand reached over to a basket, and she plucked it up, her healer supplies clattering when she placed it next to me. "Any new symptoms? Strange cough? Weird wheezing? I'm still not thrilled about the cursed water you swallowed," she said.

I shook my head. "This is the best I've felt in over a month, I think. Despite my emotional state after speaking with Orin."

Taryn gave me a knowing look before she surveyed my wounds. Her face scrunched with disapproval. "Hmm, I don't like those," she muttered, her focus on the cuts that adorned my shins.

To me, they didn't appear too awful. Not like they had been when I reached Everbloom. Then again, blood had crusted over the gashes back then, and the dirt had been washed away since the first healing.

Taryn didn't have to warn me—I knew she would place her hands on them. Her eyes darted back and forth as she started the healing. It tingled some, a subtle sensation beneath the skin.

Alba hummed to herself while she folded. The tune was off, but it made me grin. It was pleasant regardless, and it helped distract me from the sparks that moved through my skin.

Taryn pulled away after a few minutes, and her mouth puckered sideways in a way that showed her frustration. "Blasted boys and their ability to make everyone so anxious," she grumbled.

My face twisted with confusion, and she gave me an apologetic look. "Orin, Casimir, they're both a bunch of worrywarts. The General is worse, though. I wish they wouldn't have said anything to me about your bloom," she said. Her hands rubbed through her own bloomed hair. "The white is beautiful, but I don't like it."

"Taryn!" Alba scolded. She threw a cloth down and stood. "How is that any help to poor Elita?"

I resented how many times Alba attached that word in front of my name.

"What? I'm supposed to lie? It's a big job being tasked with healing the white bloom. I'd like to see you try to not feel anxious," Taryn said as she made quick work of redressing the wounds on my shins.

My fingers played with the hem of my linen top, and something about the sight of Taryn's petals made my chest clench with envy.

I gulped and took in a shaky breath when I noticed how damp my palms had become as I fidgeted. "I only have twenty-four more petals before my wilt begins." The words silenced the tent, and they both looked at me with somber expressions. The sweat on my palms increased. "I've dreaded my bloom all my life, but I think perhaps coming here made the reality more painful." It left my lips before I could shove the words away.

Guilt racked both of their faces.

"Elita—" Taryn started to say something, but I cut her off with a shake of my head and a half-hearted smile.

"It's okay. I just wish I had more time to prepare. To make matters worse, I think my father may have known. He never said anything." The vulnerability made me want to recoil and hide. But there was no shift of discomfort from them.

Taryn sat next to me. Her hand patted my knee. "Try not to go down the path of wondering what he did or didn't tell you. You won't get answers from the dead."

I averted my gaze to a spot on the floor and stared blankly until my eyes no longer ached with the sensation of tears. "I just don't understand, and it's been suffocating," I said, then braved a glance at Alba, who stood with her hands knotted into a cloth. The pity poured out of her, and I continued to war against the desire to retreat from the pain.

"The prince of the Iron Thorn visited me in my cell many times after their deaths."

Taryn winced, and I heard her gulp.

"They had my father's notebook. He insisted my father knew things. And that he knew of a hideout for Roses. It pains me to think he knew, and never told me."

Taryn's hand squeezed my shoulder, and she scooted closer. Both women gravitated toward me, and something about their presence—it soothed some of the grief.

"I wouldn't take a word Prince Talos said to heart. That family is purely wicked, and it's a shame if you let their lies taint the memory of your father. Don't let him have that power over you," Taryn said with conviction.

I nodded in reply, and in my head, I promised to attempt to rid his words from my thoughts. Even then, I couldn't get his twisted face out of my mind, and I despised speaking of him. I hadn't discussed the topic with Ronin. The wounds were too fresh, and I still managed to shiver then, when I remembered his hands on me and the torture I endured at his command.

A shallow breath fell from my lips, and I clenched my fists. Nails bit at my skin, nearly breaking it. "Sorry. I didn't mean to be so morbid," I said nervously. Both women shook their heads at me.

"Don't ever apologize for sharing your heart. I promise, even when it's painful, it's a good thing," Alba said, her grin already lifting her rosy lips.

Taryn was a stark contrast as rage swirled in her pale orange gaze. "Your demons can't haunt you here. If you let go of them, you'll find some peace. Just give it time." Taryn's words were heartfelt, but I could tell that some part of her still wrestled with those truths. "Now, you get out of here and go grab some grub before it's gone. Those wounds won't be healing any time soon if you're starved to death," Taryn said with a sideways grin.

I dipped my head and rose from the cot, heading for the exit.

Taryn swatted the cloth out of Alba's hand while she muttered under her breath that standing there didn't help. Alba didn't seem bothered, and she followed me out of the tent.

We carried on in silence, and when we passed my empty tent—to my dismay—I found myself wishing for Casimir's company. I went between saying something and leaving it, but the memories of torture left me on edge, and I glanced at Alba.

"Do you think we could find Casimir?" The question brought me a wave of humiliation, made worse when Alba snorted in response. I scrambled to explain myself. "Sorry. He's the only person I really know here, it's just easier—"

"Don't you worry, I know where to find him. It must be hard being somewhere new. I get it." She smiled at me. "It's this way."

We walked along the path, and Alba's pace quickened until I had to scurry after her as she left me behind. People continued to stare at me whenever I passed by, focused on my petals. They flashed white in the corner of my eye when I hurried alongside Alba.

I spent nearly a month in the woods trying to forget what happened in the Temple. It brought me an odd wave of guilt when the memories of torture pained me just as much as the sting of grief.

Though, in the same breath, I grieved what was taken from me. And every footfall rang in my head until it reminded me of the sound of Talos arriving at my cell. In a bout of agonizing flashes, his sneer followed me, along with the look of delight in his eye when he caused me pain. The way he watched the maids strip me, leaving me bare. My dignity stolen from me.

I once longed for a life outside of the cottage. For other people to see me. I would've traded anything to return to the life I had before the cottage burned, taking my family with it—before the Prince robbed me of any last shred of peace I had.

Somewhere in the woods, my mind had tried to erase his torture. But something about being in Everbloom, it came back with a vengeance.

When we reached a short but wide gray tent, Alba gestured to it. "He should be in there. But I should warn you—"

I didn't wait for her to finish. The echo of fear in my body after the talk about Talos made my skin crawl. It made me feel weak that I wanted Casimir's familiar presence, but regardless, I darted between the undone drapes.

Within a matter of seconds, I realized I made a terrible mistake.

Several men stood frozen in the tent, all stationed at different weapon racks or stands filled with armor. They gave me a curious look, and when I caught the movement of a figure I knew much too well, my cheeks burned a furious red.

Casimir paused a few feet away, an armor vest in his hands and his chest entirely bare. The edge of a scar peered over his shoulder, and I found myself staring for a moment too long. I opened my mouth to say something but stopped, pursing my lips.

He raised a brow. "Is something wrong?"

The heat traveled from my cheeks down my neck, and I shook my head, tearing my eyes away from his scar. "No, I...um."

A few snickers came from behind Casimir. He waved a hand over his head, silencing them. I peered back at the drapes to see Alba stifle a laugh with her hand.

"After Taryn redressed my wounds, I thought—" When I faced Casimir, he stood closer than before, the vest hanging loosely in his hand at his side. My focus fell to the long scar that continued over his shoulder.

"Was everything okay?" he asked.

I shook my head, immediately regretting it when he grew concerned. "It was fine. She just did another healing. We were talking about the Temple, and I wanted—"

Alba appeared at my side and placed a hand on my shoulder. "She's nervous with all these new people. I thought a friendly face would help calm her down." While it was a lie, I let her take the blame.

Casimir narrowed his gaze, surveying us both. His focus settled on me, searching my face for the truth beneath Alba's explanation. Despite the way his jaw tightened, his eyes softened with understanding.

Some of the tension dissipated when he went over to where he had previously stood before our interruption. He left the armor vest behind, rummaged through a pile of clothes, and threw on a black tunic.

I tried not to pay the other men any mind as they muttered to each other.

When Casimir came back to us, he held the drape open, and I ducked out. Over my head, he glared at Alba. "Perhaps next time, don't send her barreling into the men's barracks?"

Alba burst into laughter, and I added another glare in her direction. I made a mental note not to ask her for help again.

Casimir led both Alba and I through a path in the trees until we reached the Everbloom gardens just off the side of the mess hall. Despite my difficult conversation with Taryn and my awkward interruption at the barracks, I found myself in a much better mood once we were in the sunshine.

We sat outside at a weathered oak table that was empty except for the three of us, and I was grateful for the lack of extra bodies.

A stream ran a few feet behind our table. It gurgled softly, and a beautiful array of marsh marigold swayed along the edges of it. Familiar inky, black wings darted in and out of the flowers, chirping happily.

It was a decent distraction from the way Prince Talos and my father both filled my thoughts with painful memories.

The food that adorned my plate also did a wonderful job of drawing my attention elsewhere. It was the freshest food I had since the last stew I ate in Woolfolk.

Fluffy sourdough bread with honey drizzled over the top, strawberries, and a thick slice of pork filled my plate. I continued to devour it with abandon. The raven pitter-pattered closer, and I tossed it a strawberry. It pecked at it close to my legs.

Casimir's scrutiny across the table caught my attention, and I pointed my cutlery at him. "What's your problem?" I asked around a mouthful of food.

Amusement flashed in his gaze, and he shook his head at me. "I see you've traded your nightgowns for something more practical. Though sleep clothes aren't typically worn outside the tents."

I rolled my eyes. "I stand by how comfortable those gowns were, and if I had one here, I'd be in it right now." My fork dipped into another plump strawberry, and I bit into it, enjoying the burst of sweetness.

The linen pants and loose tunic I wore were much more comfortable than the leather pants and armor vests stashed away in my tent. I wouldn't change until I had to, and the first meal of the day didn't feel like a reason to swap out the comfort for tight leathers.

Alba stared at us both with a brow quirked. "What are you two going on about?"

From the corner of my eye, I saw Casimir smirk. It made my grin stretch wider.

I spent many years of my life with Casimir visiting me while I donned nothing but a nightgown and terror on my face. It was strange yet ordinary for me to be in his presence, speaking about things only us two knew.

Alba shook her head. "While I'm sure it's interesting, I promised Lyleen I'd help with garden tending today." She got out of her chair. "I leave the white bloom to you, Casimir. Don't let the girl give her entire meal to the bird," Alba said, her tone playful.

Casimir scoffed in response.

I waved goodbye to Alba while she sauntered away, her hair dragging behind her through the tall grass.

The raven came closer, and I leaned over, a small strawberry in my hand. It rolled off my palm, and to my surprise, the raven appeared to bow its head in thanks. I chuckled and sat straight.

My attention went back to the meal in front of me. The cutlery scraped on the wooden plate, which looked fashioned out of a tree stump.

Everything in Everbloom was more enchanting. From the flowers to their tables and dinnerware. It was all made from what was available to them in their underground oasis. It brought me a sense of peace, and I slumped further into my seat.

Casimir sat across from me, his body leaned back with his arms behind his head. The sun soaked against his black tunic, and I couldn't help but wonder about the scar I saw over his shoulder.

To my dismay, Casimir caught me staring at him. "Find something interesting?"

I sighed with vexation. "Not in the slightest," I replied before eating the last bite of bread.

Casimir chuckled and pushed his chair back. He stood and took the remaining plates off the table. I watched him walk the used items over to a barrel in front of the mess hall. He set them down among the other dinnerware.

When he strode back to the table, he didn't take a seat. "Do you feel up to exploring more of Everbloom?" he asked, his grin roguish.

That piqued my interest, and I nodded. The chair scraped against the stonework beneath it and the noise brought back more memories of my time in the Temple. I tried to block it out, even as my blood ran cold.

I was determined to see what I could of Everbloom before I left. Because I had to return to the Iron Thorn, eventually. And after spending so much time away from Talos, he would have even less restraint. It threatened to make me never leave, regardless of how I had to return to the kingdom—for Ronin and everyone else.

The hair on my neck stood, and a sick sensation rolled through my stomach. I avoided Casimir's questioning gaze and stepped away from the table. I didn't bother to return the chair.

"What caused the sudden sulking?" Casimir inquired.

"I'm not sulking." The way my voice pitched didn't help my case, and he raised a brow. "Does your offer to show me more of Everbloom rest on my emotional state?"

"You always did insist on making things difficult." He searched my face for a brief pause and let go of a sigh. "Fine, let's go."

We started down the path, and the raven plucked the last bite of strawberry from the ground and flew close behind.

The horrors that plagued my mind begged to be unleashed, and I had to war with my tongue to not allow the words to spill out. Talking to Taryn about Talos brought back things I tried to suppress.

I quickened my pace, almost passing Casimir. He let me stomp along the path without questioning me. He knew when I needed space to sort through my thoughts. It took him a few years of interruptions in my dreams before he caught on, but I was grateful for it at that moment.

In the chaos of running from the Iron Guard, I hadn't given myself much time to process my time in the Temple.

I didn't want to remember what Talos had done.

After moving through the thick woods, Casimir brought us to a stop at a different waterfall, one that ran out of the cavern wall and into a small pool below.

It shimmered in the sunlight, and wispy willow trees swayed near it, misplaced among the darker emerald trees at the front of Everbloom. The scene was magical. Despite the internal battle, I mustered up a smile.

"Yeah, this spot usually has a similar effect on newcomers," Casimir said, sounding pleased with himself.

"Hmm, you take all your haunts here, then?"

Casimir pursed his lips and looked away. I chuckled and watched him take a seat in the grass.

I followed his lead and sat, enjoying how the grass felt on my hands when I put them behind me. I rested back on my arms and closed my eyes to block out the beaming sun.

Without warning, another flash of Talos's snarl made me grimace. I couldn't find a moment of peace.

Sitting straight, I dusted my hands until they were free of the thin layer of dirt that clung to them. I pulled my knees to my chest and wrapped my arms around them; my chin rested on the worn linen of my trousers. I watched as the raven approached me, nestling in the grass beside me. Timidly, I reached out with one hand and ran a finger over its slick feathers. To my surprise, it allowed me to pet it.

"Are you going to tell me what's bothering you, or should I start guessing?" Casimir asked.

I turned my head in his direction, and curls fell in my face. I stopped stroking the raven's feathers and tucked the stubborn hair away.

The words kept trying to claw their way out. My body longed to spew the memories and give some of the burden away.

Unlike his typical manner, Casimir waited patiently for me to speak. I tried to push back the worst of it and talk about something easier. "I talked with Taryn briefly today," I said. One of my hands found a blade of grass, and I ran it between my fingers. "I know I won't ever get any answers, but I think my father knew about my bloom."

Confusion twisted Casimir's face. "How so?"

I shook my head and turned my gaze back to the water. "Just something the prince said." My voice caught the moment I mentioned Talos, and I hated how my body prickled. "You know, if you had visited me when I was trapped in the Temple, you would've already known." The lighthearted comment came out tinged with bitterness.

Casimir shrugged next to me. "I tried to visit your dreams once or twice. There wasn't much more I could've done."

My lips pressed into a tight line while I stared at the swirling water. It shimmered and churned in a dance that put me into a daze. But it wasn't enough to push the painful memories from my head.

I wanted to shake them free. I wanted to drown the flashes of Talos's snarl beneath the water. Most of all, I didn't want to have to shove my burdens onto Casimir. But it finally forced its way out.

"I think it may have been whatever the prince gave me." My skin crawled at the mention of Talos. "Some kind of tincture used for torture. I think it blocked everything out." I swallowed hard. "Either that or the pain—" my voice broke, and tears welled up. "The pain wouldn't let anything else in. It's probably why you couldn't reach me."

Casimir tensed, and I sensed him watching me. I couldn't bring myself to look at him while I tried to force the sting of tears back. They clung to the edge of my vision and blurred the scene.

"Elita." Casimir's voice lost its rough edge, making it harder for me to hold back the tears. "What happened in the Temple?"

I sucked in a harsh breath and shook my head. Wetness coated my cheeks rapidly, and I couldn't have stopped them if I tried.

"Some of the memories are gone, another side effect of whatever he made me consume. It felt like swallowing hot coals. I couldn't speak." My entire body shook at the mention of it. "And the day he left the marking, when they took my clothes—" I had to stop. I bit into my bottom lip to stifle a sob. Having my dignity stripped away continued to haunt me. The herbs, the bite of his nails, they didn't compare to the shame I felt when Talos watched them strip me down and force me to play the part of sacrifice and prisoner.

Casimir shifted next to me and his hands balled into tight fists.

My breath quivered. "I wish I could be rid of the marking. It brings back a lot of things I want to forget."

Fury flickered on Casimir's face, and he glanced at my neck, searching for the sacrificial marking, until he found the scar half hidden by my hair. He seemed at war in his mind, and his hands tightened more until his knuckles were ashen.

Tears continued to fall, but I didn't feel the need to hide them.

When Casimir tore his gaze from me, his jaw clenched. "The General's rules be damned. I should have crossed the border when your parents died," he said through gritted teeth.

I watched him grapple with the guilt. And even though I wanted to reassure him, the words wouldn't come.

He could have come for me. But he chose not to, at the word of a general. It was a different hurt, one that left a lingering ache in my chest.

Casimir sighed and unfurled his fists. "If I ever cross paths with that prince, it'll be his end," he spat.

In spite of myself, I offered a sideways grin. "We'll see who gets to him first. If it's a draw, we'll pull sticks to see who gets the first swing."

Chapter Twenty-Four

T
rees swayed along the edge of the backyard. I watched them as they bent, and leaves spun to meet the grass below in a delicate twirl.

Somewhere in the garden, I heard Father chuckle. His grin was one of pure joy, the lines across his face telling a story.

Close by, Mother sat on a stool, braiding a child's hair. I watched the scene, both there and not. A life I longed for.

Blonde curls and hazel eyes stared at my father as the child laughed. She looked every bit the same as me, and it made my heart ache. To exist without the Rose curse, to get to be a normal child, it was all I had ever wanted.

Giggles erupted through the garden, and the flowers opened to the sound, basking in the melodic tune.

Mother leaned forward and left a kiss on the hair of the little girl. Her rosy cheeks were adorned with freckles, and she smiled over her shoulder. It was everything I had always longed to be.

And slowly, the dream changed to something less bright, less chipper. Instead, it was Father braiding my curly black hair alone in the garden. His grin stretched wide across his sun-kissed face, and in the same way, the little girl turned and chuckled at him.

The sorrow echoed, but beneath the flowers, which drooped with grief, their roots were made of love.

The sun poured over the fabric of the tent, illuminating it in an uncomfortable manner. I grimaced against the brightness.

I ran my hands up my forehead and down my hair, counting the new petals down its length as I did so. I counted four new ones, their placement with no rhyme or rhythm.

When I looked over at Casimir, he appeared liable to keel over. He stood from the chair and stretched his arms above his head.

"Well, I hate to leave as soon as you're up, but being your guard is taking its toll on my sleep. Alba is going to show you around more today." He put his arms back down. The shadow of hair on his jaw was darker, and the circles under his eyes made his appearance all the more rough.

I nodded, not sure what to say after the previous day. The talk of Talos's torture was harrowing, and we'd spent our time exploring and eating the last meals in the stiff quiet.

"I'll be at the last meal of the day," Casimir said before darting out of the tent, the drapes left open in his wake. Feeling ill-prepared for so much socialization, I nervously bit at the skin on my lip. Nevertheless, it was enjoyable to have the chance. Even if I was part of a damning prophecy.

I got out of bed and noticed new clothes lying on top of the wooden chest. Upon completing the knot in the drapes, I approached the stack of clothing and changed into the gray tunic and dark brown leather pants, complemented by a matching leather vest to wear over my tunic.

There was a pair of black boots, and I slid them on and tied the laces, pulling them tight to my calves. After taking my time, I untied the drapes and looked out, but Alba was nowhere to be seen. The little black cat prancing my way assured me Alba wasn't far behind. Her long, willowy hair was hard to miss when I spotted her a few paces behind Astoria.

A few other people who passed by gave me an odd look. It made me uncomfortable, the way they stared, and I decided to meet Alba halfway, my strides long to close the distance.

Astoria was quick to rub against my boots, her fur sleek in the sunlight. I smiled and looked up at Alba, who was grinning from ear to ear. "Sorry, I got held up with the morning crowd. Did you sleep okay?" she asked.

After another undisturbed night, I nodded with a genuine smile.

"Perfect! I have so many fun things planned for the day," she said, her tone giddy. My curiosity piqued, excited to explore more of Everbloom.

I started to trail Alba when a tap on my shoulder made me jump. Galan stood behind me, a cloth bag in his hand, offered out to me. I stared at it and tilted my head up at him, confused.

"Sir Vanmore said you missed the first meal of the day and that you would need something to eat."

"Vanmore?" I asked, glancing at Alba.

"He means Casimir," she said with a wave of her hand. The realization that I hadn't known Casimir's family name made me bristle with embarrassment.

I smiled timidly at Galan and took the bag, opening it to see two slices of bread and an apple.

"My apologies if it isn't much. The breakfast crowd cleared much of the food."

"No, this is perfect. Thank you." I bit into the bread first, a delicious sourdough. I had to force myself not to devour it, realizing how hungry I was. "This is wonderful," I spoke around a mouthful, watching both Alba and Galan exchange amused looks.

"You have my thanks. I made it the other day," Galan said, a hint of nerves in his voice.

"Galan helps prepare all the meals. He's got a knack for it." Alba bumped his shoulder. He blushed and ducked his head in thanks. I bit back a coy grin. The way he flustered at her touch was endearing.

"Well, let's be on our way. The training grounds wait for no one!"

I nearly choked on the bread, sputtering. Alba giggled and turned with an elegant twirl, her hair dusting the path.

Galan gave me a reassuring smile and gestured for me to go in front of him. I followed Alba with hesitation, the words 'training grounds' not sounding pleasant at all.

It made the pit in my stomach grow. I ate my food in a hurry, shoveling it down to fend off the nervousness.

On the way, Alba explained the different tents to me, which Casimir had done, but I let her continue, enjoying the way she described everything as if she still experienced a fresh wonder at it all. It filled the silence, keeping my mind off the topic that haunted me.

'You are the final sacrifice. As told by the goddess herself.'

I tried not to think about how long Casimir was aware of the truth. I wanted to be naive, to believe he didn't know. He couldn't have.

I questioned how many other Rose people were aware.

Galan trailed along behind us, ever quiet, walking at a slower pace to not get ahead. He appeared content to listen to Alba recount all of their surroundings as if they both weren't locals.

At the mess hall, Alba started down a different path, a thinner one with trees looming over our heads as we walked through it.

Small wildflowers dotted the tree line, vibrant bursts of color that reminded me of home. *Windflower, butterflyweed, purple coneflower, goldenrod...* I named them in my head, beautiful flowers that weren't typical to find in the same climate, yet they thrived beneath the earth in the strange forest. Their colors were more vibrant than the dark hues in the Iron Thorn.

At the end of the narrow path, it opened to a massive field. The sight was strange. People jogged in a tight, purposeful line far off to the right, and several more sparred in the middle of the field, heads dodging a kick or a fist, their movements swift.

A line of archers practiced on targets further off to the left, their arrows singing through the air before they met with the targets.

When I noticed a man to the left slam his fist through a large rock, rubble flying in its wake, I flinched, taken off guard.

Alba giggled and put a hand on my arm. "Welcome to the Rose training grounds. We all practice and hone our abilities here."

"*Abilities?*" I gaped, my attention trailed back to everyone in the field, and I watched as a woman sparring conjured plants from the earth. Vines snapped and twisted around her opponent as she grinned manically. The captured Rose roared with the effort it took him to break free, conjuring his own roots from the ground.

I watched in awe and apprehension.

I had read books about abilities. Things the king and people like my mother feared. Witnessing it firsthand was surreal. Despite already encountering Taryn, her ability wasn't visible.

"Abilities vary among Roses. For example, Galan and I both have increased strength—well, and a few others. The General does, as well. Then there's Taryn and her healing. I can also heal, but I'm not too keen on it." She paused and tapped her chin. "Then the weird ones, like Casimir. Orin's abilities are hallucinogenic. Oh! There's one Rose I've heard of, and they can mimic an ability of Aeterna. I think it drains all the moisture from someone's body..."

Unease rolled through me.

Alba just grinned. "There's growth acceleration, which is kind of why Everbloom even exists. We can help the plants take root and grow quicker—I almost forgot, vines and roots. I'm probably missing a few. But you get the gist."

I surveyed the field, even more apprehensive than before.

"Have any strange things happened since your bloom began?" Alba rocked on her heels when she asked, eager for my answer.

"No. Nothing like that." I gestured toward the unbelievable sight in front of me as Roses moved vines from the earth. She deflated at my answer and crossed her arms, tapping her fingers on her arm.

"Not a problem at all. We'll figure it out," she said with confidence. She grabbed my arm and pulled me along. I looked back at Galan with mild panic, and he appeared to echo my apprehension.

"Alba, are you certain Ms. Blackthorne should be on the training grounds?" he asked, his voice catching in his throat.

"Oh, nonsense. Roses need to hone their skills. She'll be fine."

By his expression, Galan didn't think so.

I gulped, letting her bring me to the far end of the field, which was empty. Most of the other Roses had already stopped their training. All of them watched as Alba dragged me along.

My face burned with embarrassment.

"Let's start here, shall we?" Her voice carried a chipper tone when she released my arm and gestured at the area we stood in. I rubbed at my neck, unsure how to begin.

"Here, put your hands to the earth. Try to feel its life force. The pulse of the soil. The way the roots coil under the surface." She placed her palms on the ground and shut her eyes, taking a deep breath.

I watched her for a moment before I hesitantly reached down, placing my palms flush with the earth. With my eyes closed, a sense of foolishness washed over me while I attempted to search for the pulse or the twisting roots. All I felt was dirt.

"I feel nothing."

"Shh," Alba hushed sharply. I sighed and tried once more, breathing in and out, reaching for some kind of sensation or thrum. But there was nothing. I opened my eyes and stood, insecure with the many people observing my ineptitude.

Alba followed suit and put her hands on her hips. "How do you expect to learn if you won't try?" she scolded, her pitch too high for how serious she tried to sound.

"I felt nothing. Not even a tingle." I moved my fingers in the air in exasperation, and Galan snorted, covering his face to hide his laughter.

She huffed at us before her focus landed on the center field. "I've got it! You need something to encourage your abilities to kick in." She nodded to herself and grabbed my arm.

Galan deadpanned. "Absolutely not."

Alba waved him off and my stomach flipped when we neared the two who were sparring in the field.

They watched us with curiosity. Their clothes were covered in a thin layer of dirt and bloody scratches adorned their arms and their jaws.

My unease continued to grow.

We reached them, and Alba let go, gesturing to me with both hands. "Elita would like to spar with you."

My face paled. "I what?"

"Alba." Galan's voice was a warning, but with a wave of her hand, he clenched his jaw and shook his head.

The two people laughed.

"D'ya think that's the best idea, lass?" The man spat the words at

Alba, his accent one I had never heard. Alba stepped aside and left me standing next to the two strangers.

He let out a belly laugh and shrugged. "She can't even conjure the earth, ya' think she can spar?"

"She needs help with getting them up and going. No better way than to put her in a stressful situation. The earth will move for her."

Panic made me lightheaded, and I looked at Galan, pleading.

"A'right then," the man grunted, his arms stretching behind his back. The girl who was sparring with him snickered and moved to the side. They all left me to stand face to face with the man.

Everyone on the training grounds paused to watch and muttered to each other. Sweat prickled at my skin as the nerves built, observing the way the stout man sized me up, a flicker of disgust in his face as he studied my petals.

Alba stood off to the side, a serious look on her face, her arms crossed. Her voice rang through the field. "Sparring may begin."

The statement echoed in my ears. My heart sank, and a heavy feeling settled in my limbs.

The man chortled and charged. His footsteps thundered on the packed earth and I yelped, stumbling sideways to dodge him. My hair bristled past him as he nearly rammed into me. Dust rose in his wake, making it harder to see.

My pulse raced, and I stood, watching as he circled me. An animal on the prowl. The earth shook beneath my feet, but it wasn't me who conjured it.

Roots snapped out of the ground, dirt flying in their wake.

I did my best to dodge. My body was just quick enough, slightly more agile than his burly frame. I used the skills I'd gained from hunting with my father, and then again, the skills of dodging and sprinting over obstacles I had grown used to with Ronin.

It wasn't enough.

He was quick, his roots grabbing a hold of my ankle as I went to jump over them. He pulled me to the ground with a slam.

I groaned, tasting dirt and blood. The sudden impact made me gasp for air, and as I frantically rolled, I caught a glimpse of a root barreling toward me. I spat blood and scarcely got out of the way. I scrambled to my feet, the adrenaline burning in my veins.

The earth refused to move for me.

He chased after me, his amusement evident. Galan shouted something, and Alba's own features grew nervous while she moved to step in, waving a hand overhead. They weren't quick enough.

The man slammed into me, and the impact took me by surprise. I heaved, my lungs emptied of air while I fell once more, my vision spotty.

I groaned and tried to take a breath. I regretted trusting Alba again. The many years I spent alone made it difficult for me to say no, and I paid the price. Just as my body had been able to rest and try to heal, every muscle ached again as I rasped, begging for air.

"What the fuck is going on here?" Someone shouted above the ringing in my ears.

I spit out dirt and blood, getting on my hands and knees. My tunic and vest had a thin layer of dirt on them, and speckles of blood made a strange contrast to the light dirt.

"Casimir—"

"No. Don't say a word, Alba," Casimir snapped. His boots approached my peripheral, striding across the field in a rush. "What do you think you're doing, Novian?" he growled and closed the space until he glowered at the man I'd horribly failed to spar, Novian.

"Just a bit a sparrin' is all. She challenged me." Novian grinned, and I almost laughed, but the air wasn't all the way back in my lungs.

Casimir kneeled in front of me and put his hands on both of my shoulders to help me sit up straighter. He looked me over for wounds, his eyes livid, the dark circles prominent beneath them. Dirt-coated curls fell in my face when I met his scarlet gaze—close enough for me to make out a small scar on his jawline.

"Elita is new here," Casimir said, breaking eye contact to glare over my head at the people standing behind me. "Did it not occur to any of you that maybe she needs to ease her way into it? Or, I don't know, maybe spar with someone who isn't a total ass?"

"S'everyone but the precious white bloom is allowed to spar?"

Casimir stood, and I nearly fell face-first into the dirt when his hands released my shoulders.

"Shut your damn mouth before I do so for you." Casimir's threat echoed through the field. "Would you spar a child? Because I can assure you, any child here would know more about sparring than her."

My brow quirked, irked by Casimir's example.

Galan appeared at my side and offered me his hand. I took it, thanked him, and stood.

Novian laughed and shook his head, throwing his hands up. "Lass doesn't get special treatment, not from the likes of me." He shrugged and went toward his previous sparring partner.

Casimir took a step in Novian's direction, but Alba stood between them and shook her head, looking guilty as she said, "I'm sorry. I thought it would help her activate."

Casimir whipped around and closed the distance until he stood before me.

My hands halted their effort to dust off my tunic when he reached forward, a thumb pressed to my chin to get me to turn my cheek. Warmth rushed beneath his skin, the touch oddly tender. Using his fingers, he guided me to face the other way to survey the damage, gentle while he caressed my jaw.

Sparks of rage swam in his eyes as they flicked to mine, shadowed by the crease of his worried brow. For a fleeting second, his attention fell to my lips, likely noting the cause of the copper taste in my mouth. He lingered for a pause, then met my wide eyed stare once more.

Gods, he'd never been so close before. He'd never looked at me with such intensity.

An odd flutter quivered in my chest.

"Are you alright?" he asked, releasing me and breaking the tension to inspect the spatters of blood on my tunic.

I swallowed, a shallow breath pulling back into my lungs. When my pulse steadied, I nodded and wiped my mouth. Blood smeared the back of my hand.

"Please tell me I still have all my teeth," I muttered, running a dirty finger over them. Casimir didn't seem to find it amusing. "I'm fine, honestly. Alba meant well." I smiled in her direction and she blanched, coming closer to grab my chin.

"Oh, Elita, I'm so sorry. You look as if you've eaten a hundred beets. No missing teeth, though," she assured, letting go of my face.

Casimir stared at me, his expression wild with barely contained anger. I saw the exhaustion that lingered beneath it.

"Go rest. I'll be fine. They can take me to get cleaned up with Taryn. Plus, I need another healing anyway." I tried to reassure Casimir, shaking off Galan's hand. "I'm fine. Steady as an oak."

No one found my attempts to defuse the tension comical. I pursed my lips, immediately regretting it when I realized how sore my mouth was.

Galan stepped closer to Casimir, the mood shifting when Galan's expression tightened with newfound concern.

"Did you finish speaking to Sir Orin?" Galan asked.

I stared at them, unsure where the question came from.

"Yes," Casimir ground out, his gaze never leaving mine. "I just left from there when I heard a few others making bets that the new girl would be out cold within ten seconds." He shot another scowl in Alba's direction.

"Is the General returning?" Galan prodded in a hushed voice.

Casimir gave him a warning look that made me want to recoil. Galan swallowed and nodded.

Alba tensed, and they all exchanged worried glances. I wished so badly to read minds. The secrecy was enough to drive me mad.

Alba put a hand on my shoulder, speaking softly. "Let's get you to Taryn." She led me out of the training field, away from Galan and Casimir.

Chapter Twenty-Five

Casimir was absent at the last meal of the day. I scanned the crowd for him. My search only found faces I didn't want to see again. Novian and his friend snickered while I waited in line to be served stew full of vegetables and herbs. The pleasing aroma of rosemary and beef provided a welcome distraction.

Taryn had patched my injuries as she scolded Alba and me over the fact I was already healing at a slow pace, and I went and got my head knocked around. No one had chastised me with such intensity since my mother reprimanded me for trying to sneak off to a festival.

Alba didn't leave my side after that. Though the conversation was strained, her mood depleted. Taryn made her feel awful.

Galan joined us in the line for the meal, his normal withdrawn and stoic composure back. He appeared more like a guard, his expression grim, always searching the crowd as they moved about.

New aches echoed throughout my body, but I strangely wanted to spar again. I hated the smug expression Novian had. I wasn't typically prone to violence, but I wanted to wipe the floor with his face.

We ate in silence. Galan and Alba continued to display their upset at each other, and I couldn't help but mirror Galan after Alba got me into the mess.

Halfway through the meal, I scanned the bustling hall for Casimir again, my eyes strained in the warm glow of the candles hung overhead. He never showed, and for all the years I wished to be free of his presence, I found myself agitated without him there.

A few tables across from ours, the woman from my first night there, Elrin, glowered in our direction. I swallowed and avoided looking her way again. Alba took note of my discomfort and sighed.

"Don't take it personally. Elrin is rude to everyone," she said, pushing around her food.

"What does she have against me? I've never even spoken to her."

Galan's head snapped up, and he stared Alba down. She pursed her lips, trying to hold back a small grin. He shook his head at her.

"Well, she really takes issue with Casimir—"

"Alba, don't," Galan chided.

She chuckled and waved a hand in the air. "They were involved with each other. But it was brief. She just hates anyone who hangs around him. That's all."

I eyed the two of them while they seemed to have a silent conversation. Where Alba was amused, Galan continued to give her a look of disapproval.

Despite not wanting to, I met Elrin's glare once more. She turned away and muttered something to the person next to her. Neither of them glanced back at me, but I had the awful feeling I was the topic of their conversation. Worse yet, it made me oddly uncomfortable that she and Casimir previously had a relationship. I wondered why he never told me.

People passed by and started up small talk with Alba, asking about garden tasks the next day or what the week would entail. Those were the only words spoken, leaving me in solitude with my thoughts, which circled around the horrible truth of my bloom.

The choice sounded so obvious, but the fear crippled me. Returning to the Temple meant handing myself over to Talos willingly. When I thought of the horrible things he'd do, it paralyzed me, and I couldn't bring myself to leave Everbloom. Not yet.

No longer hungry, I stood, pushing my chair out with more force than I intended. Alba and Galan both looked at me with wide eyes, a spoon half raised to Alba's mouth.

"Ms. Blackthorne?" Galan's timid voice was nearly inaudible as I left the mess hall.

I started the trek back to my tent, ignoring the sound of Alba yelling for me to wait up, her footsteps swift behind me.

When I reached my tent, I didn't bother to tie the drapes, knowing Alba would be right behind me. And sure enough, she came into the tent, out of breath. She said nothing, and I didn't turn to address her.

I walked to the bed—the petals in my hair a flash of white as I flopped down on the cushion.

Alba sighed. "When you're done being dramatic, let me know."

I rolled over and glared at her, though she looked unphased. "Alba, I ache from my head to my feet, and due to my ineptitude, I have managed to get everyone I've ever cared about killed, or I've put them in harm's way. I've earned the right to sulk for a moment."

"You're right, and I'm sorry…but shouldn't that make you want to try harder to activate your abilities?"

I mulled over what she said. There wasn't enough time left for me to hone my abilities, not truly. But until I found the courage to leave, I couldn't deny the desire to at least know what it felt like.

And maybe when I returned to the Iron Thorn, I would be able to find Ronin and save him for a change.

I sat in the bed, working my hair into a braid over my shoulder. The petals popped out at a few of the loops in my hair. When I finished, I said, "I want to learn my abilities. I want to know what it feels like before I die."

Alba grinned an almost manic smile. "That's what I like to hear."

Alba was giddy as we entered the training field, the area drenched in black, with no sign of anyone else. Her long hair trailed behind her while she skipped, perpetually joyful. I envied her for it.

Small curls escaped the braid I had done, framing my face along with a few striking white petals.

An overwhelming sense of excitement washed over me as we neared the center of the sparring field, where the dirt had a sandy hue, which was illuminated by the moon that beamed down on it.

We ventured toward the middle of the field with the cool bite of the harvest season air on our faces.

Alba stretched her arms over her head. "I'll demonstrate my abilities first, and after that, we can work on finding your trigger."

I nodded, curious to see what she could do.

She didn't disappoint.

With a flick of her wrists, she summoned vines from the earth, their tendrils twisted and tangled before they encircled us in the field. I watched in fascination as she continued to pull more from the ground.

She gave an eager grin, and then she jumped, flipping as she did. The vines whipped at the ground, following her every move. The display was both stunning and terrifying, with thorns so sharp, they appeared deadly.

Her long hair trailed behind her, but she remained unphased when the curls danced across her vision. She dashed, flipped once more, and her vines obliterated a practice dummy, causing the wood to splinter as if it were a twig.

I watched in awe.

With another lift of her arms, the vines climbed up around her in a circle, coiling toward the sky until they made a dome above her of thorn-covered vines, closing her inside.

My heart hammered for a moment in anticipation when the thorns and vines split open with audible force. Debris fell everywhere, and Alba stood in the center of it. She did a small bow, pleased with her work.

"That was incredible," I breathed as she walked back to me, no sweat on her brow or any outward sign of strain.

"Well, thank you, it was quite fun. It isn't often I need to use my abilities. It's fun to show off from time to time."

I chuckled. "I can see why." My amazement turned into apprehension, and I tightened my braid with shaking hands.

Her grin fell into a softer smile. "You have it in you. Just gotta find it. Remember, hands on the ground, feel the earth. It only seems impossible until it isn't."

I nodded despite the trepidation. Leaning down, I placed my hands on the dirt, closed my eyes, and took a deep breath. And I waited.

The minutes ticked on, every passing second turned into unexpected anger. It boiled beneath the surface as I fought the feeling of being inept. I wanted it to be simple. The lack of time screamed at me. I wouldn't hone my abilities before my wilt. It wasn't meant for me.

My brow furrowed, and sweat glistened over my skin. The tension was unbearable, causing a deep ache in my arms. I sighed and sat in the dirt, my hands trembling. The anger forced its way over to sadness—the build-up too much.

Alba sat next to me, silent for a moment while she stared at where my hands had been, handprints left in the dirt.

"Whatever's holding you back, you can't hold on to it forever." Alba's voice was gentle.

The lump in my throat grew as tears threatened to escape. "I don't know how to move past it. When I used to dread my bloom, there was a peace knowing that my parents would be free of my curse. Instead, they died—" My voice broke, and I ran a hand over the petal-adorned braid. "Their deaths were brutal, and I brought it upon them." A shaky breath rattled my chest. "I continue to put those around me in harm's way, and I'm still too much of a coward to do what is required of me."

At my side, a familiar black figure fluttered from the sky, landing close to my hand. The raven watched me for a pause before it came closer, perching on one of my hands.

Alba ran a palm over the prints I left and cleared the spot before laying her own hands down. She breathed in and out. The movement of the dust against her skin was subtle yet deliberate.

She opened her eyes, and the dust settled. "I lost my family when they tried to protect me from a similar fate." Alba ran a finger over the dust on her palm. "They died in Tyvolia while trying to keep me safe. Their last breath was full of dust and sickness. I would have died, too, had it not been for Astoria. She led me here." She smiled somberly as she recalled the memory. Her gaze went to the raven on my hand.

"You know, I think she may be your familiar, the raven. She follows you everywhere."

I wiggled my fingers, and the raven chirped, lifted its wings, and landed on my shoulder, to my surprise. "She's followed me since my buds appeared."

Alba hummed to herself. "Sounds about right. They typically appear when our abilities begin to take root. Not every Rose has one, but many do. The raven signifies prophecy and rebirth."

Feathers brushed across my cheek as the raven moved. The significance brought me more unease.

"You should give her a name."

From the corner of my eye, I watched the raven pick at its wing with its beak. It took me a moment to think. The color of her feathers sparked an idea, and I tilted my head. "Calla." I faced Alba. "It's the first thing that comes to mind. Her feathers remind me of calla lilies."

Alba smiled. "Trust me, if the name feels right, they likely requested it." She turned her gaze back to her hands. They shook, and she flexed them. Beneath her nails had a layer of dirt, and after a moment, she started to pick at it.

I watched her, unsure if I should say something.

Silence fell over the field. It made it more obvious when Astoria appeared at Alba's side. The cat rubbed at her arm, sat, and peered up at her. Alba's breath shuddered, and she pet the cat.

There was a long pause before she spoke. "When I lost my parents and my sisters, I resented being alive. I was mad at the gods, even Astoria. The anger consumed me for a long time."

I pursed my lips and watched sadness cross her face.

"Casimir was my first friend here, though he feels more like an older brother now. He helped me more than anyone else with training and learning to let go. It doesn't mean we don't grieve the people we lost or the ones we couldn't save, but it means we do something with the life we were given. A way to honor those we have lost." She smiled and wiped at her face, clearing a few stray tears. The action left wet streaks of dirt behind. She appeared all the more a warrior for it. For being only eighteen or so, she was wise beyond her years when it came to grief.

"I'm sorry about your family, Alba," I whispered.

She nodded and stood, dusting her trousers off. She offered me her hand. I sighed and took it, getting to my feet.

"Ready to let that weight go?" she asked.

And I didn't know any other answer. I couldn't find another way. So, with a single nod from me, Alba clasped her hands together, burying the pain.

"Let's start with some old-fashioned spar moves, then."

The next few hours consisted of ducking, rolling, learning how to throw a proper punch, and agonizing time spent trying to commune with the earth. Our familiars were long gone, likely sick of the repetition.

I was out of breath when I dodged another of Alba's quick advances, liking the way it felt to move out of the way. Though it was obvious, she continued to hold back for my benefit. A teaching lesson, not a true spar.

She kicked a leg up, the force of it sprawling my hair away from my face, my braid long ago let loose as I tried to keep up with her quick movements. I panted but didn't stop moving. Every few seconds, she advanced again. Her intention was to teach me how to anticipate attacks, how to dodge them, or even counteract them.

When her fist approached me, I grabbed her wrist, attempting to turn her advance to my leverage. But her experience had her swiftly switch the advantage and flip me over, falling into the dirt with a grunt.

I rolled and sprang up, my muscles in a newfound soreness. My mind struggled to keep up, and it tried to make the connections it needed to anticipate what was coming or how to best Alba. She was well-trained and relentless.

When another hit from her heel to my shoulder sent me stumbling to the ground, she called it quits. Another round of trying to activate my abilities came next.

The sun began to rise; the dome offered a brief glimpse of the orange painted in the sky.

I heaved a breath and sat with shaking limbs.

My fingers trembled when I reached forward, a thin sheen of sweat on my skin. I pressed my damp palm to the earth, no longer needing her instruction. The only breaks I took were spent on the ground, attempting to sense the pulse within the earth.

Alba was out of breath as well. The hours spent training took a toll on her. She sat close by, giving me some space.

Again, I closed my eyes, and my mind reached out for memories of my family. I searched for the hurt and the shame I carried and leaned into the emotions instead of fighting them.

The ache in my chest burned, the kind that wasn't from physical exertion. The grief threatened to crush me. But love burst beneath the grief, the very reason I ached for my family in every waking moment. I couldn't erase their deaths; I couldn't help them. There was nothing left to change, nothing left to control.

I made room for the grief, letting the reality settle in.

My pulse thrummed in my hands. The sweat that coated them started to dry. Dirt clung to the dampness. I was able to sense my heart-beat in my palms, thudding in a rhythmic pattern.

It wasn't right. The pulse didn't belong to me.

My hand pulled back as a jolt of shock surged through me. I glanced at my palms, then shifted my attention to Alba, who appeared as though she might keel over at any moment.

"I felt something," I said breathlessly. The excitement was enough to wake me up.

She straightened, grinning from ear to ear. "It starts as just a flicker, but soon it'll be as if you two are beating in sync." Excitement laced her voice, though it wasn't enough to hide her exhaustion. "You ready to head back yet?"

I chuckled and stood, dusting my clothes. "That made me a lot less tired, but I suppose I should rest. Sorry to have kept you up."

She waved me off and stood. "It was worth it, and I feel I owed you after getting you into that mess with Novian. Plus, there's nothing quite as cathartic as staying up all night sparring."

"The sparring took it out of me." I rubbed at my arms.

"You did well, especially for someone who spent their life locked in a cottage."

I shrugged in response and left the training grounds, finding my way back to the narrow path through the trees.

The forest awoke with early risers. People made their way to the feasting hall to get it ready for the first meal. Some individuals flocked toward what looked to be a giant garden, items in hand, as they murmured on their way to their daily work.

The fatigue set in after a sleepless night. My body had not recuperated from the previous lack of sleep when I was separated from Ronin.

Astoria jumped off a market stand in front of us and pranced toward Alba, who scooped up the cheery cat.

"You lazy girl, you slept away while we trained all night. Now you're going to pester me for food, is that it?" Alba scratched behind Astoria's ear. "I'll meet up with you in a bit, Elita. I need to run to my tent and get her something to eat, if you don't mind."

"'Course not," I said sleepily, waving them off.

She hurried off with Astoria and went toward the other group of housing tents. I sighed and took a moment to appreciate being alone for the first time since I found Casimir.

While I didn't enjoy solitude much, I was unaccustomed to being around that many people. There was a sense of contentment in being present for a moment, in the stillness of my thoughts as I walked along the path leading to my tent.

Only a few people passed me by, heading toward the busier tents or gardens. While a few of them waved, most looked the other way and continued on without a glance.

It was strange being able to hold my head up, not averting my gaze to avoid others seeing what I was. I got to exist in peace. It was a gift— one my family and Ronin fought for me to have, even though it wouldn't last. I would revel in the beauty of it for a moment.

The darker wash of my tent stuck out like a sore thumb when I approached it. I continued to take my time, my pace slowed by the new strain. But the fatigue didn't outweigh how good it felt to sense the thrum of the earth beneath my hands. It was intoxicating.

"Aye, lass!"

I turned rapidly, the voice catching me off guard. Novian stood near a tent, a smug grin on his face.

"In a hurry?" he inquired, his brow quirked. "Or are you ready for another match?"

I tensed and continued to walk.

"Aye!" he called, his footsteps trailing me.

My stomach turned as my pace increased. Not enough to combat his longer stride.

"Think it's nice to walk off, d'ya?" He got in front of me, walking backward. I pursed my lips, unwilling to entertain his strange desire to fight me. "C'mon, lass, don't make me keep asking."

The nerves curled in my gut, and I glanced over my shoulder, hoping Alba would turn the corner. I continued to ignore him, which enraged him further.

"Please, leave me alone," I said.

He sneered, then tsked. "Can't back out of a spar like that. Gotta finish it. Rules are rules."

I recoiled when he stopped in front of me, preventing me from going any further. I gulped and looked past his shoulder. My tent was only a few feet away. His demeanor gave me the impression he would continue to bother me even if I made it to my tent.

"I didn't even want to spar," I said nervously and tried to move past him. He put out an arm to stop me, his hand pressed against my shoulder. I grimaced and pulled back, almost stumbling off the path. My breath trembled, and I tried not to think of Talos's hands on me. The roughness reminded me too much of the prince.

Novian laughed sickly, his face twisting in satisfaction. "Ya won't get special treatment from me because of your white bloom," he hissed.

I regretted staying out or letting Alba leave my side.

Novian went to step closer when he froze, his gaze over my head. He huffed a frustrated sigh and stepped back, grumbling under his breath. "Stupid sulking boy..."

"Would you care to repeat that a bit louder?" Casimir's voice came from behind me, his presence warm and familiar, like the many times he chased away the nightmares.

"Ya, special treatment for the forest pet," Novian spat.

Casimir stood beside me, his shoulder close to mine. "I'm going to assume you aren't aware of who she is, or what she means to some of the people here and give you a chance to leave. Otherwise, you can spar with me instead."

Novian turned pink at the suggestion, displaying his lack of confidence in his ability to spar with Casimir. I held back a chuckle at his expression. I didn't need to give him any more reason to hate me.

Novian shook his head, nearly uttered a remark, shook his head again, and turned to leave.

I sighed and released my shoulders, not realizing how tense I had become. Casimir didn't move while he watched Novian disappear.

When he was gone, Casimir faced me. "Why are you out by yourself? Where's Alba?" he asked, not bothering to hide his upset.

The relief turned to frustration.

"You know, I could even walk Eldravine on my own, and yet in a place I'm supposed to be safe, I need a guard at all times? Sounds absurd to me."

Casimir sighed and ran a hand over his face. "What are you doing up at this hour?" He tried instead.

"Didn't sleep. Sparred all night with Alba."

His expression was comical. "Ugh, Alba... You'll need to catch at least a few hours of sleep. I'll stay to guard your tent. It's a busy day and had she waited, I intended to bring you to the training grounds today for *proper* training."

I rolled my eyes and continued toward my tent. He followed, never too far behind. I looked over my shoulder, offering him a mischievous smile. "Oh, and you'll have to tell me what happened with Elrin. I'm curious."

Casimir stopped in his tracks, glanced at the sky, and shook his head. "I swear, Alba has a death wish." He met my stare and continued to follow along. "You need sleep first," he said, avoiding the conversation.

I fought the urge to prod and let him catch up until he was beside me. While walking in silence had been nice for a moment, I was grateful I didn't have to be alone anymore.

Chapter Twenty-Six

"For the last time, I didn't abandon her," Alba groaned. She didn't seem built for Casimir's scolding, and it reduced her to someone akin to a small child throwing a fit. I held back another chuckle while I watched them bicker.

The sun was kind, and streaks of glorious light poured into the dome. The warmth soaked into my skin as we sat in the gardens—which overflowed with flowers—tearing through pieces of bread Galan had brought since I had slept through the second meal of the day.

Despite Casimir's mocking, I wore a pair of loose linen trousers and a white tunic. Sleepwear, according to him, but the leather armor didn't appeal to me.

Galan and I both watched the exchange in amusement. My raven, Calla, joined me, perched on my thigh. I offered her another nibble of dried oats. Her feathers ruffled, and I continued to watch the argument unfold. Though Casimir was serious, I found it comical. Alba had already apologized many times for leaving me to walk alone after Casimir told her Novian approached me.

Casimir continued to glower at Alba when he spoke. "According to the General, someone is at her side at all times. I'd have thought you'd be able to understand something so simple; I suppose I was mistaken."

Alba's face fell, and I stopped chewing and sat straighter. Calla jumped from my thigh and perched on my shoulder.

"I'm fine, honestly," I said around a mouth full of bread.

It didn't seem to ease Alba's guilt.

"Of course," she said quietly. "I will admit, I was dead tired following the training."

"Pointless training? Foolish and a waste of time. Then you forgot your actual duty—"

"Not a waste of time," I cut in, my tone firm, disheartened by how upset Alba was. She wasn't at fault. I assured her I could walk back to my tent. I hadn't bet on crossing paths with Novian, of all people. The luck I had was staggering.

Casimir quieted and turned his attention to me, the scowl remaining on his face. He waited for a moment, expectant.

"Oh," I sputtered, dusting my hands from the flour that lightly coated the bottom of the sourdough. "I learned a lot of things last night. She wouldn't let me quit until I felt the pulse from the earth. She's a wonderful teacher." I offered her a small smile of reassurance, to which she returned, perking up at the compliment.

"And to top it off, you didn't let her quit. Nice."

"Cas." My voice came out too rough, too stern. I had to fight the embarrassment when they all stared at me, surprised. Casimir raised a brow, waiting for me to continue.

"At any point, I would have been able to quit if I wanted. It was my choice. Alba helped me find what I needed in order to awaken my abilities. It's not on her."

He clenched his jaw, a clear sign of his disapproval, but remained silent. For a pause, I was taken aback. Casimir's focus trained on me, familiar irises, no longer a flicker in my dreams. He was still rough around the edges outside of my sleep, a stonewall of a man with little room for his mask to slip.

I turned from him and back to Alba, seeing she was already preoccupied while she talked with Galan about me communing with the earth. I caught a few giggles among them as she retold it. My skills must have been amusing.

Calla bristled on my shoulder. Casimir stared at her, confused. "What's with the bird?"

Feathers fluttered close to my cheek. "My familiar? I think?" I looked to Alba, who was preoccupied with Galan.

Casimir appeared exasperated. "You let her convince you of that nonsense? All the sleep you missed for you to believe childish musings."

Calla squawked as if replying to him. I chuckled, grabbed more oats, and offered them to her. She picked at them happily.

"Say what you want, but she's followed me all the way from Eldravine. She's appeared to me since before my parents died."

The mood shifted, and his features softened.

Alba peered around Casimir and jabbed a finger at him. "Don't listen to this guy. He scared off his familiar, so he's just jealous. Aren't you, Vanmore?"

Casimir gave her a look that screamed 'shut up'.

"Scared it off? What was it?" I directed the question at Alba, knowing Casimir would be too stubborn to answer.

"It's a pity, really. It was such a lovely white owl. Poor thing is probably beside itself without a purpose now." Alba frowned at Casimir. He rolled his eyes and turned his back to her.

She giggled and returned to her conversation with Galan. Her own familiar was never too far, and I caught sight of Astoria darting through the grass close by.

After a moment, I stood, my gaze finding Casimir once more. "While I actually want to hear the rest of the story behind that, I have things I've been meaning to discuss with you and Orin," I said. Calla flapped her wings a few times on my shoulder before she took off.

Casimir's cheek twitched. "You mean your friend Ronin?" He sounded annoyed.

I crossed my arms in reply, my turn to be bothered. "The one who saved me from being tortured?" Anger boiled under the surface, mixed with guilt. Ronin had waited long enough while I sat in comfort.

The memory of the cell was never too far from my mind. The countless days spent on the stone floor and the way the guards and Talos treated a Rose, someone they weren't meant to harm—it pained me to think of what Ronin endured at their hands.

I grimaced and rubbed at my arms, soothing the way my skin crawled. "Please, Casimir. I have to speak with Orin."

He sighed and ran a hand over his jaw. "Fine, if you insist. However, we aren't permitted to go over the border, and I wouldn't expect him to be of any help when it comes to rescuing a norm."

"A norm?"

"Normal. No abilities. Not a Rose." He shrugged, and I experienced a pang of disgust, thinking of my parents, of Ronin, the woman who died on my account in Woolfolk—of all the people who were 'normal' yet kind, with full and wonderful lives. To know a Rose would leave them to suffer made me ill. I kept my mouth shut, afraid if I opened it, I would curse him to the gods and back.

Reluctantly, he gestured toward the path through the garden's wooden fences, which were overgrown with flowering vines. We trudged through them, and I stayed behind a few paces, needing a moment to compose myself.

I worried if Orin spoke the same way about someone who was in need, I would lose my temper. The pent-up frustration, fear, distrust— it overwhelmed me.

With a steady inhale, I allowed the clean air to enter my lungs, exhaling as I tried to calm myself. I intended to plead my case to Orin, hoping for his help and, if not, perhaps Casimir's. Deep down, I understood I would likely have to rescue Ronin alone.

The path twisted through the trees as we continued on a route I hadn't been before. The tents were scarce and black, hidden with purpose within the thick trees that stretched high above them. They were strategically placed, hardly visible.

Before long, we approached a different structure at the end of the narrow trail. It appeared as a menacing fortress in the woods, crafted from dark gray stones. It doubled the size of the mess hall. It was misplaced in the chipper, colorful gem of Everbloom.

Guards flanked each side of the entrance, bows across their backs, swords at the ready in a hilt, no more than a swift pull away. They caught sight of our approach, their leather armor a slick onyx. Cloaks with a single broch at the center draped over their shoulders, out of the way in case they needed to engage in combat. They gave a single nod at Casimir. They appeared to know him.

It wasn't until I was close enough to observe their attire that I noticed Casimir wore similar leather armor. They showed obvious respect for him as if he were ranked above them. In an instant, it clicked for me. He was part of their guard.

I stared at his back and studied the way he walked with purpose and ease. He had been to the stronghold many times before. He looked welcomed and at home there. His duty to guard me since my arrival didn't seem as strange.

"Captain Vanmore, sir." They pressed a fist to their shoulder in a type of salute, and I nearly choked on words as they tried to fly out. The respect and title sent me reeling. Casimir stood a little taller and gave them a dismissive nod.

They returned to their rigid stance and let us walk through, not paying me a single glance.

Casimir rapped his knuckles on the door and stepped back. His foot tapped on the stone steps. It took less than a minute for it to swing open. Another guard was present inside, who saluted him the same way the others had, muttering his title and surname once more.

Orin sat in an iron chair at the end of an oblong table, which was littered with papers, scattered weapons, books, and an oddly placed teacup. Steam swirled from it. On either side of the stone room were two wooden doors, blocking my view from the rest of the fortress.

Weapon racks lined the left side wall, and a massive map hung on the opposite side, marked up with red ink. It resembled a war room.

Orin glanced up from the papers he studied, his white hair falling into his eyes. He smoothed the slick hair back and stood, giving a nod to Casimir.

"It is rather unexpected to see the two of you here at this hour without prior notice. May I inquire the reason for your intrusion?" His tone held on to its bite, perpetually agitated.

It took a brief silence before I realized Casimir was staring at me expectantly, not a single word from his mouth to attempt to help my cause. The discomfort set in. The urgency to plead for some type of aid didn't prepare me for being face-to-face with Orin. He looked finished with the conversation before it began.

I took a steadying breath and blocked out Casimir, staring at Orin despite how intimidating it was.

"Sir, I have appreciated the hospitality since my arrival despite it being unconventional." Casimir shifted beside me. "I'm here to ask for your help." I paused and watched his face. Orin hadn't tuned me out yet, and I whispered a plea to the gods in my head before I continued.

"The only reason I made it here, the only reason I'm alive, is because of a man named Ronin. He rescued me from the Temple after my parents were killed. Had it not been for him, I would have remained captive there." I tried to hide the emotion from my voice, to keep my composure. It slipped with every word.

"And?" Orin's quick yet short reply made my stomach twist.

"Sir? He saved my life; he rescued me from spending the rest of my days in a Temple cell, at the mercy of the prince—"

"With all due respect, the Temple is where you should have remained." The words cut with a lethal sting.

I sputtered, unsure what to say. If he knew what I had endured at the hand of Talos, maybe he would see things differently. I couldn't bring myself to mention the torture.

Casimir shifted uncomfortably next to me. The respectful demeanor he held slipped. Anger flashed beneath his mask of indifference.

"But sir..." My voice caught.

"I won't risk resources nor guard on behalf of an Iron Thorn man who should have minded his own and let you fulfill a destiny chosen by Aeterna. Instead, he thought he knew better than the goddess who created him. I won't waste time on someone so arrogant, much less a norm."

The color drained from my face. The finality in his voice was cold and uncaring. He wouldn't change his mind. Casimir's silence made the harsh dismissal worse.

"Then I will find him myself and be out of your hair," I said sharply, fighting back the tremble in my voice.

Casimir's head snapped up in surprise. "You can't be serious, you wouldn't survive a day—"

"I survived just fine, with no help from you. I owe Ronin my life. He saved mine. The least I can do is return the favor."

"You think they would hold on to him in hopes you'll show up? The king has no regard for life. You'd play right into their hands for someone who is likely dead!" The words came out harsh, and for a moment, I missed the ghostly tone Casimir's voice used to carry rather than the way it rang in my ears.

"I refuse to believe that. I'll go, and I'll bargain my life for his. If I'm meant to be the final bloom, I may as well use myself as a means to grant him his freedom."

Orin cleared his throat, breaking the tension in the room. "While this debate is quite entertaining on a slow day, I ask that you both leave. I have actual work to tend to."

I gaped at him in disbelief. How could he callously dismiss my request for help to save someone? Yet, in the same breath, I realized how naive I was. I didn't know him. I didn't know any of them outside of Casimir. But even he was different.

I tried to leave with dignity and less like a child scorned. Casimir's footsteps trailed hotly behind me. I wanted space from him, time to think. I didn't know where to go from there. I would climb out of the crater in the earth just to find myself lost in the Drought Lands.

The walk through Orondal with Casimir was a blur. His existence was something my mind scrambled to accept, along with talking the entire way to Everbloom. I didn't remember a single turn or step.

Heat climbed my neck as the thin line in my patience felt ready to snap like a twig between my fingers. Every step I heard Casimir take behind me made my blood boil.

"For gods sake, leave me be!" I cried, whipping around.

He paused, his expression impossible to read. "He isn't wrong about trying to get to Ronin. It's a pointless quest, and you know that."

I glared at him, the twig snapping.

"Why did you even bring me here, Casimir?" My voice broke. "No one else wanted me here. I wasn't supposed to know about Everbloom, to feel that sliver of hope. And yet you have haunted me since I was a child, begging me to find you." My breath shuddered as my pulse raced.

"I lost my sanity when you started haunting my sleep, and now you've brought me to a sanctuary I cannot have! A life never meant for me, and you *knew*. How could you do that to me? And now that I need you, I actually *need* your help, you won't even consider it."

The stillness was suffocating. Casimir's gaze bore into me, the weight of the words hanging heavy in the air. He scanned my face and continued to say nothing. His mask hung on by a thread.

Every second spent in silence, my resolve waned. The words fumbled out of me, taking with them the buildup of anger. The words I didn't want to say out loud. *'Why me', 'it's not fair'*. The implications spun in the misplaced tranquil breeze, and I wrestled with the desire to grab them back and shove them somewhere deep down to never feel them. But they were gone, spoken out loud.

"That was never my intention." Casimir's reply was cold and formal.

No words felt right. It was impossible to convey how awful it was to need help desperately, yet no one would offer any aid. The fear set in that I would have to do it on my own.

Leaves crunched close by as someone approached us, the footsteps timid as they got closer.

I broke Casimir's stare to glance over my shoulder, seeing Galan approach us with caution, scanning the situation before him.

When he reached us, Casimir didn't stay to say another word. He walked away, sulking. *'Stupid sulking boy'*. Never thought I would think something Novian said was smart.

Galan observed in bewilderment as Casimir departed.

"Is everything okay, Ms. Blackthorne?" The formality caught me off guard.

"Just Elita, please. And yes, everything is fine." The lie came easily. I was used to telling myself the same ones all the time.

Chapter Twenty-Seven

Galan quickly became one of my favorite people in Everbloom. As if he understood what would help—after leaving the dark part of the woods—he found me something to eat and took me close to the water, where children played on rocks and old hollowed trunks, shrieking with joy and laughter.

The water danced at my ankles, my slipshoes discarded by a stump that Galan used as a seat. He didn't press me for conversation. From what I gathered, he wasn't one to talk much. Unlike Alba, who had a quip or question at every turn, a joyful and friendly demeanor.

I enjoyed the quiet company.

The water lapped up my calves. I had my linen trousers rolled up and tried to avoid water getting on my bandages. I failed horribly, and they grew damp the longer I sat. The moment of peace was necessary, and I allowed it to block my worries out.

Regardless of the fact I would have to figure out some way to get back to the Iron Thorn, to Ronin. For a moment, I let myself breathe and enjoy the grounding effect of the water.

The laughter echoed around the area like a beautiful song, not a care in the realm from children who only ever experienced life in a peaceful forest. Among the many faces by the water, I spotted a familiar head of red hair. Taryn's laughter joined a child's, his hair an exact copy of hers, with short, tiny child-like ringlets. I observed as she hid behind one of the hollowed pieces of wood, leaping out to surprise the young child.

The sight both filled me with warmth and sadness, a longing there I had long ago learned to stifle. A mother who gave me her time and presence, love and safety. I yearned for that much of my life.

Galan noticed me staring, and he got up from where he sat, folding his hands behind his back. "That's Ms. Taryn's son. Most children stay further from the entrance to the forest. It's safer that way."

I nodded, tearing my eyes from them. "She seems like a good mother," I said in a soft voice, observing the water as it moved. I chuckled, looking back at him. "Though, if she scolds a child the way she does a patient, I pity the child."

He offered a small smile and glanced at the two when they stopped for a breath, slumping down in the dirt in unison.

"Ulrik is the last child I would feel pity for. He has a strong mother. She has overcome many hardships to give him a good life here. He's never had to want for anything."

I felt a sting of jealousy but hid it. Despite how my mother was, I would trade anything to have her back.

And as if the sting didn't burn enough, he asked a question that made my heart plummet. "What was your mother figure like, Ms. Blackthorne?"

I fought the urge to request he call me by my first name.

The question hurt more than I wanted to admit. I let a few moments tick by before I went back to where he had been sitting and lowered myself. My arms wrapped around my legs.

"My mother was critical and distant. But I loved her dearly, and I miss her even more."

He watched my hands fidget with the edge of my tunic. "My apologies. I did not mean to cause you grief."

"No, it's okay. No one has asked me about them since their death. It feels good to speak about them."

He nodded in understanding and sat next to me on the log.

Sunlight danced across the water, reflecting in pools of sparkling light. The sun burned high directly above the opening of the mountains, creating a warmth that soothed my soul.

Galan broke the silence. "My parents and siblings remain in hiding near Tyvolia. They were not granted passage, as they are not Roses. I see them once every solstice."

Orin's cruelty toward norms shocked me. Galan's own family wasn't allowed sanctuary in Everbloom. Orin's absolute refusal to help Ronin made sense, but it didn't make it any more right.

I observed as Galan's fingers tumbled over each other, thumbs twisting in an anxious circle. I knew he must have hated being separated from them. He was young and on his own, training to be part of a guard, which seemed pointless.

There hadn't been a war in centuries. I understood the importance of staying prepared, but Galan appeared too hesitant, too kind.

After a while, Taryn gravitated toward us, her son in tow. He held her hand, small and nervous the closer they got.

I offered a smile and stood.

"Now, I hope I didn't just see my patient dunking her bandages into the water," she said jokingly, gesturing to my calves.

I chuckled sheepishly and looked down at the wet bandages. "Sorry about that." I rolled my trousers back down. I'd need the bandages switched another time, but Taryn didn't need to rush a day playing with her son on my account.

The small boy stood at her side, curly red hair poking up in all directions, his wide green eyes staring up at me.

"Your petals are strange," he blurted, his voice small and soft. I laughed in reply before I crouched to his height without getting too close to avoid spooking him.

"Ulrik, you can't go around saying that to people," Taryn scolded, her red hair swishing as she shook her head at him.

"It's alright, really," I reassured. "They are strange, aren't they? I'm still getting used to them myself."

"I never seen white before," he said while touching one of the petals without hesitation. The innocence on his face and his curiosity only made my smile grow.

"I've heard that a lot here. They're pretty odd compared to the red I've seen."

Ulrik shrugged. "That's okay. I think white is nice, too."

"Thank you, Ulrik. I think they're nice as well." I stood, grinning. I wasn't used to being around children, but his innocent comments were endearing. When I grew up in solitude, I missed out on many experiences and interactions, but being a part of such a close-knit group of people was one of the most wonderful experiences I'd ever had.

Taryn encouraged Ulrik to go back and play for a bit, but she stayed behind. Her body turned to where she could see him. "He's right, you know. A white bloom is unheard of."

Absentmindedly, I brushed the petals through my fingers, feeling the soft, strange, thin pieces. Delicate and misplaced, yet a part of me I was fond of. The white was striking against my onyx hair.

I faced back to the water, tuning Galan and Taryn out as they both started a conversation about their blooms. Clouds passed over the sun and cast shadows over the water, blocking out the way it glimmered.

For a fleeting moment, the night the first petal bloomed came to mind, and I wished there was time to explain the oddity of my petals to Ronin. When I found him—because I wouldn't accept any other outcome—pleasantries weren't something we'd have time for.

"Elita." Taryn's voice caught me off guard.

I twisted on my heel and tucked a loose curl behind my ear when I faced them both. "Yes?"

"We were talking about heading to the tavern. It's a bit of a walk, but the tavern is pretty empty around now. Ulrik is staying with his gran since I'm on watch for an expectant mother."

"Ms. Taryn, if you're on duty—"

"Oh, settle yourself, Galan, I won't be partaking. White bloom here looks like she could use the warmth."

I glanced between them both, confused. "I don't follow."

"Galan here is quite the entertainment once he's had a few mugs of ale. I'll meet you both there as soon as Ulrik is settled with his gran." Taryn grinned and clapped a hand on Galan's shoulder. "I don't get out much between healing and raising my boy. I probably need this more than her. Wait for me!" She laughed, waving as she went to grab up her son, who let out a joyful squeal.

Galan groaned, the most annoyance I had seen him display in my short time knowing him. "This way it is, then."

The tavern was nothing more than a shack.

Sun-bleached wood made up the crowded little building, with only room for two tiny square tables and four stools facing the tavern bar. Even Galan's lanky body had a hard time finding a comfortable position at the bar, his legs squished between stool and bar.

My height made the space seem less unpleasant, my legs not as long as his. Nonetheless, it was a squeeze for me.

I held back a chuckle as Galan tried to adjust his body in more awkward ways to fit better. The server observed with a smirk.

As Taryn had requested, we waited until she arrived, her healer smock tucked into her arms, changed into her usual linen clothing she wore every time I went for a healing.

She gave a two-finger salute when she entered, scrambling over to where we were, her height an inch or two more than Galan, yet she sat down with ease. Her limbs found their place on the stool without a struggle.

"Two mugs of ale, please," she chorused, winking our way.

Galan paled and slumped in his seat. "I'm meant to be training in the morning. Sir Vanmore will not be pleased with me."

The bartender slid two drinks our way, their frothy tops cascading with foam. It looked unappetizing, to say the least.

"Ah, man up. He'll get over himself," Taryn dismissed, watching with satisfaction as Galan downed the ale in a quick swig. Some trickled out from the corners of his mouth. Taryn clapped a hand on his shoulder, letting out a whoop of pride.

Galan shook his head and raised a finger up. The tavern server poured him another mug of ale.

I eyed mine with apprehension, the liquid a strange golden color sloshing around in the dark mug. I made the mistake of trying to sniff it. The scent burned my nose when I did. I recoiled and pushed the mug.

"I don't think this is for me," I said.

Taryn rolled her eyes playfully. "No pressure from me. What kind of healer would I be if I made all the newcomers try Pacen's ale?"

Galan scoffed and shook his head. "If memory serves me well, you have brought every newcomer here."

She feigned hurt, pressing her hand to her chest. "Forgive me for wanting to share in one of my favorite places in Everbloom. Reminds me so much of a normal life in Eldravine at the tavern there."

My eyes widened. "You're from Eldravine? The Iron Thorn?"

"We share that in common, white bloom. Not many people from here can say that. My hair and not quite-red eyes helped me not be a target. No big deal. I wanted better for my son, though. Left the Iron Thorn the moment I found out I was with child and brought Ulrik's gran along with me." She shrugged it off as if it were nothing. It came as a shock to me. Leaving the kingdom felt nearly impossible, and while I got over the Forge, it was one of the hardest things I had ever done.

I stared at her in awe before I took the ale in hand, barely raising it at her. I brought the bitter-smelling liquid to my lips and took a large swig from it.

Regret set in immediately.

Galan patted a hand to my back while I sputtered and coughed. It burned the entire way down, and the taste was unbearable.

"How did you drink that?" I forced out between coughs, looking at Galan. His face broke into a silly grin, and he patted my back once more, holding back a laugh.

As if he wanted to show off, he chugged the rest of the second one, not going up for a breath. He drank until he emptied it, and the mug made a hollow sound on the bar when he set it down.

Something strange and new tugged at me, a feeling I wasn't accustomed to. I wasn't willing to be shown up by Galan nor laughed at any longer by Taryn. And with that, I held my breath and gulped down the rest of the ale, my throat burning.

Heat pooled in the pit of my stomach as I finished it off.

Again, I sputtered, clearing my throat once I emptied the mug.

Taryn's laugh died in her throat while she observed, scarcely impressed.

"Another," I ground out.

"Ha, I knew it!" Taryn whooped, slamming a fist on top of the bar. "You've got fire somewhere in there. Can't let the boys here show you up." She grinned, throwing up her hand. "Another for Galan, and I'd bet on getting another set up for our white bloom."

I tried not to look displeased at the idea and instead held my breath, chugging until I drained another mug. I watched in revulsion as Galan downed more, setting it on the bar in another triumphant slam, the look in his eye a challenge.

Something told me I needed to know my limit.

But there was no victory in that.

So, another made its way down my throat, stinging the whole way. Each one burned a little less until the room grew a bit warmer, the heat moving from my belly to my face. My cheeks became oddly flushed. I ran my hand over them in a gentle stroke, the movement odd.

My sense of time flew out the window with my balance. The five empty ales lined up taunted me, laughing as my head swam.

No, that was Taryn, chuckling to herself like a little girl while she observed me swaying in my seat.

"What?" I slurred, my mouth feeling as if it didn't want to form words properly. "Oh," I groaned, a hand against the stool to steady myself. "What have you all done?" I huffed. Taryn laughed harder, the sound booming through the small tavern.

Galan let loose a piercing laugh as if I weren't embarrassed enough. His usual serious mask slipped as pink colored his cheeks.

"I take it you never tried ale?" he asked as his laughter settled.

I crossed my arms over my chest, the movement strange, as if every shift of my body sent me into a dizzying spiral.

"Of course not. I was hardly allowed out of my cottage, *Mr. Hayes*. Frankly, I've never even talked to another human before either, not until my parents *died*." In an awful, morbid way, a laugh burst from my chest, the timing inappropriate. They both stared at me for a pause before they joined in.

My chest felt warmer. Everything did, but the way their laughter mixed with mine was soothing. Suddenly, the taste of the ale didn't bother me.

The chortling settled, and Taryn put a hand on the bar and stood from her stool with sure legs. As she had promised Galan, she didn't drink any ale. I envied how steadily she moved.

"Well, hate to leave you all, but at this hour, I should be close to the healer's tent, just in case." She pulled her smock tight over her back and then smiled at me. "I like your spark, white bloom. Don't let your social ineptitude prevent you from getting close to people here. I promise we're not all as tight ass as Casimir." She winked and dipped her head, walking out of the small tavern.

Galan stared after her, looking displeased. He groaned and pressed his palms against his forehead. "Sir Vanmore will have my head for this. I'm not an adequate guard if I'm incapable of protecting you." He glanced over at me sheepishly.

I shrugged and went to stand, my legs feeling like water. "Just don't tell him." The ridiculous suggestion was all my brain conjured while my thoughts swam in sloshing ale.

He huffed in exasperation and stood, putting an arm out at me. I shooed him away and took an unsteady step toward the exit. Only to find my legs didn't want to function properly.

Galan grabbed my elbow. "Back to the tents with you, then, Ms. Blackthorne."

"*Please.*" I drew the word out. "It's just Elita. That works fine."

He offered a nod. His demeanor shifted back to stoic as he slipped back into his guard persona.

We left the tavern behind; the server waved us off with a grin. My legs became unsteady the more time ticked on. I groaned as the strange fog in my head made everything distort.

The novelty wore off.

Galan practically dragged me beside him. The setting sun painted the underground forest a strange hue of orange and pink. The color made the swirling in my head all the worse.

Galan apologized under his breath a few times.

From his pace, it was clear his own drunken state hadn't worn off, and my weight on his arm and elbow probably made it harder on him. I almost told him it served him right for letting me chug an obscene amount of the bitter liquid, but I refrained.

We stumbled past the mess hall, and he quickened his pace, which made it hard for me to keep up. I was aware the reason was likely to avoid anywhere Casimir might be, but once we passed the hall, there he was—donning a billowing black cloak, along with full leather armor. His arms crossed over his chest as he talked to another member of the guard.

If we were quick enough, perhaps he wouldn't see.

The gods didn't favor us.

Casimir lazily glanced in our direction. He didn't notice at first and turned back to the other guard member. I started to sigh in relief until his head whipped back toward us. His eyes widened, and his arms uncrossed as he took in the sight of us stumbling in place.

After a pause, his gaze narrowed.

Casimir dismissed the conversation and stalked our way.

"We gotta get out of here," I whispered to Galan. He raised an eyebrow at me and shook his head.

Despite my unsteady balance and swaying, we were frozen in place. We both waited for Casimir to reach us. He stopped in front of us, scanning over me, concerned.

"What's wrong? Is she hurt?" His tone dripped with aggravation at Galan. I pursed my lips to stifle a laugh. He went from concerned to bewildered.

Galan shifted, and the movement almost sent me tumbling forward. "Ms. Taryn insisted on the tavern. Elita may have had some ale."

"Some? You essentially challenged me to a drink off," I hissed jokingly. Galan shot me a look of betrayal, which made me giggle.

Casimir appeared unimpressed and glared at Galan. "I'll return her to her tent. You're relieved of your guard duty, Hayes."

Galan tensed and stood straighter. "Captain, I would never allow her to be in harm's way."

"And yet you let her drink herself into a stupor. You are dismissed." Casimir's tone was sharp. My head moved a bit too much as I glanced between the two, scoffing at Casimir.

"That's ridiculous! I chose to drink it," I said. Regardless, Galan released my arm, did a salute similar to the men from earlier, and left; his head hung low in shame.

I stumbled clumsily without his hand on my elbow. Trying to stand became an impossible feat. Casimir raised a brow at me, observing as I struggled to maintain my balance. He sighed and grabbed onto my arm where Galan had been. His hand was somewhat larger than Galan's and much warmer.

I leaned some of my weight on him and let out a breath of relief at how comfortable it was. "I should lie down."

He didn't seem to find me amusing. The argument from the morning blew over for me. To him, it remained fresh.

We shuffled over the path in the trees, and my stomach twisted with discomfort. I groaned but continued to walk next to him. Neither of us said a word, and the silence bothered me.

It was strange. The one I knew for the longest time, it was as if I didn't understand him at all. For all the nights he visited me in my sleep, the time was always spent discussing my dreams or a need for me to leave my family. Little else was talked about.

The awkward silence in his presence had me paying for it.

Another step forward and my stomach churned. The burning reached the pit of my gut. I jerked us to a stop. "I might be sick."

Casimir let out a frustrated exhale and changed directions with a quick turn to a different path, the earth less packed down, the plants more overgrown. After a few minutes of walking, a different tent appeared, to which he opened in a rush, ushering me inside.

I stumbled over to the bed, not concerned about who it belonged to. I fell into it, groaning as the world spun more.

"That was a mistake." The pillow muffled my voice.

"It tends to feel that way when you have alcohol for the first time, notably when you make a drinking competition out of it," he said from across the tent.

"You're an ass, you know? Is that why Elrin hates you?" I mumbled. I was aware it was a low blow, but couldn't bring myself to care when he mocked my misfortune.

Somewhere in the tent, Casimir rummaged through items that clattered. "I'm not having this conversation with you while you're drunk." His tone was stern, and I held back a laugh at how he tried to hide his emotions from me as if some kind of punishment.

"If you don't tell me now, you may not get the chance. What happens when I leave here and we never see each other again? I'll always wonder," I teased, my voice still muffled.

Stillness filled the space, and I thought maybe he had left me there. After a long pause, I heard him walk over to the bed. "Here. For your head." Casimir pressed something cool to the back of my neck. I shivered and put a hand over it, feeling a wet cloth.

My limbs sprawled in a strange way when I turned, my back resting on the bed beneath me. It held me there, an anchor, while my head continued to be afloat. With shaky fingers, I tugged the damp cloth across my skin and let it settle over my heavy eyelids.

Another quiet moment passed before he spoke. "You know, using imminent death to get what you want is poor taste." His voice strained.

I peered from under the cloth, seeing that he stood beside the bed. "But it's true. I mean, not the wondering part. When I leave, will you visit my sleep until I wilt, or will this be the last time I'll see you?" The question left my lips before I could stop myself.

"El…" The way he said it made my chest tighten. Ale and nerves mixed until it made the tent spin. I covered both eyes with the cloth.

Casimir sighed, low and soft. "A few years ago, before I started visiting again, Elrin expressed she had feelings for me. We were together for nearly a year."

I swallowed the lump in my throat. "What happened?"

A pause. Another sigh. "I realized I didn't reciprocate her feelings. It was unfair to continue that way. I broke things off with her. I never expected her to take it so hard, and I apologize if it's caused you issues while you've been here."

An out of place smile tugged at my lips. "No, it's okay. It's only been a few mean looks. Nothing malicious. But someone should tell her that, just because they're associated with you, doesn't mean she can shoot death glares at people she doesn't know."

Casimir chuckled. "Noted."

It shouldn't have made me feel any type of way that he broke things off with her. Alba had implied as much. But I felt less offended that he didn't tell me.

There were many things we both kept from each other. When he visited me, our talks were typically light. I needed the break from night-mares, and whenever things got too heavy, the connection broke. Many times, the most intense conversations we had focused on me leaving the Iron Thorn.

For a moment, I let myself sit with the guilt of never inquiring about Casimir's life. Whether I thought he was real or not. He gave so much of his time, his sleep, to bring me out of my nightmares and ease the weight of loneliness.

The cloth grew warm on my skin, and I realized the silence had carried on a long stretch of time. I didn't hear Casimir's breathing, nor sense him standing by me. "Casimir?"

"I'm still here," he said. The low rasp of his voice trailed from the opposite side of the tent, but it gave me a sense of relief.

Even as I thought better of it, our conversation from earlier wasn't finished, and the ale made me feel as though I could say what I needed to.

My pulse quickened when I spoke. "I'm aware you think it's point-less to try to save Ronin, but I have to anyway."

"Don't start that again—"

"I have to. He's my friend, and he saved me." The memories stung viscerally, an ache in my bones when I thought of him taking me away from the Temple. And then words fumbled from my slurring mouth. "He kissed me. No one's ever kissed me before." The silence was deaf-ening when I paused. "I mean, of course not. I've never been allowed to get close to anyone. But Ronin saw me in a way no one ever has. He's been a good friend to me."

There was no reply. The words fell out, my mouth no longer willing to work with my rational brain.

When the silence carried on for a long pause, I moved the cloth and willed my heavy head to glance around, seeing Casimir still there, staring at me. He didn't say a word or move. If I didn't know any better, it would seem as if he were made of stone.

Finally, he turned to the drapes. "Sleep off the ale. There's water on the ground by the bed. Try not to knock it over." With that, he left, the drapes flapping behind him. The scene reminded me a lot of when he visited me in my sleep—always vanishing.

I moaned and rolled back over. I laid the cloth over my eyes and hoped by morning, I would be back to my normal self, and Casimir would be finished sulking.

Chapter Twenty-Eight

Moonlight cast a strange glow in the tent, some of its light breaking through the imperfections in the fabric. I rolled onto my side, my head throbbing from the aftereffects of the ale. My hand slapped aimlessly at the ground for the water Casimir left me, desperate for something to ease my parched throat.

"To your left."

I nearly jumped out of my skin when Casimir spoke. He sat on the ground near the exit of the tent, his ankles crossed over each other and his back against a mahogany chest.

The curved shape of the mug made contact with my hand, and I picked it up, gulping it with as much eagerness as Galan had when he downed the ale.

Despite the warm temperature, it relieved the thirst. If only it were enough to rid my head of the way it pulsated. I cursed Taryn and Galan both in my mind. They failed to warn me I would feel as if I'd just sparred with a bear when the dizziness wore off.

I laid back down stiffly and rested on my side to face Casimir, who sat stoic as a statue. I wondered briefly if he ever managed to sleep when he stood guard. The look in his eyes told me the answer was no.

"It's strange to look at you sometimes," I blurted, watching the way his head turned. Every inch of his movement was solid, nothing like the way he seemed to float around in my mind before. Flesh and bones. Every change in his face and posture lacked the airy movement I was accustomed to.

He quirked a brow and unraveled his folded arms. He pushed himself up straighter. "How do you mean?"

"Just everything about you. You're not wispy anymore."

He chuckled, the sound no longer an echo in my skull. Instead, it was a soft and pleasant noise, disrupting his serious demeanor.

"Wispy, hm?" He paused, appearing thoughtful. "I suppose that's one way to put it. Dreamwalking isn't as easy as one would think." He shrugged.

"So that's what you call it. Dreamwalking...That's the best you could think up?"

He scoffed and crossed his arms back over his chest. "I'd like to see you come up with something better."

I thought for a moment, my mind muddled and lacking the capability to think up anything quick or witty.

"You're right, I've got nothing. Oh, wait! Maybe dreamstalking?"

He looked unamused. "Ha ha, very funny."

I grinned, proud of how he sulked. While my mother was certain it had been some kind of curse or evil spirit, knowing it was an ability, something Casimir had to work hard at, it brought me comfort.

It was quiet for a while. The lone sounds came from outside the tent as the night continued its song. A gentle breeze rustled the leaves, and bugs chirped happily somewhere. The melody reminded me much of sleeping in the woods, with nothing but nature around me. It was close enough, without the constant discomfort to my body.

The mattress below me was worn in, the blanket comfortable like the one I had. Years of use made it softer, and it smelled lightly of patchouli and something else I couldn't quite place.

I turned my gaze back to Casimir and interrupted the quiet. "Is it strange having me in your domain?"

"You mean my tent?" His face twisted with an amused smirk. "Not particularly. Why?"

"There were many years spent with you visiting my room, yet I'd never seen where you were from before. It's odd to me, at least. Almost like I get to be in your head for a moment."

"That would be quite unfortunate. You wouldn't want inside my head."

"A bit empty, is it?"

He rolled his eyes, but a small, pleasant grin tugged at the corners of his lips. "You know, if you intend to insult me, you could go back to sleep."

"Why, so you can dreamstalk me?" I joked. He deflated, and the small smile disappeared from his face. A pang of guilt filled me, and I sat up despite the way my head begged me not to. It weighed a ton.

Casimir turned his head and stared at a random spot in the tent. "I apologize if it ever felt intrusive to you. That wasn't my intention."

My hands fiddled with the loose seams on his quilt. "Well, what was your intention? How does one even discover they can dreamwalk, or find someone to use it on?" I asked, curious.

He shifted, switching the way his ankles were crossed. Deep in thought, he pursed his lips, contemplating his answer. I waited as he fidgeted, the first time I'd seen him appear nervous.

Scarlet eyes met mine, and they appeared almost black in the night. "I was meant to recruit you. Like any Rose."

"That's a lie," I countered. He looked surprised at my accusation. "Orin didn't want me here. He *doesn't* want me here."

"He isn't the only authority here."

I bit back another reply, despite the desire to prod for more answers. The weariness took hold of me, and every inch of my being craved a deep sleep to alleviate the fog in my head.

I laid on my side but didn't turn away. The moonlight made Casimir look vulnerable. His mask slipped as fatigue wore him down.

The nights spent awake to guard me as I slept were evident in his exhausted features. From the dark circles around his eyes to the way he moved at a more sluggish pace.

Despite my efforts to stay awake, my vision turned bleary. Casimir settled against the chest behind him and laid his head back. He didn't try to sleep. Streaks of moonlight made their way through tears in the fabric of the tent to illuminate his shoulder and jaw.

His voice cut through the silence. "My mother was the one who taught me how to master dreamwalking." The explanation was abrupt while he avoided meeting my stare. "She had the ability herself. It isn't common among the Rose people. Some correlation to the blue lotus flower." His fist clenched on his thigh. "Her beliefs and my abilities are the reasons I joined the guard."

I rested my hands beneath my cheek, listening.

"She was thrilled when the General wanted our help with finding the white bloom or other Roses in need of aid. She said it was an honor to be given such a task by him."

He met my gaze, his face unreadable, even as the cracks in his wall widened. "My mother was one of the earliest recruiters. She believed no Rose should have to sacrifice their life for the kingdom. She held such a high value for human life, much higher than most people here." He shook his head, a look of disgust on his face. "Orin would leave a Rose to starve if it meant protecting Everbloom, and he'd kill a norm without blinking an eye. If it weren't for her beliefs or the willingness of the General, many Roses would have been left to die." His tone grew somber, and his shoulders fell.

"What happened to your mother?" I whispered, afraid of the wound I may open.

He turned as if I slapped him, the cracks sealing themselves shut.

"Went on a recruiting mission, never made it back." The pain in his voice was evident despite how hard he tried to keep up his mask. A pang ached in my chest.

"It sounds like she was a wise and kind woman," I said, my voice soft. His throat bobbed as he swallowed thickly.

"She was. I made it my goal to carry on her beliefs. She sacrificed everything to give me a life here. The least I could do is try to make her proud, even in death." He let go of a heavy breath and rested his head back on the chest.

The silence was heavy, the grief a thick blanket over both of us. He stared at the moonlight pouring in, and I chose to do the same. I rested on my back once more, even as my head throbbed.

I understood and shared much of the sentiment of wanting to live in a way that would make your parents proud. Something to honor their wishes. It's why I wouldn't turn my back on a destiny I didn't want. My father fought to give me as much freedom and peace as possible, but even he knew one day I would bloom, and one day my bloom would need to be a sacrifice.

Part of me continued to wonder if he had guessed at my fate. If, in all his years of research, he had seen anything mention a white bloom, and if he begged the gods, it wouldn't have to be me.

I turned my head to look at Casimir. "Cas?"

"Hmm?" He barely glanced at the bed, still deep in thought.

"What you said when Orin told me about my bloom... Do you really think it's nonsense?"

Casimir ran a hand over the back of his hair. "I mean, a lot of what the people believe here is far-fetched. They read ancient texts and think the word of man is truth." He shrugged. "I don't take part."

My hands knotted in the quilt. "And my bloom?"

Casimir glanced over my hair. The white petals had their own pulse. Their shimmery hue, always in my peripheral.

His jaw clenched, and he shrugged again. "Who knows. But I wouldn't take what Orin says to heart."

I paused. My breath shuddered. "And if I don't return to give my bloom, what then?"

He appeared uncomfortable with the question. "Not my call to make."

"What if the prophecy is wrong, and I give my bloom, and it means nothing?" My voice caught, revealing the depth of fear in my hesitation.

Casimir sat straighter, his body facing mine. His fingers tapped at the ground while he contemplated.

Was he the only one who didn't believe the prophecy? What if it was just ramblings of someone long ago deceased, and I gave my life, and nothing changed?

The hesitation didn't serve me. It would only make the choice harder. I had to go off of the little information given to me. And my bloom was white. Had I not dreamed of my death since I was a child?

Finally, I exhaled. "It doesn't matter. I think I have to try. Right?"

Casimir's eyes searched mine across the tent. For a moment, it was just a girl and her ghost. Too many questions and no answers to them.

His silence screamed his uncertainty. If I stared at him any longer, I would let his hesitation change my mind. It'd be much easier to adopt his beliefs. To only leave to get Ronin, and hope they would let me return with him. It hurt worse knowing Everbloom could've been my home. A sanctuary for me to live freely. Surrounded by company and laughter and vibrant life. More than I had ever hoped for. But it wasn't meant for me.

The weight of wondering and the pain of digging up old wounds were too much. I let the throbbing in my head and the sound of nature lull me back to sleep.

Distant chatter and the shuffle of feet brought me out of a heavy sleep. My eyes stung from the harsh light, and every sound became amplified, intensifying the discomfort. When I sat, my skull ached, the sensation strange and unpleasant. I glanced around the tent, noting Casimir's absence.

The chaotic sounds increased when the grogginess wore off, and the sound of people talking in panicked and excited voices surrounded the tent. It sounded as if there was a stampede outside.

My feet found the icy ground—bare despite falling asleep with my slipshoes on, too ill and lazy to remove them. They were tucked neatly by the edge of the bed.

I sighed with the weight of exhaustion as I ran my hand over my face, trying to shake off the remnants of sleep and ale.

Beneath all the noises, I made out two hushed voices close by, just outside the drapes of the tent. Despite feeling as if I'd just finished sparring with Novian, I stood and shuffled over to the drapes, the ties held together loosely.

The bustling sound inside Everbloom was misplaced. Too busy, too frantic. I had to focus to drown it out so my ears could make out who the voices belonged to.

"I don't want that. She isn't ready," Casimir grumbled, voice strained. I listened in closer, trying not to disturb the conversation or alert them to my presence.

"There isn't much to be done about it. He will want to speak with her. He has said as much to Sir Orin." Galan's voice sounded grim, and I wondered how he was up and able to function.

"That isn't my biggest concern. It's too much. You know as well as I do, he won't be able to stay. Orin and the General would both agree on that. We don't keep prisoners; we do not harbor norms."

My interest piqued.

"It may give her peace to know, Captain."

"You won't say a word of this to her. Your duty is to keep her here. She can't leave the tent until everything is said and done. Alba is on her way to help keep her here."

A sick sensation rolled through me, and not from the lingering effects of the ale. My body reacted on instinct, like a cornered animal. I backed away from the drapes and searched around the tent. There was no other way out but the sole exit unless I dug at the bottom of the tent. That was a last resort. Memories of captivity in the Temple haunted me.

Hands worked at the tie, loosening it in a single tug. Casimir stood on the other side, his eyes wide when they met mine.

"Elita." He stared, searching for a sign I overheard what they said.

Galan stood behind him, his own discomfort clear.

I pursed my lips, afraid to say anything. Casimir sighed in exasperation and ran a hand through his messy waves.

"I'm sorry about this." His voice was heavy with guilt.

"Please don't." Is all I managed to say. My hands trembled.

"I need you to stay here. You can't leave for now. Galan and Alba will keep you company. It isn't safe for you."

"Bullshit," I spat, backing up further. "You said I wasn't a prisoner here. So, what is this?"

"Please. Trust me." Everything inside me screamed not to. I wanted to bolt for the exit, dart past him and Galan. My entire body burned with adrenaline, the sensation like an old friend.

The memory of Ronin's voice rang in my head, screaming for me to run. Behind Casimir, Alba approached, confusion on her face.

"What are you all doing? Didn't anyone tell you the General is back?" she asked, hands on her hips.

Casimir stared at me, eyes lit with intensity. They pleaded, pooled with his desperation. I wanted to believe he was keeping me safe. I held onto that belief with everything inside me.

"Fine," I said through clenched teeth. Casimir sighed when I agreed. He turned to leave, pausing as he walked by Alba.

"She can't leave. Keep her here."

I regretted my choice in an instant.

Alba quirked a brow, bewildered, while Casimir stormed off. I noted which way he turned, watching until he disappeared.

Galan and Alba exchanged looks, both wary. I slumped onto the bed and wrapped my arms around my legs, unsure of what to do. Two people I considered friends, and yet, somehow, they had become my captors. I tried not to get angry with them and blamed Casimir instead.

Every moment I spent with him, he grew colder. Nothing like the boy I had known, spouting off riddles and sarcastic comments. I witnessed him change into somebody else within a matter of a week. Instinct told me not to trust him.

Alba and Galan whispered to each other on the other side of the tent, and I assumed he was explaining to her the circumstances. They seemed to agree I didn't deserve to know.

Another whisper of the word 'norm' broke my train of thought, my body going rigid. *Prisoner. Norm.* My gut twisted, the hope overflowing as the thought crossed my mind. It was impossible. My heart hammered at the thought that somehow he was there. Ronin was in Everbloom.

I stood. "He's here, isn't he?" I stared at Galan. His shock gave him away when their conversation died in their throats. "Please, Galan, I need to know if he's here. I'm begging you."

His gaze bounced from Alba to me, then to the drapes that hung open. The crowd outside moved about chaotically.

Galan hung his head, ashamed. "I've been charged with keeping you here, Ms. Blackthorne. I have to follow orders."

I bit the inside of my cheek, drawing blood.

Alba glanced at us both, more confused. "What's going on? Seriously, I have no idea what any of you are going on about!"

The pull to run made my muscles ache with anticipation. Staying in the tent wasn't an option for me. I didn't want to wait for Casimir to return and lie to me.

I needed to find out for myself.

Galan sensed what was about to happen and moved to stand in front of the drapes, his stance that of a soldier.

Alba stared at us with apprehension. "Okay, what's happening?"

"If you care about me at all, you'll let me leave."

Galan's face twisted with pain as he shook his head in reply. "I cannot disobey orders." He sounded remorseful, but it stung all the same.

None of it mattered, anyway. My resolve was sure.

My heart pounded in my chest, my muscles coiling like a spring as I readied myself to flee. I ran over it in my head, recounting the direction Casimir went.

The stone fortress appeared in my mind, the path a clear vision in my head. I inhaled a shaky breath. The rushing sound in my ears drowned out whatever words Galan said next. Nothing they said would change my mind.

Determination flitted through my veins, and without another thought, I ran right for him. Galan panicked, and he put his arms out to catch me. But I saw his hesitation. I saw how his movement lacked. Not at all like Alba's fast cat-like reflexes.

The motions she taught me were committed to memory after the repetitiveness.

A night of sparring wasn't enough to prepare me to fight, but it was enough for me to dodge in a swift motion, darting under Galan's arm, his height a disadvantage.

Galan shouted, the words inaudible while I sprinted, my legs quick as they carried me forward. I fought my way through the crowd of Roses gathered. Their frantic state hid me in the flood of bodies.

I darted through, following the path I had seen Casimir take. He had disappeared around a turn, but I knew where he was going. It had to be it. There was nowhere else they would keep a prisoner.

My muscles were more accustomed to sprinting, and they carried me with ease down the beaten path, my bare feet familiar with the earth beneath them. I sensed the pulse of it against the soles of my feet, matching my heartbeat.

The forest stretched on, the path ever-changing, until I found the hidden trail. The overgrowth and narrow walkway were barely familiar, but it was enough. I walked it the other morning, a fresh memory. It would be enough to get me there.

No footsteps or voices followed me, whether because Galan chose to leave me be or because Alba made him, I didn't know. I continued on, no longer worried about them pursuing me.

The trees whipped past me as I ran, ignoring the few people who walked along the path. Their faces registered a mix of surprise and confusion as I sprinted by.

When I neared the stone fortress, I slowed, skidding to a stop at the sight of the guards in front of it. There were ten or more. The number increased since the previous morning, all but confirming my suspicion.

They had to be in there. Casimir, whoever the norm was, and possibly Orin and the General.

I hesitated, unsure how to approach the fortress, let alone how to get in. While they let Casimir in the day before without issue, something told me they wouldn't be so accommodating to me.

I pursed my lips and took a moment to breathe.

The need to see and the desire to know if I was right ate at me. I had to get inside. I wished then for more time to hone my abilities, to be able to conjure the earth and wrap the guards in vines.

I suspected they wouldn't hurt me, but I hesitated. They wouldn't allow me to enter, and I worried what they'd do if I approached.

But Casimir was inside.

Ronin may have been inside.

I had to do something.

Knowing Casimir was inside gave me the courage I needed. He wouldn't let the guards harm me. If I was sure about one thing, it was that. So, I sprinted forward, and my breath came in heavy panting.

The guards spotted me, their stance solidifying. They braced for me and stood in front of the door.

Good.

I sprinted straight at them and didn't stop. They looked shocked when I didn't slow. The two closest to the door lunged forward, grabbing my arms until I jerked back. Pain radiated through my biceps. Their grip was less than gentle.

"Casimir!" My voice caught when they pulled me back. Their hands dug into my skin. They were rougher than I anticipated.

I grimaced when one of them grabbed my arm from the other guard, pulling them both behind me. The movement hurt, and I bit back a curse. He held me there with my arms contorted to my back.

When the door flew open, Casimir's ember eyes burned with unbridled rage. "Release her," he snapped.

The guard held on for a moment longer before he released my arms, the skin and tissue in them sore.

I stared at Casimir, his face full of disbelief. After a pause, he closed his eyes and pinched the bridge of his nose. "She may enter," he said. They did a single salute, no argument from them.

A breath of relief fell from my lips, and I straightened, brushing the messy curls from my face. My pulse quickened despite the fact I had stopped running.

I took a step toward the fortress.

Every second dragged on as if time itself was in slow motion, fueling my worry as it grew. What if it wasn't Ronin locked in the fortress? It didn't matter. I needed to see for myself.

Casimir took a step back, making room for me to walk through the door. Blood rushed in my ears as I walked up the steps, my entire body trembling.

Chapter Twenty-Nine

My stomach twisted in knots. I stared at the man in front of me, his face almost unrecognizable. A gash split through his lower lip, and a bruise on the side of his face painted his cheek blue-green. Dried blood stained his tunic, and his hair was a mess of dirt and gods knew what else.

He sat bound to a chair on the far side of the room when he noticed me enter. His vivid blue eyes were ringed with deep-set shadows beneath them. There was no rest for a man so beaten.

"Ronin..." His name left my lips in a low breath, and every inch of my body went rigid with tension. Relief filled his face as he stared back at me in disbelief.

"I thought I'd never find you," he said with a slight grin. The movement pulled at the cut on his lip. I grimaced and moved across the room in a few quick strides.

I looked him over, eyeing the scrapes and bruises, the dirt beneath his nails. They had his wrists bound, and the rope made loops of red on his skin.

"I'm so sorry, Ronin. I should have come for you." My voice was just a whisper. I shook in disbelief, my mind unable to wrap around him being there. He was alive.

His bound hands reached forward, brushing over my hair in a soft caress. The petals caught on his hand as he stroked the delicate blooms.

"You look well. Don't apologize to me. You're safe. That was the goal."

The guilt devoured me, and his words offered little solace. I let him fend off the guards on his own, when the people from the village came for me. How he got away from them was a miracle.

I studied him, noting the wounds on his knuckles and face. "How did you get away?"

"Luck...and a few punches." He gave a weak laugh. "I got out before the Iron Guard showed up. I'm glad you told me of your plan to go to the Forge when we met. It wasn't hard to guess where you went."

I chuckled. The sound was strange as tears filled my eyes.

"Did they hurt you in any way?" he asked.

"No, not really." I thought briefly about Novian and offered a small smile. "Well, I did spar with a man who tried to kill me with roots. Wasn't the smartest move."

Ronin's face twisted with confusion. "Kill you with roots?"

"Rose abilities. Although, I don't seem to have any, despite trying to activate them." I shrugged. Talking with Ronin brought me comfort. My shoulders relaxed, and I relished the fact he wasn't being tortured.

"Knowing you, you'll figure it out. If I learned anything over the course of our time together, you're very persistent when you aspire to be," he said, his tone too light for the tension in the room.

My anxious gaze flickered from his. "It's okay, I'm not bothered. I'm more worried about getting you out of here."

His brow flicked upward. "Why would you want to leave? This is everything your father wanted for you and more."

"It is...but they wouldn't even consider letting you stay." The words were like poison in my mouth, but the truth didn't disappear simply because I refused to say it. A heavy breath rattled my chest. "I can't stay either. I have to go back to the Iron Thorn, and I have to give my bloom."

His eyes widened. "No," he whispered, horrified. "You can't let them do that to you, Elita. Your father fought for you to have that choice, to change things. What have they been telling you here? As they saunter around with their own blooms?"

I hesitated and ran a hand over a petal. "My bloom. It's meant to be the last one." The truth was still hard for me to accept and even harder to watch Ronin struggle with it.

No, it didn't feel fair. But the gods never claimed to be.

Casimir cleared his throat, and I swallowed nervously. His arms were crossed over his chest as he stood stoically, his face unreadable.

I looked for a sign that the man I thought I knew would offer me the help I needed. It cut me when I found none.

"Are the binds really necessary?" I asked.

Casimir scoffed. "Yes, they are. General's orders. The safety of our people matters more than a norm none of us know anything about."

"*I* know him. He saved me when you were going to leave me to be tortured." I turned back to Ronin.

I knelt and began undoing the rope on his wrists. I heard Casimir sigh in frustration, but he didn't stop me. Beneath the rough fiber, Ronin's wrists were red and sore. The sight made me grimace.

"I'm okay, really," Ronin whispered, offering a tight smile.

My hands ran over his wrists, inspecting his skin. The bruises and cuts on his arms showed signs of infection.

"Send for Taryn," I said to Casimir, not bothering to look back.

"There's a system to follow when we have someone unknown—"

"I was new here, and yet I saw Taryn within the first hour of arriving. How long has he been here?" I glanced over my shoulder.

"Since last night," Casimir answered with reluctance. "The General found him wandering too close to the entrance."

"And what is the intention here?" The panic built, and I whipped around to Casimir. "He already knows of Everbloom's existence. You said you don't keep prisoners, nor do you harbor norms. So, what then?" When he didn't answer, I paled. "No. You wouldn't."

Casimir grabbed one of the other guards, and I heard him mutter Taryn's name. The guard darted out the door, disappearing down the path.

At some point, Alba and Galan appeared, and both of them were scolded by Casimir as they entered the fortress. I tuned them out, not worried about them. Ronin was alive. He was okay, and he spent the last week looking for me, desperate enough to climb over the Forge Border.

Ronin never took his gaze off me, eyeing the petals in my hair. "Your bloom has progressed so much here."

I nodded and reached for the strange petal that adorned the crown of my hair, lying oddly at the top.

Ronin watched me fiddle with it and reached out, brushing one between his fingers. It tingled through my entire scalp and I winced at the odd sensation. His gaze darted from me to over my shoulder. I sensed Casimir's watchful eye. It brought Ronin more unease—I saw it in the way he paused, his hand leaving my hair.

"I'm so relieved you're alive," I said, filling the silence. "I can't believe you climbed the wall. How did you end up so far into Orondal?"

"My father was a hunter, remember? The markings left on the rocks leading this way aren't as subtle as they seem to think they are," he chuckled. "All I could do was hope you were the one who left them. I was worried you were lost or dead somewhere in the Drought."

"I wish I would have waited for you. Stayed closer. I should have never crossed that border." The fear crept back in over the intentions of Casimir and the others.

"Then you never would have found your way here. A sanctuary for Roses? If only your father had known. The Iron Thorn would collapse at the knowledge of a place like this."

I let the reality of that roll over in my mind, how the existence of Everbloom, and so many Roses, would change the Iron Thorn forever. For the Rose people, it would be for the worse.

I understood their desire to keep Everbloom safe, but Ronin's safety mattered to me as well. And I thought it mattered to Casimir after he told me the reason for his beliefs. I would have assumed he would at least extend his compassion to someone I considered a friend—someone who saved me.

I heard Casimir and Galan greet Taryn. She entered the fortress, appearing nervous and unlike herself. She pointed at Ronin, and Casimir nodded.

Taryn pulled her smock closer and adjusted her pack. She froze before she reached us. "He isn't bound." She looked at Casimir.

"And he doesn't need to be," I replied, not giving Casimir the chance to.

She gave a single nod before her attention went to Ronin. "I'm Taryn, the healer. I'm here to assess your wounds."

I moved out of the way but remained close to his side. Casimir glowered across the room. He observed every move made as if ready for Ronin to attack. I wanted nothing more than for him to leave. I couldn't stand to look at him.

It occurred to me Casimir knew Ronin was in Everbloom when I was in his tent. He knew and didn't plan to tell me. He was going to let him die by the General's hand.

Ronin hissed in pain when Taryn applied a cleaning salve to a cut on his arm. I observed with pursed lips as he tensed, allowing her to tend to his wounds. She bandaged a few of them that needed it, leaving the others with only the ointment on them.

He sat motionless. Patient with Taryn, even thanking her as she finished each bandage, despite how cold she was toward him. They only offered warmth and kindness to the Rose people, that much was evident.

Casimir and Galan were in deep conversation on the other side of the room. Neither of them bothered to offer a single glance our way. They both appeared as soldiers, and less like the people I thought they were. Their entire demeanor turned cold, and the change was agonizing.

I faced Ronin to find his focus on me as Taryn stitched a deep gash on his left arm. His face twitched as she worked it through his skin, but he didn't close his eyes nor glance away from me.

Taryn finished and gathered up her supplies. I noticed the number of guards outside increased, and with the influx of bodies, everyone in the room with us tensed. Casimir appeared panicked while it unfolded; his gaze fixed out the door in anticipation.

The guards lined the path, more solid than the trees, their stance one of respect. Their appearance was frightening in all black, the hoods of their cloaks draped on the back of their heads, hands on their swords. The mood in the room shifted and I tensed, my pulse quickening.

Ronin sensed it, too, and he sat straighter next to me.

Orin entered the fortress first, his white hair pulled behind him in a braid. He wore light armor, a gray cloak draped over his shoulder. He surveyed the room.

The guards outside all stood stoically, and their hands rose into synchronized salutes at their chests.

Facing the door, the tension continued to build.

From the woods came a man with thick wavy black hair, woven with streaks of gray. The strands framed his scarred face—a long white line stretched from the bridge of his nose and across his cheek. He wore black armor from his neck to his boots, his cloak blood red and hanging over his shoulder. The crimson of his eyes matched his cloak, a piercing vibrancy that made me want to recoil.

He carried the air of a general, appearing much older than Orin. Maybe twenty years my senior.

Galan, Alba, Casimir, and Taryn all saluted him, dipping their head as they placed a hand on their chest. I watched him enter the room, embodying the presence of a leader.

"General Valor," Casimir addressed him first.

Ice clawed at my spine until I froze to the spot. A sickening sensation overcame me as the room swayed. The last memory of my mother swirled in my mind, her instructions clear, though they made little sense to me back then.

Her final plea for me to cross the Forge and mention the name Valor, and yet standing in his presence, finding him was a mistake. I climbed the Forge. I followed the intense pull. But staring at the sinister man, my mother must've been mistaken. She must have intended to warn me against crossing paths with him.

My head swam while the room tipped. The name reverberated in my head as his focus fell on me from across the room.

He stared at me for a moment before addressing Casimir. "I thought I told you to dispose of the norm after you found out what he knew. This is quite an inconvenience." The General let go of an exasperated sigh. "I suppose I'll have to finish it myself."

Chapter Thirty

I n the tense silence following the General's callous words, every breath became painfully audible. All eyes trained on Valor. He only had one target; his sight locked on Ronin, who became rigid at my side.

Casimir was the first to move, stepping closer to Valor. "General, if I may make a suggestion—"

Valor held his hand up, cutting him off. Sweat beaded on my brow. I knew there was no way for me to fight off any of them. Their abilities, their strength, their weapons, I had no chance. And yet, every fiber of my being screamed at me to do something. To take Ronin by the hand and run out of the door to escape back to Orondal.

But it would be futile. They wouldn't let him leave Everbloom.

Even though every inch of me shook with fear, I stepped in front of Ronin as a barrier between him and Valor. I clenched my fists and tried to steady my breath.

Amusement flashed in Valor's eyes, but the opposite filled Casimir's as he stared at me. *"Elita, no."* His voice in my head was jarring, but I blocked him out. The intrusion made my skin crawl.

"Would someone care to explain what the white bloom is doing here?" Valor glowered at those in the fortress. Galan and Alba both looked ashamed, bowing their heads low.

"I see. It's always one of you two, isn't it? Orin, see that Hayes is stripped of his rank."

Panicked, I looked at Galan. Horror took over his features, and guilt pulled at me. Orin nodded, but no one moved.

I wanted nothing more than for Casimir to speak up, to defend me, to defend Ronin. To save a stranger's life, the one who had saved mine. But he stood motionless and said nothing. The respect, or fear, of Valor made everyone stand by.

Valor took a step forward, which made me recoil. The back of my legs touched Ronin's knees.

"Don't touch him," I hissed. Anger knotted in my chest.

Valor paused, observing my petals. "Be gone, girl. This business doesn't concern you."

"No."

"No? Guards, take this girl from my sight," Valor ordered, his patience worn thin. At the command, Casimir tensed. Taryn put a hand on my shoulder, the pressure gentle but reassuring.

"General, this man saved Elita's life. If not for him, she would be at the mercy of the prince." Casimir's response took Valor off guard, and he narrowed his eyes.

"Surely you aren't asking me to spare a norm's life after they have seen this forest?" Valor challenged.

"Ronin would never betray Everbloom," I snapped, glaring at him. Ronin rose from the chair and stood beside me, his hands shaking. The fear on his face was bare for all to see.

Valor stared at us, his jaw clenched. "We do not harbor nor trust norms from the Iron Thorn. This man might never betray our sanctuary, but it isn't something I'm willing to leave to chance. We have rules here for a reason, and I won't be taking the word of a naive girl." The finality was staggering.

Panic left me with limited choices. I scrambled for something that would spare Ronin's life. I wouldn't let them kill him. He risked his life to save me from Talos's torture, and I'd already abandoned him once.

What kind of person would I be if I let them harm him? A man I claimed as a friend? No. They wouldn't lay a hand on him.

The words forced their way out despite how venomous they felt in my mouth. "If you kill this man, my last words as I give my bloom will be to the king, telling him of this sanctuary."

Tension silenced the room. The threat hung heavy in the air. Everyone's eyes burned against my skin. Taryn pulled her hand back from me as if I'd slapped it.

Valor's expression was enough to make me want to cower and take it back, but I held my ground. It didn't make it sting any less. The betrayal was written on faces I had grown fond of in such a short time.

I tried not to meet their horrified expressions. Instead, I stared down Valor. He appeared ready to explode. The sword at his side began to look like a threat. He never unsheathed it—just a single hand rested on the hilt.

Uncertainty tugged at me. It would take but a second for any of the guard members to pull a sword and end the standoff. Minutes ticked by and I bit at the inside of my lip.

Finally, Valor let out a frustrated breath. "The norm will leave and not return. If I hear a whisper of Everbloom in the Iron Thorn, he will have lost the right to ever speak again." Some of the tension left my body, but he wasn't done speaking. "But you, white bloom, will stay here for further observation. You will not accompany him. Your bloom will end here."

My eyes widened, and I peered up at Ronin. He fixed a piercing gaze on Valor. His anger practically radiated off of him.

I gulped and faced Valor. "Just let him live, please." My voice broke, desperate not to lose him. I couldn't bear it if he died.

Ronin blanched. "No, Elita, you can't let them do this to you. What about what your father wanted? What about your bloom?"

"You have to live, Ronin. I can't lose anyone else," I whispered.

Seeing the despair etched on his face, a heavy ache settled in my chest.

He would live, and soon, I wouldn't have to remember the agony of goodbye.

When I turned back around, I was met with shameless scrutiny from everyone in the room. Those who I had become fond of stared at me as if they no longer recognized me. The threat against their sanctuary was enough to turn their stares into bitter daggers. But I couldn't take it back. I meant it.

Blood was on their hands from all the Roses they allowed to die in the Iron Thorn; their bodies limp in the center of a garden—a sacrifice they never had to offer. Children, sons, and daughters, all tortured and wilted in the Iron Thorn for a lie.

I didn't regret my choice.

Valor stepped forward, signaling the guardsmen around the room. "Take the norm to the surface," he ordered.

The guards flanked us, replacing me at Ronin's side. The room remained silent as they redid his bindings. They pulled it tight, jerking on his hands. Ronin didn't look my way. His anger boiled over as he glowered at Valor, the blue in his eyes like a stormy sky. I watched as they pulled him out of the stone fortress.

My entire body ached, my legs begging me to follow him.

Galan and Taryn both lowered their heads, no longer able to meet my gaze. But Casimir and Alba never took their focus off me, both of them unreadable.

Valor grumbled something under his breath and ran a hand over his face. "Orin, make a note that our guard needs better training. This should have never happened."

Orin nodded in reply, ever silent in the General's presence.

I slumped into the chair Ronin had been in. Many of the people dispersed, leaving a handful of guards outside, along with the few I thought I knew.

Valor talked to the others in the room, addressing issues with the marks they had left in Orondal and bringing up other safety concerns. The conversation continued, but I blocked it out and wished I had just followed Ronin.

The pull to leave was visceral.

If they had wanted me dead, I would have been. I refused to be held captive and observed. I didn't escape Talos's prison to find myself in another. Forced to be used for someone else's gain or knowledge, the very thing my father and Ronin had both fought to have me free from.

I didn't know how, but I needed to get out. If I died outside of the Iron Thorn, the realm would perish. There was no way for me to remain in Everbloom, not unless I wanted to doom everyone there, and more.

The room moved in a blur. Galan spoke to Orin. Valor undid his cloak and set his sword against the stone wall.

After some time passed, Valor glanced my way, his animosity evident. "Someone get her out of here," he demanded.

I stood, and the room went still. "Who do you think you are?" I snapped, my fists at my sides. Casimir whipped his head my way, shocked at my outrage and willingness to voice it. Something inside me clicked, a flame I didn't know I had, ignited by fury.

"Elita," Casimir warned, his voice nearly inaudible as it dripped with disapproval. My hands shook. The way he spoke to me, the change in his demeanor, it made me ill at ease.

Valor cleared his throat and gestured for the others to leave with a flick of his wrist. They did so without a word.

After a moment, only Casimir, Orin, and Valor remained.

His black hair caught a glimpse of the sunlight, inky and slick. It was oddly wavy and somewhat messy, but the disheveled appearance made him appear rougher instead of seeming aloof. The man was frightening in all his stone-like composure.

Casimir shifted his gaze between Valor and me. Worry took over his features. Something was terribly wrong.

Valor cut through the quiet. "As I'm certain you're aware, I'm Valor, the leader of Everbloom." He watched my face as if expecting me to react. He looked disappointed when I continued to stare back in confusion.

"I charged Casimir with finding the white bloom. My goal was not to have a norm sniffing around. Nor would I offer aid or help to one of them." The words were sharp and unfeeling.

"He saved my life. He was only trying to find me, to protect me. Killing him is cruel, his only wrongdoing being that he rescued me from the Temple."

"The words of a smitten girl mean nothing to me." He misread me, and my face burned with humiliation. "I care little for who you find yourself involved with. I care about the people here. You do not know the traitors we've had amongst us. What of Taryn's child? Or any of those who cannot fight? Does their safety mean less than a man you hardly know?"

I didn't answer. Of course, the lives in Everbloom mattered, but Ronin sacrificed everything to save me. He mattered, too.

"You know nothing about me or him. Why does it even matter when he risked everything to save me?" I glared at him.

Everyone went silent as Valor's gaze shifted to Casimir, both curious and frustrated. "You didn't tell her?"

A terrible sensation flooded my body. Every inch of me tingled with a strange heat when Casimir lowered his head.

"He didn't tell you it was my idea to have him dreamwalk in your sleep, that I was the one who told him to instruct you to find us?"

My shoulders sank, weighed down with disbelief. "But why would you..." It was barely a whisper. He heard it all the same.

"The white bloom is the leverage we need to combat the king's rule. The exact piece we have been missing in our search for freedom from tortuous sacrifices. Your existence is the key to the Iron Thorn's fall." Valor's eyes flickered a deep scarlet, uncanny.

I trembled, and nails bit into my skin when I tightened my fists. "You're insane. If I bloom here, everyone in the kingdom will die! The realm won't survive."

"I do not have the time nor the patience to explain this to you. We only have a few weeks left to observe your bloom before it wilts. You will remain here, unharmed. I've seen to that, as proven by your guards," he said flippantly.

My brow furrowed, and I turned to Casimir. The fear on his face didn't suit him. He remained fixated on Valor. He appeared as if he were pleading with him.

"Why even bother? What does my safety matter to you?" I spat.

An eerie silence swept through the room as Valor straightened from where he had been adjusting the straps on his boots. He fixed me with a serious stare, the scar on his face menacing.

"I once spent some of my time recruiting Roses in Eldravine," he began, the words rushed as if this were inconvenient, his mind elsewhere.

My head screamed to run, but I remained motionless, listening as he continued.

"Though I doubt she mentioned me, I was close with your mother. She was one of the first norms I encountered when scouting for Roses. Only things didn't pan out how I had expected. She chose not to follow me since she wasn't a Rose." He chuckled to himself, the sound too light and full of fondness. It didn't suit him. "Riona chose to stay, and I was forced to return to my duties. Unfortunately, a small incident occurred."

He watched me, gauging my response. My head wouldn't follow. Everything inside me screamed to leave before he finished speaking. But I couldn't. I remained rooted to the spot.

He sighed, his arms crossing over his chest. "Your mother was with child. She kept it hidden from me. I simply had to find that out on my own."

My heartbeat pounded so loud in my ears; it was as if I were underwater. The room spun around me when the disturbing realization hit me. My knees buckled, nearly bringing me to the ground in disbelief.

"When I saw she found someone else to fill in my absence, I chose not to return. But I couldn't ignore the curiosity when I saw her child was a Rose. It was my idea to have Casimir visit you, using his unique ability to dreamwalk to prove my suspicions. As I suspected, you are my daughter."

I wanted to yell and deny it and demand proof. Throw something, break anything within arm's reach. Instead, I remained frozen, my face drained of color. A single touch could have tipped me over.

But I saw it as I studied him with blurry vision. Strange pieces tried to mesh together with the information.

Where I didn't share much of my mother's appearance outside of her pale complexion, Valor's nose, the shape of his mouth, shared an uncanny resemblance with mine.

His eyes had more similarities than the scarlet irises, but the shape and the way they sat on his face. My father—my non-biological father—had brown hair and hooded hazel eyes. His nose didn't match mine either, not like I had ever wondered. Being a Rose explained it away for me.

No, I looked nothing like the parents who raised me. But I resembled the man in front of me.

Casimir said something, but it didn't register with me. All I saw were Valor's eyes, fiery red and yet somehow cold. A stern and cruel man who looked as if he'd never known happiness in his life.

In stark contrast, the father who raised me was bright, kind to a fault. His smile exuded genuine joy, evident in the way it reached his eyes. He wasn't ever too serious, and even the times he needed to be, the love in his gaze was always a soothing balm.

Valor was much different. Sharing the same blood and features meant nothing to me. I didn't even know him, but I knew I would trade a thousand Valors to have the father who raised me back.

"Elita?" Casimir's voice was timid, different from his usual tone. His hand grabbed my elbow, an anchor as my head swam with a million different thoughts and questions. Only when I tore my focus from Valor did I realize I was crying. Cloudy tears blurred my vision as I searched Casimir's face.

I didn't want to believe it. I wanted to demand proof. And maybe when I had my bearings, I would pray to the gods Valor was lying and got some kind of joy out of my misery. But the last words from my mother, a brief utterance that I looked like my father—it made horrible sense. It had to be true. A harrowing truth I wanted to forget and run from. Only my legs wouldn't work.

Valor clapped his hands together, a strange and inappropriate sound, considering the words he spoke. "While I'm sure there are questions, I don't have the time nor the desire to answer them. I have things I need to attend to. Orin?"

I gaped at him, annoyed and full of a bubbling rage. Casimir's grip on my elbow tightened, and a thumb applied gentle pressure to the inside of my arm as if he could ever have the ability to comfort me again.

Orin nodded at Valor and grabbed the pack from the floor before he stood. The room emptied, except for Casimir and me. Tightness rippled across my collarbones, and the skin at my temples prickled. Fuzz framed the edge of my vision, and I worried if I didn't relax, my nails would cut through my palms.

The panic in my body had nowhere to go, so it came in huffing breaths. If there were a way to turn back time, I would have changed it so I never heard a word Valor said. That I wouldn't have to know such a terrible truth.

Minutes ticked by before I finally faced Casimir.

"You knew?" My voice quivered.

He moved closer, his hand still on my arm.

"Did you?!" I took a step back from him.

He pulled his hand like a child who touched a flame. His jaw clenched, and when he looked away, ashamed, more hot tears obstructed my sight.

"Yes. The General asked that we—"

"No. I don't care what he asked. I can't believe you never told me. Not when my parents died, not when I was lost and trying not to die in the woods. Even earlier than that. You just let me remain ignorant of the fact you knew my real father?" Saying it out loud stung, and I cringed at the words, hating how they felt to speak.

No, the only man who was my father was the one who raised me, who walked with me at night to escape the nightmares. The only parent who loved and cared for me. His memory brought me more sorrow, and I had to turn away.

From the corner of my eye, Casimir wrestled with wanting to come closer to me but knowing he couldn't. The wound was too deep. The trust was broken.

"I was sworn to secrecy, Elita. I couldn't have told you anything without facing punishment. You weren't ever meant to find out."

I could tell by his voice that he knew the explanation was weak and didn't justify it. The formality of my name on his lips sounded wrong and nothing like his soft-spoken whispers from long ago.

Wiping my face, I squared my shoulders when I faced him, my posture stronger than how fragile I felt. I wouldn't let him ever see me vulnerable again. He lost the right.

"I can't stay here," I said. Casimir's eyes widened at the declaration, "I'm going to go find Ronin, and I don't want you to follow me.

Frankly, I don't want any of you near me. I'm going to find him, and then I'm going to go find somewhere to complete my bloom in peace. Away from more people who only want me for their gain." Rage bled into every word. "I don't want you to try to find me. I don't want you in my head anymore." My chin quivered.

Casimir looked as if I'd spit on him as he recoiled from my words, his mask of indifference gone, replaced with a hurt I had never wanted to cause him.

I whirled before he could say anything or try to stop me, and I ran out of the fortress. People turned their heads as I left, embarrassed at themselves for eavesdropping. I didn't care what they thought of my words to Casimir or what they would think of me from that point on. I didn't need their help or their friendship, which was a farce anyway, buried under lies and secrets.

I stormed off, my feet sure as I found my way back down the path through the woods. I avoided the area around the mess hall and hoped Valor wouldn't catch sight of me leaving.

When I got to my tent, I threw the familiar green cloak over my shoulders, grabbed a few things, and stuffed them into my old pack. I slung it over my shoulder, ready to head out within a matter of minutes. There was nothing to tie me to Everbloom.

The only thing to stop me was another face filled with hurt and confusion. Alba stared at me as if I'd murdered the entirety of Everbloom, the pain worn out in the open.

"You can't go, Elita, we need you," she said.

I scoffed, and the sadness in her expression deepened. Her usual bright smile pulled into a true frown. It didn't suit her. Alba was like a ray of sunshine, and somehow, I had managed to darken that.

"No one has ever asked what I need. What I needed was answers. About why I spent my life hiding in fear while thousands of Roses live in peace in some secret forest, led by my father, and no one ever thought to come and help my family." Emotions choked me, but I shoved them away. "And when I finally found my way here, after my family died trying to protect me, no one could find it in themselves to tell me that my biological father was not only a Rose but one who could've come for us long ago."

I took a breath. The tension in my body was too much. "Instead, I'm being held against my will for the very same reason the king sealed me away. Do any of you even care?"

Alba stared, wide-eyed as her tears fell shamelessly. "Of course, Elita. You're my friend. None of us wanted to hurt you or lie. Valor had made us all agree to never—"

"I don't need to hear the same excuse Casimir gave me. I thought I could trust all of you." I shook my head and let my shoulders drop. My feet carried me past Alba.

I wouldn't see any of them again, but I had to get out of Everbloom. I needed to clear my head, and I had to catch up to Ronin and help him find somewhere to start over. The king would be hunting for him, and I worried what would become of him if he went back to the Iron Thorn. I had made a deal with Valor for his life, but I couldn't stay. I wouldn't die in Everbloom and leave the entire realm to suffer.

"Can you do me a favor, please?" I asked, my back to Alba.

"Of course." Her voice was strained, tainted by tears.

"Can you tell me which way they took Ronin?"

Alba sniffed, clearing her nose. "They took the East path toward the waterfall entrance, where you first came here with Casimir."

I nodded but didn't reply. There wasn't anything else left to say.

The curtain to the tent fell behind me, leaving Alba behind. I only hoped she wouldn't be punished by Valor. I wouldn't return to find out.

Chapter Thirty-One

Each rung of the ladder echoed with familiarity. My hands slipped on them, the wood covered in moss and drops of water from the spring above. And it reminded me too much of the man I followed down, with wonder and hope in my chest.

There was no time to think about Casimir and who I thought he was. My mother had been right. He was a curse.

If I didn't force the thoughts away, they would slow me down. I needed to focus on finding Ronin. I knew Valor would send the guards to pursue me. And worse, I knew he would revoke the deal and kill Ronin.

I needed to move faster.

When I reached the top of the cavern, the waterfall trickled—peaceful despite how horrible my entire soul ached. The cave was suffocating as I scrambled to get out. I trudged through the water, dripping as I made my way out of the narrow rocks.

Too much time had passed while I sat in Everbloom, mulling over our goodbyes, and I feared I would never find Ronin. Orondal was much too vast. I didn't know where he would go. Hours had passed since they escorted him out of Everbloom.

Only when I spotted a lone set of footprints on the dusty ground did a glimmer of hope ignite. I trailed the tracks, trying to banish the thoughts of Valor from my mind. His cold, cruel eyes, the way he was quick to decide Ronin's life should end. The callous way he claimed me as his daughter yet showed no emotion regarding it.

No explanation. Not worth his time.

For years, Valor could have tried to help us before my parents died at the king's hand. But he never did.

I wondered if he knew. I wondered if it caused him grief when Casimir told him my mother had died. That I held her in my arms as she begged me to cross the Forge—to invoke the name of a man I despised the moment we met.

It was ironic how my blood-related parents showed little interest in me, their own child. The bitter sting broke something inside me. My only parent who cared had no blood ties to me. Regardless of what I was, he chose to stay and be my father.

Valor never would have been able to replace him. Even if he came for us long ago. We may have shared similar features and genetics, but he would never be my father.

I hated him for the connection he orchestrated between Casimir and me. Valor had to have known of my suffering. He never came to help. And thinking about him and things I had no desire to change was a waste of energy.

Urgency tugged at me, but I paused to assess the tracks left in the dirt, the shape of the boot print. Instinct kicked in, and tracking the disruption would be easy. As long as the breeze didn't bury the prints.

Twisted gray trees dotted the land of Orondal, a jarring scene compared to how Everbloom burst with vibrant life. The air spun with a sense of desolation as I walked through the barren land, each step punctuated by a soft crunch.

Dead twigs and pieces of ruins littered the ground. I blocked out the memory of the golden castle Casimir showed me in the dreamspace. I wanted to be angry with him. I needed someone to blame. Grief tore at my resolve. My ghost wasn't who I thought he was.

I shook my head free of the thoughts and tried to think of where Ronin would go. Despite how much my entire being protested it, chances were he returned to the Iron Thorn. He had nothing with him when he left. There was no other choice unless he wanted to die of starvation or thirst in the Drought.

So, I followed in his footsteps. The sour breeze threatened to carry away the prints, causing them to smear. Their outline matched with the marks leading to Everbloom, obvious to my eye now.

The climb to get back into the kingdom would be more difficult. There were no ladders or mysterious cats. And the number of patrol guards likely increased since I climbed it a week ago. I had to figure out how to get over it unnoticed.

They could have my bloom; I had to give it, regardless. Just not until Ronin was safe.

No matter how many times I told myself that, I wanted to run and hide—to take Ronin somewhere I could wait out my bloom.

Such a thought only brought me more pain. I tuned out the voice telling me to run, and I focused on the task at hand.

Each mark led me closer. Time passed in a blur of directions carved into stones and dead trees. When I neared the Forge, my pulse raced, growing louder in my ears with every footfall.

The terrain transformed as I distanced myself from Everbloom and moved closer to the Iron Thorn. The air changed. A horrible sting in my lungs when I breathed it in.

After being underground, the heat from the sun was blistering. It rose high in the sky, well past noon. I ignored the way it made sweat bead at my brow and continued to the wall of stone, which stood out against the orange hue of the Drought Lands.

When the Forge appeared before me, I ignored the markings. Images of the cottage in flames, Talos's snarl, my mother's mouth painted in blood—they threatened to make me turn around and never return to the wicked kingdom.

But I needed to find Ronin. And the goddess demanded my sacrifice.

On trembling legs, I made my way to the Forge, knowing it would be the death of me.

. . .

The Forge was steeper than I remembered. I had been dazed and starving when I first scaled it and standing before the formidable wall again—it was nothing short of a miracle I ever made it over.

I approached it, ignoring the pang of sadness when I recalled Casimir pulling me out of the water. The emotions warred in my mind. From the elation of finally finding him to the sting of his deceit and indifference. It was too much, and I focused on the task at hand, searching for a way over the Forge. The dead trees offered hardly any coverage, but the openness brought me back to Ronin's prints. I saw where sticks had snapped and brush was pushed aside. The area appeared as if it had been ravaged, and it was clear he had returned filled with rage.

Ronin's tracks brought me to an incline. It made a ramp halfway up the Forge and I only had to figure out the rest of the way. I would climb the stone wall itself if I had to.

When I reached the top of the incline, I sized up the remaining expanse. If Ronin had made it the rest of the way, I hoped I would as well. Even though my body already burned with exertion, it didn't compare to how exhausted I was when I first climbed over the Forge.

I took a steadying breath and reached out for the first rock. It would have been preferable to have boots on. The stones scraped at my bare feet, but I let the lack of footwear be a guide. Which stones were safe to use, and which ones were weak.

And before I could rethink it, I was climbing.

My muscles protested the movement, but I had experienced it before. I pushed past the initial discomfort and instead brought my focus back to Ronin.

The thought of the guards seeing him emerge from over the Forge made the worry outweigh hesitation until my heart hammered and more sweat trickled down my spine.

He was a wanted man, and if he were caught trying to clamber back into the Iron Thorn, he wouldn't make it far.

The fear had no time to take root when a wisp of black flew up at my side. Beady eyes stared at me, and Calla swooped, squawking in my ear. My arms trembled, and I nearly lost my grip.

Shaky breaths fell from my lips, and I pressed my forehead to a stone in front of me. I tried to steady my breathing, even as Calla swept close to my shoulder again, crying out.

The persistent raven would be the death of me.

I tried to ignore her and continued until I was close to the top. The parapets peeked into view. With each careful placement of my hands, I made it to the edge of the wall. I peered over to survey the surroundings and hoped the guards wouldn't be nearby.

Eeriness swept through the air as I took in the empty guard posts.

There were no signs of them down either side of the wall. The parapets were empty of archers. The top of the wall was deadly silent, not a single sign of life.

With caution, I pulled myself up the rest of the way, taking in the strange sight. It made the fear all the worse. If they weren't present, I worried it meant they were after Ronin.

My stride took me across the top of the wall quickly as I searched for the way down, my heart in my throat. It wasn't until I saw the ropes of a rickety ladder thrown over the wall that I paused. It should have been a relief to see, but the sight of the climb down made me ill.

The silky black raven dove close by once more. Her wings fluttered, and she circled me. I fiddled with the clasp of the cloak Ronin had given me. Stalling only allowed him to get further. I had to go.

Dizzy with worry, I clambered down the ladder, my heart pounding in my chest. My hands worked down the rails with haste. The ladder swayed with every move I made.

When I neared the bottom, I jumped the rest of the way, grunting when my bare feet landed in the grass. I whirled around, hoping for a sign of Ronin or the guards. I stood amidst the vast forests of the Iron Thorn, and the realization that I might lose Ronin grew stronger with each fleeting second.

I took a breath and tried to settle my thunderous pulse. Nothing was familiar. I had been in a state of delirium when I came across the wall, so disoriented that I followed a cat as if it were a guide.

The trees stretched on in every direction. No matter how hard I tried, I wouldn't have been able to find my way to the Temple in Eldravine. I just had to move and get far from the Forge and even further from Everbloom.

Though I knew that neither Valor nor Casimir would cross the Forge—not for me. They never had—but time was slipping through my fingers, and if I didn't hurry, Ronin would be as good as dead.

The woods swallowed me whole as I walked deeper into the sea of trees, the scent of earth and pine filling my senses. I scoured the area, my eyes scanning for any sign someone had passed through, but it was as if they had vanished without a trace. Everything remained undisturbed.

I let out a groan while I sensed time slip away, with Ronin growing more distant from me.

Until something caught my eye. To my right, some branches broke down as if someone had cut through them, accompanied by a large scuff in the dirt, as if a body had slid through it. I experienced a surge of hope, and I proceeded through the fallen brush.

With every step, my gaze darted around. So many years spent learning how to hunt or forage with my father paid off. Every life skill he took the time to teach me, building to that moment.

I was aware it could have possibly been an animal, but with no paw prints in sight, and considering how much was snapped away, I hoped my instincts were correct.

Moss appeared run through by a boot print, the first actual sign I had to prove a person had gone that way. I remained on the path, tracking the scattered debris as my guide.

The tranquility shattered when branches snapped deeper in the thick foliage. I surveyed the area with ragged breaths. The noises continued, twigs breaking in the wake of footsteps. I held my breath and watched for guards in red to emerge. But the harsh color never appeared.

The chaotic noises continued, moving closer and closer until I couldn't take it anymore. "Ronin?" I called into the woods, aware it may be a fatal mistake.

The footsteps stopped in response, and in the next instant, they picked up, nearly causing me to turn and bolt.

A figure came into view, his bruised and cut face a relief. "Ronin." It was barely a breath from my lips.

Ronin stared at me in disbelief. Our ragged panting carried in the breeze, rustling Ronin's hair from his face.

He took a step closer, appearing bewildered. "Elita...What are you doing here?"

The words caught in my throat for a moment. "I'm sorry I let you leave alone. And for abandoning you at the cottage. After everything you did for me...I'm sorry."

He stared at me. Unmoving. He didn't speak, but his hands trembled. I took a careful step closer, confused. "Ronin?"

My body stiffened in response to the sudden coldness of his demeanor. In the back of my mind, I questioned why he appeared to be returning to the Forge or why the guards were absent.

"What is this?" I asked, eyeing the pack he had and the way his hands shook at his sides. Another wave of foreboding hit me.

The sensation became familiar.

"I never did tell you about my daughter." Ronin's voice carried an emptiness I never noticed before. The way he spoke made my body twist with an ill sensation.

He didn't look at me when he continued, "She was four years old when she died. Aerilyn." A pained smile crossed his face, his cheeks blotched with red as sudden tears fell. "She was only four."

My heart ached, and I wanted to touch his arm, to comfort him in some way, but instinct told me not to.

Somewhere in the forest, a raven called.

Ronin's eyes snapped open. "She was a Rose. The goddess damned her at birth."

The wind tangled curls across my vision. White flickered in the breeze. Calla's cries echoed in the trees, and I held my breath.

Ronin pulled a hand down his face. "Her first petal bloomed when she was only four. It was too early. She struggled to voice the pain of the bloom, and my wife did what any worried mother would. She took her to a healer despite my protest." His voice caught.

I took a tentative step back from him.

"The healer alerted the king. They killed Aerilyn in the Temple garden, her hair sheared for all to see." His voice dripped with unbridled animosity. "All but us, her parents, were present. They released us from the cells with the news she died, and her bloom was unsuccessful. Her life was spent for nothing."

My vision blurred with tears, the fear and the disbelief spilling over. I didn't dare say a word. I didn't move.

Ronin erupted in sudden laughter, the sound manic. "As if they hadn't tortured us enough, we were meant to keep quiet. If we muttered a word to anyone, they threatened to sentence us both to death. But our reason for living was already gone." He ran a hand through his hair, shaking. "Melody couldn't live with the guilt. She took her life in the Temple garden. She didn't want to go quietly."

My nails bit into my palms, and I had to force myself not to reach out to him. The magnitude of the pain he endured was hard to fathom. But I couldn't touch him. Standing before him, I felt as if it were someone else entirely.

When he didn't continue, I unfurled my fists. My voice trembled when I spoke. "Why are you telling me this?"

"Because that damned forest of Roses. Because my daughter died for nothing when adults are down there, living long and full lives, flaunting blooms freely in their hair!" Spit flew from his mouth. I grimaced and backed further from him.

He countered my retreat and took a step closer, not letting me increase the distance.

Close by, wings fluttered through the trees. The sound of one raven turned into many, all screeching—as if they begged me to run.

Ronin took another step closer. "You don't know how long I've waited for your bloom, Elita. A white bloom foretold to end the drought. The king has spoken of it in the confines of the Temple. The prince has searched for it. Secrets meant to stay among the king's council." He paused, choked by the disdain. "But it was your father's notebook that said he suspected it was you. Your father damned you with his musings."

In a state of shock, I stared at him, unable to move. My mind raced with uncertainty, and my body pleaded with me to run. But I had no place to go and no one left to run to.

I stammered, "Talos...he had my father's notebook."

"And who do you think left it for him to find? Your father suspected it long ago. His selfishness cursed my daughter. Had your parents given you to the Temple when you were a child, Aerilyn would still be here." His voice broke, the only sign of apprehension.

The man underneath the grief appeared briefly when his eyes flicked to mine. He knew me more than anyone had ever been given the chance to, and I saw the way it tore at him.

But Ronin took in a sharp breath and steeled his resolve. His once warm and friendly demeanor transformed into something dark and cruel, casting a shadow over his every action. My body slumped at the sight, and my feet carried me further from him.

"Your father let me share my grief, my loss. And he said *nothing* about you being a Rose. He let me spill my heart while he harbored you away. My only regret is that Aedric isn't here to suffer the way I had to."

"You can't mean that, Ronin." The stutter in my voice betrayed me. I gulped as my back ran into the rough surface of a tree.

He closed the space. "But I do. Instead of your father, the king will suffer the way I had to, and everyone back in that sanctuary will be held accountable as well."

Ice knotted my spine. "No."

"Where do you think the guards went? What do you think I bargained for reentry?"

The realization was like a slap in the face.

Everbloom.

I blinked furiously to fight back tears. The weight of his betrayal crushed me, and my once steadfast beliefs crumbled to dust.

I gasped for air when the adrenaline rushed through my veins, causing a horrible tightness in my chest. I tried to fight such a display of weakness, but it had already begun. Tears streaked my red cheeks until they dripped from my chin to the grass below.

And in the deadly silence, I swore I heard them hit the earth.

Ronin watched the wetness coat my face, his voice broke. "You made it too easy for me to sneak my way in." He shook his head as if disappointed.

"You said—"

"I said what you needed to hear!" His resolve teetered—he no longer met my horrified gaze.

My legs buckled, and I slumped harder against the tree.

Ronin pushed fallen pieces of his hair back before he continued. "You were meant to die that night at the cottage when the first petal bloomed. If not for the man from the village, it would have already been done."

"Ronin, please, don't—"

"There's nothing you can say." He looked as if he'd gone mad. Pain tore at his expression, even as he grinned. "And now I'll shear your bloom, and this realm will feel the pain I did that day. There will be nothing left."

"There are more Roses. It won't end here. There are so many more who can—"

"No. You're wrong. You are the last sacrifice. The final one. It would change more than an old dying kingdom. You'd save the entire realm and give the Drought Lands life again. From the Iron Thorn to Tyvolia. I can't allow that."

"That's insanity. You'll die in the realm you betray!" Panic and desperation warped my words.

"What do I have left? The king took everything I had. Believe me, the last thing I care about is what happens to me when the realm dies. They don't deserve to thrive, not after what they've done."

Something glinted in the light, and I glanced at his hand, seeing his dagger catch the reflection of the sun.

The gasps and tears threatened to overcome me, but I had to do something. "You have no idea what you're doing, Ronin," I said his name softly. If I could at least cause him to hesitate, I could try to run. "I know you're hurt. I know that now. But everything you said—"

He cut me off with a taunting laugh. "You're so naive, Elita." He advanced, the dagger tight in his fist.

"Please, I'm begging you—"

Ronin cut me off when he closed the distance. His breath was hot on my face, and I couldn't think of anything to say that would stop him.

"Isn't this what you wanted? To make the king, the *prince*, and the goddess pay?" He leaned in closer, and I flinched. "You made it easy. I only had to remove your parents and take you away from the Temple, the prince's torture." He swallowed hard, his mouth inches away when he whispered, "I'm sorry it had to be you."

The forest appeared wicked. It spun around us until I was sick to my stomach. I watched it blur and shift, the trees moving as if they were alive, laughing at my misfortune.

My breath shuddered. "You killed them. You killed my family." It wasn't a question; I'd finally caught up.

"He came for your father. He came for you."

Instead of anger, the willingness to fight died out. My skin crawled, and my lips tasted like poison, both tainted by his touch. The urge to vomit overwhelmed me.

The dagger reflected the sun mere inches from my face. Ronin grabbed my hair and pulled my head back, causing me to whimper.

"Please don't do this. Don't let this consume you." The words came out high-pitched and panicked.

Ronin kept one hand in my hair and brought the dagger up sideways against the sky, poised to cut. I saw the hesitation in him while his hand shook around the hilt. The only proof of something in him being split.

It didn't matter. The hesitation wasn't enough to stop him.

Urgency filled my veins, and I thrashed against him in desperation, slamming my knee into his stomach. He groaned and stumbled forward as the dagger fell, avoiding my hair and narrowly missing my neck. The blade came down hard with the fall of his hand.

Pain seared through my side.

The blade caught, jerking through flesh as it pulled down with Ronin's loss of balance.

The steel was icy as it cut through my skin. I shrieked and pushed harder, kicking and shoving with the strength I had left in my legs. They made contact a few times and caught him off guard.

Ronin grunted and fell back onto a tree stump, toppling over. I scrambled to stand. Heat tore through my nerves. Every move I made jarred the blade.

I gritted my teeth and pulled the dangling dagger from my side with shaky hands, screaming at the way it slid out of muscle and skin. It clattered to the ground, and I backed up, heaving for air to fill my lungs.

One hand pressed to the wound as it sputtered, no longer blocked by the blade. I regretted the choice, my palm wet and sticky. The blood was warm as I applied pressure to the gash.

With my other arm, I reached out. Desperation flooded me. I begged the goddess and the earth. I needed them to move for me.

The thrum ravaged my body. Another heartbeat. A thundering pulse. It rang in my ears until it cut beneath my skin. Blackness filled the edge of my vision. It warped until waves of crimson rippled through the air.

A mixture of a sob and a scream left my throat as my hand shook. Vines burst forward from my hand and wrapped around his ankles. My entire body shook with the sheer power of it, the adrenaline and shock numbing me.

Ronin roared and thrashed, trying to break free.

My hand dropped, and the energy drained.

I didn't have time to think.

I turned and ran.

Chapter Thirty-Two

I stumbled through the woods, my feet bloodied as I stepped barefoot over twigs, rocks, and rotted bark. My vision glazed and distorted as I trudged on, whimpering every time the gash in my side throbbed, another layer of fresh blood to coat my palm. If I didn't hurry, Ronin would catch up, or I'd bleed out, and it would all be over. Rather than recoil at the thought, my body yearned for it.

Scrambling my mind, I begged for Casimir to find me once more. I begged for forgiveness in my head, and in the madness that found me in my loss of blood, I whispered it among the trees, over and over. "I'm so sorry. Please. I'm so sorry."

The adrenaline in my body dissipated. I was losing too much blood. I kept my hand pressed to the wound, hoping to stop it. But every footstep shook my entire body, and more crimson gushed, causing my head to swim.

A raven cried overhead. My skin dampened in a cold sweat. I couldn't even bring myself to look at the sky.

There wasn't anywhere for me to go. I was only prolonging the inevitable, and I continued to wander, hoping not to bleed out in the forest. It was a foolish hope.

Ronin was going to win and destroy the realm.

Though it was pointless, I begged the gods to save Everbloom. My desperation to be free, to find Ronin, doomed them all.

"Casimir, please," I whispered again, hoping he heard me through our strange connection.

There was no way to warn them. Lendorr and Talos would burn their entire forest down and take as many as possible to be used as a sacrifice. Except it wouldn't matter. Their blooms meant nothing. I would die in the woods trying to escape Ronin and become the realm's end.

In my ignorance, I had wanted to repay Ronin, to save him. But he had killed my family. He allowed the woman in Woolfolk to die. There was no shame, no remorse. A shell of a man who let himself drown in his grief.

And in a twisted way, I sympathized with him.

I wanted Talos to pay for what he had done to me. I wanted every complacent person in the Temple and the king's circle to suffer punishment for the innocent blood spilled over centuries.

Even so, the blood of my parents wasn't on their hands.

Ronin orchestrated it all. He killed them in cold blood for no other reason than to get his revenge on my family and the king. I played into his hands the moment he told me he knew my father. And instead of saving Ronin when I bargained with Valor, I doomed every Rose in Everbloom. They would be captured or killed.

More blood on my hands.

More lives traded for my desperate attempt to have a choice.

Lives lost under the guise that someone understood me.

The pain in my chest echoed the wound in my side. It reverberated and twisted until I lost my focus and stumbled.

I let out a pitiful groan and threw my hands out to catch myself. My arms were unsteady, and my elbows protested the weight of my body—they wobbled like a newborn calf trying to walk for the first time. Fresh crimson added another dark layer to my white tunic, and I winced.

The damp dirt beneath my palms sent a jolt through my veins, and I gasped at the sensation. As if the earth tried to offer something to push me on, past the tree line. If I made it back to Casimir—if I made it back to Everbloom—maybe it wouldn't be too late. The king had no way of knowing yet. It would take days to get word to him.

I had to warn them.

Hope was a dangerous thing, and it never did me any good. But I had to cling to it, or it wasn't feasible to make it out of the forest.

My muscles ached, and they begged me to rest, but the energy from the earth was enough. It was enough to get me to reach out, grasping the mossy bark of the closest tree to pull myself up, an agonized sigh breaking apart my cracked lips. It was enough to get me to stand, panting, when I reached my full height.

I fixed my gaze on the tree line in front of me where the light poured through. My feet shuffled one after the other, dragging through the dirt.

The clearing materialized in front of me, and realization swarmed me, thickening the air like heavy smoke.

The trees twisted wickedly, sinister and dark. Jagged rocks lined the other side of the clearing, like claws jutting out from the ground. Where there should have been vibrant greenery inside the confines of the Iron Thorn, it had turned gray.

Death consumed the clearing.

I had been there before. Many times, in my nightmares.

My body grew cold, and the adrenaline evaporated. A sour wind blew ragged curls across my face. They stuck to the salty tears that clung to my cold cheeks. I was too weak to summon the strength needed to push the hair off my face.

A twisted part of me wished for the Temple or even Talos and his torture. It begged for the sacrificial garden and a hundred nameless faces there to witness my death. To become one with the earth and let my bloom give the realm life. Anything but what awaited me.

Bitter resentment replaced the taste of hope and freedom I had in Everbloom. I would have traded every one of those peaceful moments to return to the cell in the Temple. I would have traded anything to have been placed with the council at birth, as I was meant to. To die the way I was destined to, rather than by the hands of a vengeful man.

A life lived in the Temple. A family never torn apart. A mother and father I never had to grieve because I never had the chance to know them. No ghost to haunt my childhood dreams—a connection forced upon me by a man who wanted nothing to do with me.

Isolation in the Temple. No loss. No betrayal.

A life untouched by love and pain. Only a duty to the Iron Thorn burned into my soul as the lone choice. I longed for it so desperately, it brought me physical pain.

Determined footsteps snapped branches in the trees behind me, and I knew what was to come. I had relived the same nightmare since I was a little girl. There was no escaping fate.

I remained motionless, rooted like a tree. Terrified yet thankful soon it would be over. It would all end as soon as the man I had mistakenly trusted found his way through the trees to me.

"Casimir." The name whistled in the fetid breeze.

Somewhere in the trees, ravens cried out.

I let my arms drop to my sides. They swayed listlessly in the stillness. I braced for the inevitable.

The footsteps came to a halt a short distance behind me, and I sensed his hungry gaze pierce through me. The vibrant blue no longer reminded me of sunny skies but rather the dark grayish blue of a lake on a cloudy day. Lifeless and cold.

"Why did you run?" Ronin's voice sent a shiver down my spine.

My bloodied hands curled, barely able to make a fist. "I figured you'd want better light, so you don't miss this time."

Ronin chuckled, dark and low.

I gulped and shut my eyes. A misplaced peace came over me at the thought of it being over. I would be free and none of it would be my burden to bear anymore.

The wind howled, brushing my petal-covered hair from my face. I took a deep breath, reaching for one last piece of adrenaline to break the ground beneath us. I searched for the thrum of the earth.

But I had nothing left.

"This won't bring her back, Ronin," I whispered, almost inaudible above the wind as it howled, throwing my hair back from my face.

Ronin huffed in anger, and I heard him lunge before the impact.

The force of his weight knocked the breath from my chest as we careened across the dirt, the dead brush scraping my face. I cried out when the movement tore through my side.

He jerked me over to face him. His expression twisted into something devilish that I didn't recognize.

Ronin straddled my waist and grabbed my hair from beneath me with shaking hands. He gathered as much as he could and sucked in a harsh breath.

"A realm where she doesn't exist is not one worth saving. You'll die here, and the king will suffer as much as my daughter had to," he rasped. "I won't stop until they're choking on the cursed air, and they have to listen to their children suffer the way Aerilyn did." He brought the dagger from behind his back.

I was too terrified to make a sound.

He pulled the strands of hair tighter, yanking my head up as he held the blade to the sky. I forced my eyes shut when the dagger fell.

It cut through my hair with little effort, shearing the petals away with the strands.

Anguish devoured me.

My mouth gaped, but no sounds came out. It felt as if he had taken the blade straight to my skull and torn it through the flesh rather than merely cutting through my hair.

Hot tears ran down my face—a shock compared to the ice that crawled over my skin.

My limbs sank into the grass beneath me.

I begged my body to fight. To kick or thrash against him, but it was futile. My tunic clung to my stomach with blood and my head swam.

For a moment, I understood why my mother never had it in her to love me. How could you allow yourself to love someone knowing what horrors they would one day endure?

I laid there, wishing for the pain to swallow me whole so I could be free of it.

Ronin growled, a guttural, animal-like noise. He pulled more hair from under me, his blade swiftly breaking through it. Black curls with flashes of white rained down on me, falling into my face and mouth. It clung to the new tears that trailed my face.

Like fog moving in after a storm, a sudden and familiar thick presence swarmed me. It was warm, a sliver of comfort in the frigid grasp of death. It sent a jolt through my veins.

The sound of sprinting erupted in the field, snapping branches in their wake. I wanted to fight harder. *I need to fight harder.*

More blood pooled my tunic when Ronin's weight shifted on top of me, and my stomach rolled with nausea.

Casimir's name left my lips in a silent prayer.

"No!" Casimir thundered. He sprinted through the trees, blurry in my tear-filled vision.

Ronin's manic laughter mixed with tears while he stood from where he straddled me. Hair and petals fell, withering on the ground, gray and wrinkled.

I wept, and my breath shuddered.

In. The wound throbbed.

Out. Heaviness settled in my bones.

The impact reverberated through the air when Casimir's shoulder slammed into Ronin, who crumpled to the ground. His body fell with a resounding thud. He gasped; the wind knocked from his lungs.

Casimir's gaze locked with mine, his eyes like fiery embers while his rage burned. His face blurred. Black spots flickered across my vision.

Ronin took his chance and jumped up in a swift movement. His hand grabbed the fallen dagger.

The ominous quiet of the field broke when Casimir pulled his sword from its sheath, his hands wrapped around the hilt. Ronin showed no fear. He accomplished his goal. He had no regard for his own life, and I watched in fear when Casimir lunged, his sword swinging for Ronin.

Ronin quickly dodged and brought his fist to Casimir's cheek, which sent him staggering to the side. My stomach churned at the sight.

It didn't take Casimir long to fix his stance with his sword already swinging for Ronin again.

Ronin brought the dagger up, attempting to block Casimir's blade. The edge of the dagger dug into Ronin's palm as the other held onto the handle. Casimir's sword locked over it, ringing throughout the field.

My vision tunneled. The torment made the forest spin.

Casimir let out a roar of frustration before he forced his blade down further, causing the dagger to slice across Ronin's hand.

The force sent Ronin to the ground once more, and the dagger soared as Casimir kicked Ronin down when he attempted to stand.

Ronin tried to kick Casimir, but he lost the upper hand. Casimir used the hilt of his sword to smack between Ronin's eyes. The horrific sound of the impact made my stomach churn.

Blood trickled from Ronin's nose as he tried to fight back. But Casimir didn't let him. His training won out. With a sickening blow, Ronin's head slammed to the ground.

My stomach dropped when Casimir raised his sword overhead, fury in his ember glare. I closed my eyes, shutting them as hard as I could. The realm spun until I was dizzy. I barely heard Ronin's wails of pain over what sounded like waves, blood rushing in my ears.

The waves carried me away. They couldn't drown out the piercing sound of Casimir's revulsion echoing through the field.

A heavy weight settled in my chest as the haunting sound filled the air. It pulled me further into a sea of sorrow.

Silently, I ached for my parents, wishing to go back in time to change what happened to them and apologize for all the pain I caused. When my thoughts went to them, I sensed Akuma's hand of death.

Losing my petals hurt so much worse than I thought it would. The anguish rippled through me. My body involuntarily tried to laugh when I thought of how pitiful it was for me to hope for a peaceful death.

That was never my fate.

The last sound to reach me was Casimir calling my name.

It made it so much worse.

Do ghosts die with you? If they tethered themselves to you?

Chapter Thirty-Three

Death was not what I imagined.

The suffocating darkness engulfed me as I floated in its midst.

In the dark, I heard Casimir's echoing plea for me to breathe. Desperation in his voice as it broke, hoarse from the amount of begging.

Thump.

The weight of death was heavy on my chest.

It pounded incessantly. It wouldn't give.

I begged for relief. Had I not earned the right to die in peace? To be carried in the waves of pain and tears. Wasn't that torture enough?

Thump.

Hot air covered my face, thick and warm like a humid breeze. The hands of death pushed against me. The weight pressed into me harder, firmer.

Fire twisted my bones as it crushed me.

Ronin's face haunted me in death; his snarl distorted by tears that clung to the rim of his eyes.

The agony followed me. I fought the memory, begging Akuma to carry me away in his hands of death. Anything but the torture that replayed in my mind.

Pools of blood. Innocent hands, dripping in crimson. Casimir's guttural scream echoed in my mind.

Thump.

Tendrils of black and crimson slithered beneath shut eyelids, disrupting the abyss. Shrieks clawed through my skull, carrying the voice of thousands in one; *"Wake up."*

The weight increased, pressing harder until my chest collapsed.

Something snapped.

A muted cry filled the silence, and it took me a moment to realize it was my own.

"Vanmore, enough. She's breathing."

Indistinct murmurs reached my ears, along with the shuffle of feet. Someone's hand ran over the curve of my neck, trembling as the other put pressure on my abdomen. Skin brushed mine, and my nerves screamed at the contact.

Swelling and heaviness in my eyes made it difficult for me to open them. I brought my hand to my face. My fingers swiped at my temple and down to my hair. Shakily, I brushed over the cut strands and winced. Heat flared through my scalp. The severed curls barely reached my chin.

A calloused hand caressed my face—their thumb ran across the expanse of my cheek. I recognized the touch and leaned in.

The realization I hadn't died was difficult to grasp. I tasted it, bitter and lonely, as it pulled me close. But the pain in my body compared to the contrast of Casimir's gentle touch was proof I somehow escaped my doomed fate.

"Elita, can you hear me?" Casimir's voice sounded miles away, but his hand never left my face.

I gave a feeble nod, scarcely able to move past the ache that rattled my bones. Each breath I took seared through my chest from where Casimir's hands pressed into them.

Shaking arms wrapped around me, and I gasped. My eyes pried themselves open, blinded by the sun. Casimir's body held onto mine as if he couldn't believe I was alive.

A strangled sob made its way up my throat, and it burned me from the inside out to cry once more.

When I curled around the wound and fractured ribs, the pain intensified tenfold. I tried to ignore it, instead, fixating on the tangible warmth of Casimir.

He was alive; he was okay.

I wept without shame. My hands shuddered as I searched for Casimir's tunic to wrap my bloody fists into, forcing him closer to me. His body heat was a pleasant contrast to the strange cold that clung to me.

Footsteps crunched as someone approached, and I glanced up to see Valor close by, his eyes unreadable and his sword at his side. Blood dried on the hilt. He made it out unscathed, his armor speckled with crimson. But his survival hadn't concerned me. He wasn't among those I searched for.

No, the one who caught my attention was Alba at his shoulder, face covered in streaks of tears that trekked through the dirt on her cheeks. I wept harder at the sight of her, and to her side, Galan appeared wounded but mostly unscathed.

I let out a staggering sigh and shifted in Casimir's arms. Air hissed through my teeth when the movement caused fire in my ribs.

When a hand squeezed my arm, I noted Taryn sitting in the dirt a few inches from me, hands covered in my blood. She loosened her grip and brushed her palm over my shoulder, much more delicate than her typical demeanor.

A dry, nervous chuckle rattled out of my throat.

Her red hair cascaded around her baffled face.

"I must look rough, huh?" My voice didn't sound like my own, and it hurt to speak. Behind us, Alba let out an uncomfortable cackle, something between a manic laugh and a sob. She covered her mouth and shook her head.

Casimir's arm tightened around my back, and his palm pressed against my wound. The pressure stung and I flinched, my breath quickening.

My gaze met Casimir's, and I noted a streak of blood across his cheek, which didn't seem to be his. Crimson made a circle around his nostrils, and one of his eyes was entirely red, with no white to balance the red of his iris against the blood surrounding it.

The sight of him sent my body rigid and the sudden tension in my limbs made both him and Taryn shift.

"It's okay, El. We're okay," he muttered. But all I could think about was the screaming. Casimir's mixed with Ronin's.

My head swam.

"Ronin?" I asked, afraid of the answer.

Casimir winced when I said his name, his grip loosening on me. He shook his head, his eyes darkening. He would never be the same, and it was my fault. The heaviness returned to my chest, and I struggled to take in a breath.

Valor approached as if he couldn't stand waiting any longer. "We need to move. She needs to be taken to somewhere that we have the means to help her. She's lost too much blood." Emotion never reached his voice. Stoic and cold.

Casimir nodded, unraveled his arms from my body, and Valor replaced him on my right side. To my surprise, Valor put an arm around my back and another under my knees.

I didn't have it in me to protest, and I let him lift me from the ground.

Until then, I hadn't realized the bottom of my tunic was ripped open, leaving my mangled abdomen bare. Timidly, Alba reached over and rested the torn fabric on me.

Valor adjusted his arms, and a hiss pulled through my teeth at the agitation in my side and rib cage. He nodded toward the woods near us. It was the first time I surveyed our surroundings.

There was a makeshift trail through the woods just outside of the clearing. When Valor started walking, the ache in my bones became unbearable. I shut my eyes and clenched my teeth. We left the dead clearing behind, and when I finally brought myself to peer through slitted lids, Valor followed a path as it neared the Forge border—a hole through the side of the stone wall. Rubble laid in the wake of whatever had broken through.

Behind the small group of soldiers, a body lay limp in the dirt, chestnut hair obscuring the face. I had to turn away.

Casimir walked in front of us, and Taryn stayed beside my head. She glanced over at me with a worried expression every few minutes. Her hand found somewhere to rest, and she continued to use her abilities.

Orin and a few others I didn't know flanked Valor. The braid was long gone from Orin's hair, the white stained with blood. The others appeared unscathed as well.

Alba and Galan stayed close to Casimir, exchanging looks with each other. I closed my eyes and buried my face in Valor's shoulder to avoid speculating their words and block out the blinding sunlight.

His arms shifted, but he never let me go or protested, and I thought of my father, the one who had raised me. I missed him desperately. More than I ever had. I wanted him to hold me while I cried. I wanted him to take away the horrific memories.

I cried silently, wetting Valor's armor, but I had no control.

We walked for hours. Every step rattled my body. Shadows passed over my face, but I didn't have the strength to open my eyes. I was bone tired. Every few minutes, Taryn would ask if I was still awake, to which I gave nothing but a single nod. The thrum of her abilities never ceased. Her hand remained on one of my shins.

The adrenaline faded fast and left me hollow.

Valor's step never faltered, even with my weight. He walked at a careful pace, and it didn't register with me at first, but it felt as if he wanted to keep me from more pain. Curled in his arms, I stayed quiet until we came to a stop. I wanted to look, and I panicked when I couldn't. I had no energy, and every move sent my body recoiling.

My breath shook, and I put a single hand on Valor's shoulder. "I can't," I muttered, my voice muffled beneath the sound of my pulse.

Valor's arms tensed, and then they let go. My back lay on a solid surface, and murmurs filled the room. People rummaged through things in chaos, hands brushed the tunic back from the wound, and frantic chatter erupted. A thrum of meaningless words.

My hearing buzzed until it numbed me.

I woke to darkness. Posture rigid, I glanced around until my sight adjusted. The flicker of a lantern created shadows outside the makeshift tent I was in, offering me the slightest bit of visibility. The dim light was piercing, and I rubbed at my eyes with sore, bandaged fists.

My body twisted with new aches, and I yearned for the solace of sleep to wash over me once again.

A shadow moved beside me, and I gasped. My torso jerked, increasing the pain.

"My apologies, Ms. Blackthorne." Galan's familiar voice filled me with relief, and I took a shaky breath. My head turned in his direction.

"How are you feeling?" he asked in a soft tone. Purple splotches bloomed beneath his skin, painting his face and hands.

The sight filled me with guilt. "Sore," I said. My throat was dry, and I placed a hand on it.

Galan grabbed a mug of water beside my cot, narrowly spilling it before he handed it to me. I grabbed it with haste and lifted my head to chug the lukewarm water, not bothered by the earthy flavor.

I emptied it, and he took the mug from me, setting it to the side.

"Where is everyone?" I asked. My head rested on the pillow.

Galan sat on the edge of the cot and brushed his hair back from his face, revealing more damage that made my stomach churn.

"Many have gone to their tents to rest. The General is trying to make a plan. They are trying to figure out what happens next." He scratched the back of his neck, then relaxed his arms at his sides. I nodded, hesitant to ask which group Casimir found himself in.

I rolled onto my side that wasn't covered in bandages, though my entire torso smarted, and short coils fell across my face. Galan reached forward as if to brush the stuck hairs away. I gasped and pulled back, my hand defensively blocking his.

"Oh, my apologies."

I shook my head. "No, it's okay. The short strands are just odd...I didn't think it would hurt so bad to have it cut." I chuckled dryly. Nothing about the situation was funny. I only wished to spare Galan from any guilt. It was, after all, my fault.

He instinctively touched his hair, pin straight and dark. "I've never bloomed and lost it by force. It's been able to run its course every time. I can't begin to imagine."

Determined to ignore the pulsating ache in my scalp, I nodded grimly and shifted my focus to the flicker of the lantern.

I was too afraid to run my hands over my hair. The curls were oily and matted against the back of my neck, undoubtedly from blood as opposed to neglect.

Instead, I steered the conversation elsewhere. "Galan?"

His head snapped in my direction.

After a moment of hesitation, I asked, "What happened in Everbloom?"

Galan tensed and averted his gaze. "I have been asked to not speak on it until you have regained your strength."

With pursed lips, I repositioned myself to face him better. "Please. Was anyone hurt?"

He fidgeted and stared at the flame in the lantern. "The border guards came down. The General was quick to take action. Unfortunately, there were casualties among our people."

The tent spun, and my fists clenched. His words swirled in my head, my chest tightened, and I struggled to take a deep breath.

Casualties.

Roses dead because of me and the bargain I made.

Visions of Everbloom filled my mind. My last hours spent there, and the man I thought I had saved. Instead of helping him, I brought death upon the Roses, and I lost my petals.

I knew it was a bad idea, but I brought a timid hand to my hair. My scalp screamed at the touch. Flashes of Ronin's snarl sent me gasping, and I sat straight in the bed, fire shooting through my torso.

My hair was choppy, barely at my chin. I pulled my hands away from my hair, and they were crimson.

Galan stood, his gaze filled with alarm.

I pulled at my hair until my hands met an early, blunt end. Tears fell on instinct, and my mouth gaped, lost for words. I stood in a panic, my legs wobbling as if they weren't even there.

Pain in my ribs threatened to bring me to the ground. I stumbled forward, knocking things over as I grasped for something to hold on to.

"Help me!"

"You're okay, Elita," he hushed, dropping formalities. He reached for my arm, and the contact made it worse.

I recoiled. Memories of Ronin's hold on me sent me into a spiral. In a state of panic, I scrambled and gasped, my mind starting to dissociate and blur the lines between what was real and what was not. I felt myself heaving for air in between pleas for help, but none of the sounds reached my ears.

Galan stood close, appearing frightened, as he tried to find a way to help me. Only something was wrong and I wasn't in the tent anymore. I was in the gray, dead forest, begging for my life.

I shut my eyes and pressed my palms to my head.

Blinding light broke me out of it, forcing me back to reality as several lanterns illuminated the tent as people charged in. Valor was the first to enter, Casimir stumbling in behind him, his eyes ablaze. A few other familiar faces appeared in front of me, all concerned as they noticed me in a mess on the floor.

Their focus went to Galan.

"She touched her hair and began to panic," Galan said in a rush. He knelt next to me, not bothering to address them.

I glanced at my hands, which were wrapped in clean bandages. No blood. I wasn't in the clearing; instead, I was in a faded black tent. The forest was gone, ripping away my sanity with it.

I blushed furiously, embarrassed by my outburst. My body ached, and I didn't know if I could stand on my own.

Valor relaxed when he realized nothing was wrong. He set his lantern on one of the empty cots near me and walked over to us.

"I can't stand," I said, my voice trembling.

Galan didn't hesitate, and neither did Valor. They both lunged toward me to help but paused when I winced at the sudden movement. They gave each other a look and moved slower, offering their hands.

I searched for Casimir in the growing sea of faces, and the way he watched me made my heart plummet, the pity more than I could bear.

Valor and Galan lifted me off the ground, careful as they helped me back to the cot, as if I were made of glass. Despite their efforts, it irritated every wound to be moved.

Taryn pushed through the crowd with worry etched on her brow. "What have you boys done now?" she scolded.

Galan stepped back from me, looking pitiful, and went over to her. He turned his back to me, and he spoke in a low tone.

Taryn nodded when Galan pulled away, her focus falling to me. "Alright then, everyone, she's had enough excitement for tonight. Let's all let her rest, shall we?" It wasn't a suggestion.

Everyone shuffled out of the tent, whispering among themselves. In the opening of the drapes, Casimir's unwavering gaze remained fixed on me.

Taryn approached my cot and gave Valor a stern look. He nodded and left my side, following Galan out of the tent.

I was left with Taryn and Casimir.

Carefully, she took my arm into her hand, pressing two fingers to the inside of my wrist. She stayed that way, her eyes bouncing from side to side. I tried to relax into the cot, but it hurt worse to release the tension than to hold on to it.

"Do you feel lightheaded?" she asked, putting my wrist down.

"Not as much as I did," I muttered.

She brought a hand to my temple to scan over me again. After a pause, she huffed to herself and peered over her shoulder at Casimir. "Mild head trauma. We're lucky it's not worse. Can't believe I didn't check for signs when—you know." Anger filled her voice, and it wasn't hard to guess where her animosity was directed.

She tried to tap her fingers around my neck, but even the gentle touch hurt. When I flinched, she apologized under her breath and focused on the exam she started. She looked over my limbs, examined my bandages, and eventually pulled back from me.

"It's not uncommon for you to have outbursts like that. Rest and time will help. But you've suffered a lot, both physically and mentally. Try to get more rest if you can. I'll grab you something for the pain." She stood, her frown deepening as she eyed my hair.

"The body and mind tend to hold on to things, even when we wish they wouldn't," Taryn whispered, squeezing my hand.

She left my side and rummaged through the supplies, gathered herbs and another glass of cloudy water. When Taryn returned, she passed them to me, and once I chugged it down, she gave me a somber smile.

"Holler if you need anything. Just maybe not so loud next time." She winked and turned to leave, reminding me again to get some rest.

Casimir went to follow her, and despite the protest of my body, I raised on my elbows, dizzy but determined.

"Don't go," I pleaded, the sound humiliating.

Casimir faced me, bewildered. Time froze as we held each other's gaze. I saw the way he contemplated.

After a pause, he sighed and swept a bruised hand through his hair, walking over to me. The familiarity was overwhelming at the memory of his visit just before the fire.

It felt like another life.

Casimir sat in the chair beside my cot. His attention lingered on my arms and hands, adorned with bandages and scrapes. He remained tense, never breaking his smooth disposition. I battled the heavy weight of his silence and sought refuge in the darkness as I closed my eyes.

Numbness washed over me when the herbs dulled the pain, causing me to drift off faster than I thought possible.

I didn't know if it was a dream, but I felt Casimir's hand brush my arm. The scent of patchouli filled the space, and hair tickled my nose as his head rested on the cot.

The distinction between dream and reality became irrelevant to me. If it was a dream, I begged the gods to let me stay there.

For a moment, all the pain disappeared, and I drifted off to the sound of Casimir's breathing. A familiar and welcome ghost.

Chapter Thirty-Four

Uncomfortable heat covered every inch of my skin in the sweltering early hours of the morning. The sunlight sent me burying my face into the pillow beneath my head. Birds chirped in a joyous tune, blissfully unaware of the tragedy that plagued me and everyone else.

"Morning." A rough voice broke the cheerful tune, and I peeked up from the pillow to see Valor propped up in the corner of the tent, a book in hand, the pages nearly falling out.

Carefully and with great effort, I rolled on the cot. My torso twisted with aches, and I clenched my teeth. The pillow folded beneath my head, and my arms burned with exertion from the movement.

The book closed, and Valor's chair creaked as he stood, grunting when he did. He put the book to the side and walked to the cot, but never too close, holding the air of a general. Nothing at all like the comfort of a father. The truth of it hit me like a punch in the gut.

"How long have I been out?" I asked, rubbing my eyes.

"Two days. Taryn has been in to change the bandages on your side. The guard has taken shifts, making sure you remain stable. Taryn insisted you shouldn't wake up alone."

"Water? Food?" I inquired.

He nodded, walking back over to where his book was. There sat a tray, a handful of berries, what appeared to be rye bread and water. He brought it to me and set it on a stool beside the cot. I stared at the tray and glanced at him with hesitation.

"I can't sit."

Valor huffed in exasperation and, to my surprise, offered me a hand. I took it and allowed him to help me.

With every twist of my torso, I winced.

When I was stable enough, he moved away, and I went for the food. My jaw ached as it broke into the juicy surface of a berry, and I paused, annoyed at the lingering pain. I brushed it off and continued to chew, moving onto the bread. It was stale, but I didn't mind.

I devoured it all embarrassingly fast, forgetting Valor was even in the tent.

He stood watch as I ate, shoveling the food until there was nothing left but crumbs from the bread. I chugged the water in a few quick gulps, gasping.

"Is there more?" I asked, wiping water from my chin.

He gave a single nod, taking the tray and mug. And despite my instincts that told me not to, I grabbed his arm with my shaking grasp, fingers bruised and scarred from attempting to fight off Ronin.

Valor froze in place and watched my hand before he looked at me, his mask holding firm.

"I didn't mean to put any of you in danger. Thank you for not leaving me out there."

He moved his arm, my hand slipping from it. "Vanmore insisted he knew you were in danger. His rescue efforts and insistence on allowing you to return is where your gratitude should lie."

I bit the inside of my cheek. His withdrawn demeanor hurt in a way I pushed down. I had no more room for it when the grief already over-flowed. There was no time for naivety. It had caused me enough problems.

Valor turned and left the tent, taking the tray with him. I relaxed back into the cot, in solitude with my thoughts.

The heat in the tent made my body sticky with sweat, and the cloth that covered so many surfaces on my skin didn't help. My hands were tight and smarted when I clenched them as if the cuts would tear if I made too tight of a fist.

None of it compared to the way my scalp pulsated.

I ignored the urge to touch the severed strands, knowing it would bring me more pain. From the limited movement of my neck, I noticed how short it was. Just to my chin and the nape of my neck.

The weight of grief for the petals I lost became overpowering. They were as much a part of me as any limb, if not more so, woven into the fabric of my being. The loss stung, and I yearned for the softness of the petals. The way they would poke at my cheeks if I laid the wrong way. Or the strange petal at the crown of my head.

I clenched my fists and willed myself to swallow the emotions that welled up, burying the wounds deeper.

The clouds overhead cast parts of the tent in shadow, creating darker patches in the fabric. Sunlight still managed to shine through the faded areas, giving them a grayish hue and intensifying the uncomfortable heat inside the tent. Sweat trickled down my temples, and I winced as it stung the scrapes on my face.

I glanced around the tent, and for a moment, the loneliness was suffocating. Even the company of Valor was preferred to the isolation.

The intent behind my actions didn't matter. In the process of trying to do what I thought was right, I managed to betray the only people I had left.

A breath shuddered past my lips, tears mixed with the sweat, and in the deafening silence, I convinced myself I was okay with solitude. Detachment was easier, familiar, and it kept me safe.

Alone in the tent, I vowed to never trust again.

Alba dubbed herself my stand-in healer when Taryn was absent.

She stayed by the cot when I slept until I woke, her and Galan swapping out, occasionally tapping in others. But I didn't see Casimir after I woke from my long sleep.

While Taryn said her near-constant presence was normal, the amount she pestered me would imply she was concerned. She had people with me at every hour. Morning or night. The least bothersome presence was Alba, her cheerful tune always close by, ready to chime in with something positive, even as the realm outside the tent began to wither.

She didn't ask me how I felt. She didn't inquire about nightmares or 'episodes' as Taryn described my embarrassing dissociation.

Instead, Alba was the first and only one to fill me in on where we were. Which was a refugee camp of sorts. Something Valor had at the edge of Orondal should things go sideways.

Alba took the time to explain the situation and the next move, which no one knew much about.

The days I was out, Valor spent them planning alongside Orin and other members of the guard. Their intention was to get the people of Everbloom somewhere safe before the king picked up our trail. And although she wouldn't give me a reason, I chose to believe it was why Casimir didn't visit. Even if Galan and Valor, of all people, had found the time. Ignorance was the state I lived in.

The afternoon stretched on. Alba kept me company, her legs swinging at the edge of a cot cheerily while I endured another change of dressings. Taryn applied another thick layer of healing salve she had made to my sutured side. It stung when it touched the tender skin, and I winced.

Alba's legs stopped swinging.

"You know, maybe something to take the edge off wouldn't be too bad?" Alba asked as she had the other times she was present for Taryn's redressing of my wounds.

Taryn rolled her eyes. "We don't have enough supplies. If we run out before the General has made a plan, we're in trouble." She looked away from Alba, put a hand on my shoulder, and smiled apologetically. "Sorry. You know I wish I could."

I nodded, my teeth clenched so tight, my jaw ached.

Taryn turned her attention back to my side, laying a piece of the wrap over my abdomen before she offered me her hands.

I pulled on them, and Alba stood, knowing her cue. She grabbed the rolled-up cloth, taking it around my torso once I was sat up. My arms shook while Taryn held onto me. The weakness in my limbs never ceased to annoy me, despite Taryn assuring me it was normal after I had scarcely made it out alive. I needed to regain my strength after losing my bloom in such a horrific way.

I tried to change my trail of thoughts to avoid them from going back to Ronin's betrayal. I didn't want to have another breakdown. It was humiliating to feel so mentally shattered, and others witnessing it made it all the worse.

A few times around my torso, and Alba finished wrapping me. She appraised her work and nodded. She smiled at me, patted my shoulder, and I promptly laid back down, not needing much more encouragement than that as my body trembled.

Taryn eyed Alba's handy work and, looking pleased with it, gave a nod of satisfaction. "You'll be a fine help to have with all the wounded that have been piling up," Taryn said to Alba as she put her supplies away, tightening the jar of salve with a quick spin.

Alba sighed and sat back up on the cot. "Oh, Taryn, you know how I feel about healing." Alba crossed her arms, her chipper mood gone.

Taryn shook her head, not glancing back even as Alba huffed another annoyed breath.

"You know we're shorthanded. General will need you if we journey too far. It's a skill that's important, if you have the inclination toward it," Taryn said as she discarded her white smock, rolling her tunic sleeves to her elbows. "It's a big job, and I need help."

My focus shifted to Alba, who wallowed.

I didn't understand her apprehension, but knowing what she could do, it made sense the healing abilities didn't speak to her. Whereas building walls of thorns and shattering wooden dummies had immediate gratification. A thrum of power I hoped I would have the chance to feel again.

The spark of power in my body still rang beneath the surface after I had conjured the earth to slow Ronin down. With any hope, Alba could teach me to be even half as good as she was.

Carefully, I raised onto my elbows, hating the way Alba and Taryn both stopped what they were doing to jump to my side, hands outstretched as if I'd fall from the cot. I reminded myself they meant well, and their kindness was more than I could ask for, especially after I almost doomed Everbloom and threatened them before leaving.

The thought sobered my frustration, and I gave them both a kind smile. "Thank you, but I'm okay. I want to sit on my own," I said, raising the rest of the way despite every rib screaming in protest. My chest was a canvas of painful bruises, overshadowed only by Taryn's hasty and ragged sutures on my torso.

They both watched with scrutiny, hands twitching at their sides, ready to help if I became faint or the discomfort was too much.

When I sat, hunched over with my hands holding the sides of the cot to keep me up, they both grinned.

Alba clapped her hands together. "Your resilience will get you far. We'll have you up and training again in no time!" Alba chimed. Taryn shot her a glare and shook her head. But it didn't kill Alba's joy.

"She's got a long way to go, but she'll get there," Taryn said, trying not to be too negative but also not trying to get my hopes up. There wouldn't be much time to train. Not with the realm hanging on by a thread.

I still hadn't looked out the drapes since the first day I woke. The weight of guilt and shame was mine to bear, yet I couldn't muster the courage to confront it. If I tried to carry one more burden, I'd shatter beneath the weight. The loss of my bloom reverberated through every fiber of my being. It left me hollow. Empty by a destiny unfulfilled. A sense of hopelessness threatened to pull me into a spiral.

Alba noticed the shift, my mood changing swiftly. She put her hands on her hips and rocked on her heels. "I think we can move her," she said, her tone serious, which was unlike her.

Taryn raised a brow, glanced at me, then back at Alba. "She hardly sat up by herself—no offense—and you think she'll be fine in that death trap of a chair?"

Alba appeared annoyed. "The chair *you* made?"

"Exactly, so I would know," Taryn bit back.

If it weren't for my wounds, I would have chuckled. The two bickered as I imagined siblings would.

Alba and Taryn glared at each other for a while before Taryn caved, releasing a heavy breath of exasperation.

"If Elita falls out of the chair, someone tries to fight her, or any other kind of nonsense, it's getting pinned on you. Got it?" Taryn pointed a finger in Alba's direction.

Alba took the win, dancing with glee. "The breeze will be so good for Elita! Some fresh-ish air, sunshine, and socializing. It'll be just what she needs."

I turned to her, an uneasy grin on my face. "Everything but the socializing would be great." I didn't want to have the entirety of Everbloom glaring at me. The blame on my shoulders for their discovery, for the loss of some of their people, made sense. That didn't mean I wanted to give them an easy target.

Alba rolled her eyes. "I'll show you around the temporary camp then. That is, temporary until we figure something better out."

I hadn't brought myself to look outside, but I knew we were on the outskirts of Orondal. There was no fresh water or gardens. And even with the ability to speed plant growth, it would take over a month's time to rebuild the gardens they would need. The water problem presented a whole different struggle. It wasn't feasible to remain there.

With my bloom gone, they didn't know what would happen. If their abilities could even sustain the gardens. Or work enough magic to bring life back to some of the land, purifying the water as the earth burst with new vegetation. There were too many unknowns. And many more issues to work out. The living quarters were in shambles, and meals were hard to make.

But I would allow myself to forget about it for the next hour. I would get to feel the sun on my face. Even if it was sweltering.

I needed to bask in the sunshine and breathe the air—before it became too toxic, Ronin's final wish coming to fruition.

Children, Roses, and kings alike, all choking on the air until it poisoned us entirely.

Chapter Thirty-Five

Taryn forced me into a contraption that resembled a poorly crafted wheelchair. The wheels were made of wood, nearly rotted down, the fabric in the seat a breath away from snapping beneath my weight. A sad excuse for a mode of transportation.

Still, I was grateful as we pushed through the drapes of the tent.

A dry breeze rolled through my severed and choppy hair, causing it to dart across my vision. It wasn't as fresh as Everbloom, but it brought some relief.

Alba took it upon herself to push me. Her abilities had more range than most, from conjuring vines to healing and her strength. With her wide array of power, she'd likely outrank Casimir if she wanted. Instead, she chose a quiet life, helping tend to the unique vegetation and flowers back in Everbloom. A purpose she also lost.

An uncomfortable stillness enveloped us through the camp. Looks of piercing anger or faces full of pity followed every creak of the wheels. Some of the Roses gave the impression they wanted to kick me over when we got too close to where they stood.

It gave me a sense of comfort to know none of them would attempt it. Not with Alba pushing me, her own glare clear as day every time we passed a muttering group who had daggers for stares.

We made our way through the crowd of busy people. They darted around, carrying baskets filled to the brim with random supplies. They pulled groups of barrels on carts down toward the tree line, sweating as they moved through the humidity and heat.

I watched, perplexed.

Taryn stood close to the right side of me, and she noticed me watching the group in disarray, many of them bumping into each other in their rush. "They're preparing in case we have to leave. There isn't enough to keep us here, and Everbloom isn't safe for obvious reasons."

I ignored the bite in Taryn's tone, despite how responsible I felt.

Ronin tricked me. How could I have known?

I ignored the ache in my chest. The disbelief and grief were overbearing. There was no time to grieve a man twisted by hatred. I never truly knew him. His kindness was a lie.

My lips pressed into a line, and I wished I hadn't left the tent where I could doze off to sleep every few minutes. Lolled into a listless state by the ache in my bones and the herbs in my system.

People continued to move around the camp, and Alba turned us along a different path, the chair protesting the change of direction. Her strength overpowered it, and we went down the muted path, away from the busyness and the glowering eyes.

Alba powered over the rough terrain with ease, taking us along a strange curved path dotted with twisted trees and the awful scent of decay. I understood it was connected to the Drought Lands. It didn't make it any better.

We didn't go very far before we arrived at an overlook. Dead trees outlined an opening that looked out over the expanse of Orondal, and to the west, the sight of the cursed sea caught my eye.

Everything was dead as far as I could see. Nevertheless, I found a strange beauty in the openness of the Drought Lands.

When we came to a full stop, I clambered out of the chair, shaky as I sat in the dead grass. It crunched when my palms rested on it. Taryn and Alba both sat on either side of me, never too far.

The sun burned fiercely in the sky. Its rays seared everything in sight until it looked as if it would drench the entire realm in flames. I tried not to think about where the fault lay.

Ignoring the truth was impossible, and the guilt spilled over. "I'm sorry. To both of you. For Everbloom. For what I said," I whispered into the stillness. Both of their heads turned my way.

"You didn't know, Elita," Alba said in a soft voice. Her hand rested on my shoulder. Taryn scoffed, and Alba glared over my head.

"Oh, come off it. Do you think that will help her?" Taryn huffed. "We all make bad decisions sometimes. She needs to own that. Let her."

In spite of myself, I chuckled. "Thanks, Taryn." I was grateful she wouldn't lie to me. I made a horrific mistake. It didn't matter that I wasn't aware. I chose the words I spoke to Valor for Ronin's release. The attack on Everbloom, their safety being taken from them, rested on my shoulders. Had I tried to figure something else out, never threatened their peace, perhaps there had been an option I didn't give myself time to see.

In my heart, I knew Ronin's death at their hands wouldn't have ever been an option. I didn't know his darkness, and I wouldn't have let them hurt him.

We let the conversation die out as a breeze rolled through the barren land, kicking up dust and dead brush.

Before I could appreciate the moment, the sound of sprinting came from the forest of decay and shouting broke through the little bubble we had formed on the ledge.

I straightened quickly. Black spots speckled my vision, making me feel faint. Alba and Taryn both scrambled up, standing in front of me, shielding me. The memory of Ronin's haunting footsteps echoed in my mind, making my stomach twist.

"Elita!"

My name resounded through the trees, though the voice was one that soothed every tense muscle in my body.

"Elita—" Casimir and Galan broke through the trees, faces dripping in sweat, eyes wide with panic. They halted, assessing the scene in front of them.

Galan sighed when he noticed me between Taryn and Alba, his shoulders falling in relief. Casimir still appeared as if he were ready to fend off an entire army.

Casimir's hand gripped the hilt of his sword. "Damn it, do you have any idea what we have been through looking for Elita? The General will be furious she was removed from the tent without approval—"

"Casimir," Alba interrupted, her voice taking on a serious tone. "She's fine. We thought she could use a break from the monotony of that stuffy tent. Taryn insisted."

Taryn glared at Alba, giving the impression she wanted to smack her. Casimir's stern expression didn't dissipate.

Galan stepped closer, visibly relieved. "I'm certain the General will take no issue with Ms. Taryn. She is in charge of healing and care. If she believed this to be the best course of action, I'm sure he would see reason." Galan's hand reached for mine.

I fought the urge to turn away from his outstretched palm. Nothing enticed me to go back to the tent.

"Can't I stay?" I asked, hating that I had to.

Galan gave me an apologetic frown while he helped me back into the chair, Alba at my other side. "My apologies, Elita, but the General is calling for a meeting in the guards' quarters. He has requested your presence."

I pursed my lips, despising the idea of it.

Everyone exchanged heavy glances.

Galan pushed the chair over the rough terrain, his abilities similar to Alba's. She stayed close to my side, as did Taryn.

With a steady breath, I prepared myself for whatever conversation awaited me in Valor's tent, and I tried to ignore the way Casimir continued to stare at me as if I were a stranger.

"As many of you are aware, we cannot return to Everbloom for the foreseeable future." Valor stood at the head of the table, and the tent held very few people, all appearing part of the guard. The temperature was unbearable. Sweat glistened on everyone's brow.

"At this rate of decline, there may be nowhere to go. However, I have connections to the leader of Mistvalle. It would be a long trek, nearly a month's worth if we can make it that far on what we have. But it is our only option."

Fear crept in among everyone in the tent. The talk of impending doom followed me everywhere I went, even when narrowly escaping death. Every expression in the tent went grim and frowns pulled at the corner of every mouth.

We all gathered at the General's tent after Alba and Taryn brought me back, Casimir and Galan leading the entire way. It was the largest tent in their refugee camp, full of scattered maps, books, and weapons.

It was hidden within the rocky cliffs of Orondal, a place I still knew little about. Everyone was much too busy to explain anything as they tried to comfort the confused and fearful people of Everbloom. All while trying to manage lack of food supplies, or clean water. Chaos reigned in the camp.

Casimir sat near Valor along with Orin. Galan flanked them—still part of the guard. They somehow managed not to melt from the heat of their armor and cloaks.

Alba and Taryn sat next to me, never too far, their eyes flickering to me as Valor spoke. The attention and pity were suffocating.

"How will the children make such a long trek, General?" someone asked, standing from their seat. They appeared as if they were roasting in their heavy armor.

"They have no other choice. We cannot stay this close to the Iron Thorn. They know of our existence, and they are on the move. My scouts say the king's armies are mobilizing and calling on the men of the villages to fight. We are fortunate enough the orders are to not kill on sight, but to capture all they can. Lethal force only if necessary. They are desperate for any way to save their kingdom."

I gulped down the weight of the unbearable guilt.

Tuning them out, I leaned over and whispered to Alba. "Are they intending to make a month-long journey on foot?"

Alba shook her head. "The General has a fleet of ships near the waterfront."

I stiffened. "The waterfront? But wouldn't it be a death sentence to sail the cursed sea?"

Her gaze darted down to her hands as they fiddled with the frays near the buttons of her linen dress. "It won't be easy. The General has sailed it many times before, though. He knows how to navigate them in the safest way possible. Roses exist not only in Everbloom, and General

Valor arrived back from his last journey to Mistvalle recently. He knows what he's doing," Alba explained, her own nerves obvious to me.

"How will they sail with the entirety of Everbloom?" The concern built the more I thought of the many faces I had only ever seen in passing. There had to have been over a thousand people in Everbloom.

She sighed and lifted her head. "General Valor will find a way. He wouldn't leave a single Rose behind. He'd stuff the ships until they overflowed if he had to." She sounded sure of her answer. Yet, from the little I knew of Valor, he didn't seem to care a great deal about anyone.

Perhaps his compassion solely extended to those he shared no connection or blood relation. The simple fact he left my mother to die showed me how much he valued a person's life.

"I can assure you; we will do everything within our control to get everyone to Mistvalle safely," Orin said in a thundering voice as his gaze scanned over everyone in the tent while they all tried to talk over each other. There weren't many present, and I only recognized a few of them.

Many more people were just outside, tucked away in tents much too small. Most made their way out of Everbloom, and the attack, unscathed. There had only been seven lives lost in Everbloom.

Only seven.

I bit the inside of my cheek so hard it drew blood.

Seven more lives. Their deaths my fault.

"And what of the white bloom?" Someone else asked, standing near Orin. Their attention made me uncomfortable.

They looked at Valor. "She isn't dead. Why is any of this even happening? Couldn't we just send her to the king and convince him she is their salvation?"

Casimir's arms uncrossed, and he glowered across the table at the man. "Try it and see," he snapped. His ember scowl was full of fury and exhaustion, the dark circles under his eyes prominent.

The man who asked grimaced, recoiling from Casimir's threat.

Valor held up a hand and glanced around the room, disappointed. "We will not be bargaining with the lives of our own people. Mistvalle has resources there we do not have here, nor in Everbloom. Centuries have passed with us searching for a solution to the constant sacrifices. Together, we may find the answers."

Looking like a child scolded, the man sat down.

Casimir's shoulders remained tense. I watched him from across the table, but he didn't glance my way.

The tent swelled with tension as silence fell. No one knew what to say. I felt just as lost. Not on any of the maps I had seen was Mistvalle ever mentioned, although Everbloom wasn't either.

Such a daunting task plagued the people of Everbloom as the reality of having to travel in such a large group set it. It seemed impossible. The heat would kill us before the king's army could.

Some people in the tent got up and left without a word. Their skin took on a sickly appearance as the disappointment proved too heavy for many of them.

Taryn rose and placed a hand on my shoulder. "I'll check up on you later tonight. I need to go see Ulrik before he's asleep," she said.

I nodded in reply, and she disappeared out of the drapes, following the others who likely needed to prepare their families.

The room continued to thin out. Valor and Orin watched many of the people depart, leaving them and the guard, along with Alba and me. I looked over at Casimir once more while he sat.

In the tent, he felt more distant from me than he ever had before, and I experienced another pang in my chest. Though I knew the people in the room, I had never encountered such a sense of isolation. Each of them looked anywhere but at me.

My unease grew, and I shifted in my seat, my ribs burning when I did. The only person who stared back at me was Valor.

"Well, what is it?" I blurted.

Valor took a seat at the table, his cloak falling over the back of the chair in a swift motion. "There are many that do not want you to accompany us, Blackthorne," he said simply and without emotion as if he were talking to me about the last meal he had.

My skin prickled, and I glanced at Casimir. His sight remained fixed on Valor.

"That said, there are leaders and rules for a reason. And while your foolish feelings clouded your judgment, we will not sentence you to die because of it," Valor said.

The wound was too fresh; the betrayal too painful. Grimacing, I dug my nails into my thighs, desperately trying to suppress the memories.

I was foolish and caused innocent people to lose their lives. People that those in Everbloom loved and cared for. Understanding it was one thing, but hearing it brought me more shame than I could bear.

I tried not to let it bother me that Valor was my father, and he seemed to not care much either way. Our blood relation was nothing in his eyes. Twenty-one years he knew of my existence and never once tried to bring me to safety. And had it not been for Casimir, he may have left me to die at Ronin's hands.

Though I couldn't wish it to be any different. Every moment spent with my parents was held and cherished. I wouldn't trade it for a cruel man who had no regard for my life.

I bit back the words I wanted to say. The questions of why they kept me there at all. In a sinister part of my mind, I wondered if the solution they needed would involve me. More lies, studying, and secrets.

Another cage where they would use me for their own gain.

I pushed back the paranoia before it consumed me.

"I think I'd like to return to my tent," I whispered, trying to stand from the chair with legs that protested the movement.

Alba jumped up, grabbing my hand to help me over to the makeshift wheelchair. I shifted my shaky body over to it, dizzy from the movement.

"If you wish," was all Valor said, his attention on something Orin showed him. It resembled a map; worn from years of use.

We moved, the wheels not wanting to make it over a single stick on the ground. If not for Alba's abnormal strength, there would have been no way for us to make it out of the drapes.

From the corner of my eye, I saw Casimir stand, his stride moving to follow us out.

Alba pushed us through the open drapes, and outside, the trees whipped around in the sour wind. Somewhere overhead, a raven called.

People moved between tents and carts, ducking through open drapes and carrying lanterns around in the dark. They worked in a disorganized frenzy, no longer having a routine. They looked like roaches scrambling.

The stars were scarcely visible through thick clouds that moved in the night, their outline just discernible by the moon's glow.

Tents were scattered and misplaced, thrown up in a hurry, some nearly falling over or drooping to the side. It was nothing like Everbloom and its intricacy. The well-tended flowers and markets were far away in a crater in the earth, likely to never be touched again.

It stung to think about, despite only getting to experience Everbloom for such a short time. I missed the safety, the simplicity. Regardless of it not being intended for me.

Alba continued to press on. People jumped out of her way as she stormed through the crowd, her own thoughts seemingly elsewhere.

We turned along a path when the earth trembled.

A blood-curdling boom reverberated through the dense, gnarled trees. Heat engulfed the camp, and light burst in the distance.

Alba shrieked as the sky lit up orange and red. Flames spilled over the rocky cliffs only a few miles away.

Another shake of the earth, and I tumbled forward, a wheel coming loose from the chair.

Shouting erupted as the fire roared in the distance. Valor charged out of the tent while yelling orders that were incomprehensible to me over the ringing in my ears. The ground trembled once more.

Hands grabbed at me, trying to get me to stand. I glanced up to see Casimir, desperation visible on his face. "You need to get up!" he shouted over the ringing.

My body trembled as I struggled to gather the willpower to do the simple thing he asked. My breaths came out in panicked gasps, aggravating the wounds throughout my torso.

Alba crouched. Her features were full of fear, and tears pooled down her face. She reached for my other arm, but I went numb.

My eyes widened as flames licked at the night sky, climbing the dead trees at rapid speed.

Before another shock rippled through the ground, Casimir tucked a hand under my knees and the other around my back, bringing me close to his chest as he straightened. He pressed through the crowd that scrambled in a mess of panic and screams. Confused shouts echoed between people as they ran out of their tents to the horrific sight at the cliffs.

The blast was a few miles off in the distance, yet it felt as though it shook the entire realm.

I trembled in Casimir's arms as he ran, Alba close at his side. It was almost impossible for me to see Valor when he vanished into the group of people, shouting for them to go to the water.

The trees whipped past us while Casimir sprinted. Dead branches shuddered to the ground, the force of the blast was enough to shake them loose. A crowd of frightened bodies swelled around us, following Orin, who ran to the front of the crowd, instructing everyone to follow him.

My body ached with every jerk of Casimir's movement. The fear drowned most of it out until it turned into a dull throbbing.

The flames disappeared the further we went downhill, despite the sky still being lit by an ominous orange, though it had been black moments before.

Casimir continued until he surpassed Orin, stopping when we reached the waterline. It stretched out in a daunting way as waves moved and crashed against the stones near the shore.

The body of water was too large, never-ending, and the scent was foul. Salt and death wafted through the air, the waters echoing the centuries-old curse.

Casimir lowered me to the ground, panting. He searched my face, a hand on my upper arm. My heart sank, heavy in my chest. It was the first time he really looked at me since the clearing, and all I could hear for a moment was his plea for me to breathe.

When my swaying steadied, he released my arm and scanned the faces, finding Alba not far behind us.

The throng of bodies continued to swell. Crying infants and fearful families moving among the dead trees. Every member of Everbloom filled the area, panic-ridden as they tried to reassure each other, to comfort their scared children.

Valor appeared at the back of the crowd.

"The prince marches on Orondal. He has destroyed the passage out of the cliffs," he spat, his rage no longer concealed. "If we do not depart, we may as well turn ourselves over."

Horrified gasps shook the mass of people.

Icy fear crept in. It twisted a part of me I had tried to bury.

"We weren't fully prepared to make this long of a journey, but now we have no other choice. The only comfort I can give is that our ships are mostly functional. Anything left back at camp will remain there, likely to be lost to the flames. But it doesn't matter what we are missing or lacking. We must leave." Valor left no room for anyone to argue.

Cries of confusion and horror rippled through the crowd. Many of the Roses shouted, crumbling at his words.

Aimlessly, my hand searched for Casimir, my fist wrapping around the edge of his cloak. I tried to anchor myself to anything steady, afraid I would drown in the panic that filled my veins.

The scent of the acidic waters overpowered my nose beyond the odor of smoke. My stomach churned at the mere thought of venturing out onto the cursed sea.

For a fleeting moment, Valor's gaze flickered to me. "We'll sail to Mistvalle. And we leave now."

"What of the wounded?" someone shouted angrily in the crowd.

Valor sighed, turning from the people of Everbloom, quiet enough for his voice not to carry. "They will adapt or die."

I paled, and my fist tightened on the edge of Casimir's cloak.

The sky awoke with smoke and ash swirling together in a terrifying dance. Sounds of wood splintering echoed through the forest. The rotted trees fell to the ground in a puff of embers.

White ash rained down, coating the ground. The shame and guilt crept in, consuming me. The emotions swirled in a similar violent dance.

Beneath the thrum of chaos around me, words rang in my head.

A warning I did not heed.

In my defiance, I had become the realm's end.

Bonus Chapter

Chapter Thirty-Six

Casimir

I watched her go, white petals shuddering when she passed through the threshold of the door. Blood thundered in my ears, and anger furled my fists.

The General would have my head. I let her go, though every bone in my body begged me to follow her. Visceral and sickening. It was weak to wish for her to walk back through the door. To wish for her to hear me out. None of us had any desire to hurt her.

It was something I never wanted. I tried hard to keep her from harm. And to have brought her pain...

Those thoughts offered no solace. Elita was gone as quickly as she appeared. The General and his rules be damned. I should have told her the truth about Everbloom long ago. Worse yet, I kept from her the identity of her father.

I pinched the bridge of my nose and took a breath. Emotions had no place in my decision-making. They never did me any good.

The neck guard of my armor appeared too tight, and I pulled at it. I swallowed, gritted my teeth, and walked to the door. I tried not to let Elita's absence bring me ill feelings, but it had been surreal to have her in Everbloom. Years spent walking among her dreams, and she finally found me.

Memories of her falling into the water made my fists tighten. The fear was fresh—her body when it hit the surface. How limp she appeared in my arms. I should have made a point to instruct her on how to swim. Any adequate adult could learn easily. And she was exceptional.

The guards outside stood straighter at the sight of me in the doorway. They saluted, though they looked bewildered.

I let the General's prisoner, his daughter, go. I didn't want to rob her of that choice. I didn't want to be another captor. It pained me when she looked at me with hurt in her eyes. I never wanted to see her look at me that way again.

A sinking sensation filled my chest.

It was likely I'd never see her again. She would wilt somewhere in the Iron Thorn, leaving this realm behind.

The realization made irrational panic quicken my pulse. I needed to get a clear head. My duty was to the guard, to Everbloom. We'd need to reinforce our security measures. Address the guard. Plan an evacuation should it become prudent.

Breathing through my nose, I steeled my resolve. My squad needed to be briefed. It remained plausible for the norm to turn over Everbloom out of spite.

Though it seemed unlikely. If the norm's feelings for Elita were true, they wouldn't allow him to put her in danger. If the guard entered Everbloom, it would have put Elita in danger. We had time to prepare.

The norm wouldn't have reason nor time to think of turning over Everbloom until Elita finished her wilt.

My boots thudded down the steps to the General's quarters. If I thought too long on her wilt, it'd drive me mad. There wasn't enough time to convince her she didn't have to. That she had a choice.

Prophecy be damned. To demand she give her life on account of words spoken centuries ago, it wasn't right. Her hesitation the night before swirled in my thoughts.

Fuck.

Elita always managed to twist my mind until I no longer thought rationally.

Before I lingered another moment, I stalked down the path.

The General would be furious. Regardless, I'd address him and admit to what I'd done before he found out. If anything, I hoped Elita got away before he caught sight of her. I didn't know what I'd do if she hadn't gotten out in time and he held her captive somewhere.

He wouldn't draw his sword on me. He owed me that much after his poor decisions cost my mother her life. If he found Elita before she left, I'd make sure she could have the freedom she longed for.

"She's gone?" the General thundered. His hand twitched near the hilt of his sword. I could see by the way he moved he wouldn't pull it from the sheath. It occurred to me by his expression that he wanted to.

Sighing, I placed a hand to my chest in salute. "I apologize, General. The blame remains with me, and me alone."

The General scoffed, shook his head, and turned his back to me. It wasn't usual behavior for him. The fool of a man cared for his daughter despite his attempts not to.

A grudge held for Elita's mother didn't seem to be enough to block out his paternal instincts. It had been the reason he made me dreamwalk all those years before—and why he didn't want Elita to return to the Iron Thorn. In Everbloom, she could have wilted in peace.

Perhaps it would've doomed the realm. And perhaps I wouldn't have let her give such a sacrifice.

A long pause held the space. The General glanced over the wall of the mess hall. He hadn't even begun the briefing before I pulled him to the side. Our preparations would change now that Elita was gone. Things became more complicated. Not once did I regret the decision to let her walk out, though. If that was the life she wanted, she deserved to make that choice. Everyone in her life, including me, had taken enough of her choices away.

When the General turned to face me, he glowered. Rage simmered in his gaze, and it brought me back to the years I spent dreamwalking in my adolescence in Elita's sleep. He insisted I didn't need to anymore. A pointless intrusion.

I didn't dreamwalk for his benefit.

The General let go of a shaky breath. "She's made her choice. My guard will not risk their lives to go over the wall. But you—" He jabbed a finger into my armor. "You're fortunate enough I swore to your mother no harm would befall you. I should have you stripped of your rank and thrown over that damn border. Take this as a warning."

I bowed my head. "Understood, General." I fought the desire to remind him my mother's death was his doing. Had he been a better leader, had he not let her go. It never got me anywhere to argue with him.

I took his dismissal and left the mess hall, trying not to think about Elita's vacant tent, the sight of her walking among the forests with me. The pain on her face when she spoke of her days in the Temple cell. Or the way she looked when she slept in my bed, her hair a mess of curls and white petals; more peaceful than I'd ever seen her.

My hands ran through my hair, and I let go of a heavy sigh.

To my dismay, Alba jogged up the path, her face red from crying. When her direction didn't change, I nearly turned back into the mess hall. She'd scold me worse than the General.

Alba stopped in front of me, glaring beneath her bangs. "Why didn't you make her stay?" She sniffled, wiping at her nose with her sleeve.

I glanced over her head, wishing for a moment alone. My tongue ran over my teeth and I met her angry gaze. "She didn't want that. Would it have been better to keep her here and allow her to be miserable?"

Alba punched my arm, taking me off guard. "Yes, you idiot!"

Her strength was enough to make my arm ache, but I wouldn't give her the satisfaction of rubbing it.

"When have we ever kept Roses against their will? She's had enough people controlling her life. It was her choice to make."

Alba shook her head, her lip quivering. "You're a coward, Casimir. You could have made her stay."

Underneath my eye, a nerve twitched.

Screams shattered the surrounding peace.

Alba froze, eyes wide. Her mouth opened to speak when I caught sight of the uniform in the crowd. I pushed her to the side as an arrow soared through the camp, hammering into a post of the mess hall.

My hand found the hilt of my sword, and I pulled it out, eyeing the guard in a blood-red uniform. Three more emerged from the woods behind him. One donned a bow, the other a sword.

Alba scrambled on the ground, gasping for breath.

"Go!" I shouted. For a moment, her gaze met mine, the terror evident. She didn't protest. The Iron Guard closed in.

Another arrow whipped past me, and Alba took off, grabbing others in the area and shouting for them to follow her. She only needed to get them to the General's quarters. There weren't enough Iron Guard to overrun us. They would be safe until we cleared the forest.

Behind me, guards poured out of the mess hall. Swords rang in the dome, echoing among the rocky walls.

The General barreled out, rage and disbelief across his face. We never had a breach.

Somewhere in the forest, another scream erupted.

I charged for the closest guard. He grinned, pulling his sword. Our blades locked, and without much effort, I twisted his until it fell to the ground.

He stared at me, bewildered, but I didn't give him another chance to attack. I slammed the hilt of the sword into his temple, and he fell to the side. Beside me, the General raised his blade, plunging it through the man's chest.

I left him to handle the others, following the shouting that filled the trees. When I reached the source, I froze.

One of my own men lay in a pool of blood, his father leaning over him, weeping and begging. Karion held onto his son, hands covered in blood. The guard was no more than eighteen.

Knots twisted in my chest, but there was no time to linger. Three more guards approached from the entrance, heading for those wounded.

The guards I charged with watching the East exit lay injured or dead. My own team. They were there on my order. It twisted akin to a blade in my gut.

Karion continued to weep. There was no time to usher everyone to safety. Not with their wounds. I'd have to take them down myself.

The glaring scarlet guard approached me, and our blades locked. I shoved back against them as another guard stalked over from the right. They outnumbered me. They also appeared too arrogant, and it would cost them.

My hand trembled on the hilt, and I cursed myself. I had a duty to protect those of Everbloom. My mother would have done what needed to be done. But I'd never taken a life before.

Before I cut down the guard in front of me, an arrow flew through the forest, cutting through his neck. The Iron Guard sputtered and fell, the light gone from his eyes.

I looked in the direction it came from, and Orin walked out of the trees, letting another arrow go. He barely spared me a glance. It was enough to see the disappointment.

Turning from him, I went over to Karion. "Sir, we need to get you somewhere safe—"

Karion hit my outstretched hand. "Not without my son!"

I gritted my teeth, and before I denied his request, Galan jogged our way. He gave me a knowing look, and using his abilities, he lifted the young guard from the ground with ease.

Blades continued to collide, ringing throughout the once peaceful woods. I glanced through them, looking for any sign of more wounded.

When I spotted a familiar raven swoop from the entrance, a chill ran over my spine. It cried out over the sound of guards in combat.

Elita left not long ago. Had the Iron Guard not seen her? Why had the norm given the location with such haste?

The raven flew close to my shoulder. Beady eyes met mine, wings flapped with fervor, and it screeched next to my ear. Horrifying thoughts filled my mind, and I turned, leaving any remaining guards for Orin.

I sprinted back through Everbloom. Sobs echoed among the dome. Guards escorted people to the mess hall and the General's quarters. It wouldn't be long before we had to abandon our sanctuary. If the Iron Guard knew, it was no longer safe.

When I reached the mess hall, I slowed.

The General stood before a pile of red uniformed bodies. Dead. Their eyes remained open, the last look of terror forever frozen on their faces. I tried to avoid glancing at them.

When he saw me approach, the General sheathed his sword. Anger flitted in his gaze, but he didn't speak. The panic must have been evident in my features. I cursed my weakness.

Reaching the General, I didn't bother to salute him. "Sir, I believe Elita is in danger." The words rushed out, and I hoped he wouldn't ask me how I knew. A bird and the assumptions didn't give me much to go on. However, when I tried to shut it all out and reach for her in my mind's eye, she was lost to me.

The General's brow furrowed. "Vanmore—"

"Sir, the norm would have had to send the guards down the moment he reentered the kingdom for them to be here in such a short time. He sent the guards down before Elita would've made it to him."

The more I thought it over, the worse it became. I tried harder to reach out through my connection with Elita. Either my worry was too much, or...

"I'm going after her."

The General tensed. "Our people do not cross the border, Vanmore—"

"I'm not asking permission."

He surveyed me, and I saw the battle in him. Elita was his daughter, regardless of how callous he tried to be.

We stared at each other for too long. Time slipped through my hands the longer I waited. And as if I needed any more prompting, the raven followed me to the General, endlessly squawking close by.

It was nonsense. Animals weren't guides. And yet, I couldn't shake the image of Elita with the bird on her shoulder, fondness in her voice when she spoke of it following her since before she lost her parents. I had never witnessed a bird act in such a manner.

It had to be hers.

When I went to leave for the East exit, the General stopped me, a hand on my shoulder.

"Help me prepare everyone first. Then grab Taryn and anyone else we may need. We cannot leave our people unprotected. When you've informed everyone, head out. We'll be behind you."

With every step I took through Orondal, I tried to tether a connection with Elita. It was harder to do when awake. My abilities weren't trained enough to break through the panic. I needed a clear head. I needed to think as a captain would. That proved fruitless.

The raven all but confirmed my suspicions something was off. It guided me through Orondal, all the way back to where Elita first fell into the cursed water.

Memories of feeling her touch for the first time flooded me. The way her arms enveloped me without hesitation, nearly tackling me to the ground, even as cursed water burned at her skin. I pushed the emotions down and trudged past it.

Never had I been over the wall before, and the raven's presence became of more use when it led me to a way up the wall. Footprints pressed into the dirt over the incline. Bare. Elita's.

If I didn't hurry, I worried harm would befall her. It occurred to me there was a chance I was mistaken. Merely paranoia driven by feelings that blinded me.

I wasn't willing to take that risk. If she was okay, I could leave with the peace of knowing she wasn't in harm's way. But something about the guard's timing and the presence of her raven left me with unease I couldn't shake.

Then there was the norm. Ronin. For a man who had given up everything to save Elita, he didn't seem to care for her. It may have been in my head, but he didn't stare at her with the concern a friend would have. He stared at her with desperation, which brought me discomfort.

Another twisted part of my own feelings? Perhaps.

I had to make sure.

When I made it over the Forge Border, it was deadly silent.

The ladder was in disarray, and I took note of where branches and brush were pushed away in the tree line ahead. Making it easier, the raven dove into the woods, leading me through them.

I pushed past branches until the bird fluttered to a sudden stop.

Without warning, it took off, darting into the sky. Hundreds of ravens cried overhead.

My brow pulled together, and I glanced around the area.

The hope I'd been mistaken quickly faded. Alarm settled in my bones when my gaze fell to a nearby tree. Blood made a puddle in the dirt at the base of it.

No.

I walked over to the blood and knelt, swiping a finger over it. Fresh. No weapon in sight. And no bodies.

I barely glanced at the sky again before I sprinted, following the trail of blood in the dirt. It marked the trees, the brush. Handprints of crimson pressed into the bark of a nearby tree. Too small to be a man.

"No, no, no. Come on, Elita," I muttered, wishing the connection would spark.

Rapid breaths shook my chest. The sense of powerlessness consumed me. I watched the bloodied hand prints smear on the trees. Unrest swelled, and I ran faster, following the line of ravens in the sky. They cried out, all heading in the same direction.

It had to be her. It had to be.

I ran until I noticed the birds dart to the right, creating a circle in the sky. They swarmed, and worry warped my vision.

Through the trees, light poured into what appeared to be a clearing. *A clearing.*

Throughout the years I knew Elita, she often shared her chilling visions of death, her hair sheared in a clearing of desolation. It never was anything more than a nightmare. It brought her much distress, but there was no explanation for it.

The realization was horrifying, and I dashed through the trees.

Horrible sobs reached my ears, and the sound drowned out everything else as my pulse hammered. The agony of it tore at me.

In the center of the clearing, Ronin's blade cut through familiar black curls adorned with white petals.

No, please.

I sprinted, my heart pounding in my chest, my breath coming out in short, panicked gasps. "No!"

Is she moving? Is she alive?

Ronin stood, laughing while tears coated his face. He left her in the grass. Blood pooled through the white of her tunic.

Rage consumed me, blinding me to everything except the glint of the blade in Ronin's hand. It glistened, blood still on it. *Her* blood.

Oblivious to my surroundings, I sprinted across the clearing and collided with Ronin, toppling him to the ground and pulling him away from Elita. He gasped for breath, and I nearly cut him down in an instant, but ruby eyes made me freeze.

Elita's gaze found mine, tears trailing over the bridge of her nose while her eyelids fluttered; too heavy to stay open. Her hair was already cut through, white petals withered to gray on the grass around her.

Blood covered her hands, her tunic, the side of her face. A breath shuddered her chest, weak, barely there.

I had to help her. If I didn't do something—

To my left, Ronin stood.

Anger ripped through my chest, and I straightened, pulling my sword from its sheath. Ronin cackled, his appearance half mad.

Hatred surged within me, propelling me forward. I lunged at him without a second thought. It cost me the upper hand when Ronin's fist cracked against my cheekbone. Adrenaline numbed the pain.

I straightened, spat blood, and went after him. The man had the gall to grin.

Our blades locked, the dagger not enough for him to properly counter me. He held the flat end of his blade to his palm, trying to block my sword. Fear flitted through Ronin's expression. It wouldn't save him.

A thunderous roar of frustration burst from my chest, and I forced my sword down harder, using my height advantage to send him staggering.

The blade slid across his palm. What a foolish man. It cut, and Ronin lost his balance, stumbling back. I didn't let him recover.

The hilt of my sword cracked his nose, sending blood pooling down his mouth and chin. Ronin sputtered and shook, trying to gather himself.

I yelled over the pounding in my head and kicked him down. My sword arced through the air, and I drove it forcefully into his chest without a second thought, the impact reverberating through my arm.

Panic filled his eyes. Blood sputtered from his mouth. Within a matter of seconds, life left his gaze.

Ragged breaths shook my shoulders, and crimson dripped from my nose. My hand trembled as I pulled the sword from the man's chest. Crimson coated his tunic. A life taken by my blade. The image of fear was frozen on his face. It seemed everyone died with the same expression.

Ice surged through my veins, and I dropped my sword. It fell to the grass below, and in a bitter wind, gray petals dusted over Ronin's tunic. Black hair clung to the blood on his hands.

Fear quickened my breath until I was lightheaded. It took all I had to turn around and look at her.

Elita's eyes were closed, her chest still. No fall or rise.

"Elita?" My voice trembled, and I moved quickly, dropping to her body in the grass. Blood coated her tunic, a harsh contrast.

My breathing was quick enough to make me sick.

Frantically, I tore the edge of her tunic open, exposing the gash that marred her side. The edges were too jagged; it was too deep. Blood coated her skin in a horrific display, and I pressed a hand to the wound.

"No, please."

I swallowed the sensation to retch and moved my hand from her side. Her blood clung to my skin. She would bleed out if there wasn't pressure to stop it.

She's already dead.

I shook my head.

There was no fall or rise to her chest. No twitch in her face. When I pressed a shaky hand to her bloodied side, she didn't flinch.

"El, please," I begged.

Pressing a palm to her chest, I waited for the feel of her heartbeat. For a breath to leave her lungs. Even with her petals sheared, I couldn't bring myself to accept it.

Carefully, I moved her arms out of the way—too limp—and I brought both my hands to her chest. The sound of running echoed in the woods behind me. I focused on her face, not turning around. If it were the Iron Guard coming to kill me, I'd let them.

I pressed into her chest, using my weight, counting in my head while her ribs dipped beneath my palms. "Come on." I pressed harder, faster until the rhythm was right.

She couldn't die. I wouldn't let her die. *I did this. I let her go. Had I tried harder to get her to stay...*

Red hair appeared in the corner of my vision, and, keeping my hands on Elita's chest, I glanced up to see Taryn. Her face paled, and she looked over Elita's body in disbelief.

"Fuck, don't just sit there! Do something!"

Taryn jumped when I shouted. She scrambled and moved the torn piece of Elita's tunic, pressing her palms to the wound on Elita's side.

To my horror, every time I pushed on her ribs, more blood gushed from the wound. It covered Taryn's hands, but she didn't falter. Taryn's eyes darted from side to side, and she held pressure on the wound.

More footsteps came to a halt behind me, and I heard Alba cry out. To my left, I caught sight of the General's crimson cloak. He didn't say a word. Everyone froze around us. They were useless.

Again, I pressed into Elita's chest. "Please. Breathe, El." Harder until her ribs tried to give way under my palms. The sensation made me hesitate, and Taryn's head snapped up.

"You have to press harder."

"But she—"

"Give her two breaths. Then press harder. You have to, or she has no chance."

My bloodied hands shuddered on her rib cage. There wasn't time to hesitate. Each second lessened the chance of bringing her back.

I tilted her chin, and blood smeared over her skin. Her lack of movement brought a chill up my spine, and I pulled her chin down to open her mouth, bloodied fingers pinching at her nose.

Two breaths and I moved back to her chest, pressing harder. It felt wrong as they threatened to snap under the pressure. She looked too delicate, too frail. Had she always appeared that way?

Close by, Alba continued to sob. The General didn't speak. Taryn continued to do what she could, stopping the bleeding. It fell on me to bring Elita back.

After another thirty compressions, I tilted her chin. Two more breaths. Another set of compressions. Repeat. Repeat. Repeat. Until I was gasping for my own breath, shaking and unable to tear my gaze from her lifeless face.

The General shifted beside me, putting a hand on my shoulder. "Vanmore...she may be in the hands of Akuma. We must—"

I jerked away, not sparing him a glance. "If you say another damn word, I'll kill you."

I felt everyone's gaze on me. I didn't stop.

"Come on, Elita, stay," I whispered, desperation in every word. Two more breaths. Then I pressed with more weight, further, until I felt her ribs snap beneath my hands. It was jarring, and I almost pulled back. But I needed to finish it.

I pressed into her cracked ribs. Relentless. Desperate. *Seventeen, eighteen, nineteen, twenty...*The compressions shook her body, her ribs collapsing with every press of my palms.

"Vanmore, enough. She's breathing."

Adrenaline rushed through my veins, and Taryn put a hand to my shoulder to stop me from pressing into her chest again. The muscles in my arms ached from the rush. Every inch of me trembled; my gaze found her face, waiting for her eyes to open.

Seconds passed, and I swallowed, straightened, and brought Elita's limp body onto my legs. One of my arms wrapped around her shoulders, and I pressed a hand to her wound, trying to hold pressure.

In my arms, Elita winced. My chest shuddered. Nothing else mattered in the clearing. It all fell away, and I ran a hand over the curve of her neck. Her lips parted, a shallow breath pulling into her lungs.

The sound committed to my memory. It was the most glorious thing I had ever heard.

Acknowledgments

First, I want to thank my husband. I know that's corny. But I really wouldn't have been able to do this without his love and support. A lot of self-doubt followed me throughout this entire process. Having him cheer me on, devour my books, and listen to all of my rambling has meant more to me than I can ever express.

I'd also like to thank all my alpha and beta readers.

I'll start with my sisters. Lorra, Sarah, and Ashley, you all hyped me up when the draft was messy and the sentences were clunky. You loved my characters with the same passion I did, plus you encouraged me and helped me shape this story. All the times I messaged about "oh no, should I make this change?" and you all were quick to reply. Your support lifted me when I doubted if this story had a place in this world. You reminded me that my words matter. Thank you for that!

To my betas: Dahlia, Kallie, Lori, Paige, and Sarah, thank you for devoting your time and energy to reading my messy thoughts turned into a story. The unhinged comments, the suggestions, the willingness to read it before it was polished and pretty—thank you, thank you, thank you!

And a super important one, Tabs: THANK YOU. I'm so sorry for all the unnecessary commas. You're the real MVP and I appreciate the care you handled my story with. Your guidance and time spent reading it over and over just means so much. I know what it's like to read it a million times and make edits. So, truly, your hard work means a lot to this first-time author!

More people I'd like to thank: My parents and their eagerness to support my dream. I know this book isn't quite to your taste, but the love and cheering continued anyway. From the time I was a teen and you bought me the notebooks and asked me about my stories, it helped me grow that passion. Also, Mom, thanks for sharing your love of books and taking us to the library so often.

This one will make me cry, but that's okay. My three little ones, I follow my dreams to show you how. It's worth it, I promise. To Luna and Koda, who spent many car rides listening to the robot voice read my book, and they adored it—thank you. (Sorry, Atlas, you were too young to notice.) It might not mean much to others when a child says they loved their book, but dang. Hearing my own kids enjoy my story and say they loved it brought me more joy than I thought possible. (And don't worry, it was the censored version)

For 2023 Olivia...you survived it. It was hard and messy (and still is), but you pulled yourself out of the fire, burns and all. Yeah, there are emotional scars left. Trauma isn't easy. But you found yourself again in writing. It doesn't heal it all, it doesn't remove the hurt. But you did the damn thing.

Thank you to my readers for taking a chance on a debut author. It means so much to me!

Trigger Warnings

Mention of suicide.
  Death of a child mentioned.
  Torture.
  Violence.
  Swearing.
  Death of parent.
  Mention of nonconsensual removal of clothes (No SA)
  Forced reproduction mentioned (But does not take place)
  Thoughts of death.
  Betrayal.

www.ingramcontent.com/pod-product-compliance
Lightning Source LLC
Chambersburg PA
CBHW030044130726
47901CB00007BA/1862